BIMINI MAN

BIMINI MAN

C. M. Jonnard

iUniverse, Inc.
New York Lincoln Shanghai

Bimini Man

iUniverse, Inc.

For information address:
iUniverse, Inc.
2021 Pine Lake Road, Suite 100
Lincoln, NE 68512
www.iuniverse.com

ISBN: 0-595-27360-2 (pbk)
ISBN: 0-595-65670-6 (cloth)

Printed in the United States of America

To my family and friends,

whose support, patience and understanding

made writing this book possible,

and to Danielle DePasquale, Shawn Hickey and

Tracey O'Keeffe who assisted in the copyediting.

C ONTENTS

▼

PART III: THE DEATH OF BIMINI MAN

PART I

▼

THE RETURN OF AMISON RUEBEN JONES

CHAPTER I

▼

CECIL SPINS A STORY

"Tell us the story of Bimini Man," the students begged.

Cecil Fergueson smiled. Short and squat and shaped like a bull dog, he sat cross legged on top of the picnic table under the shadow cast by the tall obelisk shaped monument and studied the relaxed faces on the students lying about on the sand and waiting for him to respond. So this was how it felt to be a professor leading a bunch of anthropology students on a field trip. It was a wonderful feeling, even if he was merely a last minute stand in for the actual instructor who had taken the day off to go shopping in Alice Town in North Bimini on the other side of Porgy Bay.

The monument was taller than the palms covering the tiny island in the middle of the bay where Cecil was holding court. And now it threw its long shadow to the east, as if to point a long dark finger at a patch of land beginning to rise from the deep in the receding tide. To the west, the sun was melting into a field of crimson over the bluffs in whose shade the hamlet of Alice Town lay huddled. Another day was passing. Lorraine and Bill Small came by earlier. They introduced themselves as amateur anthropologists and asked if they could join the outing. Cecil, always eager to please, invited them.

They were tall and attractive in matching khaki field jackets and fatigue trousers tucked into boutique hiking boots. She was strikingly beautiful and he was darkly handsome and their carefully tailored ensembles could have clipped out of a high fashion magazine. Cecil had no idea where they were from except that they were not from poverty. He could not help but notice the similarities between them: the same height, the same brown hair, the same facial and body features. Maybe they were property shopping. And business was slow. He could use customers.

A female voice brought him to attention. It came from the direction of a launch and several inflatable dinghies tied to the rickety dock on the beach. "Put on your sweater, dear. It's getting chilly."

"Yes, Charlotte," Cecil replied in an accepting voice. He winked at the giggling students. "My wife watches me like a hawk," he said.

More smiles. The students continued to lay about, drawing their bodies to the last rays of sun. They were in no rush to leave. Cecil had promised them a story, and story telling is what he liked to do. Story telling was important in his job as a full time real estate agent and essential as a part time tour guide. On this occasion, he was helping to shepherd students from Las Olas University in Fort Lauderdale through the Bimini islands.

"Who did you say owned this island?" Cecil turned with a start. It was was Bill Small who had asked the question.

"Centurion Trust, a title insurance company in Miami. This is the place where archeologists from Las Olas University dug for the lost civilization of Atlantis and for Bimini Man."

"Wow!"

A long ocean going catamaran with battleship gray hulls in need of cleaning and paint rested on the beach near the dock. The name *Phoenix*, written on the forward section of each bow, was covered with dirt and barely visible. An anchor chain ran from the hawse-eye of one of the bows to a palm tree around which it was coiled and secured with a lock.

However, the hulls' undersides were clean and barnacle free. So were the two bronze propellers, one for each hull, fitted to sturdy shafts extending out from the bottom of the hulls. They must have been recently polished because their surfaces reflected the setting sun's blinding brilliance. Their size suggested that they were driven by a pair of powerful engines.

The catamaran's after deck and its main cabin, with heavily tinted one-way port holes, straddled the hulls and was connected forward to a smaller wheel house in front of which a steel platform supported something like a gun emplacement that seemed as if it once hosted weaponry of sorts, perhaps a heavy caliber machine gun or rocket launcher.

The cabin was raked back, giving it a streamlined shape to reduce windage, and centered on its flat roof was a small tower shaped like a submarine cone.

Directly in front of the cone over the cabin's forward bridge was a wheelhouse. Below the wheelhouse and in front of the cabin and mounted on a steel platform extending across the hulls was an armor plated frame. It bore a remarkable resemblance to a gun emplacement, perhaps one that could accommodate a heavy caliber machine gun or rocket launcher.

Chain plates were riveted to the outside of each hull, suggesting that the cat once had a mast. One could only guess that it was a high-tech spar that stepped inside the cone that could automatically telescope out when called into use. The mast was nowhere in sight, but its long boom was lashed securely on the port side deck.

Cecil studied his watch. It was almost six o'clock and he wanted to be back by nightfall. It was warm. He pulled a handkerchief from his pocket and mopped the perspiration on his round face and partially bald head. The toothy grin under the slightly off center Groucho Marx moustache stalled just long enough to allow him to work the handkerchief over his puckering lips.

"Is this island we're standing on for sale?" Lorraine asked.

The smile returned to Cecil's lips. "Yes," he replied. "But it is designated as a historical landmark by the Nassau government. Construction would be restricted to one single family home with guaranteed public access to the monument."

"Who owns the island over there?" Bill pointed to the reef rising out of the water.

"The Bahamian government."

"This is part of the Bahamas?" a student asked, not quite sure of the correct answer.

"Yes. The Bahamas is actually an archipelago of over seven hundred islands that stretch like a crescent shaped necklace from Grand Bahama Island to the Turks and Caicos. About 255,000 people live in the Bahamas. The Biminis where we stand are forty five miles east of Fort Lauderdale. Two thousand people live here."

Cecil paused to make sure his listeners were absorbing the geography lesson. "Skin color runs from black to white. Most of the people are West Indian like me and we all speak English. The economy is tourist dependent, and everyone is well off relative to the other West Indian nations. I read somewhere that the Bahamas is the fourth richest nation in this hemisphere after the United States, Canada, and Bermuda."

Another student asked. "You say the country is rich, and there's not much here besides tourism, and that has to be seasonal. Do you think drugs have anything to do with it?"

"Absolutely not!"

Lorraine Small asked about the catamaran. "That's a big boat," she noted. "It looks as if it's been here a long time. Does it have an owner?"

"It's over eighty feet long," Cecil explained. He added as an after thought. "And it's not for sale."

"Can one live on it?" she asked.

"Yes. It's an ocean catamaran. It's designed for speed. It can do forty knots."

"What does the name *Phoenix* mean?"

Cecil slowly began to maneuver his guests to the launch. "Well, according to legend, *Phoenix* was a giant bird. The only way to kill it was by fire. But it would always rise from the ashes and spring back to life whenever its owner returned to claim it."

Lorraine was persistent. "Is that all there is to it? It really looks abandoned."

Cecil smiled. "Looks are deceiving. The cat is napping. It will spring to life when its owner returns."

Bill joined in. "Who owns the catamaran?"

"A guy named Jonesey."

"Is he still around?"

"He's around somewhere, I'm sure."

"Is Jonesey his real name?

"We call him Jonesey. Women call him Ruby. His real name is Amison Rueben Jones."

"How did the monument behind you get here," A student inquired.

"It's an obelisk, a memorial to Bimini Man, to the archeological dig team and to everyone else who died here."

"Wasn't Bimini Man a hoax?"

"Well, that's what some say. And that's where Jonesey comes into the picture."

Cecil looked longingly at Alice Town across the bay. Its evening lights were starting to twinkle in the gathering dusk. He estimated the trip back to the ferry dock at the seaplane landing next to the End-Of-The-World Bar could take at least an hour. It would be dark by then.

"Tell us about Bimini Man," Bill requested.

"Yes, tell us the story of Bimini Man," Lorraine chimed in with a chorus of students.

"Well, several years ago," Cecil began, "This archeological team from Las Olas University thought they found not only the lost city of Atlantis but also evidence of its people's African origins. Bimini Man was the name given to a human fossil they claimed to have found. The team claimed it was one of the area's pre-historic inhabitants who came from Africa.

"However, according to rumor, a cache of sealed heroin was also buried near Bimini Man's remains. Some of the dig team operators got greedy and joined up with a band of drug traffickers who arrived to move the stash. The official version is that white supremacist terrorists suddenly appeared on the scene, murdered the dig team and blew the dig up. They were in turn were drowned in a storm and tidal surge that swept over the site and destroyed it."

"What happened to the heroin?"

"Some believe Bimini Man and the heroin are still here; others say everything was moved in advance to an old freighter called the *Casa D'Ora*. It went down in the storm a few miles from here."

"How much heroin was there?"

"A couple of billion dollars at wholesale, or so I was told," Cecil replied. "I was here when it happened. And so was Jonesey."

"Were you in the real estate business back then?"

Cecil shook his head and laughed. "Nope. I was a cop. This is my retirement job. And Jonesey was a hired gun."

"What's a hired gun?"

"A hired gun? That's a hit man on retainer. But, it's getting late. So let me get started. It began several years ago. Jonesey lived here but not by choice. He left Florida for the Bahamas to avoid murder charges. He did marine salvage work for the Bahamian government and was also a bounty hunter. He pursued drug runners.

He did pretty well in fact. He picked up ten percent of the salvage or insured value of the abandoned vessels he recovered and a ten percent bounty on the wholesale value of the narcotics he picked up. He made more money in the Bahamas than he could have dreamt of making in the States.

"Anyway. Let me get back to my story. I shared a common problem with one of Europol's director, a Frenchman named Jacques Leroux.

"What's Europol?"

"Oh. Europol is an international police intelligence organization. It's located in Paris. Its mission is to help local police investigate crimes involving two or more countries. It also cooperates closely with your CIA and FBI in areas where their intelligence is lacking. What happened here was that Europol had dispatched an agent to the Biminis in response to an FBI inquiry about possible irregularities at the dig site. To make a long story short, the FBI had received a report that some of the bones being uncovered at the site were allegedly stolen from a museum in New York.

"The Europol agent was found dead on a beach in South Bimini shortly after he arrived. Leroux then hired the services of one of our part time police officers who met the same fate as the Europol agent.

"I had two possible murders on my hands and Leroux had pressure from Paris to resolve the matter quickly. This is where we stood when Leroux suggested to me that Jonesey be recruited for the job. He was familiar with these islands and knew how to take care of himself. There were details to be worked out, of course. "Leroux agreed to speak with U.S. officials to drop all charges against Jonesey. My role was to convince him to enter the investigation. I was the chief constable for the Biminis back then. When I finished speaking with Leroux, I flew to Nassau where I heard Jonesey was given a new salvage job by Reginald Lang, the newly appointed regional commander of the Bahamian Defense force....

CHAPTER 2

▼

OUT OF EXILE

It was early Sunday morning. Amison inhaled deeply and looked out Domino's bathroom window. The air was clean. It reminded him of a distant tropical island after a cleansing rain, where the air smelled fresh and where he met a girl whose face he could not remember, a long, long time ago. But now he was distracted by a shadow on the ground below. He stopped shaving. The shadow belonged to the card sharp at the casino where he had taken Domino last night.

He snickered. The sun was out. At least, it promised to be a beautiful day.

This was today and he was rich. In fact, it had been a good couple of weeks. He and Ojo had brought in two abandoned vessels and claimed salvage rights. Only the first one brought him cash from a cocaine cargo. The second vessel, a trawler also suspected of carrying cocaine, was totally empty. It even seemed as if it was deliberately stripped before having been set adrift.

For some reason Cecil Fergueson had showed up moments before he and Ojo were about to set out from the commercial dock at Potters' Cay under the bridge that connected Paradise Island with Nassau. There was no choice but to take him along.

"Who sent you the call on this one?" Cecil asked.

"Reggie Lang," replied Amison. "It's a trawler. One of his cutters sighted it the other day. We have to tow it back. It shouldn't take long. Are you up to it? There might be some action out there."

Cecil bristled. "Are you saying I'm not up to the job?"

Amison backed off. "Whatever you say, chief."

Without further ado, he took the helm inside the wheelhouse as Ojo let loose of the dock lines and *Phoenix* set sail with the sun rising high and the trade winds driving them westward at twenty knots with the mast up and sails unfurled.

It took less than a half hour to reach their target. In the distance they saw the trawler bobbing aimlessly in the choppy water. Ojo hoisted the salvage flag on the port spreader and the Bahamian flag on the starboard side. The ship's burgee, an eagle with outspread wings and curled claws clutching the letter "P"over a field of gold, clung to the stern backstay.

Ojo handled the sail trim from the center hull's after cockpit while Amison and Cecil huddled in the wheelhouse to escape the ocean spray as the big cat circled its prey.

"It's a nice piece of change for you," Cecil shouted over the din of the sea. Ten percent of whatever you find, including the boat. How's that for dinner?"

Amison ignored him. The locals were nice but they had little to do but count other people's money.

"How's Charlotte and the kids?"

"They're good. Thanks for asking. How's Domino?"

Amison's face lit up. "She's good. I'd like to get more serious with her but she already has kids. I don't mind her dating Nassau big shots. She'll give that up, but what am I going to do with a woman with kids?"

"Cecil rolled his eyes. "You raise them, Jonesey. That's what Charlotte and I do. That's what family is about."

"Well, I have a wife. And until her situation changes, I'm stuck. It would be nice to say that I'm in between wives, but I can't."

Cecil opened his mouth to say something but Amison stopped him.

"Save it, Cecil." He pointed into the distance. Out of nowhere two fast moving yachts appeared and began converging rapidly on them. He grabbed several jelly beans from his pocket and popped them into his mouth.

Amison's initial thought was that the yachts had intercepted the trawler earlier, killed the crew and then left to avoid detection when another vessel passed by. The danger of apprehension gone, they were coming back for the loot. He studied the yachts through a pair of binoculars. "Is this a setup, Cecil?"

Cecil shook his head. "Not on my side," he said. "Perhaps we should leave. It doesn't look good."

"Why? You're a cop. You stop traffic violators. You can arrest them."

"Not funny, Jonesey. This isn't the kind of traffic I handle. Do you have a plan?" "Yeah. Go back into the cabin."

Cecil obediently followed instructions and ducked through a small rear door to the relative safety of the main cabin where he passed Ojo with a rocket launcher on his shoulder. He had a big grin on his face and patted the weapon lovingly with his free hand.

Amison was in top form. "The problem today is that people have no respect for the property rights of others. Don't you agree, Ojo?"

He pulled out a cigarette from a pocket, lit it and inhaled deeply.

The diminutive Bolivian smiled and said nothing. He carefully made his way to the gun emplacement below the wheelhouse and anchored himself securely and braced the launcher on his shoulder.

"Are you sure we should stick around for this?" Cecil called up from below.

"We have an obligation to uphold the law," Amison said. "Besides, if we bag the boat, I get a bounty and it'll be a payday for all of us."

"Just don't get us killed," came Cecil's howl from the cabin.

The two yachts were close enough to spray the catamaran with machine gun fire. The rounds missed although a few shells hit but bounced harmlessly off the steel reinforced wheelhouse. The closest vessel tried to cut off the cat and crossed into Ojo's sights. There was a "whoosh" and it was broadsided by a rocket.

The yacht exploded on impact, disintegrating in a ball of orange flame and black smoke.

Birds circling above screamed and flew off in the direction of the second yacht which promptly turned tail. Before it disappeared over the horizon Amison caught a glimpse of the name, "*Flyer,*" on the vessel's stern through his binoculars.

"Damn! I know that boat," he said out loud to no one in particular.

He put the glasses down to exchange high fives with Ojo, but Cecil raced out to the after deck and threw up over the lifelines.

Amison brought *Phoenix* alongside the trawler and Ojo threw over a tow line. He jumped over the side, landed on the vessel's deck and tethered it to the cat.

Cecil jumped on after Ojo, disappearing with him inside. They emerged a few minutes later.

"The damn thing is empty," Cecil exclaimed.

"Empty?"

"Empty."

That was the operative word. Empty. The trawler was a shell. Its instrumentation and electronics were gone and its tanks were dry.

Amison looked at the horizon around him. "We walked into a trap," he said to Cecil.

Leaving Ojo at the helm in the wheel house, he and Cecil went on deck to mull over their next move.

"Where to, Jonesey?" Cecil asked.

"Whoever is after me isn't after you. No one knows you're here unless you left a trail."

Cecil shook his head. "I didn't tell anyone I was meeting you on *Phoenix* or in any particular place. Let's head for Bimini. It's safer there for both of us."

Amison agreed, motioned to Ojo through a wheelhouse porthole to set a course westward for the Bimini islands and followed Cecil to the afterdeck where they sat down on the banquets along the cockpit coaming.

"Anyway, I'm glad you're here, Cecil. I missed you. How are things at home?"

"Not so good. The Las Olas archeology team is still digging away and our friend Sanford Jack is raising hell with his Rastafarian guards."

Amison snorted. "We should have killed the guy when we had the chance," "Now, now, my friend. We must give law and order a chance. But that's not why I'm here. I've come to bring you out of exile. Leroux asked me to speak to you about a mutual problem."

"What's that?"

"Two guys in Bimini died, Luther Guenther and Dwayne Douglas. Their deaths baffle me. Leroux and I need help."

Amison stared at Cecil. "I heard the story. Accidental drowning? Their bodies washed up on a South Bimini beach about one or two weeks apart? Dwayne was Frances's husband. How is she taking it?"

"Not well. She's thinking of leaving Bimini."

"I worked with Luther a few times. He was a professional. But Dwayne was a part time cop under your command. He couldn't make a jay walking arrest. How did he get involved?"

"Leroux hired Guenther to check out rumors about alleged irregularities going on at the Bimini Man dig site. When Luther died, Leroux asked Henry Alstrum to find a replacement. Henry asked Dwayne, and he agreed. He needed the money."

"Damn. Why didn't Henry consult with Luis Santiago?"

"Your brother-in-law? He was away. But, it's awful anyway. Dwayne leaves Frances a widow with two kids. And of course, there's her sister Domino who is also a widow with two kids and has to keep company with creeps like Lang to stay flush. Bimini is a small place, Jonesey. It can't afford too many widowed mothers. And it's not right that Domino has to do what she does. It's not proper."

"I'm no detective, Cecil. Murder is your bailiwick. Why me? Henry Alstrum is Leroux's West Indian coordinator. Why doesn't he get directly involved?"

"He's a doctor, not a knee cracker. Besides, he also thinks you're the best man for the job."

"What about his medical assistant, Dudley Haynes? Isn't he also on the Europol payroll?"

Henry isn't too sure about his integrity."

Amison grinned. "I'm honored. Is this a pro bono job or is Europol paying?"

Cecil coughed and a look of embarrassment swept over his face.

"You'll have to travel most likely. Maybe to the States to solve this one. Leroux arranged to have your American passport restored."

"Indeed."

"Charlotte and I were at a reception at the American embassy in Nassau to honor its new drug enforcement attache ."

Amison smiled. "Oh? Who's that?"

"Jack O'Brien."

Amison's smile faded.

"That's right. O'Brien, your old CIA mission chief. All our mutual friends were at the party, Jonesey. Harold Levy from Alliance Insurance, Ignacio Bencivenga and Captain Jack…"

"Sandford Jack? I guess he got bored in Bimini. What was Bencivenga doing there?"

"He's a major depositor at Madsen Bank a majority of whose shares are owned by Alliance. Bill Nigel, Reginald Lang, and Jonathan and Rodney Sykes were also there. So was Leroux. He and I spoke privately to O'Brien about having all those old charges against you dropped. He agreed when we told him about the situation in the Biminis."

Amison looked suspiciously at Cecil. "There must have been something else on the party's agenda besides toasting Jack's new job and my return to grace."

"Yes. In fact they all left briefly during the reception for a private meeting."

"What about?"

"It's speculation on my part," Cecil answered. "A game of musical chairs is on, I think. Jonathan was just appointed commissioner for the Biminis. Brother Rodney made it as Madsen Bank's corporate counsel and snuck Bill Nigel in as president. The trouble is that Bill is a thief and Harold wants him out, but Harold lost on that one. However, my take is that O'Brien, don Ignacio and Harold were unanimous in having you re-activated. Alliance owns the land on which the dig is being held; Bencivenga is financing it and being very influential in Venezuela,

O'Brien wants to keep him happy. The three of them have a vested interest in making sure that the dig is clean, so to speak. The Bahamian government, speaking through their new Bimini commissioner, has the same interest. You're a very lucky guy. If it wasn't for the dig, you might never get those charges dropped. You might even end up dead here."

"Why do you say that?"

The Sykes sister, Martha, is Lang's wife. Lang is a big shot these days and he, as you know, also keeps company with Domino. The Sykes and Lang are very close and they hate you, Lang especially because you're more successful and make more money chasing down drug runners that he does and because you're muscling in on his personal woman."

Amison shrugged. "That's the way life goes, Cecil. I have to choose my women carefully in the Bahamas. Many broads hanging around pick up johns off the street and are HIV or AIDS infected. Domino is a kept woman, and so I figure that she's pretty clean and doesn't work the bars and clubs. That's important. It's no skin off my ass If Lang can't hang on to his women, and if he's upset, that's tough. He's a jerk anyway. Domino is the pick of the litter. As far as money goes, I've never stopped Lang from running his own bounty and salvage business. He just doesn't have the balls for it."

"Your logic as usual is impeccable, Jonesey, but they hate you nevertheless and I wouldn't be surprised if it wasn't Lang who staged that little ambush today."

"That's life. So what?"

"Well, Jonesey. Considering that you're tapping both women and have a pretty bad relationship with Reggie, and given that Jack O'Brien and don Ignacio want you dead for their own reasons, I'd say the meeting could have been about taking you down. Leroux was able to convince them of his need for you. Frankly, I think they have bigger fish to fry and also need you to help them, at least temporarily."

"What bigger fish?"

"Listen. All those guys are heavily invested in the Bimini Man dig one way or another and most of them are also directly or indirectly involved in the drug trade. The unexplained loss of two Europol operatives in the process of investigating a rumor of wrong doing at the the archeological site can create an embarrassment if drugs are somehow mixed up with the dig."

"You're very polite, Cecil," Amison noted. "You should have been a diplomat.

Let's face facts, friend. Bencivenga doesn't grow carrots in Venezuela and our old friend Captain Jack doesn't haul tomatoes on his ship. The Bahamian islands are an entrepot for drug trafficking between South America and Florida. If Guenther and Dwayne were murdered, it must have been because they were on to something big."

"You're probably right. You want to know what I think?"

"What?"

"I think O'Brien wants you back for a special job related to the Bimini Man dig, and I don't know what that is. The Europol investigation works for me and Leroux but it's only an excuse. O'Brien made it clear after the party that I should ask you if you want in, and to give him a definite answer."

"Where did you tell him you would meet me?"

"In Bimini."

Amison smiled. "That's where we're going. You can tell him that we did meet in Bimini."

"I can?"

"Yes. I take it that the Europol investigation is a side show and that you're not sure what the main event is."

"That's about it," said Cecil.

"Is O'Brien is pressing you?"

The police officer frowned. "No. He's too smooth for that. Reggie's adjutant, Wayne, passed the word to me. If you say 'yes,' I keep my job as chief constable in the Biminis. If you decline, Charlotte and I get shipped off to the Out Islands."

Amison mulled silently over Cecil's story for several minutes until Ojo started knocking on the cabin's outside wall to signal they were approaching Nassau.

"Well then. Tell Leroux and O'Brien I'll investigate those deaths in Bimini."

Cecil looked wide eyed at Amison. "You will?"

"Listen, my friend. I've been shit canned here for five years. My wife lies in a coma back home and I haven't seen my kids. I want in."

"Come to think of it, Jonesey. Who is looking after them?"

"Sid Stone, Mark's brother in New Jersey. In any case, I want to go home. I'm also curious about this Bimini Man gig. And besides, I owe you one for letting me make a living."

"You'll also be able to touch base with Mark Stone and Luis Santiago if you get to Fort Lauderdale."

Amison winked at his friend. "You're right. It's been five years. What do I do next?"

"Meet with Henry Alstrum. The good doctor is in Bimini. He'll brief you and probably ship you off to Philadelphia for more detailed instructions."

"I want my passport."

"I have it. O'Brien gave it to me." Cecil dug into his pocket and extracted a blue official looking booklet encased in a transparent plastic envelope and passed it to Amison. "It still has five years to go on it."

"You guys waste no time, do you?"

Cecil ignored his remark. "Henry has Leroux's carte blanche. Make sure it gets into your hands; you'll need it."

"That's Europol's international license to kill, Cecil. I guess this is going to be more than a simple murder investigation.?"

"Leroux and I are nearsighted, Jonesey. We have zero tolerance for murder. But Leroux is not stupid and knows O'Brien wants you for something else. The carte blanche in your hands will keep guys like O'Brien in check. They know you kill better and faster than any of them can. But still watch your back. What we have is a gathering of wolves. So try to stay off the menu."

"I am on the menu," Amison emphasized. "That trawler was a trap and the boat that ran off was *Flyer*. It belongs to Frank."

"Hoffman? The president of Las Olas University? Are you sure?"

"I know the boat. It's a sixty foot Hatteras. He had it custom made six years ago when my cat was built. I'd recognize it anywhere."

"Hoffman wouldn't compromise his position to kill you. Besides, what would be the motive?"

Amison scratched his chin. "We aren't exactly buddies but I don't think he has it in for me. It could have been someone else using his boat."

"Who?"

"Who and why are what I aim to find out, Cecil. If I live long enough. I'm going forward to help Ojo get us to Bimini."

A few minutes later, its great sails unfurled in a steady following wind, Phoenix skimmed over the sea like a giant bird following the setting sun.

CHAPTER 3

▼

THE SETUP

Amison stepped back to the bathroom sink and started working the straight edge over his lathered face in front of the mirror. Now and then he would go back to the window to have a peek outside. The apartment's second floor bathroom window overlooked a wrought iron fence and gate with spiked end posts. Against the fence were bunched several garbage cans guarded by alley cats arguing over breakfast.

He could not take his eyes away from the shadow and was reluctantly forced to admit to himself that this was no social call.

He was in trouble and he had no plan. Of course, this predicament could have been avoided had he stayed in Bimini and invited Tucker Anderson and Hank Lawrence there. But they were on a gambling junket and wanted to stay in Nassau. Besides, they had gossip for him, and he knew Domino was aching to give him an update about who she was seeing and what she was doing. Anyway, it was too late for regrets.

Amison looked into the bathroom sink mirror. He temporarily forgot about the stalker outside and began thinking of Reginald Lang and Frank Hoffman. Did they think he was alive or dead? Or, were they totally innocent and ignorant of what had happened a week ago? He kept shaving as he recalled his conversation with Tucker and Hank who had some eye opening answers for him.

He had decided to spend a long weekend with Domino and arrived in Nassau on a Thursday, parking the cat as he usually did at a bulkhead slip on Potters'

Cay, a stone pier between Nassau and Paradise Island. They dined out and visited the hot spots. Saturday morning Domino went shopping and dropped him off by cab at a local eatery where he was to meet his friends.

A festive parade was getting started and the streets were filled with floats, bands and tourists snaking through the streets. Amison made his way through the crowd blocking the restaurant's open doorway and stopped at the cashier's counter to find his friends. It took only a few seconds to make eye contact with a huge barrel chested bear of a man with a thick walrus moustache sporting a weathered suede blazer.

He was sitting in a booth, nursing a bowl of conch chowder and munching on a chunk of Bahamian bread. Next to him was a slim, sandy haired man with soft features in a trim blue suit and a red and black regimental tie over a white button down shirt. He was young in appearance but lines on his face and gray in his hair whispered his years to the world.

Amison howled. "Tucker Anderson and Hank Lawrence!"

The two diners rose to their feet. The bear shaped man called Tucker Anderson held out a thick paw of a hand. "Man! Jonesey in the flesh. Back from the dead."

"It's been a long time," the other said quietly, shaking his hand in turn.

"Five years and counting," Amison exclaimed.

He slid into the seat opposite them. "You guys look like ten million dollars each after taxes. What's up?"

Tucker crossed his fingers. "Surviving," he said.

"What about you, Hank? You should be pretty close to the top spot at Alliance."

Hank shook his head. "That's not going to work for me, Jonesey. I turned in my resignation last week. I came with Tucker to clear up any misunderstanding about my leaving Alliance."

"Whatever, Hank. I'm glad to see you. I wouldn't care less if you killed the pope as long as you pay for breakfast. I'm broke."

"I know," Tucker joked. Your assets are all tied up in cash."

Amison laughed. "Same old Tuck." Then he turned to Hank. "What happened at Alliance? I thought you were well fixed with Harold, what with all those missions you organized for us."

A waitress wandered by to refresh their coffee and Amison asked for an order of grits.

"No grits after eight in the morning." the waitress announced.

Amison grumbled and ordered scrambled eggs and coffee.

"We heard a rumor you were killed, drowned a couple of weeks ago when your boat went down. We didn't think you'd show this morning," said Hank.

"I heard that myself," Amison noted, helping himself to Tucker's doughnut and some of his coffee. "The rumor was wildly exaggerated. Who put out the word I was dead?"

"It came to me from the big man," Tucker informed Amison. "He asked me to check it out. He said that if I found you dead, I should arrange for a proper burial. But that if I found you alive, I should tell you to see him in Philadelphia for your new marching orders. I think Harold wants you back in action."

The waitress brought over Amison's eggs and coffee. "Any idea what for? I'm supposed to be working for Europol."

"You mean those unexplained deaths in Bimini? I heard about that one. It may have started as a Europol assignment," Hank answered. "But you know Harold. He won't let anyone upstage him. That's one of the reasons I'm retiring."

Amison lost his smile. "No one retires from Alliance, Hank. You know that."

"I am."

"Man. That's a suicide wish. What the hell for?"

"Thirty years at Alliance is a long time, Jonesey. You and I had good times, but it was time to walk."

"We have to talk, Hank. But in the meantime, how's Sid Stone and my kids?"

"Oh, he never changes. He sends his regards. He says Bernice is doing fine but is still comatose."

"How's Mark?"

"Oh, he's holding up. He'll be all right."

"And Luis Santiago?"

"Great. He was made chief inspector at the Broward County sheriff's office. You need an appointment to see him now."

"That's good to hear." Amison looked closer at Hank. "Man. You would have been up for retirement soon if not for the top spot."

"Just about. Just like you and the others, Jonesey."

Amison banged the side of his head with the side of his hand. "Damn. You're right. But still, I would have thought you would have taken over Alliance by now or started your own operation, with your smarts."

"Thanks, Jonesey. But Harold pays well and that makes us all lazy. It's easier to crack kneecaps on someone else's dime. Besides, his first cousin's kids, Vincent, Roger, and their mother Mercedes, have the inside track at Alliance now that Max and Dominick are dead; and then there's Marvin Childs, the company's numbers cruncher. I didn't want to wait."

"What about you, Tucker? Are you still working the tables?" Amison asked.

Tucker grimaced. "I'm trying to, Jonesey. I got lucky at a private poker game last night, but I still didn't break even, and I have to catch a flight to Miami. How come you took a job from Europol?"

"It got me my passport back. Now I can get back to the States and see what I've been missing, beginning with my kids."

Tucker took a couple of tablespoons of soup, making strange slurping sounds. "I know. Well, you look good, Jonesey. Your face is bigger. Have you been growing more brain?"

Amison rolled his eyes up to the ceiling. "You think?"

They all laughed.

"How are the twins?" Tucker asked.

"Gordon finished college and grad school on a government scholarship and is completing his CIA training. He's still unmarried. And Debbie did the same but decided to get married and now has two kids. Her husband is a cop."

"And Bernice? Any hope?"

Amison grimaced. "You know what I know. It's touch and go. As Hank says, she's still in a coma. It's just lucky that Mark was able to get her admitted to his brother's place after the accident. Debbie lives nearby and looks after her. What are you doing here besides losing at the tables?"

Tucker looked over at Hank. "I needed a job. So Mike Quinn talked to Harold and Harold spoke to Frank Hoffman who got me in as head of security at Las Olas University and then farmed me and Mike Quinn out to Leroux for your backup."

"Backup? Mike Quinn is in this too?"

"That's what the big man says."

"What? For a lousy murder investigation?"

Tucker's eyebrows arched up. "You mean you don't know?"

"Try me."

"You're supposed to close down the Bimini Man dig."

Amison looked at Tucker. "Is that so?"

"That's what I hear, Jonesey. But what I don't get is that Quinn does explosives. He closes down things by blowing them up."

"I didn't hear anything about having the dig destroyed," said Hank. "That could end up a suicide mission if you're not careful."

Amison curled his lips. "Not on my watch. We'll be fine if Quinn hasn't lost his touch." He studied Tucker carefully. "Are you in?"

"I'm in."

"It looks like the old gang is being brought for one more job," Hank remarked ruefully. "I wish I could be with you guys."

Tucker turned to Hank. "I don't think you'll like this job, old buddy." He looked back at Amison. "That's what I'm here to talk about, Jonesey. We're supposed to take down the Bencivengas along with the dig."

Amison's face was emotionless. "The entire family or just the old man?"

"The entire family. That's the word from Harold."

"That could be a blood bath, folks," Hank warned.

Amison sighed. "We specialize in blood baths," he said.

"Does Henry Alstrum understand what Alliance wants?" Hank asked.

"Don't know." Then Amison leaned forward. "And it doesn't matter, Hank. Now that you're retired, you can go home and grow roses. No need to doubt everything anymore."

The waitress came over with a check which Hank picked up. He looked at the clock over the counter. "Well, I have to go."

He was about to get up when he seemed to have second thoughts. "I don't know how to put this, Jonesey, but Tucker and I have lingering questions about your wife's accident. Are you still sold on that accident story?"

Amison was caught off guard. "I'm not sold on anything. What have you got?"

"Nothing, except that the accident story is too neat. Bernice goes to the Alliance Insurance building in Philadelphia upon hearing of your death, becomes hysterical and tries to commit suicide by jumping out a window?"

"She's one lucky broad," Tucker noted. "Those two stone gargoyles on the ledge two floors down broke her fall. I hear she actually loosened one of them when she hit. Otherwise she would have done a swan dive forty three stories to the street."

Amison winced and Hank coughed loudly. "Let's not get descriptive, Tuck. The fact is that her fall was no accident."

"How do you figure that, Hank?"

Hank cleared his throat. "For starters, women don't usually commit suicide by shooting themselves or by jumping out of buildings. Guys do that. Women slash slash their wrists or overdose on drugs and pills. Anyway, what did you do when you and Mark got back after your encounter with the Bencivenga yacht five years ago?"

"I called Bernice to tell her everything was all right, but she wasn't home. And then I called Tucker and told him to keep trying and to relay my message."

Tucker nodded. "Right. And I also called Hank in Philadelphia and asked him to try to reach Bernice."

"Which I did," Hank confirmed. "I had her cell phone number and reached her that evening at a mall. I told her you were alive and well but that you might have to stay away for a while. I told her we had monies set aside for such contingencies and that Harold said she should come down to Philadelphia to settle up."

"What are you saying, Hank?"

Hank tapped the table top repeatedly and emphatically to make his point. "What we're saying, Jonesey, is that Bernice knew you were alive before she ever went to Philadelphia. She didn't try to commit suicide. Nor did she have an accident. She was thrown out of that office window."

Amison said nothing for the longest while. His eyes narrowed to slits and his nostrils flared. "Why didn't you say something before?"

"Our lives were on the line," Tucker confessed. "We had to keep quiet." He slurped down the remains of his soup. "We went to see Frank but he said we had to sit tight."

"I've had my own suspicions," said Amison. "I told Harold back then that I was going to take down whoever was responsible for turning her into a vegetable, and that's still a fair warning."

Hank was more cautious. "Why not tell the police and let the law do its work."

"What law, Hank?" Amison asked. "We're in the killing business. That's what we do for a living. The law doesn't work for us!"

"Hell," said Tucker in support of Amison. "I'm surprised, Hank. You know how we operate, one shot ahead of the law."

"I have to go," said Hank.

Amison followed Tucker and Hank out of the diner into the crowded street where there was barely enough room to walk.

"You're not telling me everything, Hank. What happened at Alliance."

Hank threw up his arms. "There's a power struggle at Alliance. I don't want any part of it."

"For example?"

"It concerns the murder of Harold's cousin, Max Neals and the disappearance of his son Dom last November. Rumor has it that Harold issued the contract and you were the hit man. What happened to Dominick, Jonesey?"

"Shit, Hank. I've been holed up in these islands. Everyone knows that."

"That's true. But your deaf mute side kick has Bolivian friends in Florida. We heard that Ojo and his buddies sailed your boat north and made the hits."

Amison laughed lightly. "I plead not guilty."

"No matter. I'm close to you guys and in the line of fire if and when the Neals family comes after you. Those hits also killed my promotion chances at Alliance. But those aren't your problems. Listen. This business has no friends. Someone is after you."

"Who?"

"If I knew, I'd tell you. Off the record. Watch O'Brien."

"You're kidding."

"You didn't hear that from me," said Hank.

Amison was perplexed. "What the hell am I getting myself into, Hank?"

"You're stepping into a snake pit, Jonesey. But the pay is good. By the way, do yourself a favor and see Estrella Gomez when you get to Philadelphia. She was on duty the day your wife visited Alliance."

"I will, Hank. But why are you telling me this?"

Hank Lawrence smiled mischievously. "I'm lobbing a few grenades behind me as I leave, Jonesey. It's a way of getting even for being treated like a nerd all these years." The smile evaporated and he turned serious. "Besides, you and I go back years. We have to hang together. If we don't, we'll hang separately."

"Where do I find you?"

"Oh, I'll be around. I'll be working part time as a consultant for Centurion down in Miami."

"Mel Weinberg's outfit? Doesn't it compete against Alliance?"

Hank nodded. "Yes, but it'll keep me alive until things settle down at Alliance."

Amison grabbed his hand and shook it. "Good luck, Hank, whatever you do."

Shaking Tucker's hand in turn he asked. "Are you going to be hanging around Las Olas University?"

"You have the address, Jonesey. You used to teach there. Give me the word and I'll be ready."

There was a slight commotion. In one moment, they were standing arm-in-arm on the sidewalk and in another moment Amison was separated from Tucker and Hank by three men in tropical shirts and a crowd of revelers. They surrounded him and blocked his view. Out of the corner of his eye he saw Hank fall into Tucker's arms and being pushed into a cab which had pulled up. Everything and everyone dissolved in the crush of the festive crowd before Amison had time to react. It was as if nothing happened, and if it did, it was over.

CHAPTER 4

▼

THE HIT

Domino was preparing coffee in the kitchen. So far as he knew she worked alone and had no pimp. He learned over the months that these were her own digs, a two bedroom condominium paid for with generous gifts from wealthy Nassau clients and minor help from him whenever he came to town.

He rinsed the straight edge razor under the steamy water pouring into the sink from the faucet and resumed shaving as the sun poured through the slightly open bathroom window. He opened his mouth slightly in a sort of stiff smile to allow his lower lip and his chin to jut out so that the razor could easily reach in the cleft like dimple in his chin without cutting the flesh. His smile exposed a set of cheap, removable partial upper dentures that looked like the mail order teeth. He liked the "clip-ons" as he called them but promised his daughter that this year he would spring for better fitting teeth.

Amison looked out the window again and the shadow was still there. So much for anonymity. He sighed with resignation, walked back to the sink and rinsed off his face. Did Domino know? No matter. The card sharp stepped into the open long enough to adjust a silencer on his pistol before dropping back against the wall. Amison cursed silently. There was always something to spoil a nice day.

The sun cast a sharp beam of light directly on the mirror to help him with the final touches of removing the stubborn remaining pieces of stubble and soap from under his chin and nose with the straight edge. Sounds from a televised choir singing "Amazing Grace" in the next room mixed with the whistle from a kettle of water boiling on the kitchen stove. He began whistling the tune as he admired his handiwork in the mirror.

"Not a single cut," he complimented himself aloud.

He examined the face in the mirror like a jeweler inspecting a diamond and tossed his shaving gear back into its toiletry bag, leaving the straight edge on top of the sink. The whistling grew more insistent and a sermon consigned the world to eternal damnation unless sinners repented and renounced their sins. How was that for guilt by association.

"Come forward and be saved!"

Amison snapped the straight edge shut and slid it into a side pocket of his slacks as a large brown water bug tried to cross the bathroom floor. It never made it. A determined foot encased inside a highly polished black leather loafer stopped its journey dead. "I hate roaches!" He muttered, "even if they are God's creatures."

A strong female voice called out from the kitchen over the noise of the whistling pot. "You know, Ruby, you're actually not bad. How old are you anyway?" The voice was sultry and slightly sensual. It was easy on the ears.

"Old enough to know better," he growled.

"I noticed the monogram on your shirt and the initials on your cuff links, Ruby. What do they stand for?"

Amison went to the bedroom for the rest of his gear. "Amison Rueben Jones," he replied.

He finished dressing and packed his toiletry gear inside a nylon duffel. "And don't steal the links, Domino. They're not real."

He spoke slowly and haltingly with a slight drawl as if he was hunting for words. He was nursing a slight cold, and his voice, a bit hoarse and nasal, suggested the hint of a slight lingering lisp.

She laughed. "Like your teeth?" she asked sarcastically.

"That's not funny, Domino."

He walked into the living room-dining room combination, his dark blue blazer slung over a shoulder and packed duffel in hand. He lay the bag down on the floor and the jacket over it as the woman joined him, carefully balancing two cups of steaming hot coffee and an apple in her hands.

"How do you like your coffee?"

"Black, no sugar. You're sweet enough for me."

Another laugh. "Black and instant, we have. Milk, sugar or cream, we don't have. I also have one apple. Care to share?"

"Apple," He took it and put it in his pocket. "For later," he said.

She set the coffee down next to her canvas string bag on the round glass coffee table, stood on tip toes in her slippered feet and placed her arms around Amison, bracing for a hug or kiss. He drew her close and gave her a lingering kiss before sitting down on one of the tan leather sofa by the table to watch the morning news on the TV screen. He stared at the screen and Agnus stared at him.

Theirs was a quid pro quo relationship. He paid the market price for her services and made the rounds of the local clubs with her to boot. He enjoyed showing her off and willingly paid her way. When they parted company, he always left her with extra money. She never asked how he made a living, and he never inquired about her affairs. They also made a point of never dating in the Biminis where she had a home occupied by her mother and sisters who took care of her children.

Domino was tall, slim and long legged. Yet she was strongly built with ample enough breasts and a soft oval face under curly black hair cut pixie style. Her color was that of rich chocolate and her dark eyes danced with wonder and anticipation.

The TV news was dull, the commercials stale, the weather forecast spotty. It was an unusually cool February and rain was predicted. Amison turned away from the tube and looked at Domino.

"We haven't had much of a chance to talk since I got here," he began, taking a sip of coffee. "What's been going on in your life?"

"Funny things," she replied. She placed her hands in his. "Reggie Lang has a business associate, a big fat sloppy guy who says he's a banker."

"Oh?"

"His name is William Nigel and says he's the president of a bank here. He's a real queer bird and was very pissed when he tried to date me last night."

"Maybe you should have gone with him."

Domino shuddered. "Not my thing. He likes to have sex parties with his other queer buddies but he never touches women. He gives me chills."

"Does he at least pay well?"

"I wouldn't know and that's not the point, Ruby. He showed up several Sundays ago at the church I go to when you're not around."

"Oh, which church?" Amison was all ears. Domino was always a good source of information.

"Saint Matthews Episcopal church on Shirley Street, around the corner from the American embassy. I go there because a lot of rich and important people go there. After church, he invited me to an embassy reception."

"Was anyone else interesting there?"

"Yes. A big, tall man with broad shoulders who owned an insurance business."

"That would be Harold Levy," said Amison.

"That's strange," she continued. "He said he owned the bank Nigel worked at. Do insurance companies own banks, Ruby?"

Amison chuckled. "This one does."

"Reginald Lang was there. He's my steady client, like you. But I like you more," she added hastily.

"I know Lang. How about Jonathan and Rodney Sykes?"

"They came and went. But Lang stayed there with Sanford Jack. I know him, a great big black bearded sea captain who calls on me sometimes when he's around. But there were three men I never saw before. One guy had a funny accent. I think he was French. The other guy was a dapper older gentleman with silver white hair from Venezuela and the third was an American. He had the coldest ice blue eyes I ever saw and said his name was Jack O'Brien."

"What did they talk about?" Amison asked.

"That's what was strange. They talked about you, about someone by the name of Frank Hoffman and about something called the 'Bimini Man' project. I couldn't understand what they were getting at except that the Venezuelan turned a pouch filled with money over to Captain Jack who counted it and then gave it to the big insurance man."

"Did Harold Levy say anything?"

"He seemed mad about something. He held up one hand and said, 'One month. That's all you get. One month.' Does that mean anything to you, Ruby?"

Amison shook his head and Agnus went on.

"He looked at Bill Nigel and said something about wanting to see the books no matter what. I have to say, Ruby. There were no happy campers at that party."

She looked at Amison. "Did any of them speak to you, Ruby?"

He leaned forward and gave Domino a peck on the cheek. "Not yet, cookie, but I'm hopeful."

"Are you mixed up in something?"

Amison shook his head. "Not yet."

"How did I do, Ruby? Was I helpful?"

"You did great. I think I'll hire you as my personal information director."

She was beaming with Joy. "You can hire me anytime, anywhere. Where are you off to next?" she asked.

"Don't know yet?"

Just then, a news bulletin flashed across the TV screen and the scene shifted to a makeshift podium with hastily mounted microphones erected in front of a church.

"Damn," Amison exclaimed. "That's Alice Town."

Their eyes became riveted to the screen.

Behind the podium was a tall, distinguished tousled haired man with glasses in a seersucker suit. Next to him was a statuesque blond woman of about the speaker's height in her heels, also wearing glasses, with her hair neatly tied in a bun.

"Frank Hoffman and Leslie Sandler," he muttered. "Damn. She's now a blonde."

The news narration voice-over declared that this was a great day for Bahamians, a historic day for Africans, for people of African descent, and a momentous event in human history.

"We can announce with confidence," the Las Olas University official was saying in a voice filled with solemnly serious professional certainty, "that the preserved skeletal remains of a pre-historic male have been uncovered here in North Bimini. Dr. Sandler's team completed the excavation of the intact skeleton yesterday and has a statement she wishes to make."

Amison broke out laughing as he listened to the female archeologist explain how tests were proving beyond doubt that the male skeleton was of African origin. That suggested, she maintained, that the original inhabitants of the Bahamas came from Africa, probably several hundred thousand years ago."

He turned off the set. He began to relish the prospects of putting Frank Hoffman and Leslie Sandler out of business.

Domino waited for him to say something else and then asked, "A penny for your thoughts, hon?"

Amison shook his head. "I'm sorry. I was day dreaming."

"You look sexy when you're day dreaming. Are you married?"

"No. My wife is ill."

"Every guy has a dead wife or one who's in a permanent vegetative state."

"Matter of fact, she is comatose."

She suddenly burst into tears. "Oh, Ruby! I'm so sorry. You're serious, aren't you. You're telling me the truth."

"I never lie," he responded.

"I didn't realize…I thought…"

Amison gave her another kiss to console her. "That's all right. However, I do have two kids back in the States."

He got up to stretch his legs and walked over to the window and took a long look outside. The shadow was still there.

"What do you do for a living, Ruby?"

"I'm a salesman," he replied, returning to his duffel where he removed a pair of surgical gloves and slipped them on when she was looking the other way."

"Are you sure you're only a salesman?" she asked.

He grabbed Domino where she stood and kissed her again.

"What was that for?"

"For a delicious breakfast with a beautiful woman."

She gave him an aggravated look. "Where do you live?"

"On a boat. A catamaran. Its name is *Phoenix*."

"On a boat?" She was temporarily at a loss for words. But she pressed on. "How come you live on a boat, Ruby?"

"Because it's free, and it's the only home I have right now. Besides, it gets me where I want to go. I get around on my boat."

Domino was unsatisfied with his response. "You're foot loose and fancy free. And yet you always have money. Are you sure you're not a pirate? I've known you for five years and I don't know what you do for a living."

Amison held her closely and tightly. "I'm a pirate. Now, tell me more about what you know."

She took advantage of his grip around her and pressed ever more closely to him and whispered. "I shouldn't be telling you this, Ruby. Someone is hanging around outside. He was following us at the casino last night. So be careful, hon."

He gave her another peck on the forehead and maneuvered her away from the window.

"You set me up, Domino," he said. "I don't need to know why and I'm not going to hurt you, but I do want to know who paid you and how much."

Domino tried unsuccessfully to break out of his grip and her face filled with fear and anguish. "I was out of my mind, Ruby. I wasn't thinking straight. Lang gave me ten thousand dollars…"

She tried again to break loose but Amison tightened his hold.

"Where's the money, Domino?"

"Under the sofa pillow."

"Ten thousand dollars. Is that all I'm worth?"

"All right. It was twenty thousand dollars."

He smirked. "That's better," he said.

Domino was sobbing hysterically by now. "They said you were no good. They said you were wanted for murder and that you were going to kill me and my kids." "Where are they now?"

With my sister Frances in Alice Town. You're a hit man, aren't you?"

He smacked her across the face so hard she went flying into the sofa.

"You're going to kill me," she cried.

"I'm not going to kill you, Domino. I'm falling in love with you. But I sure don't want to die today. So tell me. Lang doesn't have that kind of money. Where did he get it from?"

"I guess from the Madsen bank."

"Fascinating."

"What do you want me to do?" she asked plaintively in between sobs.

"I don't give a shit. What were you supposed to do?"

"I was to signal the guy from the window when you were leaving."

Great. Do that. Just give me time to get down the back stairs through the service door in the kitchen. I'll handle the rest. Can you do that for me?"

"Yes. What then?"

"Leave Nassau. Return to Bimini and go see Cecil."

"But he's a cop."

"He's my friend. Tell him exactly what happened and he'll protect you. You can trust him even if you can't trust me."

"That's not fair, Ruby."

"Listen closely. Your life isn't worth a dime if I get out of here alive. You'll give yourself running time by spreading the word I'm wounded. They'll spend more time looking for me than for you. Get to Bimini. I'll meet you there. If you're too scared to return to the Biminis, then hide out in Florida for a while. You told me once your folks were in Miami."

She dried her tears and pulled a bag from under one of the sofa pillows.

"Here. Take it. It's the money Lang gave me."

"I don't want it. You might still earn it."

"You're a real bastard, Ruby!" she shrieked. "Take the money."

"Fair enough." He opened the bag and examined its contents. It contained ten bands, each tied around twenty fresh one hundred dollar bills. The bands bore the Madsen Bank imprint.

He threw the bag into his duffel, picked up a carving knife lying on the kitchen counter and bolted out through the rear door to the back stairs.

A slanted ray of yellow light from the stairwell window crossed his unblinking eyes as he glided silently down the steps like a jungle cat. Duffel in his left hand, he drew the straight edge out of his pocket with his right hand and snapped it open when he reached the bottom. The exit door was ajar and offered a view of the iron gate with the spiked end posts outside.

Something moved ever so slightly behind the door. Amison dropped the duffel, kicked open the door and pinned whoever it was against the building wall. He slammed the door against the wall repeatedly until the man stumbled out, his hand barely able to hold his weapon. With straight edge in one hand and carving knife in the other, Amison slashed his face and hands until the gun dropped.

He moved like greased lightening. He snapped the straight edge shut, slipped it back into his pocket, threw the duffel over the fallen gun, and grabbed the dazed man's head in a hammer lock. He rammed it into the wall l over and over again until he heard the skull crack and then heaved him full force into the iron railing over the garbage cans where he impaled himself on one of the spikes. It pierced his chest and burst out his back like the head of a spear.

Amison took the apple from his pocket, planted it on the protruding spike and sneered at the bleeding body. "Bon Appetite, scum bag!"

He straightened out his clothes, grabbed his duffel and walked briskly to Potters' Cay where *Phoenix* was docked, ready to sail. A bright sunny day, Amison noted. A good time to move on. Ojo was waiting on board and seemed to read his mind. He released the lines as his boss jumped on deck and took the helm inside the wheelhouse. To the rumble of throaty diesels, the catamaran slipped away from the dock into the main ship channel and headed for open water.

CHAPTER 5

▼

THE BIMINIS

Phoenix sailed west northwest past the Berry Islands the through Providence Passage and then southward past Great Isaac Light to the Biminis. A steady trade wind allowed the vessel to race under sail at speeds up to forty knots and landfall was made early the next morning. The cat reached a shallow bay between North and South Bimini in the grip of a strong tidal current. Ojo was at the helm and, not having Amison's experience, he was understandably jittery. The fact that the tide was first moving in made him even more nervous. He used the reverse thrust of the vessel's powerful diesels to slow it down but was fearful of crashing the boat into one of the many reefs hiding under the surface of the water at the entrance to the bay. The waves breaking over submerged reefs could be heard but not seen and Ojo sighed with deep relief when his boss took the wheel and proceeded to effortlessly guide the cat the rest of the way through the unmarked channel.

The Biminis consisted of two main islands and several smaller islets. They faced the Gulf Stream to the west and the Bahama Bank to the east. Limestone and coral based, they were barely above sea level except for a low line of spinal bluffs that ran above white sandy palm tree shaded beaches along South and North Bimini's western shores.

From the air, North Bimini resembled a left tilting letter 'A' without the cross bar, in place of which were several tiny mangrove cays that looked like stepping stones between the two legs. The Sound, used by smaller craft as an anchorage, lay above the cays. Porgy Bay lay below the cays and separated the two islands.

North Bimini's south western leg hung over South Bimini's northwestern shore by a quarter of a mile. This meant that mariners coming in from the Gulf Stream had to make a mean dog eared turn to enter Porgy Bay and North Bimini's Alice Town on its left leg and Buccaneer Point, a spit of land on South Bimini's north shore facing the hamlet. The cut between North and South Bimini was also used by the ancient seaplanes of Chalks' Airlines that made daily runs between Miami Harbor and Paradise island with an Alice Town pit stop.

All of North Bimini was about ten miles long with Alice Town and Bailey Town sloping gently down from the bluffs to Porgy Bay. Alice Town was the Biminis' main hamlet and official port of entry. Its hotels, shops and restaurants, built with overhangs over raised walks, flanked the King's Highway a block away from the the docks. The road was dusty on dry days and a mud puddle filled when it rained. Locals lived behind the main road in small clapboard homes with blue, green and pink shutters, surrounded by flowering gardens and cooled by shade trees and palms.

Narrow lanes of private residences ran up the slope from the King's Highway to the Queen's Highway, a scenic but narrow lane running along the bluff line. Both roads merged at the police barracks and Eunice's diner and lead to Bailey Town near the top of North Bimini before turning down its right leg which was swamp and mangrove filled and sparsely populated. Roads were impassable when wet and travel was mostly by boat. Most of the people lived in an around Alice Town.

South Bimini lay perpendicular to North Bimini, underlining the island. It was shaped like a slice of pizza with the pointed edge facing east and its crust facing west. It was seven miles from crust to point and two miles from Buccaneer Point to the Bimini Reef Hotel at Round Rock on the island's southwestern tip. Mangrove, swamp and low lying scrub pine broken up by natural canals covered most of South Bimini to the bluff line. A small marina and a pier hosting an old jitney ferry to move people, animals and vehicles between the two islands stood on Buccaneer Point. The canals crisscrossed the island and flowed into Cavelle Pond to the south, a small lagoon emptying into Nixon's Harbor just east of the Bimini Reef hotel.

Two hard surface roads crossed South Bimini. One paralleled the western bluff line between the hotel and Buccaneer Point. A few private homes were scattered along the road's land side and were backed by canals whose bulkheads hosted large yachts equipped for game fishing. Their tuna towers and out-riggers stuck out prominently over the trees behind the houses. Some homes were spacious but most were shacks, trailers and modular affairs with rusty pick up trucks and old cars parked in front. A second road made ran east from the ferry landing through heavily wooded and dense mangrove swamps to a clearing and customs hut by an airstrip not far from a secluded beach at the island's eastern tip.

Because North Bimini's left leg was longer than its right, entry into Porgy Bay from the east was through a broad unmarked channel filled with shoals and reefs concealed from view at high tide. Ojo was more comfortable negotiating the narrow cut from the west than the treacherous eastern access. Amison smiled to himself. He rather liked this approach, especially on mornings when the sun was behind him. It gave him a clear view of the baby blue transparent waters and of the dangers that lay below. But this morning his mind was elsewhere.

Years ago, after he married Bernice to have a mother care for his infant children, and before Domino materialized, while he was teaching at Las Olas University, he had an affair with Leslie Sandler. She had gone to Bimini for a long weekend with him and asked him why he liked going there so often.

Amison had replied, "It has the best game fish in the world. Otherwise, there's nothing much around. Yet, people have fought over this little stretch of nothing for centuries. A branch of the Arawak Indians, the Lucayans, migrated here after they were pushed out of Jamaica by the Caribs. The Spanish came and killed off all the Indians and brought in slaves from Africa. The French came and kicked out the Spanish and then the English came and kicked out the French and imported more slaves. Then came pirates, privateers, renegades, thieves, fugitives, refugees from the American Revolution and Civil War and just plain bums, scoundrels and con artists. They all came to the Biminis for mischief, murder and good old fashioned mayhem.

"More recently, Ernest Hemingway played in Bimini and hunted game fish with machine guns. The de-frocked black congressman, Adam Clayton Powell, lived out his days in North Bimini. And the islands were where Presidential contender Gary Hart and his bimbo girlfriend waved goodbye to his political career and to his wife and family from the stern of *Monkey Business*."

"Just like you're going to wave your wife, family and career goodbye one of these days, Ruby?"

"Don't hold your breath, woman," Amison had shot back. "That's not going to happen any time soon, if it all happens at all."

Little changed over the centuries, he reflected. The setting was the same. People came here for laughs, for elbow room, for fame and fortune and for treasure. The plots varied slightly, depending on whether the actors were scam artists, fortune hunters or just plain escapees from reality. They were all playing and fighting for pretty much the same things. In his case, he was a fugitive from justice, at least up to now.

Amison's mind kept wandering, causing him to momentarily lose his focus and almost run *Phoenix* aground. An excited and panting Ojo raced up to the wheel house to see if his boss was all right. Amison blushed, smiled bravely and waved him away. Everything was fine, he motioned.

The wide expanse of the eastern entry between the Biminis was deceptive. It was reef and shoal filled and a bar, passable at high tide, lay barely submerged at low tide. Alice Town came into view as the catamaran passed Pigeon Cay on the right with Porgy Bay behind it. The two Biminis now drew closer together as the cat advanced cautiously toward Alice Town and Buccaneer Point just off to the south.

Amison kept *Phoenix* at a bulkhead slip at the Jolly Roger Marina, a small beat up boat yard on the edge of Buccaneer Point owned by Ginny Peters and a senior partner who was known in the islands only by his first name, Winslow. This was where he now headed.

Most yachts slipped up in Alice Town along narrow finger docks from Brown's Docks at the End-Of-The-World Bar to the Bimini Big Game Fishing Club near Eunice's diner and the telephone center. Deep draft craft anchored in Porgy Bay and shallow draft boats wove their way between the cays to drop their hooks in the Sound.

Tourists staying at the Bimini Reef hotel were already gathered and waiting for the ferry at Buccaneer Point to take them to Alice Town when *Phoenix* arrived and tied up at its usual slip. Tourism was good for the Biminis, Amison reasoned. Its population of two thousand normally doubled in season and he reckoned that it had swelled to five thousand with all the publicity surrounding the Bimini Man dig. He and most other residents accepted the visitors as welcome contributors to the economy but he shared their angst about the in-your-face obnoxiousness of the Jamaican guards hired to patrol the dig's perimeter. They rudely kept everyone at bay during working hours and routinely got drunk and terrorized the townspeople when they were off duty.

He navigated *Phoenix* slowly to its reserved slip, leaving Ojo to work the dock lines. Another uneventful trip, he thought. At sea, uneventful was a good thing.

There were chores to be done, like cleaning the boat and helping Ojo install an awning over the boom to shelter the after deck from bad weather. Domino's fate preyed on his mind, and once all was done, he tried reaching her several times at her Bailey Town home on his cell phone, VHF and CB radios, all without success, even taking into consideration the haphazardness of telecommunications in the Biminis.

He cursed and jumped to his feet. Cat claws scratched his innards but he knew that getting jumpy was no answer. He bounded off the boat and walked briskly toward the marina office where he saw Ginny in a cotton print dress sitting a at a picnic table with a grizzled marina rat guzzling a can of beer. It was Winslow.

Ginny excused herself and rose to greet Amison with a big kiss.

"How's my favorite sailor?"

"Not bad," he replied. And he tucked a wad of bills into her dress. "This should take care of my slip charges and other bills."

She gave him another kiss. This one lingered. "Business must have been good in Nassau," she said.

Amison waved a hand indecisively. "More or less. How's Winslow?"

He waved at the old mariner who grinned and waved back.

"Maybe, if you're free, we could have dinner or something," Ginny suggested.

"I could go for something," he added cautiously. Sex, he knew she wanted, but she was also a smart woman and he felt she was up to something.

"I'm going to the States to see my sister," she informed him. "Are you heading Stateside any time soon?"

That was a leading question if he ever heard one. Amison liked Ginny and found her attractive. She was a heavy breasted woman with a full body, long thick brown hair and ruddy cheeks, and he had often thought of her even after he had started seeing Domino. Her personality wasn't great but at least she was no hooker.

"What about Winslow?"

"Oh, don't worry about him. He's a distant cousin."

That was the thing in the Biminis. Everyone was a cousin. Black, white, brown or purple, everyone was related. Winslow, he had heard, hailed from Georgia and Ginny came from Mississippi in her teens. She had married and then divorced a Bahamian and had no children. Beyond these few historical details he knew little about either of them.

He was about to reply when he happened to see someone pacing back and forth on Phoenix's after deck. He excused himself and retreated to the boat where he found himself looking at a man with a Santa Claus build and beard who returned his stare through a pair of twinkling eyes behind a pair of steel spectacles.

Amison's face broke out in a grin and he jumped on board.

"Henry. What a pleasant surprise."

Henry Alstrum sat down on one of the banquettes on deck while Amison drew a cigarette out of his shirt pocket, lit it and sat down opposite him.

"I was told to see you about Bimini Man, doctor," he said. "But I didn't expect you to come to me."

He blew smoke rings over Henry's head, giving him time to reach for his pipe. He promptly stuffed it with tobacco from a pouch, lit it and started puffing away.

Ojo brought up two cups of hot coffee and repaired to *Phoenix's* bow to check the anchors.

Henry stroked his beard. "Cecil tells me you're working again, Jones." His voice betrayed the hint of an English background. "I called Leroux and he was pleased to hear the news."

"I'm sure. I was planning to see you in the Abacos, doctor. What happened?"

"I came early to make sure I have a place to sleep when the Triple A conference meets here late next week."

"Isn't that the Atlantis Artifacts Association?"

"Yes. Those folks are all hyped up about Bimini Man. And I also have patients to in North Bimini. I'm covering the islands for another physician who retired and it's tough getting to all of them. I spend more time waiting for inter-island flights than in the air. I think I should get myself a seaplane or a fast boat like yours."

"Why doesn't Nassau get you some assistance?"

"The government tries to. But it's difficult to find a doctor who wants to do a circuit of the out islands, and the population in these towns is too small to afford resident health services. But I do have some help," he added. "Dudley Hanes is my medical assistant and handles coughs and colds as well as the logistics of handling our Europol agents in the West Indies."

Henry took another puff on his pipe. "I'm hitting four birds with one rock here. I can see my patients. I can take a look at the two dead bodies that Cecil has on ice. I can brief you on your mission before sending you off to Philadelphia and I get to attend the conference."

"You're still Leroux's West Indian coordinator?"

"Yes, but only part time. However, I help wherever and whenever I can."

He dug into his pockets, produced a leather portfolio and gave it to Amison. "Don't lose this. It has a airline tickets to from Fort Lauderdale to Philadelphia and a credit card with cash advance privileges. The card has a nice draw limit of one hundred thousand dollars. Dudley made the arrangements."

"I've been thinking of retiring, Henry. So this job better pay well."

Dr. Alstrum's face clouded. "Don't bargain with me, Jones. You know the drill. We don't retire in this business; we get retired."

"Well, let's leave it at that, Henry. Tell me about Bimini Man."

The doctor paused. "Have any of you ever heard of Cyrus Gordon?"

"Yes."

Henry continued. "Gordon's research suggested that Hebrew-Phoenician fleets sailed many thousands of years ago around Africa where they picked up crew on various stops before heading west where they made landfalls in Brazil. He claims that some expeditions made it as far north as the Bahamas and Florida. I attended a cartographers' conference once and examined a set of old charts. The Bahamas and Bimini in particular were shown as being about one hundred to five hundred feet higher above sea level than they are today. If that's true, early voyagers may have come upon a much larger land mass than we see today. Thousands of years ago, the Bahamas could even have been connected to Florida. And there could have been a flourishing civilization in the Bahamas. That would be the legendary city-state of Atlantis."

"Fascinating." said Amison.

"Well," said the doctor. "There's more. There is an underwater six hundred feet long rock formation off North Bimini. It consists of identical boulders with carved ends set equidistantly apart from one another in a perfect reverse 'J' in thirty feet of water. The precision with which those rocks are set is amazing. Now, someone put them there but not recently. What I'm saying is that there could have very well could have been primitive human beings living here eons ago, and finding that out is what the Las Olas University project is all about."

Amison yawned. "What's my starting point, Henry?"

"Start with Cecil's problem. Determine if the Europol agents were murdered and if they were, identify their killer or killers."

"Terminate with extreme prejudice?"

"No. Just find out and advise us. That decision may come later."

Amison leaned back in his chair and grinned. "Sounds good. I could use drink and date money. Now what's the pay? I have bills to pay."

"Well, Alliance has been keeping you on its offshore payroll and you'll stay that way. However, Europol is sweetening the deal with a two hundred thousand dollar bonus, half payable immediately after your briefing in Philadelphia is completed and the rest after the mission's completion. Those amounts will be added to your credit card so you can draw cash advances."

Henry did not elaborate. Instead, he looked at Amison and asked. "How long have we worked together?"

Amison leaned back, extinguished his cigarette, stretched his legs and folded his arms. "Over thirty years?"

"Correct. And I've always backed you and you have always trusted me."

"That's true. Then, can you explain Leroux's carte blanche?"

Henry spoke slowly in a low voice. "There's more to this Bimini Man thing than meets the eye. It's an earthquake waiting to happen with you at the epicenter. You might have to take a few people down."

"I thought you said there should be no terminating with extreme prejudice."

"That's what I said. You didn't hear anything else." Henry's tone softened. "You can still back out, you know. Cut and run. I'll make the appropriate excuses."

"No way. I'm in. I promised Cecil."

Henry cleared his throat. "Well then, welcome back to the fold."

CHAPTER 6

▼

A MATTER OF CONSCIENCE

Amison unfolded his arms and leaned forward. "But tell you what. I want my compensation doubled."

"You're being greedy, Jones."

"Not really. I ran into Tucker Anderson who said that he and Mike Quinn will be working with me. I understand our real mission is to close down the Bimini Man dig and to kill the Bencivengas."

Henry looked squarely at Amison. "I won't comment on that. That is not exactly what Europol has in mind for you to do."

"I figured. You guys have to get together and iron out your differences. When you do, double my pay!"

"That may be difficult."

Amison ignored his words. "And I should also give you fair warning, Henry. I plan to revisit the issue of Bernice's so-called accident."

A look of rising concern registered on Henry's face. "That's a Pandora's box and you want to keep it shut, Jones. It's been five years and Bernice will probably stay comatose. You're safe so long as she stays that way."

"How come?"

"If she recovers, she might start talking about her accident. Supposing it was in fact a case of attempted murder as you imply. What steps are you prepared to take in righting the wrong?"

Amison was adamant and looked at him coldly. "Attempted murder? Those are your words, not mine. What made you think attempted murder?"

Henry was at a loss for words.

Amison continued to press his point. "Look," he said. "Bernice is my problem, not yours, and I'll never fault you for knowing more about her than you're letting on. However, you would do the same in my shoes. I'm taking this assignment for Cecil's sake, whatever it is, but I aim to reopen my wife's case. I was not a great husband and was never there when she needed me. This is something I need to do. It's a matter of conscience. How about it, Henry? Deal?"

"Deal," agreed the doctor reluctantly. "It's fine with me, but Harold or Marvin get the last word on this. I can talk money to an extent but vengeance is not in my department. But getting back to Bernice. What if by some miracle she recovers? It's no secret about your current flame. What are you going to do with Domino?"

Amison thought in silence for a while. Henry apparently was unaware of what happened with her in Paradise Island.

"That's a tough one," he answered haltingly. "She knows I'm married and that our relationship is temporary."

Henry shook his head. "No woman looks upon a relationship as temporary, even if it involves a married man."

"Right, Amison said. "But we had an incident. She inadvertently set me up to be killed in Nassau the other day and I had to leave in a hurry...." And he went on to describe the episode in Domino's apartment. "Frankly," he concluded regretfully. "I don't know if I'll ever see her again. But you want to know something? I miss the woman."

"That's too bad," said Henry. "Cecil and I thought for a moment you guys were going to make a go of it, even though she makes a strange living. But this casts a different color on the picture. And it also means you're in someone's sights."

"That's part of a larger puzzle, Henry. I have several pieces but no picture. The first piece is my wife's fall. If it was no accident, who tried to kill her and for what reason. The second piece is my being suddenly railroaded to the islands right after Bernice gets hurt. That never made any sense to me. The third and fourth pieces I can connect: the failed ambush with the decoy trawler in the waters off

Nassau and the thing in Domino's apartment. But who wants me dead? I haven't started working yet."

"Cecil told me all about that trawler business," said Henry. "I don't think Frank had anything to do with it."

"That's good, but it doesn't make me feel any better. The last two pieces I can't match are the Europol assignment and the hints I keep hearing that the real reason I'm being re-activated is to end the Bimini Man project and kill the Bencivengas. Can you shed any light, doctor?"

Henry Alstrum looked straight into Amison's eyes. "We are facing a god awful mess with Bimini Man," he commented. "The Europol investigation is the way to get you into the loop. It's naive to believe that Leroux's two agents accidentally drowned. They were murdered because they found something. They were silenced to keep their mouths shut. I keep hoping Bimini Man is for real but I'm no longer sure."

"Well, let's talk about Bimini Man and the Atlantis legend that all the media is harping on."

"I'm not an archeologist," said Henry. "Speak to Mark Stone. He's the expert.

Cecil Fergueson thinks the dig is a cover for moving heroin. But you know cops, they're a suspicious lot. I'd like to think he's wrong."

"Cecil may have a point, doctor. Bencivenga has been hanging around a lot and Nassau has taken over the security detail around the dig perimeter. The dig site is heavily patrolled by Rastafarian guards who for a Jamaican security company owned by Sanford Jack."

"Treat Bencivenga and Captain Jack delicately. They are well connected."

"Thanks," replied Amison. "What about Las Olas University? Is it clean?"

"A bunch of pin-headed professors would be out of their league with Captain Jack and don Ignacio. You might be over reaching."

"Well, why do Frank Hoffman and Leslie Sandler keep the dig site off limits?"

"You'll have to ask them."

"I can't. They keep me at arms' length. I haven't seen them in five years."

"Ahem!" Henry cleared his throat. "I detect sour grapes. I attended a Triple A meeting at Las Olas University six years ago. It was a fund raiser for the dig idea. Frank was the new university president, but Leslie Sandler ran the show. Ignacio Bencivenga was there and put up ten million dollars in seed money. You must understand that once he invested his own funds, corporate contributors and the U.S. government followed suit.

"Bear in mind that Bencivenga has been Washington's darling up to now and if supports this dig so does Washington. Thus, whatever your final instructions may be, move carefully. Your last encounter with the Bencivenga family cost you five years."

"Who in Washington? Anyone in particular?"

"Jack O'Brien, of course."

"You're smart, Henry. Tell me who you believe wants to see me dead before I get started?"

The doctor counting on his fingers. "Let's see. You killed Pauli Bencivenga, don Ignacio's eldest son in that famous shootout outside Miami harbor five years ago.

I wouldn't blame the old man for coming after you, especially if he's hearing that you've been hired to shut down the dig and to terminate him.

"Then there's Bill Nigel who is on the outs with Harold. He may have tried to bring you down as a preemptive strike if he believes Harold has a contract on him with you as the hit man.

"Then we have the Neals family which is not very fond of you, and last but not least, we have Reginald Lang with whose wife you've been banging."

"What about Jack O'Brien?"

"He has real concerns about you, Jones. But right now he needs you as much as you need him. I don't believe he's involved in a plot against your life."

Amison was about to respond but Henry stopped him. "Look, Jones. Keep it simple and do what you're told. Don't reopen any blood feuds. Insofar as Sandler goes, you're annoyed just because Frank stole her away from you. You need to get into the dig site so renewing old acquaintances would be good. But do try to stay away from too much tail. It's going to kill you. How many women can you handle at one time anyway?"

"I'll take my chances, Henry."

"Personal errors of judgement can be more lethal than professional lapses."

Amison smiled wryly. "You think?" He got up to stretch his legs. "What's going on in Philadelphia?"

"Harold is top dog now. Incidentally, is that rumor about your helping Harold kill Max and Dominick true?"

Amison got up, walked over to Henry's side, placed a hand on his shoulder and gave it a squeeze. "Rumors can be harmful to your health, Henry."

"I know, I know," Henry Alstrum said quickly.

"Good. Now tell me how Marvin Childs and the two Neals brothers are doing."

"Marvin is CEO. Vincent is controller. And Roger is into drugs and sex."

"Is Harold secure?"

"For now. He's a homicidal maniac, but social workers don't run in our circles, do they? And if it makes you feel better, Harold still calls you his hired gun. That's what has Bill Nigel scared. He thinks you're after him."

Amison laughed. "Harold hasn't given me any orders to take him down."

Henry seemed relieved. "I'll tell Nigel if I see him."

"You do that. Now, how's the weather up north?"

"It's snowing in Philadelphia. Do you have warm clothes?"

"I'll think of something."

"While you're thinking, how about a ride to Alice Town?"

"Will customs do? I'm taking the Zodiac over to the customs dock."

Ojo lowered the inflatable dinghy from *Phoenix's* davits on the cockpit stern and held the boarding ladder as his boss followed by Henry climbed down and settled into the Zodiac and started the outboard motor.

The dinghy quickly covered the short distance from Buccaneer Point to Chalks' seaplane landing adjoining the customs dock where Cecil Fergueson was helping Frances Douglas on the tarmac prepare for the incoming Chalks flight.

Cecil turned when he heard the Zodiac approach and gave Amison and Henry a hand getting off as the small boat banged against a bulkhead.

"Breakfast later, Jonesey, Henry?" he asked.

Amison shook his head. "Not today, Cecil. I'm off to the States."

Cecil and Henry exchanged glances. "Jones is working again," said Henry.

"That's good. Is everyone finally getting excited about the Bimini Man dig and my two dead bodies?"

Frances was nearby and overheard. Still teary eyed over her husband's death, she cleaned her glasses and came over. "Hi, Ruby. Good morning, doctor. I hope you guys find the bastards who killed my husband."

Amison gave her a kiss on the cheek. "Don't worry, angel. We'll find them now that Superman is here."

"Is this like releasing the monster from the deep to save the city?" Cecil asked.

"Something like that." he turned to Frances. "Have you heard from Domino?" Frances nodded. "She called from Miami and gave me the whole story. She said she's terribly sorry but she's scared. I'm looking after her kids while she's away. But she is worried about you."

Amison became defensive. "Listen. She knows exactly what I do for a living and she understands my personal circumstances. She had..."

Cecil raised his hands in despair and repeated the phrase in unison with Amison. "I know, I know. She had 'fair warning', Jonesey."

Amison grinned. At least she was safe. "I'm holding her money," he confided. "Hang on to it," replied Frances. "We might yet need it."

"Why is that?"

Cecil took Amison by the arm and lead him outside. "This place is falling apart and I'm up to my eyeballs in shit," he groaned. "The town is filled armed creeps running amuck in the streets. They've turned the End-Of-The-World Bar next door into their own city hall. The jail is filled with drunks and bone breakers and they get released as fast as they're busted. Things may get even messier if these guys act up when the Triple A people start arriving in a few days.

"To top it off, I have Guenther and Douglas on ice and a medical examiner who is dragging his feet on getting here to confirm the cause of death. I have to work with Dwayne's widow every day and I can't look her straight in the face. And I have Luther's family in Switzerland making noises about lodging an official complaint. Whose ass do you think is going to go through the wringer when this is over?"

"I guess you're a little disappointed in this wonderful scientific expedition."

Cecil rolled his eyes. "Are you stupid or what? There's nothing here but heroin." Amison nodded grimly. "How is Bimini Man playing with the Triple A?"

"Those guys are wearing blinders. Bimini Man is their black messiah."

"Then maybe I should tell you what I told Henry."

"What's that, Jonesey?"

"You've been duped, Cecil, and so was Europol. The murder inquiry is the lead into the real mission which is to shut down the the Bimini Man dig and terminate the Bencivengas."

Cecil's eyes widened. "Are you sure?"

"I'm positive."

"Shit!"

It was one of the few times that Amison heard a curse leave Cecil's lips.

"That's why I'm going to Philadelphia, to get my official instructions."

Several moments of silence passed between the two men.

"I want you to understand, Cecil," Amison went on, "that I plan to execute the mission faithfully. You need to relay that to Henry and Leroux. Europol, Alliance and the CIA are in bed together it's essential that we're all reading from the same page. We have no way out."

"Is the mission that important to you?"

"You bet. It'll give me a chance to settle some old scores."

"A private vendetta is not a good enough reason to drown us in blood, Jonesey. Scores settled create new scores to settle. The last man wins, and then the last man dies. That's the final score."

"Excellent, Cecil. Just don't forget you asked me for a favor."

Cecil did not reply.

They stopped to listen to the roar of the Chalks seaplane as it dropped from the sky into the cut between North and South Bimini.

"If you get to Fort Lauderdale, go to the Esplanade," yelled Cecil above the din. "I was there last month with the wife. We went with your brother-in-law Luis and and Mark and their wives to the new theater for the performing arts. It was terrific. They were playing La Boheme."

Amison sneered, "What the hell do I care about La Boheme?"

"You know, Jonesey. Now I understand what women love about you. You're a wonderful guy. Way down deep, you're very superficial."

Amison showed Cecil the international finger of ill will, threw back his head, grunted incomprehensibly and walked back to the dinghy.

Cecil laughed. "I love you, Jonesey!" he yelled after him.

Amison looked back with a broad smile on his face. "Fuck you, Cecil."

Cecil waved. "Good luck anyway."

Amison climbed aboard the Zodiac, started the outboard and made his way back to Buccaneer Point. His mind drifted back to the time five years ago when he was at Eunice's diner in a booth sitting across from Frank Hoffman and Leslie Sandler. He had just arrived in Bimini and the Las Olas University archeological team was about to start excavating on one of the cays in Porgy Bay.

"I'm putting you on indefinite leave for reasons of health, Jonesey. Mark Stone can teach your courses," Frank explained. He sat close to Leslie Sandler with his arms around her and she was not shy about coddling up to him.

"It's the best way, Jonesey. You can't go wrong with the deal Harold is offering you. It'll keep you flush. And don't worry about your job. It will always be there."

Frank gave him a slap on the back on the way out.

It was more like a slap in the face. He was jolted out of his day dream when the Zodiac bumped into *Phoenix*.

CHAPTER 7

▼

HARBOR BEACH

Amison's mind was made up. He would take a Chalks flight to Miami and from there fly north to meet with the Alliance people in Philadelphia. His plan was to go alone. But Ginny Peters, who he found waiting for him at the Jolly Roger, had other ideas.

"My sister called," she informed him. "She arranged a doctor's appointment for me."

"Yeah? What for?"

"Ginny sidled up to him and gave him an enticing smile . "You know. Woman stuff and all that. I called Dr. Alstrum for a checkup but his medical assistant said he was too busy. So I'm going to the States. That's where he said you're headed. Mind if I tag along?"

Amison sensed an opportunity. "By all means. But I'm flying. Tell you what. I'll pay the airfare. That should settle all our bills for a while."

"Great," she said. "My duffel is packed. Another Chalks flight to Miami will be here soon. Where are you heading?"

"Chicago." He lied.

"I'm going to New York. You can give me a preliminary physical on the way."

It was an offer too good to pass up. Leaving the catamaran in Ojo's care, they boarded a west bound seaplane an hour later.

Ginny fell asleep immediately when the plane took off, leaving Amison to wonder how and where this episode was going to play out. He dozed off and one daydream lead to another and soon events long buried in the recesses of his mind emerged to set a perspective from what had been to what was now.

There was his last dinner with Jack O'Brien five years ago. He was on a Miami street trying to hail a cab after leaving O'Brien at the restaurant where he was told that because a drug intercept mission back-fired and caused several high profile deaths, he had to be temporarily cashiered to avoid a murder indictment.

The CIA mission chief had a plan. Amison should leave the country before an arrest warrant was issued. He could live in the Bahamas for a while. Leave now, Jack had urged. Just get in that damn boat and go! They shook hands, and Amison left the restaurant only to be shot at on the street a few minutes later. The shooter missed and got away.

He had called Harold Levy at home later that night. Harold's booming voice resonated over the telephone and thundered in his inner ear as he now recalled the conversation. "Listen, Jonesey," Harold had said. "We've been down a long road together. I love you like a brother, but you screwed up. Jack is right. You may end up in prison. Your wife's situation also complicates things for us. If she fell out of our office window accidentally, or if it was attempted suicide, that's one thing; but if she was pushed out, as she might have been, that's attempted murder. A murder investigation on Alliance property at this moment wouldn't be cool. We have too many things cooking. The matter must be closed at least temporarily to prevent a public airing of our arrangements with the CIA and Europol.

"Here's what I propose, and Jack agrees. You're banked for five years. Sail off to Bimini. The police chief there, Cecil Fergueson, is a Europol man like Henry Alstrum. Surrender your passport to him. He'll send it to our embassy in Nassau. "Believe me. You'll do great. You'll do drug intercepts for the Bahamians. It's bounty work and it'll also earn you redemption points with the feds. You'll be a hero and back in no time, richer than ever.

"Besides, I'll need you for some housecleaning down the line. So stay alive and healthy, you hear?"

There was no time. No time for goodbyes and no time to see his wife and kids. He left for the islands before dawn and arrived with a blistering rising sun in his eyes.

It was not Ginny's head against his shoulder. It was Dolores whose head leaned on his shoulder. She too was sleeping. They were on a small plane going across the islands from the Dominican Republic to Miami where they hoped to marry. That was thirty years ago. That's who the twins resembled. Dolores. Damn! What had happened to his life? Where did it go?

The seaplane landed in Miami Harbor under a sunny sky. He half expected to be arrested on the spot, but U.S. Customs was cleared without incident.

The customs agent merely smiled and said, "Welcome back to the United States, Mr. Jones. We hope you have enjoyed your stay in the Bahamas."

That was all there was to it.

They hailed a cab for the airport in Miami only to learn that a nasty winter storm up north was creating massive delays. After several attempts to reschedule, they were finally able to book for the next day but then only out of Fort Lauderdale.

"What now?" asked Ginny.

"It's okay," Amison answered. "I can take care of some business there."

"Oh?"

"I need twenty four hours. I'll put you up at the Lago Mar. It's a great place."

"Sure?"

"Positive."

They found another cab and headed north to Fort Lauderdale. The cab ride took them through the Port Everglades harbor district off the inlet where they passed an old freighter with the name *Casa D'Ora* on its bows. It seemed deserted and stood alone at an old decaying pier on the Dania Cutoff Canal before depositing them in front of the ocean front Lago Mar. The resort-conference hotel all Ginny expected and more and when she saw its setting and facilities she readily agreed to stay in one of its suites.

Amison left her in a one bedroom suite overlooking both the pool and the beach with his duffel, gave her a kiss and left for the lobby where he pulled out his cell phone to make a call.

It was early evening and he knew that Leslie Sandler, who lived in the Harbor Beach Towers overlooking the Port Everglades inlet less than a quarter of a mile away, might be at home. She taught morning classes at Las Olas University early in the week and would not be going to the Biminis for several days to participate in the Bimini Man dig. This was a golden opportunity to see what she was up to. He tried one call but there was no answer.

He had been physically attracted to Leslie from the day they met. Aside from being attractive, she was a great talker and was a natural as a teacher with great rapport with students and colleagues. This Bimini Man business could of course launch her on the way to academic fame and commercial fortune. Married once, divorced, never remarried, no kids, she was always in debt. But she had street smarts, and Amison knew she could take care of herself.

What he really wanted was a hooker for the night. Even Ginny would not fill the bill. That brought Leslie back to mind and he tried calling her again. This would be the right time to start rattling Frank Hoffman's chain. He thought she might be in Bimini, on campus or with Frank because the phone kept ringing. But no. She was indeed home and she picked up the phone on the sixth ring.

Amison heard her distinctive voice. "Hello. Dr. Sandler here."

"Dr. Leslie Sandler, Ph.D.?" Amison started in a low voice, trying to disguise it. "This is a used bone salesman."

"Ruby, you big oaf, what a surprise!"

Amison looked at his phone in disbelief. "I'm in town," he continued. "I thought I'd give you a call and see if a famous person like you has a few moments for a nobody like me."

"Ruby, you're just as phony as ever. What do you have in mind?"

"How about a night of heavy sex? I'll spring for dinner." He liked that line. It rarely worked, but he liked it anyway.

"I'll settle for dinner first. We'll see about the rest later. Where are you now?"

"Nearby."

"Come on over; I'll dress for dinner."

"Same apartment?"

"Same place. You helped me move in, remember?"

Amison hung up and jogged the short distance to her building entrance. He often wondered how it felt to live in the Harbor Beach condos with a commanding view of the city of Fort Lauderdale with its beautiful beaches, its famous inlet and the harbor filled with giant cruise ships and great white yachts parading up and down the waterway.

When he finally arrived at her door, which was open, he found her standing in a black, low-cut, shift-like, knee length black dress with her long, tanned legs thrust into spiked heels. With the heels, they were the same height. They embraced like new lovers, almost passionately, he thought. One thing had changed. The long hair was gone in favor of a short blonde page boy cut.

"More suitable for the academic world and my more mature self," she said with a twinkle in her eye. "It hides the gray. Besides, they say blondes have more fun."

"Nice digs," he observed. "And you manage all this on a teacher's salary?"

Leslie laughed. "It's a struggle, but I manage." She waved at the furnishings. "I cleaned the place up a little, and added a few things since the last time you visited. Where are we going?"

"You pick it," said Amison. "I was thinking of the Old Heidelberg Restaurant. It has good food and 'oompapa' music. We had dinner there when you first came to town."

"That's it, then," she agreed. "Heidelberg it is."

The food and drink was always good and plentiful at the Heidelberg, a Bavarian eatery dressed up as a restaurant and nightclub near the Fort Lauderdale airport. It was a popular hangout for German and other East European tourists that flocked to South Florida every winter.

The restaurant featured vintage champagnes but Amison opted for the German Henckel which he preferred. Of the many dishes they offered, he liked their rack of lamb the best, mainly because it was a complete rack that was a meal in itself. Dining at the Heidelberg was not a high a culinary experience, but it was a feast complete with Bavarian music and complimentary shots of Ausbach, a German form of cognac, at the circular bar after dinner.

"I never had the chance to call you to say how sorry I was when I heard about your wife," Leslie was saying during dinner.

"It's just as well," replied Amison. "I had to leave in a hurry. It wouldn't have helped to talk."

"Why did you just let me go when you left?"

Amison shrugged his shoulders, and watched some couples moving to the band music on the small dance floor. "It was tough to compete against Frank. For me, there was no sense fighting a losing battle."

"I know you're living in the Bahamas," continued Leslie. "And you certainly know I spend all my time in Bimini when I'm not teaching. You could have come by."

"I did. I came over once to see if you could get me to the dig site, if you recall. You told me to drop dead. Frank was there. He too told me to drop dead."

"I didn't mean what I said. Besides, you caught us at a bad moment. Frank and I were screwing. That's how I am. I don't like interruptions. But tell me about your life. Frank tells me you have a colored chick. Does she fuck better than I do? Or does she only clean?"

His jaw tightened. Leslie was getting to him."Not better, but different."

"How nice but I think I still have better moves. Listen. Frank is away for a few days. We can do some catch up. Unless you're having your period."

"My dear woman," said Amison. "I'm always having my period."

They ordered another bottle of Henckel.

"That's true." Leslie nodded. "What about work? I hear from Frank that you're basically retired."

"Correct. But I'm working while retired." Amison did not elaborate. "Let's talk about you," he suggested. "You're more interesting. How are things at Las Olas University? I hear you're quite a big shot."

"You mean the Bimini dig?"

"Are you digging anyplace else?"

Leslie laughed. "I'd like to dig into your pants, but Bimini will have to do. To answer your question, I'm surviving. This is my tenure decision year, so this is an important semester. But you know, you still could have called me in Bimini to say 'hello.' You didn't have to give me the cold shoulder."

"Well," replied Amison somewhat cagily. "I didn't think it was my place to butt into your life, if you pardon the pun. And besides, I was busy."

"Busy? You mean busy fucking your Bahamian chick."

Amison winced a little. "Fair," he replied. "But what about Frank? I understand the university is backing you in this Bimini project."

"Yes. Frank's behind it. It's my key to tenure, so I don't want to mess up. And Frank? He is backing me for tenure, so that's good. But there's a price. He wants to get married. It may not be such a bad deal, you know. I may just marry him, but after I get tenure. He has money and position."

"How is the tenure process moving along?"

Leslie's smile disappeared momentarily, and her lips turned into a sneer. "You know who's against my tenure?"

"Who?"

"Your buddy, the wise old professor, Mark Stone."

"Mark? What's he got against you?"

"Ask him. He thinks I'm a fake and that the Bimini dig is a phony."

"Can't your sister Marlene work on him? She married the guy."

Leslie shook her head in despair. "She can't shake him," she replied. "Marlene said he's even thinking of going to Bimini to the Triple A conference for the sole purpose of discrediting the Bimini Man project. Maybe you could speak to him, Ruby."

"I'll try." Then he continued. "Tell me about Bimini Man. Is it the real thing or is there something else going on?"

"It's real, Ruby. We're making history. The media spilled the beans ahead of time, but it's ok. Just wait until the fossil is exhibited at the Triple A conference in Bimini later next week. It will turn Las Olas University from a diploma mill into a world class institution. And it will guarantee my tenure."

"The Bimini project wouldn't be a cover for something else going on, would it, Les?

"Like what?"

"Like drugs?" Amison was groping. "I hear a rumor that there's a cache of drugs buried in Bimini and that it's going to be moved to Florida."

"I hear rumors like that all the time. Someone is always trying to run drugs from the Bahamas to Florida. What else is new?"

Amison was unconvinced.

"Any connection between Bimini Man and heroin is bullshit," she insisted. "Is this something you heard or something that you're working on?"

"I'm working on it. I'm interested in two Europol agents who died in Bimini."

Leslie frowned. "I heard about that one. They might have been snooping around the dig site. Few people are allowed in. The Jamaicans have orders to shoot people who don't belong there."

Amison remained skeptical. "Just to protect a few relics from outside eyes?"

"Special relics, Ruby."

"But the they weren't shot. They drowned. Maybe accidentally. And the drugs, Les? I never said anything about heroin. That would be news to me. Is there any heroin in Bimini?"

Leslie's smile returned to her face. "What can I tell you, Ruby? I'm just guessing and trying to help."

"If you want to help, get me into the dig site. I want to look around."

She looked at him sweetly. "I can speak to Jonathan Sykes. I'm flying to Bimini tomorrow."

She suddenly lost her good humor. "What are you really doing besides fishing for dead bodies?"

"Alliance has me back on the payroll. Frank knows the outfit since he was once part of it. Alliance is managing the investigation for Europol. That's why Bimini Man intrigues me. And by coincidence, I'll be there soon and I'll look you up this time. Maybe we can go for a long romantic walk on the beach."

Leslie made a face. "Don't shit on me, Ruby," she snapped. "I know you much too well. You don't screw on the sand. You hate the beach. And you don't figure out how people died. You already know how they died. You kill them!

"You've been in the Bahamas for five years doing didley squat and now all of a sudden you're working again? I know all about Alliance. It's a CIA front. They get their marching orders through Europol when the CIA can't do its own dirty work. You're the exterminator! You were out for a while but now you're back. You're not going to be a threat to me and my career, are you?"

They sat there, glaring and snarling at each other, like two jungle cats who could not decide whether to fight or mate.

It was Amison who retreated. "I wouldn't categorize it that way," he protested, raising his glass. "In any case, here's to the most beautiful ditch digger in the world. May I suggest a truce for the night."

Leslie Sandler raised her glass, laughing. "You're a real bastard, Ruby, but you have a way about you. And, I'm going to tell you something you don't know."

"What's that?"

"Your wife didn't fall out of that Alliance office window up in Philadelphia. She was pushed!"

"Oh, yes? By whom?"

"I wish I could tell you more, Ruby, but I can't because I don't know. You have to figure it out for yourself. Come, pay the bill and let's go home. And don't talk to me anymore about Bimini Man or drugs, or you're going to get me pissed."

They arrived back at her apartment a half hour later.

"Do you still keep the vodka in the the refrigerator?" Amison asked.

"Yes." Leslie pointed to the kitchen. "Take the bottle and two glasses and go on the terrace. I'll join you in a few minutes."

He walked out to the terrace where a cool breeze was blowing from the sea. He could see across the way the other high rise building where people were moving about in those apartments that were still lit.

"Are you engaging in a little voyeurism?" asked Leslie. She came out on the terrace wearing a black negligee.

"I keep thinking how we look to folks from other worlds when they peek into our everyday movements," said Amison. "We move about like mice or hamsters in a cage, going from one corner to another, performing what we think are unique and important functions. But we all do pretty much the same things. Sometimes, we go to the kitchen for food, sometimes we go to the bathroom, then we watch a little TV. We have different reasons for doing things, but we the same things."

He passed her a glass of iced vodka, and they drank in silence. Then Leslie slid her body into his, saying, "I'm not into philosophy tonight," she said. "You owe me a night of heavy sex to make up for lost time. That's why I let you take me out for dinner."

Leslie awoke at dawn before Amison. Rousing him, she asked, "What do you think, Ruby?"

He was still drowsy, but her question made him jump and sit up straight as an arrow on the edge of the bed.

"Think about what!"

He got up from the bed and immediately put on his pants.

"About us."

"Us? There is no Us."

"How can you make love to a woman and then say there is no 'us'?"

"There is no Us with Frank around. He shoots better than I can. I don't plan to be in his cross hairs."

"You know, Ruby, there was a time when I would have followed you to the ends of the world."

Amison finished dressing. "That was long ago, Les. Too many things have been happening since then. Listen, a few weeks ago Frank's boat tried to take me down in the waters off Nassau. I don't need more trouble."

Leslie burst out laughing. "That wasn't Frank, you big coward. I've been with him constantly. It was Miguelito."

"Don Ignacio's kid?"

"Right. He uses Frank's boat with George Gibson, Marlene's cousin. Now, what about us?"

"I don't know, Les."

"But you sure like to screw anyone you get your hands on."

"Right. All men are sleaze," said Amison. "But here, I do give you fair warning about that Bimini Man business. You and Frank are at risk, especially Frank. And if Frank goes, your career goes."

"I can take care of myself," Leslie said defiantly, putting on her clothes. "Tenure is the only thing I'm interested in, and Frank is going to get it for me."

"Not if the dig is a phony."

"Oh yeah?" Leslie fumed. "Prove it. You'll be dead before you get close."

"Like the two Europol agents?"

"As I told you before, they were probably not minding their own business."

"What about Mark Stone? Do you still want me to speak with him?"

"That little creep? I hope he croaks. Yeah, you can talk to him."

"Is that a death threat?" Amison gathered his things together.

"Ruby. You don't get it. You can fuck me anytime, even after I marry Frank. I like you. But don't fuck with me! Now, are we going to fight or have coffee?"

"I'll take a rain check." He gave her a kiss on the cheeks and began heading for the door. "Knowing you is always exciting," he exclaimed.

A smile returned to her face and she walked him to the door.

"Where are you going?"

"To work," he replied.

Out of nowhere Leslie suddenly gave him a kiss.

"Watch yourself," she counseled. "You're not a coward, but you can be stupid. You don't want to die over this. For whatever it's worth, I still love you."

Amison grinned. "That's good, Les."

"We have a good thing going, Ruby. With tenure, I can do anything. We can even be rich."

"Tell you what," Amison said. "Get me into the dig site, and I'll speak to Mark Stone. What about it?"

"Ok," Leslie said finally. "And what I say still goes. I can be yours, even after I get tenure and Frank Hoffman. And even if I can't be yours, you can still do me from time to time."

They kissed again and Amison left the apartment. He shook his head. She was hard to dismiss from his mind. Too bad life had no do-overs.

CHAPTER 8

▼

NORTHEAST DIRECT

Ginny was pleased with her surroundings at the Lago Mar and was reluctant to leave. But after some cajoling and the vague promise of a new wardrobe, Amison was able to check her out of the hotel.

A waiting taxi took them to the airport on the way to which they stopped briefly at a second hand store where he picked up an old gray belted overcoat, a brimmed hat, a worn blue suit, a cheap shirt and tie plus some socks and a pair of shoes. At the airport, they learned that all flights were canceled except those to Washington D.C. which the storm had not reached.

They chose the flight to the capital where Ginny indicated she would stay with friends before continuing on to New York.

"How are you going to get to Chicago?" Ginny asked.

"Probably by train or bus. I'll see."

Amison had already decided to use Amtrak's Northeast Direct train for the last leg to Philadelphia from Washington but hought it best not to tell her. The nation's capital was not a wildly popular destination in mid winter. Their flight, except for themselves, one more passenger and the attendants, was empty and they were able to make themselves comfortable in a row of center seats towards the back of the cabin near the rest rooms.

They were an hour into the flight when Ginny said she had to go to the bathroom. "Walk with me," she requested. "We can fool around back there."

Amison was tired from his tryst the night before but he felt it wiser not to make a fuss. He followed her to one of the vacant cubicles and waited outside the door, half expecting a cabin attendant to walk up. No one did.

A whispered voice came from behind the door. "Ruby. I need a little help."

He opened the door. Ginny was seated, perched on top of the metal sink, her panties dangling from one ankle, her skirt gathered up around her waist, legs raised and spread, her blouse opened and her full bare breasts sticking out. "Interested?"

"Interested!" He repeated. He entered the bathroom, and closed the door and dropped his trousers at the same time that she wrapped her legs around him.

They emerged from the rest room a while later as the plane began its approach to the capital. Ginny straightened out her hair and remarked, "We must do this again, Ruby, real soon."

Amison agreed. "You bet."

"This can be the start of something good, Ruby, now that Domino has left."

"Shit." Amison muttered to himself.

They returned to their seats. Out of a corner of one eye he noticed that the other passenger sitting in the rear was a West Indian who had been seated near the front of the plane. Strange, he thought. It was noisier in back behind the jet engines.

The snow was starting to fall when the flight landed. He and Ginny embraced before she left the terminal. Invigorated but exhausted, he hailed a cab that took him directly to Union Station he boarded the Amtrak commuter train that made the nocturnal milk run between Richmond and Boston.

He was alone in the car and decided to take a nap. Women paraded before him. There was Dolores followed by Bernice, Domino, Ginny and Leslie Sandler, all in conductors' uniforms, walking down the aisle collecting train tickets. One by one they stopped by and asked for a ticket. He smiled and gave each one a ticket until he had none left. In the distance he heard an amusement park carousel organ.

The train lurched into Wilmington and Amison awoke with a start. A passenger bundled up in a navy blue pea jacket with the collar raised entered from the wagon in front and took a seat two rows behind Amison. They were alone.

The passenger was small, reminding slightly of Ojo. He studied the man's dark stocking cap and thought back to a different time a long time ago. How different life would have been had Dolores lived to raise their children. He might have been a cookie cutter college professor without its cover for his real. And what would Luis Santiago, Dolores' brother, be doing had he not pursued police work after his sister's death? Use his experience as a hotel concierge in the Dominican Republic to open a restaurant?

He and Luis were not close. But Luis was dependable and Amison was forever grateful to him for looking after his children when he traveled. Luis shared that responsibility with Mark Stone, Sidney Stone, and with Frank Hoffman. What a team. In his fantasy world, he envisioned one more grand mission with all of them together.

He sat up in his seat and stared vacantly at the ticket stub in his hand and then out the window into darkness broken by mournful whistles and blurry light flashes from trains passing in the opposite direction. Moisture streaks on the window and white blankets over the track beds reminded him that snow was dogging the train as it slugged its way north to Philadelphia.

The new arrival had fallen asleep with his head propped up against the window moments after the conductor checked his ticket and placed the usual destination receipt into the molding strip that ran the length of the luggage rack over the seats.

The conductor returned to check the car one more time. "Boston?" he asked.

The man's reply was muffled but Amison thought he detected a West Indian lilt. The conductor looked around one more time and retreated to the other car.

Amison was now wide awake. He pulled a pair of surgical gloves out of his coat pocket and put them on. Why did the Alliance people want him in Philadelphia in mid winter when they could have called a meeting in Florida or the Bahamas?

All except Marvin Childs. He was a workaholic who rarely traveled. He was sure to be at the office with Vincent Neals who also rarely wandered far away from his executive offices. Harold Levy, however, was a rolling stone who might be away. Amison disliked Marvin and Vincent and thought they were dull witted gnomes. But that was in keeping with his general opinion of people in whose circles he traveled.

He once had an animated discussion with Mark Stone regarding the differences between friends and acquaintances. The exchange ended when Mark insisted that Amison take the time to list all his friends on the back of a postage stamp. Mark was right and Amison snickered. Basically, he did not like people.

In contrast to Harold Levy, Marvin Benjamin Childs, the numbers cruncher. He was short and skinny with dark slicked back hair and looked like a weasel. Gray gun metal suits and monogrammed French cuffed shirts were his daily wardrobe. That once prompted Amison to point at his monogram and quip, "I see you're still having trouble remembering your name."

Vincent Neals was another of his least favorite people. Fat and rabbit faced, the insurance executive worked with Marvin in Alliance's internal auditing section. Vincent infuriated Amison whenever he reviewed his expense reports. At another meeting where the two disagreed over an expense account item, Amison lost his temper.

"Tell me," he yelled. "Those high collars you wear. Are they to hide the bolts sticking out of your neck?"

He suppressed a smile. Vincent went wild and pulled a knife. Harold stopped the fight and was accidentally stabbed for his intervention. Amison was sure Harold would kill Vincent for that some day.

Amison peered into the train window's reflected light and a pair of unblinking eyes returned the stare. It was time to make a move.

He rose to his feet, coughed and walked slowly to the rear of the car for a smoke. His gray overcoat was open and dragging slightly behind him. The train's rocking motion accented Amison's slight swagger as he moved up the aisle and passed the snoring passenger.

He never turned his head but he knew that the man had risen and was shuffling silently behind him, body slightly bent forward, following like a shadow between the rows of empty seats to the sliding door leading to the exit vestibule. Amison reached the rear and raised his right hand to press the "open" button on the side of the door. His motion never stopped as he wheeled around and delivered a sharp chop directly above the man's left ear.

Stunned by the blow, the man's head jerked right and the stocking cap flew off and a thatch of dread locks fell around his neck. He grabbed the top of the seats on either side of the aisle for support and a small knife in his right hand dropped.

Amison turned clockwise and delivered a fast double-fisted chop, this time to the right side of his head.

A groan escaped the West Indian's lips as he fell into Amison who grabbed him in his arms and pulled him into the darkened vestibule. He lay the West Indian face down and removed a noosed wire garrotte with a dowel handle from his pocket.

He dropped the working end over the man's head and around his neck, put one foot between his shoulders and gave the dowel handle a hard yank as if he was tugging at an outboard motor's starter cable. The man shook and thrashed about for a few minutes and then lay still.

Amison then kneeled over the West Indian, and to make sure the man was dead, he grabbed his head and rammed it against the vestibule door jamb, slammed the door into it and cracked his skull.

He knelt down to have a closer at the face. Damn! It was the West Indian on the flight to Washington.

Dragging the body into the vestibule and peering behind him to make sure the car was empty, he rifled the dead man's pockets and found a folded wad of bills. The money was fresh and wrapped with paper bands with the name Madsen Bank stamped on them. Twenty thousand dollars in all, half in Bahamian dollars and the rest in U.S. currency. He was at least getting richer.

Leaving the corpse in the vestibule, Amison whispered "Bon Voyage."

He closed the door shut, returned to his seat, the money now stuffed in his own pockets, where he picked up his duffel and walked casually to the next car forward which was also empty. The train was entering Philadelphia's station where it came to a stop a few moments later.

A sign on the platform read, "Welcome to The City Of Brotherly Love."

Nice place, he mumbled to himself. He stepped off the train and disappeared into the night.

CHAPTER 9

▼

PHILADELPHIA

A few hours' sleep at a cheap hotel under the glare of neon lights from a local bar had to do. A real bed in a real home with a nice manicured lawn was never a real option for Amison who awoke to the crackling noise of a clock radio and a forecast that announced that later today, Wednesday, the blizzard would end.

He left the hotel shortly before seven in the morning and called Debbie in New Jersey from his cell phone. She was up, preparing breakfast for her children and husband.

"Dad! This is terrific. Are you back in the States for good?" She had a fresh, cheery voice.

"Yes. They returned my passport."

"That's wonderful, dad. When are you coming up?"

"I could come up tonight after my meeting with the Alliance people. How's the weather?"

"Not good, dad. I don't think you'll make it with all the snow. We're pretty much closed in here. Why don't you wait?"

"I'll do that. How's mom?"

"No change."

"Mitch and the kids?"

"They're great. They send their love. There was a brief pause before Debbie continued. "Dad?"

"Yes?"

"Take care of yourself; you're five years older…"

"But not any wiser, sweetheart. Have you spoken to Gordon lately?"

"No. He is out on some sort of bivouac. He's probably stuck in the storm."

"I'll catch up with him later," said Amison. "Incidentally, I'm going to re-open the investigation of mom's accident five years ago."

Another pause. "Do you think that's wise, Dad?"

"Why not?"

"Maybe we should let things be and move on with our lives."

"Maybe. I want to speak with you and Gordon first before making a move."

"That's a good idea. I have to run, dad. The kids are screaming. Call me soon."

Amison sighed. His family which was already sufficiently stressed with the care of a comatose wife even if she was in a rehabilitation facility. Maybe no one really cared any longer about Bernice. Keeping a vegetable alive was no joy ride for his family and friends. The trouble was that he was unprepared to pull the plug on the woman.

A cab took him promptly despite the blinding snow storm to the old, gray gothic style office building in downtown Philadelphia that housed the Alliance Insurance Company. It was early, and the Depression era skyscraper's lobby was dark, empty and silent.

Familiar with the building, he trudged through an alley to the back and snuck in through an unlocked fire door that opened into a utility room. He was going up the emergency fire stairs when he ran into Estrella Gomez, one of the cleaning girls. Her shift was over and she was going off shift.

Estrella was a short, pleasant faced woman in her late thirties or early forties with long dark hair tied in a pony tail, and an attractively plump figure on slightly heavy legs in short white socks and work sneakers. They recognized each other from five years ago when she worked the day shift and ran into him at meetings.

"How come you're working nights?" he asked.

"Not my choice," she complained bitterly in halting English. "We're all being fired. The company hired an outside service. They said I could work nights until April and that then I must go."

"That's too bad," said Amison. "I might be able to arrange another job for you if you wish."

"Si. I think I am ready," she replied. "Are you here for el senor Childs?"

Amison nodded. "And Harold Levy as well."

Estrella shook her head. "Oh, I don't know, senor Jones. He is away. He has not been here for weeks. Only el senor Childs and el senor Neals are here."

Amison did not comment. He pulled a pen and piece of paper out of one of his pockets and wrote down his daughter's telephone number. "Call this number and give Deborah my regards. She's my daughter, and she may need someone to help her temporarily with her children and with housekeeping. When she longer needs you, I can get you a job at my friend's hotel in Fort Lauderdale. But call her first and say I suggested you call. She will help you….and give me your home number, Estrella. I may need your help sometime."

The cleaning woman wrote down her telephone number on another piece of paper that Amison produced and then returned to him.

"Is Ojo still working for you?"

"Your cousin?" Amison smiled. "Oh, yes, he stays on my boat."

Estrella thanked him and then gave him a hug. Amison was about to pull away and continue upstairs when he randomly asked. "Tell me, were you here five years ago when my wife fell out one of the office windows?"

"Si," she said. "It was the forty third floor. I was cleaning the office next to the one she was in. Poor woman. How is she?"

"Hanging in there, thanks. But tell me who else was in the office at the time."

"Senor Childs may have been there, but I am not sure," she said. "He told me he was at a meeting in another part of the building with el senor Neals."

"Vincent?"

"Si. But they both spent time with her because they went into the office together. They were there for a while and then left, leaving her inside. But I think el senor Levy was there as well."

"Harold? I thought he was overseas at the time."

"Creo que si tambien, pero….Oh, I'm so sorry…I said I thought so too but in cleaning the office after your wife's accident, I found a Cuban cigar still burning in one of the ashtrays. I know of only three people who smoke cigars at the office. You smoke Jamaicans, el senor Neals smokes Dominicanos y el Senor Levy fuma Cubanos. But I remember something curious."

"What is that, Estrella?"

"El senor Levy was here with someone else that day."

"Who was that?"

"I don't know his name. But the eyes were the color of ice. I will never forget the eyes."

Amison gave her a peck on the cheek. "Did you tell the police?" he asked.

Estrella shook her head. "No police. Senor Childs made me clean up. He said he would call the police. He was very nice and generous. He gave me one thousand dollars cash and told me to take a long vacation so I could forget about that terrible accident."

Amison smiled. "I have a meeting upstairs," he said. "You have that telephone number, use it, and I'll see about getting you a permanent job in Florida where you can say 'adios' to winter forever."

He gave her a big friendly kiss and started up the stairs.

He reached the forty-third floor and entered the cold unlit suite now occupied by Marvin Childs. A yellowish grey light from the storm shrouded morning seeped into the office with the wintery chill through the windows and filled it with long brown shadows and a melancholy gloom. A chill entered his spine and seized his body.

He tossed his hat, coat and duffel on the forest green leather sofa near the door and sat down on the matching armchair facing Marvin's mahogany partners' desk and executive swivel chair to await his arrival. Massive mahogany pieces, chairs, tables, sideboards and wall units filled the high ceilinged cavernous office. Behind the partners' desk and chair was a bank of tall double-hung windows two feet off the floor that faced a wall of buildings across the street. The windows could still be opened from the bottom for ventilation although central air conditioning had been installed throughout the building years ago.

The snow was falling hard and clouds of steam rose from pipes that spewed heat exhaust to a ledge guarded by evil looking stone gargoyles two floors down. They must have been the gargoyles that broke Bernice's fall. One of them was knocked loose and was slightly lopsided but was still holding.

Amison waited patiently, motionlessly, as the minutes ticked by and he didn't move even when the main door opened behind him and two men came in. It was Marvin Childs and Vincent Neals.

"It's too bad Bill Nigel was cooking the books. I think it's clear what old Harold wants done," one was saying.

"Assuming Jones shows up," the other commented. "If he doesn't, we have Quinn as backup." Their short burst of cynical laughter stopped when they turned on the lights and saw Amison sitting calmly in the green leather arm chair.

"Damn you, Jones," shouted Marvin Childs. "How long have you been here?"

"Don't you believe in being ushered in properly?" Vincent Neals chimed in.

Amison yawned. "I arrived early, so I let myself in. I know the way." He looked past Marvin and Vincent and out the windows behind the desk. He hardly listened to their agitated chatter and thought about what his wife must have been thinking when she went through the window.

Despite his talk with Debbie, his mind was made up. "Where's Harold?"

He pulled a cigar out of his jacket pocket, lit it and started blowing smoke rings into the air.

"In the Bahamas," Vincent replied.

"At his condo," said Marvin.

"What about Hank Lawrence? He's usually around."

Vincent looked glum. "Hank quit and the big man wants him dead."

"What for?"

"Hank found out that Bill Nigel was embezzling and covered for him. Harold is going to kill Hank and Bill. That's why he quit. He needed a head start. But we'll get him. You know how the big man is. He likes fast justice. He wants Nigel taken down for stealing and Hank taken down because he knows too much."

"Who knows, Jones," Vincent added. "You might end up with the contract on Hank."

"I haven't been given a contract on anyone," Amison insisted. Thinking it best not to dwell on the subject, he asked, "Now that I'm here, what can I do for you two gentlemen?"

Marvin cleared his throat and sat down behind the partner's desk while Vincent paced about nervously.

"This assignment we have for you, Jones, comes from Europol, as you already know." Marvin Childs was saying. "It requires your background and experience in the Bahamas."

Amison sat up. "Is that a fact?" He feigned ignorance.

Marvin had a remote control unit in his hand. It was shaped like a derringer and he was vainly trying to turn on more lights with the trigger mechanism but started trembling when he saw Amison's eyes lazily following his movements like a cat. Marvin put the unit down, cleared his throat and began to describe the mission. "It's that Bimini Man project. Europol asked Jack O'Brien and Harold for help, and Cecil Fergueson found you on your boat. Jesus, man. Why don't you live on land like normal folks?"

"A moving target is hard to hit," Amison commented lightly.

"I appreciate your concern," said Marvin. "By the way, you should have called when your train reached Philadelphia. I would have sent someone to pick you up. Anyway, I'm glad you're here."

"So am I."

The telephone rang at that moment, and Marvin excused himself to take the call. It was Harold Levy, he said.

"Let me explain what we are." Amison remembered what Harold told him many years ago.

"The intelligence community is an extended family living in an onion. The outer skin is smooth and sweet smelling. Here we find diplomats and cabinet ministers in their penguin suits making foreign policy. Peel off that layer and we have senior intelligence officers engaged in the highest levels of espionage through embassy, diplomatic, corporate and celebrity functions. In deeper layers are the professional assassins, mission specialists and the explosives, demolition and sabotage experts. And at the onion's rotten core are the back alley operatives: the thieves, hookers, swindlers, mercenaries and killers who do the real dirty work on a daily basis to keep the outside skin pink and sweet. But we, from the onion's surface to its core, have one thing in common: we kill on command. Our role is simple. The CIA calls on Europol and Europol calls on us. We do the heavy lifting when and where no one else is willing. We are the killers of last resort."

Marvin completed his conversation with Harold Levy and turned his attention to Amison. He swivelled around in his chair and tried one more time to use the remote control unit. He squeezed the trigger. A screen was supposed to drop down but nothing happened. He threw the derringer down in disgust.

"Harold wants you to call him from the airport before you leave." he said.

"I'll do that," Amison replied drily. "Now, what do you want to tell me?"

"We want to brief you about Bimini Man. Henry didn't have the full story."

"Ok. Shoot." Amison returned to his armchair and sat down.

Marvin smiled secretively. He thought he knew something Amison did not.

"Europol's interests in Bimini are important but there are other matters at stake. Alliance is Las Olas University's insurer, and Las Olas has guaranteed that Bimini is where humans lived long ago in a place called Atlantis. Alliance must repay its investors if Bimini Man is a fraud. If the university cannot pay, Alliance pays."

Vincent coughed. "There's another facet to this, Jones. The island upon which the Bimini Man dig is taking place was given by the Bahamian government years ago to the Bencivenga family who sold it to Alliance for a cool one billion dollars. Alliance in turn leased the property pro bono five years ago to Las Olas University for its archeological excavations in return for selling it an insurance policy whose premiums the university pays. That lease expires soon.

"Meanwhile, Alliance resold the land to Sol Weinberg's Centurion Trust in Miami for $1.1 billion but kept the policies. Now, Madsen, our Nassau affiliate, loaned the university forty million dollars to finance its general operations and put in another ten million dollars for the Bimini project. That deal was made directly between Madsen and Frank Hoffman. We were never cued in. The loan collateral is about $50 million in cash and securities that the university has on deposit with Madsen through its agency bank in Miami. Although Alliance no longer owns the Bimini Man site and the property it's on, it has insured all the university's paper currently held by Madsen against default. It also insures mortgage paper on many of the university's properties in Florida. If the university defaults, Alliance has to make good. If Madsen pulls the plug first and calls the loan, the university goes under and Alliance is left holding the bag filled with worthless paper and still has to make good."

"If I'm following you correctly," Amison noted. "We're looking at a house of cards. Bimini Man is part of this house of cards. If it's a phony, then the house collapses and Alliance falls."

"Exactly, Jones. The Bimini Man dig site is a hot property right now. If Bimini Man doesn't exist, it's worthless swamp land. While we no longer own the damn place, we're nevertheless chained to it. In effect, we are Centurion's surety."

"Why would Alliance deal with drug traffickers like the Bencivengas? We've been trying to take them down for years."

"We were and we weren't," Vincent replied. "That's what you were unable to understand about our relationship with don Ignacio, Jones. Friends are friends, and enemies are enemies, but business is business. This whole thing made sense at the time. They were cash deals."

Marvin and Vincent both beamed. "Not bad, huh?"

Marvin added while Amison was digesting the full impact of those revelations, "The problem occurs only if Bimini Man is a fraud, not if it's real. But we can't take a chance one way or the other with all those rumors floating around."

"Even without Bimini Man," said Vincent. "Madsen right now wants to call its loans and freeze the university's accounts. That alone could close could be the trigger that closes down the university and forces Alliance to go belly up."

"I thought Alliance owned Madsen."

"True," said Marvin. "But Madsen is a bank operating under Bahamian and U.S. law. It is obliged to call bad loans, even those made to majority stock holders. The Madsen bank could end up either ruining or running Alliance. Harold Levy sits on the bank's board and is being pressured to close the books on the Bimini Man.

"Now, let me give you the latest. Madsen is offering to forgive the Alliance debt and to assume some of Las Olas University's financial obligations connected with the dig in exchange for title to the Bimini dig site. They want to seal the deal this week. But Centurion is refusing to sell."

Marvin wrung his hands. "Let's put it this way, Jones; it would be wonderful if Bimini Man would just go away."

Amison yawned. "That would be nice, wouldn't it?"

Marvin and Vincent looked at Amison and then at each other. "This assignment is threefold, Jones. First. Harold is going to need you for some housecleaning in Nassau. He's going to speak to you personally about that. Second. Take care of Europol's business and find out how their agents were killed. We don't want to let Leroux down. Third. Close down the Bimini Man dig."

"Close it down?"

"Let's put it this way," said Marvin Childs. "Do you believe in happy endings?"

"Like in fairy tales?"

"Exactly. Make the bad dream go away. We want to get back to where we were before this all started."

"I assume this is what the CIA and Europol wants?"

"Forget Europol. This is what we want."

"And the Bahamian government?"

"Nassau will go along so long as we sell a plausible story to the Afro-centrists and the Afro-American community about what happened. We're working on that.

Can you turn Bimini Man into history?"

"That depends," said Amison. "How much are you paying?"

"We got your message from Alstrum and have no problem with your fee."

Amison smiled blandly, rose to his feet, walked to the windows behind Marvin's desk and stared at the falling snow, "That little spit of land must have a gold mine under it for it to be worth over a billion dollars. I want one hundred million dollars up front!"

"You' re crazy," Vincent screamed.

"I know. And, I want more…"

"More?"

"That's correct. I told Henry Alstrum I plan to look into my wife's accident."

"It was an accident," Vincent insisted. "She fell or jumped out the window when she heard you were killed. Besides, Alliance paid you on its insurance policy."

"I know that. But think for a moment. When did a woman ever commit suicide by jumping out a window?"

They did not reply.

"This is not a smart move," Marvin finally insisted. "You have your son and daughter to consider. Besides, if it was attempted murder, we would question the payments Alliance made to you. We might have to ask for it back, with interest."

"Tell you what," said Amison. He spoke calmly and slowly. "Hire a boy scout."

There was a long silence. Marvin and Vincent fidgeted and exchanged glances. Vincent coughed. "We'll speak to Harold. But we can't make any promises."

"Don't promise," insisted Amison. "Just do it."

"We're just hypothesizing, you under understand," said Vincent. "But what would you do if your wife's fall was actually a case of attempted murder?" And then he added, "Hypothetically speaking, of course."

"Of course," Amison answered. "Hypothetically speaking, I'd kill everyone responsible; I give you fair warning." And he smiled again. "Naturally, that's all hypothetically speaking."

His eyes moved from Marvin to Vincent and back again. They squirmed like worms but said nothing. "And," he added. "Supposing there is heroin buried in Bimini, and I find it?"

They squirmed uncomfortably. "We want you to tell us before you tell anyone else."

"Well now. Supposing I told you the exact location of the heroin—assuming it existed in the first place—what would that knowledge be worth to you?"

They were at a loss for words. Finally, Marvin asked, "How much do you want?"

"Another one hundred million dollars, payable on delivery."

"You're full of shit, Jones!" cried Vincent.

Amison just smiled. "Not a problem. Just ask Harold."

"You're pushing your luck, Jones," Vincent said, his voice rising in anger.

"Am I?" Amison laughed hoarsely. "Try me!" He rose to his feet.

Marvin was more conciliatory than Vincent. "All right. I'll speak to Harold if you agree to the mission as we laid it out."

"Of course."

Vincent heaved a sigh of relief. "Excellent. What about a cover?"

"No. Bimini is too small for a cover. I'm playing it straight as an Alliance agent for Europol to check on two possible murders."

"I agree. Now, what do you need?"

"I'll figure it out in the next few days. By the way, who's my handler?"

"Harold said you'd find out in time."

"What's my time line?"

Marvin went over to his desk and checked the calendar. "Las Olas Uinversity is going to exhibit the bones at the Triple A reception at the end of the conference. The dig needs to be gone by then. I'd say you have a week and few days."

Amison gathered his hat, coat and duffel and started for the door.

"Don't forget," Marvin reminded him. "Call Harold from the airport. He's waiting for your call at the Paradise Island Country Club."

CHAPTER 10

▼

LUCK IS NOT FOREVER

Amison left the Alliance building and was about to catch a cab to the airport when a black limousine pulled up to the curb. A darkened rear window rolled down and he found himself being scrutinized by a pair of piercing eyes over a masterful nose. "Monsieur Jones?"

"Well, I'll be damned! Jacques Leroux himself!"

"May I offer you a ride?" It was a decidedly French accent behind the lyrical voice. "You might have to wait a long time for a taxi."

"I'm going to the airport," said Amison. The rear door opened and he climbed in next to the Europol director. "What brings you to Philadelphia?"

"I followed you," Leroux answered. "I was at the French consulate here on other business when Henry called with your itinerary. We realized you had made some changes because of the weather and thought also you might call your daughter. So I called her earlier and she told me you had a meeting at Alliance. I took a chance, 'et voila!' Here I am, your personal chauffeur. By the way, how did you get here from Washington? I learned that your flight ended there."

"I took a train."

"Ah. That was smart."

Oh. I don't know. Someone tried to take me down. A West Indian, I think. Any ideas?"

Leroux laughed. "Somewhere I have a book filled with names of your enemies. You must read it." He looked at Amison carefully. "But I see you have survived the experience. Where's the West Indian?"

"Probably in Boston by now."

"Ah. Boston is a wonderful city with many fine restaurants. But now, shall we talk about your meeting at Alliance. Has the mission been spelled out to you?"

"The part about the deaths of your two agents? Yes. Can you fill me in a little?"

"Et Bien. I need two possible murders investigated and some housecleaning," he declared. "That is why I have asked O'Brien and Levy to hire your services."

"Murder and housecleaning?" Housecleaning is Harold Levy's term. People die when he cleans house. I do that for Harold, but murder inquiries are not my forte. I hope you realize that."

"I use the expression in Harold's context. The alleged murders? I lost two agents and I want revenge. Cecil is out of his element on this. I need you to look into the matter. You are the best man for the job under the circumstances."

"So I hear."

The Europol director coughed. "I do not take the death of my agents lightly. I believe they found something odd at the Bimini Man excavations."

"Can you be more specific?"

The director sighed. "It began with a phone call to the police from a museum in Fort Lauderdale concerning a shipment of human fossil bones shipped to them by the Museum of Natural History in New York for an exhibition. It never arrived in Fort Lauderdale. Your brother-in-law, Luis Santiago, was given the case. Since there was a possible inter-state theft situation involved, he alerted the FBI. And since there was a rumor that the bones might have been diverted to the Bahamas, the investigation went international and the CIA was called with the case thrown into O'Brien's lap. For some reason, the CIA didn't want to be involved directly so Jack called me and asked me off the record to launch an inquiry. I sent Luther Guenther. When he died, Henry tried his luck with Dwayne Douglas who also died."

The director's eyes narrowed and his voice hardened. "I am desperate. I am also deeply angered. I want this matter resolved."

"I heard about Guenther's and Douglas's deaths, but no specifics."

"I don't know much more than you. Their bodies washed up with the tide a few weeks apart."

Amison was skeptical. "Why would Luther Guenther's talents be wasted on old bones. He's a demolition expert like me or Mike Quinn. We blow things up."

Leroux was evasive. "I thought of hiring Quinn but he was busy. Besides, he's Jack's cleanup man. O'Brien likes to keep him in reserve."

Amison pondered the director's response. "Why didn't you use Mark Stone or Luis Santiago, or Henry's medical assistant, Dudley Haynes?"

"I'd rather use Mark Stone," Leroux replied. "But his diabetes is iffy."

"Luis and Haynes would be good."

"Luis? He was recently promoted to police inspector at the Broward County's Sheriff's office and has his hands full. Dudley Haynes? He does want to become more involved in Henry's non-medical business. But he is inexperienced, and I don't know enough about his background."

Amison was sure the Europol director was holding back and decided to put him on the spot. "I'm supposed to close down the Bimini Man dig," he said.

Leroux was exuberant. "Aha!" he yelled. "I thought so."

"Tell me, what kind of housecleaning we are talking about."

"Europol is a global police investigatory agency," Leroux stated gravely. "We cannot afford to jeopardize its international relations because of...what would we say.... a few bad apples?"

"Can you elaborate on that, Director?"

"I can. I am suspicious about the archeological team from Las Olas University in the Bimini islands. It arrived shortly before you were exiled five years ago. I have reason to believe the project is a cover for illegal activities."

"Like drugs?"

Leroux laughed. "Ah, again, you are a man to the point."

He became serious. "Yes. Drugs. I believe drug traffickers are in Bimini. That would explain why my agents were murdered. They discovered a drug trafficking plot mixed up in the Bimini Man project."

He waved a long finger in the air. "I also believe that certain Alliance and CIA functionaries are part of that plot. This is where you come in. You will continue where my agents left off. You will be an Alliance agent but you also work for me."

"As a double agent?"

Leroux winked. "Those are your words, not mine. But hear me out. A few bad apples will contaminate the entire crop if they are not rooted out. You may not be a good detective, but you are an excellent hit man."

"I'm no longer a spring chicken," Amison noted.

"No. You are an experienced rooster."

Amison lit a cigarette. "Any suspects?"

Leroux eyed Amison carefully. "Ah. That, you must find out, Mr. Jones. I will pay your fees apart from those of Alliance."

"And the housecleaning?"

Leroux had a twinkle in his eye. "In time, yes, but not right away. Report to me before taking action. There may be a special bonus for your work."

"What kind of bonus?"

"If my hunch is correct, there could be a bonus of a few million dollars in your pocket provided you and I have a perfect understanding."

"Like a partnership?"

"A partnership," he echoed. "And a chance to set old matters to rest."

"Like what, Director?"

Leroux sat back. "Like what really happened to your wife five years ago."

"The accident?"

"Ah, so I heard as well." Leroux sat back.

Amison looked out the limo's window. They had reached the airport. "Let's play this by ear. I want to avoid a conflict of interest between Alliance and Europol."

Leroux nodded. "Of course. It is difficult to serve two masters."

"I've been lucky so far, Director."

The Europol director smiled. "Luck is not forever, monsieur Jones." He tapped the plexiglass divider and informed the driver. "Let our friend off here."

Amison found himself standing with his belongings at the Continental terminal at Philadelphia International Airport. The snow had stopped falling. He stopped at a 'Dunkin' Donuts' kiosk where he where he called Harold Levy at the Paradise Island Country Club on his cell phone. It was Harold himself who answered the phone.

Amison's assumption that Marvin had called him the moment their meeting was over was correct.

"Great to hear from you, Jonesey," he was saying. "You have to excuse Marvin. He's new at being top dog at Alliance. He'll improve. But watch out for Vince Neals. He can be deadly. How's the family?"

"Hanging in," replied Amison.

"I hear your daughter is making money hand over fist as a stock broker."

"Someone has to make a living in the family," joked Amison.

"What about Gordon? How is he doing?"

"He's finishing his training."

A big hearty laugh from the other end. "That's what the world needs, Jonesey. Another spook. Is he still a bachelor?"

"Yes."

"That's good. I have an unmarried daughter, you know. We should get those two together." A short pause. "Anyway, I like good news. Now, Marvin told me about your needs and wants. There'll be no problem meeting your needs as long as you haven't become too rusty. I hope you'll be happy with this new assignment. You can use the action. With regard to your wants, we'll talk about it."

"Good. It will give me a chance to look up old friends and enemies."

There was hesitation at the other end. Then Harold went on. "Look up who you want. Just don't tell me about it. I want you to follow Marvin's script closely. We don't need the mess you and Stone got us into five years ago."

"I'll keep things under control this time," said Amison.

"Good. Now, I need a favor. I want you to fly down here right away. Bill Nigel and I are going fishing tomorrow. I want you and Mike Quinn to join us. Matter of fact, Mike has my jet ready at general aviation near the main terminal where you are and he's waiting for you."

Amison was caught off guard. "Mike Quinn?"

"Yeah. Jack O'Brien loaned him to me. He's going to work with you after we finish up in Paradise Island. So, cancel your return flight if you have one, and go find Quinn. Hey, this call must be costing you a small fortune, and I'm going to hate paying you back when the bill comes in. Well, I've got to go," said Harold. "I'm wanted on the golf course. Find Quinn, and I'll see you guys in a few hours."

Amison hung up the phone and sat in the booth musing for a few minutes. He really was in no mood to return to the Bahamas but there seemed no way to refuse Harold's request. When one takes the king's shilling, he had once been told, one does the King's bidding.

He drew his cell phone from his duffel and called his son who had just returned to his dormitory.

They engaged in small talk until Gordon asked, "Dad, Debbie called me a few minutes ago. Are you serious about reopening mother's case?"

"I'm thinking about it," Amison replied. "But she feels it's not a good idea."

"She may have a point, dad. Why don't we wait? Mother may be able to tell us something when she regains her memory. We may be reading too much in this."

"You might be right. How's the class work going?"

"Great. I'm looking forward to graduation and starting with the CIA."

Amison laughed. "The country will sleep soundly when that happens, I'm sure."

He suddenly remembered what he had told Estrella Gomez.

"Can you do me a favor?"

"What, dad?"

"I promised a cleaning girl at Alliance who is being fired a nanny's job if Debbie needs one. Debbie might get a call from her. Can you give her advance warning?"

"Is she one of your girlfriends?"

"Don't be smart, Gordon."

They continued chatting for a few minutes until Gordon informed him he had to leave for a meeting. "Lets keep in touch through Debbie, dad. I'll see you soon."

He hung up and his thoughts moved to Mike Quinn. He remembered him from the old days when Mike worked as a chopper pilot, dropping Amison and his team to blow up various installations. He concluded that Harold had more than a friendly fishing trip in mind if Mike Quinn was in the picture.

He had an open return ticket but no firm booking so there was nothing to cancel. He gathered up his things and walked past several news stands on the way to a taxi stand outside the terminal building.

Bimini Man had made the headlines. Front page columns dealt with everything from the origins of the human species to stories about an Afro-based civilization called Atlantis that once flourished off the coast of Florida. Travelers clustered around television sets where talking heads gave the Bimini Man happenings their favorite spins.

"Forget Africa!" a pundit yelled. "The first humans were Black and came from Florida."

Another suggested that Bimini Man explained Florida's "large Afro-American population."

The rhetoric, filled with emotionally charged racial innuendos, was at fever pitch and Amison was amazed that a race riot did not break out. But bystanders, waiting for flights, were good natured and absorbed the commentaries with indifference and detachment. This was, after all, a form of reality TV entertainment.

On impulse, he began randomly rummaging inside his duffel without knowing exactly what he was looking for when his hand came into contact with an object the size of a silver dollar.

"Damn!" he said aloud.

It was a tracking sensor, the kind that work off satellites. That helped explain many things except to identify the person who gave the order to have him tailed. Amison returned it to the duffel. It would make a good decoy, he thought.

He bundled himself up against the cold and was about to leave the terminal for the general aviation building when he happened to glance over at the kiosk where a squarely built pilot was holding a doughnut and coffee in his hands and studying a TV monitor broadcasting the latest news from the Bahamas.

There was concern now, the anchor was saying, about an un-seasonal tropical depression forming off the coast of Africa and moving slowly in a northwesterly direction. The scene shifted rapidly to the network's meteorologist who followed up the commentator's statements with the suggestion that such storms rarely pose any threat this time of year, but that the hurricane center in Atlanta was following it.

A local weather update followed, and then a commercial about a product to ease menstrual pains.

A broad grin crossed Amison's face. It was Mike Quinn and he looked the same as he did the last time they met, ruddy faced, medium height and solidly built with smiling eyes but now with a touch of gray peppering his curly brown hair. Heavy hands with short fingers stuck out of his navy blue parka, holding the coffee cup in one hand and urgently munching on the doughnut with the other.

Amison nudged him and said, "That's just about where I left you five years ago, eating," he noted.

Mike looked up, that grin fixed upon his face. "Hey, Jonesey! I wasn't expecting you for another half hour. Matter of fact, I wasn't sure you were going to show."

"Why is that?"

"The word on the street is that there's a contract out on you."

"You think?" Amison looked over his shoulder. "Shall we get out of here?"

"Well, I'm sure glad you're here," Mike Quinn said.

He pointed to the TV. "What do you think of that bullshit over in Bimini? Isn't that something else? And that storm brewing off the coast of Africa, in the middle of February. How do you like that for the ultimate bullshit?"

"It's certainly making news," replied Amison.

"Those goddam niggers!" said Mike Quinn. "They always have to prove a point! So who cares if they were on earth first. All that means is that they had a head start and still haven't caught up!"

Amison put his arm around him and cautioned, "Keep it low, old buddy."

He looked around. "This isn't the place to discuss race relations."

"Well," grumbled Mike Quinn. "It will be good to get out of this shit weather."

"You and me both," said Amison. "What's up?"

Right then another news bulletin interrupted the regular programing to proclaim that the archeological team from Las Olas University headed by the university's president, Frank Hoffman and his chief archeologist, Dr. Leslie Sandler, had just confirmed the origin of Bimini Man. It was from Africa.

Amison shook his head. He had heard it first in Nassau weeks ago.

Mike Quinn smiled. "Old Frank never changes, does he?"

He finished the coffee, gobbled down the doughnut and turned to Amison. "The big man wants us for a job. We should try to get out of here while there's a break in the weather. What do you think?"

"I'd say it's a plan, Mike. Shall we go?"

They were air bound in the Alliance jet an hour later, flying in bright sunlight way above the gray storm clouds that engulfed the land below.

Amison sat alongside in the co-pilot's seat trading gossip while he changed into a short sleeve shirt and lightweight slacks. "This is an expensive way to travel," he said. "What is this thing? A Lear?"

"You bet," answered Quinn. "Alliance has a bunch of them. We can go round tip to Europe without refueling, but we're only going to the Bahamas. That will take us about ninety minutes. But this isn't new. I started flying it five years ago."

"You sound like an advertisement."

"It's important to know your product. I even do submarines. Do you need one for this mission?"

"Not that I know. Does Alliance have one?"

"You know the big man," said Mike Quinn. "He can get one. How's the wife?"

"Much better, thanks." Amison lied. "It looks as if she's going to recover."

"I'm speaking out of turn, Jonesey, but the rumor among us little people is that your wife's fall was no accident."

Amison frowned. "How do you figure that?"

"That's all I can say, Jonesey. I'm just telling you for old times' sake."

"I understand. How's with you? Hear anything from our old group?"

"I'm good. You already know about Frank. He made out real well with his deal at Las Olas University and he hasn't done anything with us in years. I hear he has a sixty-foot sport fishing yacht, a Hatteras, I think. And he's been tapping Mark's sister-in-law, Leslie, since she joined the university. But Mark also lucked out. Frank got him a teaching job at the school. I suppose that's good, what with his diabetes and all. And of course, Mark has Marlene; that's one piece of ass, even if the poor guy has to share her with Frank who's also tapping her. At least Mark has the Riverside, and that's good money for his aggravation. Anyway, those two guys sure knew when and how to bail out."

Amison agreed. "For sure. My problem is that I move too fast and I can't quit."

"That's your style," Mike noted. "You make quick calls and bring things to a fast finish. Frank and Mark work more slowly. Same with Hank. But he has the smarts, though."

That he does."

"They know this business never ends. Even the scenery stays unchanged except maybe for a fresh coat of paint. Only the players get replaced."

"I never thought about it that way," Amison said. "Are you a poet?"

"You know how it goes. Supposing someone has to be taken out. The setup is the same. The best place for the job is a crowded street at lunch or quitting time. That's when Max Neals and his son were gunned down. During lunch on a busy street. The assassin's profile is non-rescript and blends into the crowd. And the best backdrop is an office building, a busy department store, or a bunch of retail stores and eateries. We have the crowd, the killer and the victim. The victim goes down and the killer gets lost in the crowd. Neat, isn't it?"

"I suppose."

"Now you, Jonesey. You're a good hit man but you're not neat. Your problem is that you have a heavy foot. Something always gets blown up along with the people you blow away."

"That's what I do for a living," Amison said. "I blow things up, like you do. The killing is incidental. I'd rather stay away from it. Everyone I have taken down was always pretty much in self defense."

"Well," continued Mike Quinn, "The Neals hit doesn't bother me whether you did it or not. You usually do the big bang thing. But don't get a complex. I'd still follow you in a fix. You never know which way the wind blows with Frank. He is too much of a politician. And Mark? Too indecisive."

"Thanks," said Amison. "By the way, did you get a briefing about what we're supposed to do?"

"Not really. Just bits and pieces from side conversations and that sort of thing. I spoke with Mark the other day. He says that we're supposed to shut down the dig in Bimini before the Triple A conference ends. At least, that's what he heard."

Amison shrugged his shoulders. "That's what Marvin Childs and Vince Neals say. Plus we're supposed to terminate the Bencivenga family."

Mike grinned. "That's what O'Brien says also. You know, I've wondered about you, Mark, Frank, Hank and Sid."

"What about?"

"You guys are pretty tightly woven together. How did you all meet?"

Amison looked out the cockpit window at the sun falling in the west. "We went to college and into the army together," he explained. "We met Harold Levy years later after finishing a job in the Dominican Republic for Jack O'Brien."

"Is that where you guys got started with Jack?"

"Yes. Our first mission chief was Jack O'Brien. His contact with us was Luis Santiago, a local CIA agent with a hotel concierge job for a cover. We met Harold Levy and Max Neals in Kingston when we left Santo Domingo. When we got back the States, Luis became a cop. Harold and Max settled in Philadelphia where they started Alliance selling insurance to foreign service employees. They hired hit men and a team of covert intelligence operatives and expanded by taking on CIA jobs on contract.

"We joined Alliance on a freelance basis except for Sid who went into business but continued to help us out whenever he could. Hank went with Alliance full time and Frank, Mark and I became academics, using our teaching positions as covers for work with Alliance. Harold tried to recruit, O'Brien but he decided to stay with the feds. Harold also tried to bring in Henry Alstrum, but he went with Europol. Mark got sick and was semi-retired when Frank became university president. And I, of course, had to drop out of teaching five years ago."

He gazed wistfully into space. "That's about it in a nutshell," he said softly.

"Mark has no kids, does he?" Mike asked.

Amison shook his head. "He married Marlene rather late in his life. And neither does Frank. He did marry, but his wife died years ago. Hank never married and neither did Jack O'Brien. Luis and Harold have two children each and Marvin Childs also has two; I don't know much about the Neals side of the family."

"I guess Frank did well for Las Olas University. He's certainly putting it on the map."

"I guess so," Amison conceded. "Aside from Bimini Man, he turned the campus into a repository for free lance intelligence agents for Alliance."

He drew himself up straight in the co-pilot's seat. "You know, Hank didn't do guns well, but he was the brain and did the planning. Mark was the best shot, and then Frank. I was mainly good at blowing up things. By the way, I hear Tucker is working with us."

"That's right. Have you seen Hank recently?"

"In Nassau. With Tucker."

"Do you want some advice?"

"Shoot."

"Stay clear of Hank. The big man has it in for him." Mike Quinn changed the subject before Amison could comment. "How about Ojo? Is he still around?"

Amison nodded. "Yes. He works for me. What happened to Bob Byrne?"

"He got shipped off to Alaska," added Mike. "But he's back now."

"He is? What about the rest of the gang?"

"All the rest? Sick. Retired. Dead. Dean Jordan grows sprouts in California but Tucker Anderson is back as you say."

"Any other news?"

"Not much. You know, we're like brothers in this business, even when we have to kill one another. But it's in the line of duty, Jonesey. You must understand that. We still love each other. We're brothers and we cry."

Amison found it strange; Quinn sounded almost apologetic.

The flight to the small airport on Paradise Island took under two hours. The sun dropped below the horizon and the Lear effortlessly landed in Paradise Island.

"What kind of folks are we talking about here?" Mike asked Amison.

"Plain folks, Mike. Plain folks, just like us."

PART II

▼

THE DECONSTRUCTION OF BIMINI MAN

CHAPTER 11

▼

FINAL RECKONING

Paradise Island was a welcome change. Harold Levy was standing on the tarmac in a damp breeze to greet them in an over-the-trousers short sleeve guyaberra shirt similar to the one Amison had changed into.

"So, who's your tailor?" Amison joked.

"Same as yours," was Harold's friendly retort.

Harold was big, half a head taller than Amison and broad shouldered. He had a look of congeniality that camouflaged a nasty temper.

"You guys look terrific," he said, giving them each bear hugs. "I wish I had your jobs. Come. I bet you're exhausted, Jonesey. We'll go to my place and you can get some sleep. Tomorrow is Thursday and we're going fishing. Mike will stay here. He knows our schedule. He's going to get the plane ready for departure tomorrow afternoon. He also has to get my boat ready for our little fishing trip. I keep it at a dock near the Chalks Seaplane landing ramp at the airport. We're going to use it to meet up with Bill Nigel's yacht."

The Customs duty officer was half-asleep and cleared them without bothering to examine their passports. A few minutes later, Harold and Amison were shuttled by cab to the Alliance condominium.

"Busy, busy," exclaimed Amison as they walked rapidly to the condo. "What's the rush?"

"We're in deep shit, Jonesey, and there's going to be a lot to do in the next few days if we're going to bail ourselves out. We have to move fast before everyone figures out what's going on."

"Talking about figuring things out," said Amison. "A West Indian tried to take me down on the train between Washington and Philadelphia. So someone must already know something. Any ideas?"

Harold shook his head. "No. But that makes things more difficult. It could have been Bill Nigel. He's in bed with Ignacio Bencivenga who has wanted you dead for the longest time. Bencivenga suspects what I'm up to and figures to make life for me miserable by wiping out my best hit man."

Amison did not reply.

"How's the family?" he asked as they entered the condo.

"Great," replied Harold. "My ex-wife can't spend money fast enough. And the kids are fine."

Then, all of a sudden, he became all business. "I'll be brief," he said. He turned on the lights and they sat down on rattan arm chairs around a glass coffee table on he set down two glasses of lemonade.

"I don't mind your looking into your wife's accident. It's over due. I would have looked into it but I've been too busy minding the store."

"I'm sure," said Amison.

"What I'm saying is that I don't want Alliance interests compromised. Kapish?"

"I understand. Now, if you don't mind, Harold. I don't think I'm here on a joy ride, so why don't you tell me what's up for tomorrow, and then point me to the right room for some sack time."

"Fair enough, but don't get cranky on me," said Harold. "I need housecleaning. That's why you and Mike are here. "We're going to replace Bill Nigel."

"Really. I thought he was doing a good job."

Harold's face darkened. "He's doing a magnificent job," adding, "stealing from Alliance." We've have a long standing arrangement with your old friend Ignacio Bencivenga that was set up by the CIA through Jack O'Brien. The Bencivengas support the Venezuelan government and Washington looks the other way when his organization deals drugs in the States through operatives in Las Olas University. All proceeds from the drug sales are collected by a bagman and the cash ends up in a special Madsen account. Nigel manages that account for us. The problem is that he's been making loans to a Bencivenga owned export firm from the account. They were never repaid and he would write them off as bad loans. Every time he did, he would receive a kickback from the old man himself.

He and don Ignacio milked us out of more than fifty million dollars this way in the past five years. I'm going to kill them both!"

"How did you learn of this?"

Harold's rising voice showed his rising excitement and anger.

"Hank Lawrence hired some independent auditors through Europol. They found out. They thought your old buddy Frank Hoffman was helping himself to the till, but dirty as he is, he's clean here. Anyway, Bill Nigel's thievery creates cash flow problems, and to make matters worse, we have this Bimini Man nonsense."

"I'm supposed to be closing it down."

"You're damn right, you're closing it! But Madsen, through Nigel, is threatening to call its loans to Alliance by midnight, Sunday. That's not going to be. And you know what else? Your buddy Hank just quit on me. I'm going to kill the bastard when I find him. Nobody ever quits Alliance alive!"

Harold was working himself into a rage. "All that Bimini Man crap? That thing is bogus! It's one big cover for a bunch of cocaine or heroin that's going through Bimini. The Bencivengas have their fingers in that gig, and me like a jerk I went along with the old man and with Jack O'Brien. Well, I don't give a shit about some stone age nigger buried in Bimini!"

He was bellowing incoherently like a lion robbed of his kill by hyenas.

"I own a runaway bank. I have a thief stealing my money. And I have a shit ass university president who is into bones and broads and who deals drugs with your Venezuelan friends who are protected by the feds!"

His face turned crimson. "I'm suffering, Jonesey. I'm suffering! I'm pissed. And I hate being pissed! This shit must cease, and it must cease now!"

"Have you met with Frank?"

Harold Levy regained his composure and smiled. He took a sip from his glass of lemonade.

"Sure did. I meet with him and the university trustees every month. They should have their balls cut off with dull scissors. And Warren Kilpatrick, their chairman? I swear, Jonesey, he's a fag. I know one when I see one. And old Frank is either blind or blind. It's that damn director of his, Leslie Sandler. She spreads her legs and he takes a dive!

"But he does make some sense. His position is that the university has gone too far and spent too much to officially jettison the Bimini Man program. He says that the entire Afro-American community will be galvanized against us if we pull the plug. He says we have to see it through. But he also says that if we decide to pull the plug, he doesn't want to know about it. He knows he's on thin ice on this one. If it goes bad, he'll have to go back to breaking legs for a living.

"You know, it's my fault." Harold was almost apologetic. "I listened to Marvin and Vincent who convinced me this thing would make me rich."

Harold banged his head with his fists. "Shit! Shit! Shit!" What could I have been thinking?

"Frank is counting on a long shot, but I'm not betting on him. We're going to lose everything unless we stop both Madsen and the dig dead in their tracks. The dig is a total fabrication; I'm convinced now. Frank is either a liar or stupid. And, I don't trust don Ignacio, O'Brien or anyone else. And I trust your buddies even less. They're all scum bags! You have too many crooked buddies there, Jonesey! And sometimes I even wonder about you."

"You're right, Harold. Do you want to kill me now or after I get rid of the dig?"

"You're not being funny, Jonesey."

"So, what do you want me to do?"

Harold calmed down. "You're going to help me take over Madsen," he said in a low, steady voice, "and then you're going to get rid of Bimini Man and kill the old man and his kid, Miguelito. They are the last remaining Bencivengas."

"How about the federal protection they enjoy," said Amison.

"Fuck the feds. I'm telling you what I want. The dig goes, the Bencivengas go, and so does Bill Nigel!"

"Has the Madsen board voted yet?"

"Yes. The board went Nigel's way by one vote, his vote. That's unacceptable. I convinced the board to take another vote on Sunday."

"What's happening tomorrow?"

"We're going fishing."

"Look at me, Harold," said Amison calmly. "I took a big chance last year to help you solve your problems with the Neals family. I never asked for money because you needed help and I owed you a favor, but this is different."

"Ok. What is it?"

"I don't want money. I want something else."

Harold sounded exasperated. "What?"

"I have Leroux's carte blanche."

"So?"

Amison pulled a small folded note out of his pocket. He opened it and read it to Harold.

This is to certify that the bearer of this letter, Amison Rueben Jones, under the powers granted to our organization by international treaty, has the authority to do what he has done and to do what has to be done.

The letter, in French, bore Jacques Leroux's original signature. It had an issue date but had no expiration date. He refolded it carefully and put it away.

"That's an international license to kill, Jonesey," Harold observed quietly. "It also places you outside our control, if that's what you want."

"That's what I want, Harold. I'm telling you now that I plan to kill everyone who was responsible for turning Bernice into a vegetable."

Harold caught his breath and said, "Well then, there's something I want."

"What's that?"

"If heroin is buried in Bimini. I want the whole thing!"

"How much heroin are we talking about, Harold?"

"Two billion dollars at wholesale. It's buried at the Bimini Man dig site but I'm not sure exactly where. Find the heroin and steal it before you blow up the dig."

Amison smiled inwardly. The entire Bimini Man project was a charade.

"How did it get to the dig?"

"The Bencivengas shipped it over from Venezuela over the years. The idea was to use the dig as a ruse to eventually move the heroin to Florida. The deal was that we would do the real estate deals, the Bencivengas would do the drugs trafficking and the CIA through O'Brien would provide the cover. We agreed to a three way split."

Harold continued. "Look. You're probably aware that Centurion Trust owns the Bimini Man property. We bought it from Bencivenga and sold it to Sol Weinberg at a hundred million dollar profit. In reality, he gave us a loan provided we turn over two billion dollars after the dig is over and the heroin is removed and sold, maybe for four million dollars on the streets. The original plan was for us to split any excess over two billion with the Bencivengas and the CIA, who through Jack O'Brien who would keep its share in offshore accounts to fund covert operations.

"Now, I hear you want one hundred million dollars. I'll do you one better. I'm offering you one hundred million dollars or an even split, whichever places more cash in your pocket when this shit all blows away. We're going to steal the entire stash and sell it. And Frank is going to help us."

"Sounds good to me! Are you sure about Frank."

"Yes." Harold slapped his thighs. "There's work ahead. Let's hit the hay."

Sunlight poured into Amison's room early Thursday morning when he awoke to the smell of freshly brewed coffee and scrambled eggs and bacon being readied downstairs. He cleaned up, dressed and went down to find Harold serving William Nigel breakfast.

"It's a day off for the help," said Harold. "So I'm the cook and server."

The banker smiled. He stood briefly and extended a limp hand to Aimson. "I can loan you some of my servants," Bill Nigel said to Harold, totally ignoring Amison. "I'll take you up on that," Harold replied.

A beefy, jovial type, William Nigel radiated happiness and smugness with his lot in life as a well-heeled banker in a city overflowing with offshore money. He had, in his mind, outsmarted Harold for control of the Madsen bank and seemed not the least surprised to see Amison.

They sat down and started eating. "We're going fishing with Bill Nigel and he needs crew," Harold explained to Amison. "And you're it."

Bill Nigel was wearing white deck shoes, white slacks and a marine blue blazer with shiny gold buttons and opposed to the old slacks and short sleeved shirts Harold and Amison had on. A small bulge in small of Harold's back suggested he was sporting a piece.

"I don't really fish," said Bill Nigel. I just like being on water. I bought this new Silverton because it's all fiberglass. There's not an inch of wood on it."

"I bet that saves on maintenance," Amison commented.

"Yes, and the other reason I like it is because this model is easy to for me to handle alone. Some days, life gets so hectic, one just wants to be alone."

"I understand," Amison said.

"What we're going to do, Bill," Harold continued Bill, "is to let you take your yacht out, and we'll meet out in the water," said Harold. "I want to give my old derelict boat and its tired engines a workout. Then, we'll drop anchor and you'll pick us up for a short cruise on your yacht. How does that sound?"

"Splendid," said Bill Nigel.

An hour later, Amison and Harold were back at the Paradise Island airport where Mike Quinn had already prepared Harold's old Chris Craft docked at a crumbling slip near the Chalks landing strip. It's engines were running, the outriggers were up, and all the rods and reels were in place around three fighting chairs that were bolted to the floor of the after cockpit deck.

Harold looked at his watch. "It's time," he said. They jumped aboard and a few minutes later, the Chris Craft had circled around Paradise Island and dropped anchor in in flat waters under a cloudless sky.

Mike Quinn was at the controls on the bridge while Harold and Amison tended to the equipment in the cockpit, keeping An eye out for Nigel and his Silverton.

The sparkling white Silverton appeared on the horizon in Harold's binoculars shortly before noon. Through the glasses Harold saw that Bill was alone. The big yacht came up alongside theirs and Harold climbed aboard with Amison following behind.

"Do you want Mike aboard while we talk business?" asked Harold. "We have our boat anchored."

"That would be great if you could do that," replied Bill. "I hate to drive."

With Mike Quinn aboard and at the helm on the bridge above and guiding the vessel in long circles around the Chris Craft, Amison, Harold and Bill Nigel sat around a small table in the cockpit.

"This is one hell of a ship," began Amison. "Thanks for having me aboard."

"You should spend more time here, Mr. Jones," said Bill Nigel, smiling. "Your Mr. Levy could arrange it for you."

"Great idea," agreed Harold. "But to do that, Madsen must make more money." William Nigel smiled broadly. "This was our best year yet."

"Yes, it was," Harold nodded. "But, it could have been much better."

Bill Nigel lost his smile. "I don't follow."

"Bill," continued Harold. His tone was serious now. "We have two concerns. One is that loan Madsen has extended to Las Olas University. I hear that the bank may call the loan over some question about the university's activities."

"We have to, Harold. We're under pressure from the board."

"Who may they be?"

"Some represent our major depositors, including the Bencivenga family from Venezuela who you know well. They and other major depositors want to spread their funds out in the Caymans and other islands. We have to call the good loans or else we may not have enough reserves to pay off depositors. That could force a run on the bank."

"I appreciate that," said Harold. "But that's not good for Alliance. I do have a say in this, William. After all, Alliance is the bank's major stockholder."

"I'm sorry, Harold, but Marvin Childs was always kept abreast of what was going on. He is the one who suggested that the Bimini Man project might be a problem. We here in Nassau suspected that for a long time. The bank and Marvin expressed their concerns directly to Frank Hoffman many times. And I do recall you sat in on several university trustee meetings where you expressed the same misgivings. And of course, that leaked FBI report does make things look even worse. It makes for very poor publicity. Unfortunately, Harold, my hands are tied."

"I have another concern, William," Harold continued on in an even more somber tone. "It's the cash leakages from Madsen. They have averaged ten million dollars each year for five years. That's a lot of money, William."

Bill Nigel became all puffy and indignant. "You're crazy. You have no proof."

"I'm also concerned about the fact that your hit man tried to kill my very valued associate here, Amison Jones."

Nigel's eyes flashed. "You're truly mad."

"Who put out a contract on me?" Amison asked, slipping on a pair of surgical gloves he kept in his pockets.

Bill Nigel started to tremble. "It was don Ignacio Bencivenga who passed the word to me through an intermediary that he wanted to kill Mr. Jones."

"Who was the intermediary?" Harold asked.

"Captain Jack. I told him I had no contacts and Captain Jack said he'd use one of his men. But as I told Harold, I never issued a contract on your life. I swear on my life I didn't. Even though I thought that you might try to take me down on Harold's orders."

Harold gave the table top a resounding slap that made Bill Nigel jump in his seat. "No contracts are issued by anyone unless I approve them," he bellowed. "No one kills anyone unless I say so. I never gave orders to take you down, my friend. But let's return to the subject. Tell me, how are you going to pay me back for the money you stole?"

Bill Nigel' hand moved quickly, very quickly, much to Amison's amazement who did not think he had it in him. Before anyone could blink, Bill had a pistol in his hand.

But Nigel never had a chance. Amison was over him in an instant and wrestled the weapon out of his hand. A fist caught Bill Nigel on the chin, cracking it. The banker fell back in his chair and then flopped to the deck as the chair toppled over.

"Gag him!" ordered Harold. He threw a roll of tape and some rope he had in a fishing bag at Amison who bound the banker. He also drew a revolver from under his shirt and gave it to Amison. "Here, use this if you have to."

Mike Quinn called down from the bridge. "Is everything all right below?"

Amison stuffed a cloth into Bill's mouth and sealed it with the tape. "Everything's fine. We'll be done in a few minutes."

Harold found a long coil of halyard line that Amison used to tie Bill Nigel's feet. He metered out two hundred feet of line and then tied the bitter end to a cleat on the Silverton's transom while the Alliance chairman took a pail from a corner of the cockpit, tied a long cord to its handle and tossed it overboard and filled it with water. Pulling up the pail, he doused Bill Nigel's face with sea water. Bill came to his senses heaving and coughing.

"We want him wide awake for this," said Harold, as Amison tied Bill's hands behind him with another rope. "Here. Use the fish knife to gut him for the sharks." He passed Amison a serrated knife from the freezer console against the cabin.

Bill Nigel started crying and shaking . "What are you doing? Please don't kill me...I can explain. The Bencivengas were blackmailing me...I'll pay you back, with interest."

He went on blabbering and blubbering as Harold told Mike Quinn to take the vessel further out at about ten knots.

"Not a chance, Bill," said Harold. "This trip is costing me plenty and I want to have some fun. I want to see your face when the sharks tear nice meaty chunks off your fat body. We'll keep the boat in motion, Bill. We don't want those fish to eat too fast and get indigestion. Do we?"

He laughed hoarsely.

Amison cradled Bill Nigel in his arms like a dying tuna. "Come on, Bill. Be a man. It's not that bad. Make like a fish when your head hits the water. Keep your eyes and mouth open. It will be faster that way. You'll pass out before your lungs explode and you won't feel anything. You want to die before the sharks close in. You really shouldn't have placed that contract on me, you know. Here, have some jelly beans. It'll sooth your nerves."

He dropped a few jelly beans into Bill's mouth and gagged him before grabbing the fatty part of his belly in one hand. He gave it a twist before making two small cuts with the knife.

Nigel's eyes bulged and muffled sounds escaped his taped mouth as blood began oozing from the wounds. He struggled hysterically as Harold and Amison scooped him up and threw him into the water behind the yacht.

The Silverton picked up speed until the line was taut, the roar of its engines drowning out any sounds Nigel might have been making. It dragged Nigel by his bound feet with his head face down and skimming along the water's surface until the dorsal fins of several sharks appeared.

The vessel slowed and the sharks closed in. Harold found some large pieces of frozen meat in the boat's cockpit freezer used as chum for game fish and heaved overboard and then helped Amison pull Nigel back up over the transom.

The gag was gone, giving him time to catch his breath. The hapless banker was bleeding, choking and spitting up water when they untied him. Still, he was about to thank them when they suddenly dumped him over the side again, leaving him to thrash about in the foamy water with the chum and sharks.

Harold cracked jokes and Amison chewed on more jelly beans they watched Bill flail his arms and legs and listened to his falsetto shrieks.

The sharks nosed around in curiosity and then, driven wild by Nigel's kicking, they attacked the chum first, ripping off large pieces of meat, devouring them and then, in a feeding frenzy, they lunged into the banker's quivering body.

A shot rang out and the screaming and kicking stopped. Nigel's body bobbed around lifelessly as the sharks tore him apart until his remains disappeared in a pink tinted circle of foam and flesh.

"Why did you do that for?" Harold complained. "I wanted to see the show."

Amison returned the gun to Harold and pointed to a boat moving rapidly in the distance.

"Company," he said. "Might be a government boat. Let's move out of here."

Harold agreed and helped Amison coil the line. "I'm getting too old for this kind of work," he said, huffing and puffing.

"That's the problem with all this sun and fun," remarked Mike Quinn who had climbed down from the bridge to lend a hand.

"There's always heavy lifting. We had this job a few years back. Matter of fact, you and I did it."

"That's right," recalled Harold. "The guy must have weighed over three hundred pounds. We stuck him belly down on a meat hook in an ice house, took some bats and played baseball with his body. The bastard was so heavy he bent the hook. He wouldn't talk and we couldn't kill him. So, we took him down and pulled the hook out of his belly. I think we took out some of his guts out with the hook. Then you came up with the bright idea of chopping off his arms and legs one by one. It took another twenty minutes before he finally went, and still he didn't talk."

"A real hero," observed Amison, popping still more jelly beans into his mouth.

It unnerved Harold. "Can't you eat something else besides those damn beans?"

"How about steak and caviar?" Amison retorted.

"Fuck you, Jonesey. You're too expensive for me."

With the halyard line back in its original coil, they placed it in the sun to dry, washed down the cockpit and headed back to the anchored Chris Craft.

"Shall we sink the Silverton?" asked Mike Quinn?"

"Slowly," said Amison. "Just loosen a sea cock and put the boat on remote. It should head out to sea and sink in deep water."

They were back in Paradise Island on the Chris Craft shortly after the noon hour. "What's our schedule?"

"I'm sticking around for a while. But I want you guys out of here now."

They parted company without ever so much as a brief farewell. Harold returned to his condo, leaving Amison and Mike Quinn to return to the jet.

"Incidentally," Mike Quinn remarked, "That was no government boat out there."

"I know," Amison said. It didn't make any sense to make the guy suffer. I'm not even sure he deserved to die."

CHAPTER 12

▼

THE QUID PRO QUO

An hour later, Amison and Mike Quinn were waiting to be cleared for takeoff in Harold's jet.

"I set a flight plan for Fort Lauderdale via the Biminis," said Mike, "in case you want to make a pit stop there for any reason."

"You read my mind," Amison nodded. I'm going to pick up my boat and sail it to Florida. We're going to need it to carry explosives to the dig."

"I guess this means we're going to blow the place up."

Amison sighed. "I guess so."

He pulled the sensor out of his pocket that had been planted in his duffel a few days earlier and showed it to Quinn.

"Ever see one of these things before?"

Mike whistled. "It's a new three way high-tech devices. It links the object, you, with a satellite based guidance system and a smart ground or air sensor seeking weapon. It's still experimental, but it works. I've used it. How did you get your hands on it?"

"I'm the object," answered Amison.

"That's not good for us, Jonesey, especially on this plane. Get rid of it."

"Not just yet, Mike. Can we immobilize it?"

Not really. We can create some radio interference for a while. That might work."

"Lets try that. I want to hang on to it for a while."

"It's your funeral."

They were cleared for takeoff.

The flight to the airstrip in South Bimini took less than a half hour. No sooner had the jet gained altitude when it dropped to make its approach to the deserted strip.

"Incidentally," said Amison. "I never mentioned this when we were on the way to Paradise Island, but that meeting I had with Hank and Tucker in Nassau ended badly."

"What do you mean?"

"We met at a luncheonette. When we left, Hank was sandbagged by several guys I never saw before. I think Tucker did him."

Mike Quinn spoke without removing his eyes from the landing strip. "I wouldn't doubt it. The big man has a contract on Hank. Tucker does that type of work. He gets real friendly with his target and then zaps him."

"With me as bait?"

"Mike threw him his usual enigmatic smile. "At least the bait lived, Jonesey."

"This isn't right, man."

Mike Quinn lost his smile. "Let it go, Jonesey. Don't start getting sentimental on me. Know what I mean? Now, what are we doing, boss?"

He brought the jet to a rough landing on the uneven dirt runway.

"I want to give you a list," said Amison.

He waited until the jet landed and came to a stop before giving Mike a materials shopping list.

"This should do to blow up a small island. You can add to the list if you want. I also need depth charges, about six or eight of them and multi-purpose automatic low and high caliber weapons. Load them on *Phoenix*. It'll be parked behind the Riverside in Fort Lauderdale."

"How much time do we have?"

"The Triple A conference starts Monday. That's when I'm leaving Florida. At dawn. Call me on the cell or call Mark Stone."

"But, you haven't seen him in years."

"I will real soon."

Mike Quinn said nothing. He studied the list and ignored Amison as he pulled out a pen and a piece of paper and copied down some serial numbers from above the cockpit's instrument panel.

"Is that all?" Mike asked when he finished digesting the list.

Amison pulled some jelly beans out of his pocket and dropped a couple into his mouth.

"Want one? They're good for the nerves."

Mike Quinn shook his head.

"You know what this mission is about," said Amison, munching away. "You're also O'Brien's man…"

Mike started to protest.

Amison placed a finger on his lips. "Don't start with the bull shit or else I'll kill you on the spot. So, hear me out. You're O'Brien's hit man. So you know what I know. There's a load of heroin buried somewhere at the dig. I'm supposed to steal it for Harold. I'm sure O'Brien has his own plans for the stuff and ordered you to steal it for him."

"I didn't ask for a war, Jonesey."

"Neither did I. So, I'm proposing a truce until we find the heroin. Then we can decide to fight or not to fight."

He stuck his hand out. "Can we shake on it?"

Mike Quinn, much relieved, eagerly shook his hand.

"Great," Amison remarked. "We are now a team."

He picked up his duffel, jumped off the jet and began half walking, half jogging through a rough path in the woods to Buccaneer Point.

Poor Bill Nigel. Embezzlement was not a crime worth dying for. Now he was dead. Amison was sure Nigel never tried to have him killed. He was a braggart but not a killer. Hank Lawrence was another issue. He had crossed Harold Levy and ran out of luck. The big man was in the midst of one of his housecleaning fits.

It was late afternoon when he reached Buccaneer Point where Ojo had finished scrubbing down *Phoenix* and getting it ready for its next trip. Two messages were on the voice mail and Cecil had dropped over, he indicated with hand signals. The first was from Luis Santiago and the second was from Mark Stone congratulating Amison on his return to grace and inviting him to stay at the Riverside. Cecil had left a note asking Amison to stop at the customs office when he returned.

Cecil did not usually make idle requests and Amison promptly hopped the ferry to Alice Town where he found Cecil and Frances. They had finished checking passengers from an incoming flight and seemed happy to see him.

"Some folks are passing around the word that you were killed," said Cecil. "It's good to have you back."

"The rumors are really stirring up with those Jamaican guards," Frances added. "They've been acting like they own the place."

Amison could see that Frances was still saddened by the loss of her husband. He took a deep breath. "Well, Im back. How's your sister, Eileen?"

"Oh, she's fine, Ruby. She took a hostess job at the Reef Hotel."

Cecil added. "She wants to land a husband," he said. "Any ideas?"

Amison grinned. "Yes, but they're all married, some of them many times."

"Well, at least they're experienced."

"What about Domino?" Amison dared to ask. "Is she all right?"

Frances replied matter-of-factly. "She's flying back next week, Ruby. She wants to pick up her kids and take them to Miami. She's worried about what's going on here. And I don't blame her. I'm also thinking of leaving with my kids."

Neither Cecil nor Frances seemed to care to elaborate so Amison dropped the subject.

"We have a serious problem," Cecil started to say, but Amison anticipated his statement.

"Captain Jack?"

"Yes. He started the rumor about you being dead. He holds court at the End-Of-The-World Bar next door. As a matter of fact, he's there now."

"Who put you on a short leash?"

"Commissioner Jonathan Sykes from Nassau. He got here while you were gone. He sailed in aboard a large cutter that your Coast Guard donated to help fight this damn war on drugs. The ship is anchored in Porgy Bay in back of Pigeon Key under Reginald Lang's command."

"You're kidding."

No. Lang also heads a special assault unit out of Nassau. He's here with part of that unit. They stay on the cutter. Captain Jack and his Jamaicans are part of that command and they report directly to Lang.

"Is the Bimini Man dig perimeter still heavily guarded?"

"More than ever. Trespassing in not only a crime; one can get shot for even coming close to the dig site."

Amison smiled cynically. "Those old bones must be valuable," he commented.

"Don't be funny, Jonesey." Cecil threw his hands up in disgust. "You know my thoughts on the matter. I just hate to believe this hullabaloo is all about drugs and that my government is playing cozy with crooks and killers."

"It wouldn't be the first time, for any government," Amison responded. "Shall we have a chat with the good captain?"

They had walked back to Frances, who was within earshot, had overheard the last part of gtheir conversation. She started sobbing and blurted out. "Be careful, Ruby."

Amison gave her a soft kiss on the cheek and started to leave as Cecil called after him. "We'll follow you with a couple of men."

The bar was a minute away. Amison strode through the western style batwing doors and into the dimly lit interior. Crude wooden tables and chairs were lined up around a small dance floor. A juke box was in one corner, and a mountain of a man sat on a high stool in another, hairy arms folded and watching all movements around the room. Armed Jamaicans were seated at the tables and at the bar, and the sweet smell of marijuana and hashish was in the air.

Sure enough, Sanford Jack was standing at one end of the bar, drink in hand and speaking to one of the Jamaicans. The place fell silent when Amison sauntered in and slipped in between the captain and his companion.

Captain Jack was taller and more heavily built than Amison. His dark heavy beard and moustache and the jolly roger tatoos on his arms and on the back of his big hands gave him an old fashioned piratical appearance. He put his drink down on the counter to face Amison who grabbed the glass and tossed its contents in his face with one hand and grabbed his crotch with the other.

Turning to the Jamaican behind him, he threw him the empty glass, drew a snub nosed revolver from under his guyaberra shirt and aimed it at his head while he held the speechless captain by the scrotum.

"I'm only going to take a few minutes of your time," Amison told Captain Jack. And to the Jamaican next to him he said, "Be smart, and we might meet again. Be stupid and I'll attend your funeral today! Your call, pal."

The Jamaican hesitated in the face of the gun muzzle. Finally, he backed off and moved over to one of the tables. The big guard at the other end of the room tried to sneak off his stool but found himself facing the same business end of the gun. He tried to draw a knife from behind his back but Amison fired and nicked his elbow. The knife fell and the guard grabbed at his wounded arm.

"I have five bullets left," announced Amison, "for five dead heroes!"

He then turned his attention to Captain Jack whose testicles he still held firmly in his hand.

"We're not misbehaving again, are we cap?"

He squeezed and Captain Jack screamed.

"Good. Your voice is good. But you don't have to say anything but 'yes' or 'no' to a few questions. Like for instance, what's really buried with Bimini Man?"

There was silence. Amison gave a squeeze and Captain Jack screamed.

Amison repeated the question. "What's buried out there, cap? You can tell me. I won't tell."

Another squeeze followed by a long scream of agony.

"Heroin." The huge man started sobbing hysterically.

"I didn't hear you."

"Heroin, you mother fucker!" Heroin! Heroin! Heroin! Now let me go!"

"Not yet, big guy. Who put a contract out on me?"

"I don't know."

Another squeeze.

Captain Jack shrieked. "I can't tell what I don't know."

"Well. Tell me what you do know. What happened in Nassau?"

It was obvious to Captain Jack that Amison was well informed. He whispered hoarsely. "Don Ignacio gave Harold Levy an envelope with one million dollars."

"What for?" One more squeeze followed by more groans, cries and sobs.

"It was a bribe."

"What the hell for?"

"To keep the dig open. Harold spread the word that he wanted to shut down the Bimini Man project but said he'd wait until the end of the Triple A meeting. The money was to buy him off and give us time to move the heroin out of Bimini."

"How does Bill Nigel fit into the picture?"

"He doesn't. Harold told him you were going to kill him unless he gave back the money he stole from Madsen."

"So that's how Bill Nigel got involved?"

"Yes. He asked me to arrange the hit. I sent one of my Miami boys to get you on the way to Philadelphia. What happened to him?" He winced as Amison tightened his grip.

"He's dead, cap."

Amison gave the sea captain's testicles one final squeeze, but not so hard this time. Sanford Jack fell cursing to the ground, rolling around and clutching his groin as Cecil Fergueson and two local police officers burst through the batwing doors with guns drawn. Amison put away his revolver.

Cecil's eyes moved from Amison to Captain Jack on the floor to the wounded bouncer in the corner rubbing his arm. "We heard a shot," he exclaimed.

"Not here" said Amison, going to the door. "The good captain and I reached an understanding, didn't we, cap?"

The skipper struggled to his feet and regained his composure. "Yeah," he growled. "Yeah, we have an understanding, for now."

It was a standoff, nothing more, but Amison felt better. His presence was felt and that was good for his ego. At the very least a modicum of civil order in Alice Town was restored, at least temporarily, and to Cecil Fergueson's amazement.

He returned to *Phoenix* with a self-satisfied smirk on his face. It was good to do a good deed, if that could be called one. Amison was about to board the cat when Ojo pointed to a short, silver haired man in a French cuffed shirt, silk tie and a dark blue double breasted blazer leaning on a cane on the dock near the boat. A gleaming white yacht was anchored in the middle of the lagoon harbor.

"Don Ignacio Bencivenga! To what do I owe this visit after all these years?"

"Buenos dias, senor Jones. I usually tell people it is a great pleasure to see them after so many years, but in your case it is not such a pleasure. In fact, you are not the primary purpose of my visit. I have come to witness the resurrection of Bimini Man at the Triple A conference." He spoke in a crisp Spanish accent.

Bencivenga pointed to the marina's makeshift outdoor bar and café. Winslow was duty and was serving a couple at a picnic table and seemed unhappy to see him. Amison said nothing and followed him to the café where they sat down and ordered two coffees.

"Winslow," he called over. "How's Ginny?"

"How the hell should I know?" Winslow grumbled. "Ask her."

Don Ignacio looked slightly embarrassed. "Am I interrupting something?"

"Oh, nothing at all." Amison put on a smile. "So, don Ignacio, what gives?"

"I am here to spare your life."

Amison sat back in his chair and laughed. "That's not your style, friend. Does Does Sanford Jack's health concern you?"

"News travels fast, senor Jones. I heard. I see you have not lost your touch. This is why I am here. I want to spare your life since you will not die easily."

Amison chuckled. "That's mighty generous of you."

"Sometimes, only sometimes," the old man went on, "I wish you had worked for me."

"I suppose I should be flattered."

The older man went on. "I was terribly angered when you, Ojo, and your team destroyed my trawler fleet in Venezuela seven years ago. I lost many good men."

"Your trawlers were moving heroin, don Ignacio. My orders were to stop them."

"But I was to be protected by your government in exchange for my financial and political support to the Venezuelan government. I am a farmer. I once grew sugar but your country's sugar quota put me out of business. I now produce heroin. The money I make supports Venezuela and your country's foreign policy goal to make sure the Venezuelan government does not collapse. You were to take down one of my boats, not the entire fleet."

Amison drew a cigarette from a pack in his pocket and lit it. "That's news to me. Had I been informed, you can be sure only one boat would have been sunk."

He leaned back in his chair, inhaled deeply and blew a line of smoke into the air.

Don Ignacio pressed on. "Why did you kill my son, Pauli?"

Leaning forward in his chair, Amison replied. "That was five years ago, friend. I was not paid to kill him. I never touched Pauli. His boat was chasing us. I had no idea he and your other son, Miguelito, were on it. We had no choice."

"An interesting story, senor Jones. I was told by an informant your boat was on a personal mission to destroy my yacht and kill my sons."

"What informant?"

"Dudley Hanes, Doctor Alstrum's medical assistant."

"He was wrong, don Ignacio. I had no personal reason to harm you or your sons. Anyway, I heard that Miguelito escaped."

Ignacio nodded over his coffee. "Whatever happened, one son is dead and his death must be avenged."

Amison took another puff from his cigarette. "Someone tried to take me down in Miami before I left for the Bahamas five years ago. Was that your call?"

"Yes. But it was a shared decision. I am not the only one who wants you dead. But as you can see, we failed."

"With whom did you share that decision, don Ignacio?"

"I have many partners, senor Jones." Bencivenga replied.

"One more thing. Someone is still trying to kill me. Is that your call?"

Don Ignacio smiled. "I leave your fate to others. Certainly, you must appreciate my position. Your departure from earth would be good. But that does not seem to be happening. So, if the devil will not die, I must work with him."

"Fair enough. What do you propose?"

Ignacio smiled. "You are a grandfather, are you not?"

"Yes. I have twins through my first wife: a married daughter who has blessed me with two grandchildren, a boy and a girl; and, I have a son, still single."

"Miguelito too is single. He is my only son besides three daughters. Pauli left me with grandsons, but they are young. Jocalinda, my youngest daughter raises them. My other daughters live in your country. We say that when a man has children, he is blessed. He is doubly blessed with grand children; but when he finally has great grandchildren, he becomes immortal."

Don Ignacio stopped to take another sip of coffee.

Amison squirmed in his seat. "Speak to me about sparing my life, don Ignacio."

"I want you to retire, permanently, and away from here."

"Why, don Ignacio?"

"Bimini Man is very important to me. I am therefore prepared to pay you one hundred million dollars in cash to either retire or to come work for me. If you work for me, you can manage some of my business affairs, but not here."

"That's a lot of money, don Ignacio. Much more than the value of a few fossil bones. What's the real story with Bimini Man?"

"That is not your affair. I will not have you meddling."

Amison finished his coffee. "Murder is my affair, don Ignacio," he said. "Two Europol agents have died. My job is to investigate their deaths. That's why I must refuse your offer."

"Are you asking for more money?"

"No. Money and threats mean little at my age."

Ignacio Bencivenga looked tired. "In a way, I would have been disappointed had you accepted. Tell me. Will you kill my son Miguelito if he comes after you. He is so young and impetuous."

"I will try not kill him," Amison promised.

Don Ignacio rose to his feet, supporting himself on his cane. "That is good to know. Favors and candor among enemies are rare treats."

"It is rarer among friends, don Ignacio."

"Yes. You should watch out for some of your friends. Some of them are more anxious than I to see you dead."

"We must all die one day, don Ignacio."

"What a pity. Some day, when this is over and if we are still alive, I will tell you the true story about Bimini Man."

The old gentleman tipped his cane in Amison's direction and left.

CHAPTER 13

▼

BREAKFAST AT EUNICE'S

It occurred to him after don Ignacio left that he still did not have his handler's identity. On a lark he called Mark Stone at the Riverside. Much to his surprise, the call was picked up on the first ring. The voice at the other end was unmistakable and it also recognized Amison's.

"How are you doing old buddy? Has the phoenix risen from the ashes?"

"Yes it has. How did you hear?"

"Cecil called. So did Henry? Where are you?"

"In Bimini. If you know so much, who's my handler?"

"Don't know. But the limerick has changed. When are you coming over?"

"In a few days. I'll let you know."

"Watch out for Dudley Hanes. Henry doesn't trust him."

"How's Luis Santiago?"

"He's fine. We'll talk when you get here."

Early Friday morning, Amison grabbed a handful of jelly beans, stuffed them in his pocket and ferried over to Alice Town after instructing Ojo to dinghy around the Bimini Man dig site, preferably without being caught. Cecil, as usual, was at customs helping Frances.

"Hi. I thought you might have left after your resounding victory yesterday." The tone of his voice had changed.

"No. I'm leaving this weekend. Did you know don Ignacio is in town."

"Yes. I heard he paid you a visit."

"Is Henry around?"

"Cecil nodded. "As long as you're here, you're in time for breakfast.""

A ritual developed over the years. It consisted of weekly breakfasts meetings at Eunice's with Cecil and Henry and other regulars. But Amison had a purpose and an agenda today. While Ojo was poking around the dig Bimini Man dig perimeter, looking for places to bury detonation charges, Amison planned to use breakfast as an opener to bring up the issue of the dead Europol agents.

He was not unduly concerned for Ojo's safety, believing that the little Bolivian would be closely observed but not interfered with by Captain Jack and his men who were not ready for an open fight with Amison and Cecil.

There were also few secrets left. The bearded Jamaican had clearly confirmed that heroin was mixed up with the Bimini Man project, and in all probability, the it was hidden at the dig site. So the task was to guesstimate where it was buried and to remove it before blowing up the excavations. The question of what to do with it when and if it was found was now entering his mind. He also figured that Mike Quinn would be right behind him in his quest for the treasure. He could not assume for a moment that Jack O'Brien buy into Harold's demand without first making sure that the heroin stayed safe.

Cecil informed Amison on the way to Eunice's diner that Frank Hoffman and Leslie Sandler had arrived on a chartered cruise ship at dawn along with over one thousand tourists and Triple A conferees. This lead him to wonder how the site could be detonated without inflicting casualties.

"Where's the vessel now?"

"It dropped anchor in Nixon's Harbor. Some of the passengers are staying on it; Frank and Leslie have taken rooms at the Reef. Every spare room on the island is booked," said Cecil with a sheepish grin on his face.

"Who says crime doesn't pay?" Amison responded.

Cecil scowled. "That's what I want to talk to you about."

Bimini's six man police force and four part time customs officials worked out of the police barracks which had an infirmary and a seldom used holding pen in back of the reception room. A refrigerated icehouse that sold crushed and block ice to fishermen, and featured a new coin machine outside that dispensed cube and block ice to the public, doubled as a mortuary. Luther Guenther and Dwayne Douglas' bodies were its only current occupants.

Amison broke the silence of the ride over the uneven streets by offering Cecil a few jelly beans. "Have some. They're good for you."

The jeep almost left the road.

"What's with the Guenther and Douglas investigations?" Amison asked after Cecil regained control of the jeep and refused the candy..

"Fred Peterson, the medical examiner, is here. He says he spoke with Jonathan Sykes who wants to review the case in Nassau after the conference."

"What about Reginald Lang?"

Cecil sounded exasperated. "He agrees with the commissioner. Our friend the captain complained to Lang last night and Sykes called me in. He's mighty pissed at what you did."

"So where do we stand?"

"I've been thinking, Jonesey. This Bimini Man thing. It could just be for real."

"What do you mean?"

"I mean, Sykes wants us to exercise caution. Sure drugs might be involved, but we don't know for sure and Bimini Man is bringing us a lot of business,"

Cecil went on, almost apologetically. "I realize that drugs are bad, but you have to understand that many people here in the islands supplement their incomes from the drug trade. Perhaps Sykes is right. We shouldn't be hasty. It doesn't mean that Bimini Man is only about drugs."

"What about Luther Guenther and Dwayne Douglas? Do we forget about them?"

"No. We must find out what happened. But that's all Leroux and I want to do. I don't want to get in any deeper, and we all want to keep an open mind on Bimini Man. It could be that he's for real."

Amison said nothing. Cecil parked the jeep and they walked into Eunice's diner where they were greeted inside by Henry and Dudley Haynes who were there with Fred Peterson.

The medical examiner was friendly enough. Well built and looking younger than his years, Amison sized him up as an exercise freak. A waitress had set up a round table and Fred sat next to Henry and Dudley with Cecil and Amison on the other side.

It was Henry's turn to buy breakfast and he ordered breakfast pastries, toast, tea and coffee.

Dudley spread marmalade on his toast. "Do you realize," he was saying cheerily, "We are being evicted from our precious homeland."

"Only temporarily," Henry interjected. "The conference ends next weekend,"

"It will be good for the economy," Fred Peterson observed.

Cecil agreed. "We would be dead in the water here in Bimini if not for the dig and the Triple A. The weather is so bad, we can't attract bugs to a garbage dump."

"The conference should bring some a lot of money to the Biminis," Fred noted.

"The meeting is good," said Cecil. "But so far as the white world is concerned, it's just a communion of black people. Who cares? The dig is the drawing card. Everyone here believes that the world's oldest human being is an African and may have migrated here thousands of years ago. That's why Bimini is prospering this season. It's Bimini Man. Let's hope a storm doesn't rain on our parade."

"What's the view from Nassau, Dr. Peterson?" Amison asked.

"Oh, I agree completely," confirmed the medical examiner. "This is a splendid event for the Bahamas. It will definitely put us on the map. Despite all the rumors, we're all rooting for Bimini Man in Nassau."

"Same here," added Dudley. "Would anyone care for more marmalade?"

Amison thought it appropriate to change the subject. "I'd imagine you guys are staying for the big event."

"You bet," said Dudley. A thin man with thick glasses on his hawkish face, his myopia forced him to stare closely and intently at anyone and anything.

Henry dug into his pockets for his pipe, tobacco and a wooden match. "It'll be a show stopper, that's for sure."

Amison lit a cigarette and stretched his legs under the table. "Good luck finding a room."

The doctor grinned. "We're staying the Fergueson Hotel," he quipped. "With meals prepared and served by Mrs. Fergueson."

Cecil winked at Amison. "Must we put up with you guys so soon, again?" Then he said, "You guys know how to find our home. My wife will be expecting you. And I'll join you later today after work."

"I'm lucky," said Peterson. I'm staying at Government House. The place is open while Sykes is in town."

Henry looked up from his tea. "Are they finished at the dig?"

Cecil shook his head. "No. I hear Frank Hoffman's dig team ran out of money. That's why he's here. He's going to announce the project's termination at the conference. When they get more funding, they can always return and look for the rest of Bimini Man's family. What do you think, Henry?"

Henry Alstrum stuffed more tobacco into his pipe, struck a wooden match against the side of his shoe and relit his pipe. "I think Frank is going to play safe, declare victory and quit while he is ahead. What would you do, Jonesey?"

"That's up to Frank," replied Amison, lighting a cigarette. "I'm curious about one thing, Dr. Peterson. Why not ship the Bimini Man remains to Nassau where it belongs instead of to Florida?"

"Here, here," chimed in Cecil, looking straight at Peterson. "What do you say to that?"

Peterson threw Cecil a disapproving look. "I haven't the vaguest idea. Maybe, there's an agreement between Nassau and the university."

At that, the conversation shifted to the two men lying in the ice house next door. "You know, Fred," Henry said softly, puffing away on his pipe, "It's time for an autopsy on our two bodies. I just don't think they drowned. Very little water came out of their systems when we pumped out their stomachs. Moreover, the water we found was brackish. It wasn't our local water, and it certainly was not sea water."

"This thing is out of our jurisdiction if they died outside the Bahamas."

"We do have a problem with the idea they died in Bimini," said Dudley. "Those bits of plant debris hanging to their clothes are not appear native to Bimini. Isn't that what you found, Henry?"

"That's true," agreed Dr. Alstrum. "But it would not hurt to perform a complete autopsy to settle things."

"Let me speak plainly," said Peterson. "This is the tourist season, and Nassau wants to keep the matter quiet."

"Aren't the two cases similar?" asked Amison. "If so, the killer or killers might be the same in both instances. But since Dwayne Douglas is a Bahamian, I would imagine you would be interested in finding out what happened to him. He was, as you know, a police officer and one of yours."

"Amen, to that," said Cecil.

Henry added, "Fred. It would at least be nice to have some clarification about the origins of those bits of flora that somehow got into their clothes."

"I agree with the good doctor," said Dudley, turning to Henry Alstrum, "We should have a closer look."

Amison added. "I understand the bodies were found lying face down on the same stretch of beach on South Bimini near the cut leading into the harbor."

"What's more," said Henry, "both men had apparently stripped or been stripped and then dressed again in a hurry. One had his drawers on backwards; the other had his on inside out. These things don't happen naturally. There must have been something going on."

He turned to Amison. "Are you going to Florida any time soon?"

"This weekend. Saturday or Sunday."

Henry smiled and nodded. "I want Jones to take their clothes along with samples of hair and skin scrapings so that he can get them tested in Florida, just to satisfy our curiosity. What do you think, Cecil?"

Cecil shook his head. "I'm going to defer to Dr. Peterson on this one."

Peterson sighed. "I have no problem. But Nassau's position stays the same."

"There's a sad side to this mess," explained Henry, looking squarely at Peterson. "The Biminis are a tiny community with five bars and fifty houses of worship. We work all week and we worship on Sundays. Not knowing how Dwayne died means he cannot be buried. He is being denied that which is granted to common criminals, a Christian funeral. It slaps us, the people of Bimini, in the face!"

"That's right," said Cecil. "It's the least we can do for Dwayne Douglas and his family."

"Amen to that," added Dudley with finality.

Fred Peterson looked around the table and finally relented. "All right," he said. "I'll sign a death certificate for Dwayne Douglas so long as we show the cause of death as 'unknown'. But Luther Guenther stays as is for now. Cecil, you can tell Dwayne's widow to make funeral arrangements. And you, Henry, you can do the autopsies, and Jones can have some tests done in Florida."

They all sighed with relief as they allowed the conversation to move to other subjects. After a few minutes, Amison rose to leave.

"It's been a great, gentlemen, but I have to get back to my boat. "Henry, you were going to give me some specimen to take back to Florida?"

"Dudley put something together for you," said Henry. "We were counting on Dr. Peterson's consent."

Fred shrugged. "It can't hurt," he said as he too got up.

"I'm expected for at Government House for a meeting with Sykes and Lang. I'm leaving also."

"Me too," said Henry. "I have house calls to make. As they say, I have promises to keep. Dudley. Are you coming?"

Dudley followed Henry. "Yes. Wait a moment. Let me fetch the bag from next door."

He went to the barracks across the street at the barracks and returned with a big canvas bag.

He handed it to Amison and walked out outside with him. "Do you need a ride back to the ferry landing?" Dudley asked.

"No. I'm walking. It will do me good."

"Do you enjoy poetry?" asked Dudley.

"From time to time," Amison replied.

"Here's one of my favorite lines…'You are old Father William,' the young man said. Your hair has become very white. And yet, you incessantly stand on your head. Do you think at your age it is right?' What do you think of that?"

Amison looked at Dudley and continued, "It's good. Now try this. 'In my youth, Father William replied to his son, I thought that I had a great brain. But now that I'm perfectly sure I have none, why I do it again and again.' Well? How does that sound?"

Dudley nodded. "Marvelous. I'm glad we'll be working together. When do you plan to leave for Florida."

"Tomorrow."

"You told them you were going Sunday."

"A diversion."

"Very clever. Do you have a final destination?"

"The Riverside hotel. But, let's keep it quiet. We don't want to tip off the bad guys, do we?"

Amison left Eunice's with the canvas bag and started to walk down the road back to the ferry landing. He passed an outdoor café where Frank Hoffman and Leslie Sandler happened to be finishing breakfast. He wished to avoid them but they waved incessantly and he felt compelled to stop at their table.

"Hello, Ruby." Leslie smiled, half rose from the table and extended her hand in a handshake. "It's been a long time."

Amison shook her hand and give her a kiss on the cheek. "Not that long, cookie, has it?"

"I take it that you both met again recently," said Frank icily.

"We've met," replied Amison. "What's up?"

"How about coffee, old chum?" asked Frank.

"I'll take a rain check."

"I hate to bother you, old chum. Can we have a chat?"

"Talk on," said Amison, leaning back in his chair and folding his arms.

"We, I mean, Leslie and I know why you are here," Frank said.

"I like it here."

"Right. But you're also on the Alliance payroll. We also know about the Europol connection and about the two agents who were found dead on the beach. Very sad. However, you're in a position to make or break this project. I'd like to know that we can count on your support by not pursuing your investigation."

"You know, Frank, you sound like a university president raising money."

"How is that?"

"Like a total ass hole."

Frank sprung to his feet, and Amison followed suit. "I could break your face for that crack!"

"Am I being threatened?" asked Amison quietly.

Then he looked at Leslie. "Am I being threatened? Am I hearing right?"

Finally, he faced the street, asking no one in particular. "Is my good name being sullied?"

Leslie got up between them to prevent the discussion from degenerating into a brawl.

"Boys, boys," she said. "Let's sit. Let's not fight." They sat down again. "Now, where were we?"

"Frank was telling me he'd like my support, now that I'm so popular. What kind of support do you want?"

"Ruby," said Leslie imploringly. "We're on the verge of making an important announcement. Our future could depend on it."

"Your future too," added Frank.

"I'm impressed by your clairvoyance, Frank. Aside from my future, who else's future may be at stake?"

"Mark Stone's," answered Frank gravely.

There were several moments of silence. The sun was making its way to the top of the sky, shadows were shrinking and the heat was rising.

"Frank. Let me ask you a question. "Are you mixed up with Bencivenga?"

"Jonesey. You can make life easy for you and for us," Frank said gravely. "I can offer you a nice clean position at our university with instant tenure, a great salary, fringe benefits, a health plan, everything."

"I always said," commented Amison. "Being a teacher is the next best thing to being a bum. Does your offer come with a VIP parking permit?"

"Then, what do you think?" pressed on Leslie Sandler, letting allowing a bit of breast peek out from under her blouse. "You really don't need all this shit at this stage of your life."

"What about Mark?"

"If I'm safe, he's safe, and you're safe." said Frank. "Do we have a deal?"

"Level with me, Frank. I understand that Bimini Man's credibility is in question in view of the disappearance of human fossil bones from a New York museum. Is there a connection?"

"Sheer coincidence!"

"And what is Bencivenga's interest in Bimini Man?"

Frank Hoffman shook his head vigorously.

"You have him all wrong, Jonesey. The old man turned a new leaf years ago. He is one of the dig's original backers. He sits with our board of trustees. I guess you didn't know that."

"Right. Now try this. Nigel has been milking Madsen for Bencivenga. That's how the old man pays himself back for the money he fronted for the Bimini Man project. Harold found out and is mighty pissed."

"I'll call Bill Nigel today," said Frank. He'll fix things up."

"It's too late, friend. He's gone!"

"Gone?"

"That's right. He's dead! Now, who else do you want to call?"

"You dumb shit!" Frank growled in a subdued voice. "If you killed Nigel, you signed Mark's death warrant! Mark was our bag man in all these operations."

"Mark, a bagman? When the hell did that start?"

"Shortly after you left for Bimini," Frank replied impatiently."He replaced a woman who was killed. I'm calling Hank Lawrence."

"He's gone too."

"I'll call Harold."

"It's too late, Frank. Harold called the hits on Nigel and Lawrence, and he has taken over the bank."

"Then, Mark is dead. Bencivenga was keeping him alive because he agreed to be our bagman. The arrangement even had Jack O'Brien's blessing. If Levy has taken over the bank, Mark's job is gone. I'll have Harold talk to Bencivenga."

Amison shook his head. "No dice, Frank. Bencivenga, Levy and O'Brien have a deal going and you're not part of it. If you stick around, you're going to go down. This is bail out time, Frank! We also have to protect Mark."

"You're bull-shitting."

"Wake up, man! I never bull-shit" Amison retorted. "You're just plain stupid if you believe that drugs are not what Bimini Man is all about. And, you're crazy if you and Leslie are going to get your hands on the heroin. You guys are way over your heads. The mission I was handed is as phony as Bimini Man. It's a cover to move the heroin out of here."

Frank's jaw tightened.

"I don't know anything about that, Jonesey. I really don't. Drugs aren't my bag. They never were. I'm a university president and for old times sake I allow the CIA to use our institution to park its assets. That's my deal with Jack. If I could get out of it, I would. But I can't. I truly believe Bencivenga is supporting this dig because believes in it. Leslie convinced me and many others, including

Jack O'Brien who was responsible for getting us government funding, about her Bimini Man theory, and we're going with it. Even if you're right, unless you have a workable option, we have to see this thing through."

Amison shook his head sadly. Then he took a deep breath and a mischievous grin covered his face.

"However," he said. "I can get you two out of this mess for a small favor."

"What's that?"

"You let me jump Leslie's bones once a week."

"Ruby!" exclaimed Leslie. Her face turned beet red.

"Fuck you, Jonesey!" Frank jumped to his feet but Leslie pulled him down.

Amison over the table and whispered, "Fuck you too, Frank. If anything happens to Mark, I'm going to take you and everyone else responsible down! I give you fair warning. And…"

"Just exactly what are you prepared to do?" Leslie interrupted.

Amison smiled mischievously and said, "I'll huff and puff and blow your house down."

CHAPTER 14

▼

PORT EVERGLADES

Amison rushed back to the cat. Staying in Bimini longer was useless. Frank was either a true believer or a consummate liar and Cecil was back pedaling. He could not deny the reality that drugs were the islands' dirty little secret, and he realized as he climbed aboard *Phoenix* that while he might be tolerated, he was not truly welcome. Bimini Man might or might not be a charade, but for the sake of making the most of an otherwise lackluster tourist season, it was the key to the economic salvation of the islands.

The small Bahamian community, quietly and subtly, supported the dig despite Sanford Jack's excesses. Amison was in many ways a threat to an economy that was as dependent on drugs as it was on tourism. He threatened in this sense to become a pariah and no one seemed upset when he announced his plans to leave.

The islands were convenient entrepots between the sources of drug production in South America and the markets of North America. Almost everyone dealt or used drugs in one way or another, from the big time traffickers who shipped bulk heroin and cocaine to the local residents, merchants and boat yards who serviced their needs and wants. They were all part of an informal but elaborate network for the transport of drugs from South America through the West Indies to Florida. So long as demand in the States was high, the islands were destined to prosper.

Ojo had returned from his tour of Porgy Bay ahead of Amison and presented him with elaborate hand drawn sketches of the islands he surveyed. In each sketch he placed tiny crosses around where he thought something was buried. Each cross pinpointed the location of a possible site to conceal explosives that could be wired to a central point of detonation.

Amison examined the drawings and smacked his lips. Being familiar with the cays in Porgy Bay, he found the sketches remarkably accurate and concluded that if heroin was hidden anywhere it would be on the one in which the dig was taking place. That made sense because the greater number of Sanford Jack's guards were deployed in small patrol boats around the cay. Further, for added security Lang's cutter lay at anchor within shooting range of the tiny island.

He folded the drawings, put them away and gave Ojo instructions to prepare the cat for departure. The revealing discussions at the diner and his chance encounter with Frank and Leslie convinced him it was time to leave.

The marine forecast on the weather channel was good for the next few days. The storm off Africa was on the move but the forecast predicted it would blow itself out over the Atlantic before reaching a land mass.

The encrypted e-mail message flashing on the computer screen was more critical and Amison studied it carefully. It contained instructions from Jacques Leroux to meet his new handler in Fort Lauderdale along with the new communication codes replacing those of the past five years.

He gulped down a soft drink and went out on deck, holding the sensor that was stored in his duffel. "We're leaving with the tide," he signaled to Ojo. He took the sensor into the brush behind the dock and buried it under a rock. "Now, let's see what happens."

Ojo smiled politely and shook his head in doubt.

They waited until the sun was down and the tidal current was beginning to turn west. Slowly, silently the catamaran inched out into the bay and drifted into the bay. A dinnertime glow from Alice Town bounced over the harbor's still waters in the twilight between day and night. *Phoenix* ghosted gently through the cut and a half hour later the battleship gray cat was ghosting over the darkening flats of the Bahama Banks and into the blackness of the night in front of it. In open water, the mast rose out of its tower and its great sails unfurled. Winds from the east drove the vessel. With engines silenced, the cat picked up speed and lunged across the high steep swells of the Gulf Stream in its westward track to Florida.

Amison's thoughts drifted to Centurion Insurance who owned the tiny island in Porgy Bay where the dig was taking place. Sol Weinberg, Centurion's founder and CEO was bound to surface sooner or later. He had never worked for Centurion but he knew him. He was a former Mosad agent, a big man with a heavy, sad hound dog face. Sol offered him a job once but Amison refused it to stay with Alliance.

Amison liked jelly beans but Sol preferred peanuts.

He sent Mark Stone a coded message at the Riverside. Another message went to his brother-in-law, informing him that he was in transit and expecting to arrive by morning. More sail was raised and the big cat leaped forward and raced silently through the night towards a halo over the invisible horizon.

His thoughts turned to Domino with whom he fancied he was in love. Or, was he? He had once been told that there was a difference between being in love and loving someone but had forgotten what it was. Perhaps he was merely obsessed.

An hour passed and the Gulf Stream was crossed without incident. Another hour passed and Amison surrendered the helm to Ojo and went below to listen again to the weather forecast.

It had changed suddenly. It predicted abnormally cooler temperatures and better than a forty percent chance of rain, An ominous note of urgency seemed to come through the recording's male monotone staccato voice. It went on to make a long reference to the storm from the African coast.

It was now upgraded to tropical storm status and was barreling into the eastern Caribbean. The weather channel announced that tracking centers were no longer predicting its imminent break up.

But right now the air was clear. *Phoenix* cleared the Stream, the seas calmed and the halo on the horizon grew into the brilliance of south Florida's lights from its high rise buildings that ranged from Miami to the Palm Beaches.

He had no plan beyond going to Fort Lauderdale to load on the explosives being assembled by Mike Quinn. The time table was simple. His idea was to be back in the Biminis by Monday, to lay a field of explosives around the dig site perimeter while ferreting out the heroin if there was any to be found, and blow up the place. If along the way he could divine how the two Europol agents died he would have achieved all mission objectives. If not, well, those were the breaks.

He waited until they were within a few miles of the Port Everglades inlet before calling his daughter Deborah who told him that Estrella Gomez was working for her.

"I think she'll work out well at the house, Debbie," he said. "But I want you to ask her about who was in the Alliance building when mom fell out the window."

"You're going ahead with your inquiry into mother's accident?"

"Yes. You remember Hank Lawrence, don't you?"

"He's the guy from Philadelphia?"

"That's right. He's gone. But his parting shot was to tell me he called Bernice to say I was alive before she went to Philadelphia. She was lured to Alliance, Debbie, where someone tried to kill her. If she ever regains consciousness, that someone is going to try again, this time to shut her up for good. We can't wait for that."

"What do you need?" Debbie asked after a few moments.

"I want Estrella to obtain copies of the Alliance Building's entry or sign-in logs for the weeks before and after the accident. There should be three sets. One for the street entrance, one for the executive floors and another for the roof-top chopper landing covering access through the fire door. I want to find out who'd been going in and out of that building. There should be some time clock records. Estrella will be able to retrieve that data with help from co-workers. Since they're all about to be fired, they won't be fond of their bosses. I'm sure they'll cooperate."

"What if they ask for money?"

"I have money. Promise them jobs in Miami or Fort Lauderdale. I can arrange it through Mark."

"How's Mark doing? Sid Stone never talks about him."

"All right, I guess. I spoke with him."

"Does he know about your plans to give them work at his hotel?"

"Not yet, but he will."

"Dad?"

"What, cookie?"

"Be careful!"

"I'm trying to, kid, I'm trying to. In the meantime, say hello to my grandchildren and take care of yourself."

He found it strange that she never asked the obvious question why anyone would ever want to kill Bernice.

Amison blew her a kiss over the telephone and hung up.

He could understand don Ignacio. He was an aging lion trying to protect his kill. Jacques Leroux was more obtuse, sneakier, more like a hyena. He smelled a kill, but was unsure of what to do except to lamely propose a bribe, probably worth far less than the value of the kill. Harold Levy was more open. He needed to consign Bimini Man to history for Alliance to survive. If there was heroin, he wanted it to boot.

Sure, there were other players but the joker was Jack O'Brien, and Amison had no idea what position if any he had staked out. With Mike Quinn in the picture, his interests had to be competitively identical to those of Harold. That could be a a lethal combination.

It was also possible that Levy, Bencivenga and O'Brien once shared a common agenda with respect to the Bimini Man dig, assuming heroin was the trophy, and that was to split the proceeds of its sale among themselves. A more recent scenario might be that they, each in his own way, were now planning a double cross. If the circulating stories about heroin being buried in North Bimini were correct, their original strategy would have been to move it off the island before blowing up the dig, destroying all evidence behind them. But even now, If they were attempting a double cross, their separate plans would mirror the original strategy. Amison was certain of that.

Two questions nagged him. Who tried to kill his wife, and why? And, who was trying to kill him, and why?

The giant cat reached Fort Lauderdale Inlet a half hour later where Ojo returned the helm to his boss who powered up the engines and guided the cat to a berth at the U.S. customs dock in Port Everglades sandwiched between the empty cruise ship terminals and Burt And Harry's Restaurant.

The evening was drawing to a close and the port's terminals were deserted. It would be daylight before pleasure craft and cruise ships would be once again be fish tailing out the inlet for another day of sun and fun.

Three customs officials emerged from the compound. Two of them assisted Ojo in tying down *Phoenix.* The third jumped on to the cat's rear deck. He seemed to know Amison.

"Well, well, well! Amison Jones! Welcome back to the United States!"

The officer gave him a long, hearty hand shake. The shield pinned to the pocket of his short sleeve shirt identified him as the duty officer. He, like the other two officers, one male and one female, had a nine millimeter pistol resting in a waist holster.

"Well, if it isn't Bob Byrne," remarked Amison." When did you start pulling weekend duty here?"

"I was transferred here a few weeks ago. Jack O'Brien arranged it."

"How come you ended up in Alaska?"

"Our team was disbanded after that incident in Miami five years ago, "the duty officer explained. "Jack thought that in Alaska I would be out of sight and out of mind. I guess he was right, but I'm glad to be back. The funny thing is that I was given a one month furlough starting this weekend. What gives?"

"You tell me, Robert. I have a new mission. Maybe you're part of it."

"Oh, oh," said Bob Byrne half mockingly. "Is the country in trouble, again?"

"So I'm told," replied Amison. "Has anyone else from our old group surfaced?"

"Yes. Mike Quinn stopped by to say you'd be surfacing. What's the mission?"

"We're going to rock and roll in the Bahamas."

"C'mon, Jonesey. This is your devoted servant you're talking to."

"Well, we are going to the Biminis." And Amison went on to tell him about the events of the past few weeks and about the Bimini Man dig.

The young man whistled. "That's going to be one messy party. By the way. I heard about your wife. How is she?"

"Hanging in. Anyway, Mike Quinn did tell me about your going to Alaska. I'm sorry I caused you grief."

He offered him some jelly beads which Bob Byrne readily accepted and dropped into his mouth.

"No problem. We're all proud of you, and I'm glad you did what you did. Those guys you took down were scum. I have no regrets." He waved to Ojo. "How's my main man?" He and Ojo exchanged high fives.

Phoenix was now firmly tied up at the dock and the other two Customs officers returned to the compound. "Lets go to the office. We can talk there."

Amison pointed to Ojo. "I have a bag filled with presumably interesting bits of evidence for analysis. Is there a lab that can do the job this weekend?"

Ojo handed him the bag Dudley had given Amison.

"I can find one."

They left Ojo on board and walked to the customs building.

"How's Ojo doing?"

"He's fine. He doesn't speak, but he hears a little, he reads and he understands everything. I have his papers if you need them. He's a Bolivian citizen and resident of the Bahamas with a multiple entry visa for the States."

"That won't be necessary."

Bob Byrne, shorter, stockier and much younger than Amison, was an electronic and communications expert with ten years of government service under his belt.

Brown haired, well muscled and trim looking, he was a poster image of the clean-cut and square jawed all-American patriot.

They entered the customs building where they settled down in a small office. Bob Byrne's face turned somber. "I hope you don't mind, but on a whim I tried to get a profile on you guys from the computer after I saw Mike Quinn.

"Which guys?"

"You and Mark Stone."

"Why Mark?"

"Because I figured he'd be part of our team, like in the old days. The curious thing is that your computer files seem to have been erased."

"On the two of us?"

"Yes. Almost as if you and Mark never existed."

"How about an obituary?"

Bob Byrne laughed. "Not yet, but I'll keep looking."

Amison wryly at Bob Byrne. "Did you check your own file?"

"No. I was afraid of also not finding anything."

"Well, check it out."

"I'll do that," replied Bob. "What's your next move?"

"I have none until I connect with my handler. I don't know who that is yet."

Byrne groaned. "No plan?"

"There is one but it's not mine. I'm not even assembling my own team. Have you heard any good rumors?"

"Just the usual hype about Bimini Man." Then he remembered. "There was one thing that happened. A Jamaican flag tramp steamer named the *Casa D'Ora* and commissioned as a marine biology vessel left for the Bahamas from here a few days ago. Its papers showed the skipper to be an Albert Sanford Jack Johnson. I did a background check on him, and you'll never guess. This Jack Johnson is our old friend Captain Sanford Jack. Strike a bell?"

"Yep," said Amison. "He's in Bimini."

"Well, I was curious, so I did a computer check into the vessel's registry and found it belonged to a company owned by Bencivenga and a Jamaican chicken farmer named Max Neals."

"Interesting," Amison noted. "Neals is dead. He was Harold Levy's first cousin and partner. What else do you know about the *Casa D'Ora?*"

"It's a research vessel. I don't think Captain Jack is a scientist, do you?"

"No. I don't think so. I saw the boat here last week, but I didn't pay attention."

Bob Byrne added, "I bet it's going to Bimini to pick up cargo."

Amison arched his eyebrows. "Strange," he commented. "It's too big and draws too much to fit in Bimini's shallow harbor. It has to lay outside in deeper water. That would be off Round Rock in South Bimini. Not many boats pass by there."

Bob Byrne went on. "There was something odd about the freighter. We pulled an inspection on it before it left. That rust bucket is a derelict. I don't see how it could make a short round trip to Bimini in its condition. And what's more, it was carrying just enough fuel to take it fifty or sixty miles off shore, that's all. It didn't have enough fuel for a round trip. I don't think it's supposed to return to Florida."

"Neat, Robert. I think you have just laid out the whole thing for me."

"I have?"

"Yes. If there are drugs in Bimini, the plan must be to ship them out on the *Casa D'Ora* in sealed containers and then sink it on a ledge off the Bahama Bank for future recovery. That ship is going to be an underwater warehouse. Have another jelly bean."

Bob smiled. "Let me know if there's anything else I can do."

Amison smiled. "There is. Get the bag's contents checked out by Sunday."

"What's in it?"

"Don't know yet. Clothing, plant debris, and skin tissue from the dead Europol agents. I also want the contents and the bag checked prints, DNA, anything that might identify anyone. It should have the prints of Dudley Haynes. It's important that you get me the information in total confidence."

Bob nodded. "By Sunday?"

"Yesterday. At least by Sunday. Now, I have other names for you." Amison gave him a note. "I need a computer check on them also. Now if you don't mind, I want to get some shut eye on *Phoenix* at your hospitable dock. Is that possible?"

"No problem. This republic welcomes the downtrodden and the weary. But, you know, I have a better idea since you're obviously working this weekend. I'm going off duty in a few minutes. Why don't you give Ojo a break for the weekend and have him go home with me. The wife and kids will love him, and there's plenty of room. We have a nice condo at Bay Colony. Here's my number." He scribbled some numbers on a piece of paper that Amison stuffed in his pocket. "Come by our condo Sunday afternoon. I'll have answers for you by then."

"Good, And since you're part of our team, we're sailing for the Biminis at dawn on Monday.

Amison returned to the cat and consigned his deck hand to Bob Byrne. Ojo was thrilled. He relished the idea of spending a weekend in a real home on dry land.

CHAPTER 15

▼

AMBUSH

Amison had a good night's sleep but missed Ojo Saturday morning when there was nobody to bring him his usual coffee. He called Luis Santiago on his cell phone and left a message that *Phoenix* would shortly be arriving shortly at the bulkhead docks on the New River behind the Riverside before noon. A light drizzle began falling.

The catamaran was underway again with Amison at the helm in the wheelhouse. It headed north under power, past the cruise ship docks and in the direction of the Seventeenth Street causeway bridge.

The rain fell harder. The outlines of the Marina Marriott and the Pier Sixty Six Hyatt hotels flanking the bridge came into view. Amison peered through the wheel house ports. The bridge was stuck in the closed position with workmen in yellow slickers working frantically to fix the problem. He took advantage of the delay to call his daughter. Mitch, her husband, answered the phone and asked how he was doing.

"We were worried; Debbie thought you were going to call earlier."

"Well, here I am. How are the kids, and how's the weather?"

"The kids are fine and have colds, and the weather is lousy. This damn snow just doesn't let up. Hang on a minute; let me get Deb."

Amison's smiled happily when he heard his daughter's voice.

"I have some information for you," she said. "But first. Tell me everything is all right."

"Everything is all right," replied her father.

"You're lying."

"Ok. Everything is all right as we speak. How's mom?"

"She seems better, but it's hard to tell. Sid Stone spoke to the doctors, and their long term prognosis is not optimistic. I wish we had better news, Dad. Sid thinks we're going to have to make a decision concerning her life support."

Amison was silent for a few moments. "I don't want to make any decisions right now, Deb," he said finally. "We should all be together if and when the time comes for that."

"I agree, dad. Listen, I have some news."

"Shoot," said Amison.

"The new cleaning woman, Estrella, found out some things. She has a boyfriend who works for a company that handles Alliance's information systems. He was working in the office adjacent to the chopper landing on the Alliance building's rooftop the day of mom's accident. He's a former marine guard. He was stationed at Langley and is familiar with all types of aircraft. He told Estrella that a chopper flew in early that morning, hung around a few hours, and then flew out again. He remembers the day because it had started to snow and the pilot was nervous. He's certain the helicopter was military and originated at Langley. It discharged a single passenger: a man of medium height wearing an overcoat and hat; he could not see the entire face except for the eyes. He said they were ice blue. An attendant got off first and saluted the guy as he stepped down from the chopper."

"Anything else?"

"Yes. Two things. The guy was alone. But when he left, two more passengers boarded. The woman's boyfriend believes that they were Vince Neals and Harold Levy. Dad? Are you there?"

"Yes," answered her dad. "Anything else?"

"The boyfriend did a routine check of the chopper's log and manifest and then of Alliance's computer banks to make sure all systems were in synch. He says there was no record shown anywhere of the flight's arrival and departure. The boyfriend swears that this was a military craft. What do you think, dad? You don't think that Harold and Vincent had anything to do with mom's accident, do you?"

"I don't rightly know. But you did well. However, this is a real mind bender. I'd like to know for sure where that bird flew in from and where it was headed after leaving the Alliance building. It couldn't have gone too far with the weather, and it would have been nearly out of fuel, especially if it came from Virginia."

"Is there anything else you want me to find out?"

"Yes. I want to track the movements of an Alliance owned or leased jet around the time of mom's accident. Someone somewhere must have filed a flight plan. A guy named Mike or Michael Quinn would have been the pilot."

He gave her the numbers he had copied when returning to Bimini from Paradise Island on the jet. Call your local senator's office and concoct a rumor about some environmentally damaging object like a live shell being accidentally dropped in the Delaware River or Delaware Bay five years ago. They'll panic and investigate the rumor and check out every flight in that time frame."

"I hope Harold and Vincent aren't involved. Don't you, dad?"

"I hope so too, Deb. But the guy in the chopper. That sounds like Jack O'Brien."

"I don't know what to say, dad."

The conversation ended with Amison swearing to call her before the end of the weekend.

The bridge opened and *Phoenix* powered under. On the other side it passed the *Jungle Queen*, a sight seeing stern paddle wheeler. It was slowly getting underway despite the drizzle with a load of tourists singing and swaying to the lilting rhythm and music of a reggae band. He narrowly avoided a collision with the vessel and then chanced to look down to make sure one of his custom-made, long-barreled revolvers was resting in its holster strapped to the pedestal of his stool.

The catamaran accelerated and turned westward into the New River. It passed an unbroken line of large mansions and luxury yachts docked alongside that made it seem that no poverty existed in the world. Finally, off in the distance on the right, he could see the early twentieth century style Riverside hotel with its green and white awnings over its windows. A wooden sign on the river bank bordered by red flowering shrubs informed approaching boats that this was the Las Olas district of Fort Lauderdale.

Phoenix was almost at the hotel when Amison's concentration was broken by the crackle of small arms fire and the banging and whistling of bullets bouncing off the wheelhouse. He took a fast look and saw three men running along the river walk, firing automatic weapons. One of them as Miguel Bencivenga.

"Damn!" Amison pulled back the hand throttles and *Phoenix* slowed to a crawl.

Grabbing the gun from its holster, he ran out of the wheelhouse and knelt down behind the mast tower. He aimed at one of the shooters and squeezed off a single round. He thought the second shooter was Miguelito. He aimed for his legs and fired his second round. The first shot caught one of the shooters above the eyes and blew off the top of his head. The man's knees buckled under him and he fell into the river. The second shot hit the man who Amison thought was Miguelito in the knee. It seemed but a flesh wound but it was enough to drop him screaming and cursing in Spanish.

The third shooter panicked and dove into the river after being picked off with Amison's third round shot that coincided with another shot from shore.

He rushed back into the wheelhouse to guide the vessel the last few yards to an empty bulkhead slip. By the time he docked the air was filled with wailing sirens and screeching tires heralding the arrival of police.

Squad cars raced to a parking area near the river behind the Riverside and about a dozen uniformed and plain clothes police spilled out with weapons drawn, trying to figure out where the firefight was.

Luis Santiago and Marlene Stone were standing and chatting in the drizzle under the police inspector's golf umbrella near the water taxi stop at where his brown, un-marked county sheriff's sedan was parked. They were about to return to the shelter of the hotel lobby when the shooting started.

Luis dropped the umbrella and forced Marlene down behind one of the pilings, covering her with his larger bulk while he drew his service revolver and peeked out. Under him, Marlene unhooked her cell phone and called for backup.

They saw the first shooter fall into the canal and Miguel Bencivenga drop to the ground. The third shooter was panicked and running blindly toward them. Luis jumped to his feet and ordered him to freeze. The shooter, caught in the crossfire between Amison and Luis, panicked and dove into the river.

The police moved in and in seconds, Miguelito, cursing in Spanish and English, was cuffed. By then more police cars and two EMS vehicles had converged on the parking lot.

Suddenly, the *Jungle Queen* appeared, moving rapidly with the tide. The gunfire on shore could not be heard on board, and only a few passengers leaning over the side near the bow saw bodies in the water, one dead and the other possibly alive. They were sucked under the bow, drawn to the stern, caught in the paddle wheels, and then diced by the vessel's propellers.

"Man, I hope they were dead when they hit the water," muttered Amison as he watched The *Jungle Queen* pass by. Its music was now stopped and its passengers watched the bloody tragedy in stunned silence.

Amison tied up the cat at the dock and jumped off. Good old Luis, always in the nick of time. He was surprised to see Mark's wife with him.

Luis was a husky, totally bald six footer with a thin moustache, a gold tooth, a diamond pinky ring and a Cheshire cat smile. Expensively garbed in a blue silk suit and brown lizard shoes, he looked more like the prosperous night club owner and bouncer than a cop. He quickly flashed an inspector's badge and commanded the police to cordon off the area and issued orders for police divers to come and try to retrieve the remains of the two bodies from the river. He also made sure that Miguel Bencivenga was booked on a disorderly conduct charge.

"What about this man on the boat?" An officer asked, pointing to Amison.

"He's the intended victim. I'll get a report from him."

Amison gave Luis and Marlene big hugs. "Luis", he said, "I see that prosperity hasn't passed you by. And you, Marlene, you look more beautiful than ever. When are you and Mark breaking up?"

Marlene laughed and shook her long wavy hair. "In your dreams, Ruby."

"I received your message," said Luis. "But I didn't exactly know when you were arriving. Mark Stone is running late, but we're here."

"Well, thanks for my welcome home party." He turned to look at Marlene and gave her a wink and a mischievous smile. "Is she my prize?"

"You haven't changed at all, Ruby," Marlene observed. "You're still a dirty old man." She turned to leave.

"Where are you going?" he asked.

"It's raining, you big lug. I'm going back to the hotel until you guys finish your manly work. Here, take the umbrella." She gave the umbrella to Amison and blew him a kiss before leaving, her chestnut colored hair glistening in the light rain.

"Some woman!" observed Amison, as they walked away with him holding the umbrella over them.

"You don't need more women," Luis Santiago warned. "Besides, you tried your luck with her sister. You should give it a rest."

Amison had some jelly beans in his hand.

"Have one," he said.

"Thanks."

Two police officers came over and one of them asked. "What do you want to do with the one you caught, Inspector? Are you serious about the disorderly conduct charge?"

"Well, I know who he is," said Luis. "It's Miguelito Bencivenga. Book him on suspicion of something like possession of an unregistered firearm or a controlled substance, or just public lewdness, it doesn't matter. But, stay away from any type of assault with a deadly weapon charge. And, get him patched up at the hospital, or his people will have all of us up on police brutality charges. His dad will have him out before dark anyway."

"I thought that was don Ignacio's kid," exclaimed Amison. "Does that guy have a death wish, or what?"

"Everyone who comes close to you has a death wish, Jonesey," Luis noted.

Miguel Bencivenga, from inside a squad car, glared at Amison and screamed as he was being driven away.

"We will meet again, mother fucker!" he yelled, this time in fluent English laced with a thick South American accent.

"Amazing," remarked Amison. "His English is excellent."

Divers arrived and began the task of recovering remains from the canal.

"I don't know the dead guys," Luis informed one of the divers. "We'll have to find them first and then have the lab make a positive identification. Let's clear out of here 'muy rapido' before the media arrives."

A public affairs officer from the Sheriff's department came up and asked Luis. "Inspector, what do we tell the press when they catch up?"

The inspector shrugged. "It was a gun fight and we're looking for suspects."

With sirens at blasting, several squad cars left while a police van and the EMS vehicles stood by. Other police personnel taped off the area with the usual yellow crime scene tape to keep bystanders at bay. The rain was now falling steadily, and the crowd of onlookers rapidly dispersed.

When a TV camera van and crew arrived followed by press reporters they found the area deserted except for several sullen police officers patrolling the scene. The press people waited around for a while, and then not sensing a story, left.

Amison turned to Luis.

"Luis, I need a favor."

The inspector smiled. "I can't remember the last time my brother-in-law asked me for something."

His smile disappeared. "What's up?"

"I want you to place security around Mark."

Luis's smile returned to his face.

"Already done," he said. "Frank called from Bimini and brought me up to date. I know what happened to Nigel and Lawrence. I also know what Mark's been up to all these years. Frank says you signed his death warrant over that Nigel business. But Mark is going to be all right. I'll make sure of that."

Amison took a deep breath and put his arm around Luis's shoulder.

"That's a load off my mind. So now, what am I hearing? 'Inspector Santiago'?"

"Si, amigo," smiled Luis, exposing his gold tooth. "Homicide, no less."

"Well, if you're so smart, what do you know about Leslie and Marlene?"

"Interesting question. Marlene and Leslie are sisters, so Marlene might know something or could be involved somehow. Leslie? She might be guilty of having some fake bones shipped to Bimini but we have no real proof. I did run a check on the women and found that they were orphaned at birth and raised by several foster families until adulthood. They originally came from somewhere in Europe."

"You know," said Amison. "We've known them for years and yet never knew them."

"Love and sex are blinding, aren't they? But tell me about Bencivenga. Cecil says you ran into him."

"Yep. He offered me one hundred million dollars to work for him. I declined."

Luis whistled loudly. "That's a lot of money."

"Correct. It makes one wonder why I'm worth so much. Harold let on that two billion dollars worth of heroin is buried in Bimini. What do you hear?"

Luis smiled, exposing his gold tooth.

"Many things. Drug dealers here are in a party mood. They're talking of a large heroin shipment about to come in. I would tell you more, but I have promises to keep...."

Amison ended the refrain. "And miles to go before I sleep."

There was a pause. "We have to talk," said Luis.

"I think so. You say when and where. How come you took the Europol job?"

"For money, amigo. I have a wife who eats and shops and kids in college."

"That's putting your life and career on the line. What happened?"

"Jacques Leroux arranged it. He says it will give me a leg up when Bencivenga comes gunning for me and for all of us."

"You think?"

"Si. He wants revenge for what happened to his son Pauli five years ago."

"You realize that according to Harold our mission is to close down the Bimini Man and kill the Bencivengas."

The police inspector shrugged his shoulders. "So I heard. What if we fail?"

He sighed. "I have a family. I made a career for myself. I'd hate to see anything go wrong at this point of my life. This thing may get downright nasty!"

"That won't happen," said Amison. "I have a simple plan."

Luis snickered. "It's a wonderful trait you have, Jonesey. You have very simple answers to complex problems."

Amison placed his arm around Luis's shoulder again.

Walking him back to his car, he said softly. "I'm not going to compromise your family or hurt my friends. You might as well know that there's a contract out on me. You're not the only one at risk. Someone has been trying to take me down for five years. I used to think it was Bencivenga, but It's not. Once I'm out, I suspect that the same person will pick the rest of us off one by one, you, Luis and probably Frank. I also think that special someone has a vested interest in the heroin. I plan to strike preemptively by stealing the heroin myself."

"You're crazy!"

"Maybe. The heroin is our passport to survival. So I want your help to steal and hide it. As long as we're the only ones who know where it is, we'll be worth more alive than dead."

Luis's gold tooth flashed through his smile. "It could work, Jonesey; it could just work."

"It will work, friend. But right now, I need marching orders for this mission."

Luis looked up. "You know it already. Destroy the dig and the Bencivengas. It has to be done by the end of next week. That's when the Triple A meeting ends."

"And my team?"

"Me. Bob Byrne, Tucker Anderson and Mike Quinn. But Quinn wasn't my call. Jack and Harold placed him. He's Jack's man. He terminates agents after jobs are done to destroy evidence. And Tucker isn't far behind. He's a contract killer, but his heart might be in the right place this time."

"I don't know about that. He killed Hank Lawrence in Nassau."

Luis shook his head. "No. That was an act to keep Harold Levy happy. Hank is alive and working for Centurion. Tucker made sure of that."

"Damn! That's a relief."

"By the way, Mark wants to fly to Bimini. Marlene is opposed to that due to his poor health. And I can't protect him unless he stays in Florida. Can you convince him to stay in town?"

"I'll see what I can do. Now, what about the Bencivenga kid? I never asked him for a date. How come he knew I was going to be here?"

"Someone must have tipped him off," replied Luis. "His timing was perfect. But I'm working on it. Do you want him to have an accident?"

"No. I promised his father to keep him alive."

"You're mad, amigo. Why?"

"For pity? The kid is basically stupid."

"And a killer."

"We don't know about that. He missed."

"You're losing it, Jonesey."

"Perhaps, Luis," said Amison. "But he gets a second chance. Don Ignacio and I have an arrangement. He kills me or I kill him but we leave family alone."

"Was that a financial arrangement?"

"No. it was a gentleman's agreement. It's open season on everyone else."

Lou Santiago threw up his hands and groaned. "I hope you're right. And I hope old man Bencivenga sticks to his word."

"So do I, Luis. But we can handle Miguelito. If necessary, we'll kill him."

"I'd like that." Luis looked at his watch.

Amison smacked his lips. "Good. I'm going to clean up before to the hotel. You going somewhere?"

"I want to call in an incident report on this thing from the car. Then I'm going to see Marlene. And oh, by the way. Rustle up a tuxedo on that battlewagon boat of yours."

"What for?"

"There's a black tie function tonight. I have two tickets."

"The tux I have. The date I don't."

"You won't need one. Jack O'Brien and Harold Levy will be there. One of them can be your date."

"Neat. Shall we meet this afternoon before the function?"

"Yes, amigo. After lunch. Maybe at three. How's that?"

CHAPTER 16

▼

THE RIVERSIDE

Amison had visited the Riverside in five years. The squat gray stucco walled building with the green and white awnings over its windows was a landmark and was downtown Fort Lauderdale's only full service hotel. Its front entrance on tony Las Olas Boulevard was guarded by two tin mustard colored lions watching the action on the busy street where shoppers and browsers roamed from one boutique and bistro to another. A second floor terrace shaded the hotel's sidewalk café.

The canopied rear livery entrance faced Southeast Fourth Street and led to the lobby and reception counter through a narrow hallway with terra cotta floors and walls. The hotel's executive office was to the left inside the livery entrance and past the elevators to the new wing near a stairway to the second floor.

The hotel's original elevator, across the hall from the stairs, was old and slow, but it ferried guests to and from the upper floors of the old wing. Guests tended to avoid the creaky affair for the stairs. A third entrance lead to the lobby from a side street through a tropical garden between the hotel's front and rear wings.

On the river side of Southeast Fourth Street was a parking lot, pool and cabana club and a two-story, french-windowed apartment building perched over a small car parking area on tall lolly columns. This was the Sagamore House where Frank Hoffman kept an apartment.

Several bulkhead slips, one of which was occupied by *Phoenix*, hugged the river bank from the pool to the Sagamore House. Another space was taken up by a large sports fishing yacht named *Flyer*, the vessel which had tried to intercept the cat in Nassau.

The river walk, now emptied of joggers and strollers by the rain, was lined with bougainvillea vines, hibiscus trees and the pretty blue flowers of the Florida potter weed. Their radiating colors could not be muted by the rain and cloud cover.

After freshening up on his boat, Amison darted across the street in between the rain drops and ducked inside the hotel's livery entrance. The door to the executive office was ajar when Amison arrived to find Luis and Marlene chatting inside.

He walked behind the desk where she was seated and gave her a big cheeky kiss.

"You look terrific, even if I only saw you a short while ago."

Turning to Luis, he added, "Kiss yourself for me. We already met."

Luis Santiago looked at Marlene and complained. "I know this guy for a half a life time and he still insults me."

"You can do that with relatives," Marlene noted.

They laughed.

"When did you become an innkeeper?" Amison asked her.

Marlene sighed. "Mark inherited this place but he never wanted to run it. I play manager while he plays teacher at the university."

Marlene Stone was an attractive woman of medium height, smartly dressed in a dark blue suit.

This is a work day," she said. "Two weddings and a meeting,"

"Has Mike Quinn been around?" Amison asked.

"Yes. He asked for Mark and for you."

"How's Mark holding up?"

"He's good. He knows you're here. He just got back from the doctor. Maybe you guys can spend some time together."

"And how is George Gibson?"

Marlene smiled understandingly. "Cousin George? He's still here, Ruby. And you be nice to him. He tries. He really does. And he looks after me."

"Bueno," said Luis, slapping his thighs as he got up. "I think it's time for me to go."

He shook Amison's hand, saying, "Two things, amigo. I'll be at the Floridian at about three this afternoon for coffee. And don't forget eight o'clock tonight, It's theater at the Esplanade. I'll leave tickets at the box office."

"I can hardly wait," Amison muttered.

Then his eyes lit up. "Marlene, will you join me?"

"No date, Ruby?" Marlene asked. "What happened to all your women? You're usually flush."

"Well," responded Amison. "Luis says this is business. No dates, just friends. Besides, some people are in between jobs; I'm in between women."

Luis laughed. "Jonesey. You are a man with problems. I'll see you all later." He blew Marlene a kiss and left.

"I guess he has become a man of culture," Amison observed.

Marlene got up and sat down on a chair near her desk but close to Amison. She crossed her legs.

"Everyone has different interests. What are yours?"

Amison stretched out on a nearby armchair. "Actually, I was thinking of getting laid, cookie. Any ideas?"

"You're a persistent bastard, Ruby. And don't call me 'cookie' like you call your other women."

Amison laughed. "Give me a break. I call them 'cookie' because I can't recall all their names," he teased.

"Talking of breaks, Ruby, how's Bernice?"

Amison knocked on the armchair side. "No change, according to my daughter. Thanks for asking."

"She's probably going to kill you when she wakes up."

He threw his hands up in protest. "No way. I've been living almost like a saint."

"Almost isn't good enough," said Marlene.

"I don't have a wife like Mark to take keep me honest. Incidentally, I hear Mark wants to go to the 'Triple A' in Bimini."

"Yes. And don't encourage him. His diabetes is getting worse. And besides that, his life may be in danger."

"How's that?"

"Mark says the dig is a fraud and he wants to expose it. I'm not an academic, but if what Mark says is true, the university could be in big trouble. He might be killed to stop the word from getting out. Sid can't talk sense to him. For old times sake, Ruby, now that you're here, you might be able to talk him out of it, or, if you can't, you could perhaps look after him in Bimini."

"I'll see what I can do, but isn't Frank looking after Mark?."

Marlene rearranged herself on the chair, showing a little more leg. The falling rain rattled the aluminum awning outside.

"Well," Marlene answered. "Frank asked him to check out the rumors about the Bimini Man project. I think Frank kind of expected Mark to give it a clean bill of health. After all, he did get Mark a teaching job. For gratitude, Mark damned the project, and now he refuses to give my sister a tenure recommendation. That has a lot of people pissed, including my sister. Frank was forced to distance himself to protect the integrity of the dig."

"I can imagine. What do you think?"

Marlene shrugged her shoulders. "I think Mark should stay home and make his point in scholarly journals. After all, who cares about this crap except for a bunch of cranky pencil headed intellectuals? None of this is worth dying for. I hope you can do something, Ruby."

Amison couldn't help studying Marlene's features and wondering how things might have been had she not married Mark.

"Bimini Man is about history, careers, egos and drugs," a soft voice murmured from the door.

It was Mark Stone. They did not hear him enter the office.

He walked through the door, leaning jauntily on a cane and carrying a leather portfolio under his free arm.

Amison jumped up and they embraced. "My lord!" he exclaimed. "Am I glad to see you. You look terrific!"

"You were always a bad liar, Jonesey, but thanks anyway."

Mark Stone was of medium height and build and sporting a short beard and a sloppy moustache. A rumpled sport coat over a wrinkled shirt and regimental tie gave him a look of genteel shabbiness.

"Okay. You look awful. Now, shall we do lunch?"

"How about the Indigo? We can catch up with old times? Are you going to join us, Marlene?"

His wife shook her head. "I have work to do. I'll catch up with you guys later."

Mark walked slowly and Amison had to lead him through the lobby, under the ceiling fans and around the rattan and antique oak furnishings, and to the hotel's outdoor café where they sat down at a table next to one of the sentry lions.

An uneasy feeling gripped Amison. The street glistened from the rain and was now deserted except for a few skittish shoppers trying to avoid the rain by jogging from store to store. The café's white jacketed waiters stood anxiously by the tin lions staring at empty tables while Amison could not help but notice a distant and almost vacant look in Mark's eyes. He sensed an air of finality about their reunion. It was as if they were playing out their last scene together in a piece of theater.

Mark was speaking in a whisper.

"What's up?" Amison asked. "Sore throat?"

Mark shook his head. "The walls have ears," he replied. "I'm hardly ever out of ear shot. Marlene hired a new front desk manager at Jack O'Brien's urging, a guy named Charlie Kane who just retired from the CIA."

He leaned forward and closer to Amison's ear.

"I don't trust him," he added.

Amison attributed the paranoia to Mark's advancing diabetes. A waiter came over with tea, coffee and a tray full of finger sandwiches along with a bottle of wine and two glasses.

"How are the legs?"

"Still there. But I don't know for how long. Had you waited another year to visit, you would have been in time for my funeral."

Amison tried to put a positive spin on his friend's grim outlook. "Don't be such a pessimist. Shit! We had great times, and there are more to come."

Mark smiled. "Same old Jonesey. You're still playing cops and robbers, just like we did when we were kids. I recall you preferred to play the robber."

"We played war," Amison corrected him.

"And then you played the enemy. Whatever. But for me the robberies and the wars are over." Mark heaved a heavy sigh.

"I can't believe you're saying that, old friend."

"And you're in denial, Jonesey. You're a kid who refuses to grow old. You're a fucken Peter Pan. You should be playing with your grand kids."

"You think?" Amison dug into his pocket and came up with some jelly beans.

"You should go into the jelly bean business, Jonesey."

He studied the sediment in his tea and took a small sip.

"I hear that you're a bagman for Bencivenga. How did that happen?"

Mark stared at him strangely. "I had to accept the offer or die. There was no choice. I replaced a woman five years ago."

Amison's interest was aroused. "Does the woman have a name?"

"I...I don't recall."

Amison thought it smarter to change the subject.

"Well," he said. "if you know so much, tell me about Henry's Atlantis theory?" He drank a few drops of wine and attacked one of the finger sandwiches.

Mark's eyes lit up. "The Atlantis theory is something else. There are actually several stories. One of them has its origins in a Phoenician tale that preceded the Greek myths. A land mass was supposedly identified by Phoenician sailors west of Gibraltar. Bimini Man supporters like that version, as you can imagine. The story is that the fates ordained that if gods were to have issue born out of wedlock, their offspring and all descendants would be cursed forever. Well, Zeus ignored the fates and fathered two sons through his girlfriend Europa behind Hera's back, his wife. The sons shared ruling Atlantis. Hera got her revenge by casting a curse on any children the two brothers might have.

"One brother had two daughters who fell in love with a great white bull. To satisfy their lust, the gods ordered built a hollow wooden bull for the girls. It was covered with scented hides and a hole in its rear. That opening enabled the girls to enter and to expose themselves after bending down and spreading their legs within the cow's hindquarters. The wooden cow was wheeled into a field where the great white bull grazed. The women took turns inside the cow being ravished by the bull until they were fully satiated. One daughter gave birth to the Minotaur, a monster with a bull's head on a human body with human sexual organs. The second gave birth to a Centaur who had a human head and a bull's body and sexual organs.

"The other brother had two gay sons who wanted to consort with the Minotaur and the Centaur." Mark laughed. "We're talking about a dysfunctional family here. Finally, Zeus's sons built an escape proof labyrinth under Atlantis and threw in all their offspring. They became cannibals, so now and then prisoners and slaves were dropped into the abyss for entertainment and food. The gods ended the depravity with an earthquake and tidal wave that destroyed Atlantis except for a string of islands that today some say are the Bahamas. The only problem is that the story is the distortion of another myth set in the eastern Mediterranean."

"It's a great story. But what does it tell me?"

Mark stared into space. "Legend reflects the human condition. My story is only an allegorical tale. It may help you out."

He shook as if he had caught a chill. "The ghosts of Atlantis are here. I feel it in my bones."

He recovered his composure and added quickly, "But if you're asking me if this Bimini Man is a fossilized refugee from Atlantis, the answer is negative. Bimini Man is Piltdown Man, the ultimate fraud."

Amison raised the cup of coffee to his lips. "Who was Piltdown Man?"

"It was a bogus dig in England that claimed to have discovered a million years old human fossil, proving that early humans lived in the British Isles. It took fifty years to debunk the hoax. We are talking about the same thing here.

"Whoever thought up this scheme was a rank amateur. The geology of North Bimini is such that fossilization cannot occur. The only thing there is heroin."

"think you're right. Anyway, I'm closing down the dig."

Mark looked up. "How the hell are you going to do that?"

"I'm going to blow it up."

"Well, I sure as hell want to be there for those fireworks. I'm flying to Bimini tomorrow."

"Marlene doesn't want you to go. If you do, she wants me to look after you."

"I know. That reminds me. Don't forget to take this file before you leave."

He motioned to the portfolio under his arm that he now placed on the table. "Now, bring me up to date. I heard about your welcoming committee."

"Yes. Miguelito and two of his friends were there."

Amison went on to relate his adventures up to the moment that he arrived at the hotel.

Mark listened carefully, asking questions here and there to fill in his friend's sketch.

"And Bernice is still comatose?"

"Yes."

Mark folded his hands as if in prayer and stared up at the ceiling as if in a meditative stance.

"That Miami caper five years ago was the last time we got together."

"You got that right. That was six months after we took out a fleet of Bencivenga trawlers on the Orinoco. You shot; I drove."

"That's right. And our team was disbanded shortly after."

Mark fixed his gaze on Amison and delicately nibbled at the finger food in front of him.

"What I'm saying is that the encounter with the Bencivengas was not accidental. We were set up for an ambush."

Amison agreed. "Looking back, I suppose it was. Cecil and Luis monitored our communications. They think our dedicated channels and codes were compromised and that the DEA's interdiction orders were fake."

"You know that Washington never wanted us to put the Bencivengas away."

"I know that now."

"That's the point. The Bencivengas must have had clearance from someone high up in Washington to go after us five years ago. I think Jack O'Brien is the one. He probably also called the failed hit on you in Miami. You didn't die, and so you were shipped off and out of the way. Now, you've been brought back at Leroux's insistence to solve a couple of suspected murders. That puts you in the way again, and the contract on your life is renewed. In the meantime, you're given the job to close down the dig. But the fact is that you've also been brought in from the cold to be killed. Two birds are killed with the same stone: Bimini Man, and you."

"I follow the story line. But why the attempt to kill my wife?"

"Be damned if I know. But you're going to have to watch your back if you want to live to find out. Mike Quinn is Jack's cleanup man. I'm sure the plan is to kill you after your job is finished. Quinn has been picked to do it."

"What about the heroin?"

"Ah, now, we get to the heart of the thing. The heroin. That was a Bencivenga, Levy and O'Brien deal. Ship it to Bimini, hide it, and then sell it stateside when the heat is off. The deal went sour somehow and they started double crossing one another. So Bencivenga is in a rush because he finds out that he's losing federal protection and wants to jump the gun. I bet that the heroin is being hauled away as we speak and stowed on that freighter you told me about."

"Where does Miguelito fit in?"

Mark finished his tea. "I have a headache from all the thinking I'm doing for you. That Miguelito thing? That's a revenge hit and probably has nothing to do with Bimini Man. He's one of many bit players who are bouncing around doing their own thing and following their own agendas."

He gazed absently at the wet street.

"I'm curious," he said finally. "Harold Levy. He's a Jamaican. How does a West Indian end up with a Jewish name?"

Amison fell back in his chair and burst out laughing.

"What's so funny?"

His friend leaned back, laughed, and lit a cigarette. "It's simple," he explained. "There was a Jewish plantation owner in Jamaica during the slave days named Levy. When the slaves were freed, many took their former masters' last names, just as it happened here in the States. Harold and his family descended from slaves like Max Neals, his cousin."

"Interesting." Mark waved the cigarette smoke away. "One more thing, Jonesey. It's no secret that you seem to prefer the company of women of color. Is that the luck of the draw or something else?"

Amison took a breath and responded slowly.

"Let me tell you a story. When I was a kid, I dated a colored girl named Rita. My mother never said anything, so we kept dating. At that age, I was grateful to have a date. But my mother, who was French and spoke little English, would ask quietly in French from time to time, 'comment va t'a petite negresse?'"

"I'm sorry," said Mark. "What does that mean?"

"Loosely, it means, 'How is your little nigger girlfriend?' So, I stopped seeing her. Maybe I'm making up for lost time. I'm not quite sure."

"You never told me that story," said Mark.

Both men said nothing for a long time. Finally, Mark felt he had to break the silence.

"I never knew how you felt. I regret bringing up the subject."

"It's all right. In any case, I figured there was no future with Rita. You know, a cat and a fish may fall in love, but where are they going to live? Maybe I am a racist, who knows. But, let's talk about you and your trip to Bimini."

Mark looked up and smiled. "Perhaps we can take some time off there and go fishing."

"That would be nice."

"You know, you don't have to tell me about your plan to blow up Bimini Man."

"Ok. I won't."

"That means you don't have one."

"I'm working on one."

Mark shook his head.

"Always going by the seat of your pants; You'll never change. By the way, are you going to stay in the spook business after this job?"

"Don't know. I have a few tricks left in me, but I'll think of something. Maybe peddle sea shells in the Keys or open up a beer, bait and tackle shop. That's what Domino wanted us to do. I don't know."

"Would you ever go back to teaching?"

"Maybe. Right now I have a full dance card. I've also been thinking…"

"You? Thinking?"

"Don't be a wise ass, Mark. I do think from time to time."

"Thinking is good. What about?"

"I'm thinking of making a run for the heroin myself. Two billion dollars is a lot of money. I've spoken to Luis about it. Do you want in?"

"Damn! Jonesey. You'll be killed for sure."

"Answer my question. Are you in?"

Mark grinned. "Go for it. I'm in."

"We'll save your share for Marlene and Sidney if something happens to you."

"Ah, Marlene. She'll be rich when I die. I'm worth more dead than alive. I figure that my pension's death benefit and a life insurance policy is worth five million dollars to some very lucky person. And then there's this hotel, a good business when times are good."

Amison finished his glass of wine and wiped his lips. The rain on the street had stopped.

"Marlene seems to care for you."

"My wife?" Mark grunted. "That's another story." A crazed look crept over his face. He looked around to see if anyone was listening. "I'd kill her if I could. Short of that I should stage my own murder."

"You're out of your mind," remarked Amison. "It's the diabetes."

"I'm dead serious. If I die, she gets everything, If it's murder, she gets nothing."

Amison was shocked. The man was sick.

"What's George up to these days?"

Mark giggled. "He has a pad at the hotel. Marlene made him dock master and he takes care of the boat slips."

"That's neat. A real family business. And Frank is at the Sagamore?"

"Yes. Your boat is parked under it, next to his. Frank and George are partners," Mark volunteered. "Six months ago they went out and bought that Hatteras. It's name is *Flyer*, and their idea was to run fishing charters. They must have gone into the hole for over a million on that boat."

"How is that working out?"

"Don't know. I no longer speak to either of them. Listen, I've got to take a nap and then pack. I'm leaving on Chalks early in the morning."

"What about sailing with me on Monday?"

Mark shook his head. "Too late. The conference starts Monday morning and I need to be there to start exposing the Bimini Man hoax."

"Are you staying at the Reef?"

"Yes. I'll see you there, if I'm still alive."

"Hell, man. Don't be so morose. Things will work out."

"Yes," Mark replied. "Don't forget the file! It's important."

Amison picked up the leather portfolio from the table.

"If we survive this, you, me and Frank, we should talk."

"You sound as if Frank is still one of us," said Amison.

Mark grinned. "Oh, he is. What's more, you're going to need him."

"You think?"

"I know."

CHAPTER 17

▼

THE FLORIDIAN DINER

The rain stopped for good and the two old comrades parted company without ever so much as a hand shake.

He watched Mark slowly disappear inside the hotel before walking across the street to do some window shopping. A short burly man with an unruly thatch of reddish hair and a pair of shifty eyes sidled up to him and extended a thick hand for a crude handshake. It was George Gibson.

"Hi," exclaimed George with a big smile, "Remember me?"

Amison smiled cordially and shook his hand limply. "Yes, George. It's good to see you again."

"How are things?" George asked, trying to strike up a conversation.

Amison kept walking and George tried to keep up with him. "Too early to tell," he replied.

"Can I drive you somewhere? My cousin tells me you have no car."

"No thanks. I'm walking. What's on your mind, George?"

"I need a favor. Marlene says you may be sailing to Bimini soon."

"Right," Amison said.

"My partner Frank left a mess of expensive fishing reels and rods on our last trip there. I want to get them before our next charter. Can you give me a ride?"

"Why don't you fly out with Mark? He's going tomorrow."

"I would, but I couldn't get a reservation. I'd take *Flyer* but that's going to cost us a fortune in fuel. You have that high speed sailing cat. I'll pay you a hundred bucks!"

"You're very generous, George," said Amison. "Keep your money and just show up Monday at dawn."

"Terrific," said George, gloating as if he had just won some sort of victory.

Amison sighed. "Listen, George, I have run. I'll see you Monday morning. And bring the coffee."

He knew little about Marlene's cousin. He had heard long ago that George had once been indicted for embezzlement but never convicted. George was unmarried. He had simply appeared out of nowhere about ten years ago at about the same time that Marlene and Leslie came on the scene.

"I see you've run into George."

Amison swung around. Luis Santiago was standing next to him.

Amison lit a cigarette as they walked. "He wants to sail with me to Bimini."

"I'm not surprised. He stays close to Frank. Frank's in Bimini. So George is going to be in Bimini."

"Is he a Bencivenga stooge?"

"He may be but I don't think so."

"Strange. I can't see Frank and George as partners. They are partners, aren't they?"

"That's what Mark says, and they do own *Flyer* jointly." Luis pointed to a neon sign. "Here's The Floridian."

They walked into the restaurant and sat down at a small corner table.

"I wonder, Luis, about Mark's health and about Marlene's wifely interest. She doesn't ring true."

"You're right, amigo. If he dies, she ends up rich and gets the hotel. Sidney hates the woman."

A waitress came over for their coffee order. It was way past lunch and there were few other diners in the twenty four hour eatery. The Floridian had a long horseshoe counter and an assortment of odd sized tables and booths spread over two rooms.

Its interior was done in chrome, Formica, black vinyl, and pink neon. Cheap brass chandeliers and planters surrounding Casablanca fans dangled from the ceiling. A tinted mirror filled one wall. The other walls were of cheap pine paneling and were covered with prints of famous deceased actors and actresses like Marilyn Monroe and Humphry Bogart. There were curiosities as well. A German Cuckoo clock in one corner, and several Tiffany style lead glass lamps on some tables. There were no menus and customers ordered from chalk boards on the walls.

The Floridian featured grits but never after eleven in the morning, and never on weekends. Amison was already turned off.

The waitress returned with coffee and asked for a food order.

"Are you buying?" asked Amison, lighting a cigarette.

"I'm buying. I don't want to you to chew those damn jelly beans in public."

Luis ordered sandwiches. "You haven't changed. You're the same cheap bastard who married my sister."

"I'm saving for my old age," said Amison.

Luis grinned. "With all that heroin, you won't have to save."

"I guess you have decided to go for it."

"I have to run with you. I want to keep the father of my niece and nephew alive." "Well then, clue me in. What's with Mark?"

"Mark is dying. His eyes are going and his legs are shot. He goes several times a week to Broward General for treatment, but the doctors who see him tell me he's too far gone for anything to do him any good. He wants to expose this Bimini Man thing for the hoax it is and I think he's ready to die for it. It's a death wish."

"Have you spoken to his brother?"

The police inspector nodded. "I did. There's little Sid can do. It's all too damn sad, Jonesey. Too damn sad."

Amison fell silent, rubbed his eyes and took time out to drink his coffee. "What's this Mark tells me about the Atlantis legend being some sort of a sexual freak show? Did you hear that one?"

"Many times. I dismissed it at first, but now I realize he's spinning the story for a reason. He won't speak out because he thinks Charlie Kane at the hotel is a stool pigeon for Jack O'Brien. He may be right."

"I'm going to kill O'Brien when this is over," Amison declared solemnly.

"Even after we steal the heroin?"

"Before or after. It doesn't matter. I'm positive he's the one on my case. I can't prove it but I know I'm right. But right now, tell me about those bones from New York?"

"That's an easy one. I believe Mark when he says there's no fossil type rock in the Biminis. He insists that any fossils allegedly found would have been recently imported and planted. It started was with a phone call to Mark from the curator at the New York museum several months ago. He also called Roger Brooks, our own museum's curator here in town. It was about a crate filled with prehistoric human fossils they loaned our museum for an exhibit that never took place. The shipment vanished before it got to the museum. That's how the rumor about the bones being brought to Bimini got started. Roger called me. My guys tracked the consignment to a Port Everglades pier through an unsigned way bill issued by a local trucker. The receiving agent at the dock said the crate was placed on board a yacht that departed soon after. My guess is that the crate ended up in Bimini without clearing U.S. or Bahamian customs. If the story holds water, it would have been off-loaded in one of North Bimini's coves by now."

"Any names?"

"Well, according to Roger Brooks, it was Leslie Sandler who asked to borrow the fossils for the exhibit. Incidentally, call him. He has something to tell you."

Amison stared at him impassively and lit another cigarette.

"This brings me back to Mark's Atlantis legend," Luis went on. "I've figured out who the women are in his delusional vision."

The waitress returned with their sandwiches and more coffee. Luis took a bite of his sandwich and waited for her to leave before going on.

"Leslie and Marlene,"

Amison took a deep breath. "How do you figure that?"

"They both appear from nowhere about ten years ago. After making the rounds, Leslie settles on Frank and Marlene takes on Mark. Leslie gets good action from Frank, but Marlene probably gets very little from Mark. I would have screwed the broad myself had it not for the fact that old Frank's been tapping her for years." Luis smiled and threw his brother-in-law an all-knowing wink.

Amison's eyes widened. "Man! Life is full of surprises, isn't it?"

"Si," continued Luis. "Leslie and Marlene are the sex-crazed dames in Mark's myth and Frank is the great bull. But in all honesty, Marlene was looking forward to seeing you again when I told her you were arriving. I think she was still has the hots for you. She doesn't really give a shit about Mark and she probably knows that Frank's options are running out. You're her next best bet. But now with old Harold in control of Madsen and with you out to blow up Bimini Man and hot to trot for the heroin, I think everyone is out of running room, including Marlene and Leslie."

"Who are the two queers in the myth?"

"I suspect George is one. And if you pardon the pun, I haven't fingered the other yet."

"And what about the two brothers born of the union between Zeus and Europa?"

Luis tapped his head and replied. "I have to work on that."

"Whatever. But I'll tell what I know. Harold admitted to me in Paradise Island that he, don Ignacio and Jack originally hatched the plan to gradually seed the Bimini Man site with heroin over the years. That's how it got there. You can bet your bottom dollar that they're now looking for ways to screw each other as we speak."

"A triple cross? I can buy that. Are you sure?"

Amison nodded. "Yes. Because that's the deal I have Harold, to steal the heroin for him. You have to figure that the other two guys have their agendas. That's why Jack put Quinn on me, and why don Ignacio wanted to buy my services. Talking about them, I'm waiting for Sol Weinberg to rear his ugly head. He must know a fix is in."

Luis smiled. "You're smart, Jonesey. Why the hell did you take this assignment anyway."

Amison drank some more coffee. "I took the job for five reasons, Luis. First, I wanted to help Cecil. Second, I wanted to get back in action. Third, the money is good. Fourth, I wanted to bring my wife's situation to closure; and fifth, I wanted to steal the heroin."

"I can see that, Jonesey. But about Bernice, I have a question that's been on my mind for years."

"Such as?"

"Let me say first that I'll always be grateful for your help in getting me to where I am today. And I'm also grateful to have played a part in helping you and Bernice raise your kids. But tell me, why did you remarry so soon after my sister Dolores died?"

Amison sat back in his chair. He spoke slowly.

"Dolores was my first love. I was entirely devoted to her for the few wonderful years we had together. You too were part of that life. I have never stopped loving her after she died giving birth to the twins. But I felt they needed a mother. I met Bernice. I liked her. And so I married her."

"But did you love her?"

"Yes, but never like I loved Dolores. I…I don't think that kind of love hits a man more than once in a life time. It's not in the cards for me any more, Luis."

Amison took a deep breath. "What else do you want to know?"

"What's going on with you and Domino these days?"

"She wants to get married, and I can't. That's the bottom line."

"Is that why you took up with that chick, Ginny?"

"How the hell did you find out about her?"

"I'm a cop, remember?"

"So? I still like women, Luis. And I do need someone to hold on occasion. Don't you? Doesn't everyone?"

Luis drew back and the Cheshire cat grin fixed to his face disappeared. "I'm sorry, Jonesey. I never knew how you really felt about things. I'm out of line. I think I understand you a little better now."

"Shit, Luis. These are uncomfortable subjects for me. Can we talk of something else? Where's Mike Quinn?"

"He's hanging around. I told him you're here. His plan is to load your boat this weekend, most likely tonight."

"Good. I'm leaving Monday morning. The dig goes before the conference ends."

"Take Bob Byrne with you. I told him he's on call. And watch George."

"That's why I'm dragging him along."

"What about Quinn?"

"We have a truce until the dig goes."

"Where do I fit in?" Luis asked.

"I'd rather you pull out of this mission and try to save your neck. Your police job is more lasting. Money is no problem if you need it. You don't have to stake your life on a high risk bet. This could end up being a suicide mission."

Luis waved him off and shook his head. "No way, amigo. If you're in, I'm in. And if you go, I go. We all go."

"All right. Now what about communications. My life seems to be an open book these days."

"I can help you there, Jonesey. We caught a signal from Bimini this morning. It was using a code we discontinued five years ago. You must have left Bimini ahead of schedule because your reception committee had to scramble to meet the boat. Whoever was tracking you in Bimini had poor timing, and must also have been the same person who planned the ambush outside Miami Harbor five years ago when the code was still valid."

"I think I know who that person is. Now, about George. Anything on him?"

"George's name comes up as an account holder in several offshore banks where Bencivenga cash is parked. George also has an account in Nassau under the name of a shell corporation. Now, he isn't very bright, so his power of attorney is vested in a Nassau lawyer named Rodney Sykes."

"Rodney Sykes, Jonathan Sykes's brother?"

"Right."

"That's interesting. Jonathan Sykes is the one stonewalling the Guenther and Douglas investigations."

"I wouldn't doubt it," said Luis Santiago.

"There are a few other things I found out," he continued. "There's this Reginald Lang. He and the Sykes brothers work closely. Lang is the de facto commander of all Bahamian land and sea forces in the Out Islands including Bimini. His wife happens to be a Sykes sister."

"That's history," Amison said. "And I know Lang. He's a prick with an ego. But his wife is some piece!"

Luis snickered. "Do try to stay away from the broads for a while, Jonesey. You might live longer. Incidentally, Did Harold really call the hit on Nigel?"

"Yes. And Harold has taken direct control of the bank."

"How did Bill Nigel die? Frank never spelled out the details."

"He drowned."

The police inspector leaned forward in his chair, speaking in a voice that was hardly above a whisper.

"I wanted to tell you this before. You're an idiot! And so is Harold. That hit was dumb. Harold could have just as easily shipped Bill Nigel off to a bank in some Indian Ocean island and let him work off any debt he owed Alliance."

"That wouldn't have worked. Madsen was closing the books on Alliance."

Luis flashed his golden smile. "That means Sykes and Lang know about the heroin. They too might have their own thing going."

"Everyone seems to have something going with someone else," said Amison.

"There's something else that's interesting, Jonesey."

"What's that?"

"How many years ago did Leslie, Marlene and George surface?"

"About ten, we said?"

Luis flashed another smile. "Correct. So, listen up. Didn't Marvin Childs show up at Alliance ten years ago?"

Amison folded his arms. "That was around the time that Dudley Haynes took a job in the Bahamas. And ten years ago was when the Bencivengas began to cause trouble. You know, Luis, I find those coincidences fascinating."

He unfolded his arms. "In the meantime, Mark may be in danger. Can you stop him from going to Bimini?"

"The only thing I can do is arrest him, maybe."

"Then do it. Anything."

"I'll think of something," said Luis. "Now tell me more about Bimini."

"There isn't much more except I'm going to need you when the shooting starts."

"I'll be there. I'm your mission chief. What's the game plan?"

Amison nodded. "It's simple." He sat back and explained, waving his hands as he spoke.

"I'm assuming the heroin is now being moved to an old freighter called the *Casa D'Ora* lying at anchor outside the Biminis. My best guess is that the ship will start moving out the moment the dig is blown up because that seems to be the script. We're going to blow up the dig site, but by the time we do, the heroin will be on board the *Casa D'Ora*. I aim to follow the vessel out to the Bahama Bank and sink it with all hands on board."

Luis blinked. "What happens after the ship goes down?"

"We wait a couple of years and then we steal the heroin for ourselves."

"That's international piracy and mass murder."

"I have Jacques Leroux's carte blanche. If you're fussy, Luis, the letter stands as a letter of marque on the high seas. Furthermore, knowledge of the heroin's final resting place will keep us alive."

Luis's gold tooth flashed through his grin. "I like it. What about Frank?"

It's his choice. When push comes to shove, he'll throw his chips our way. Are you still in?"

"I'm in."

"Terrific." Amison raised his empty cup and toasted. "To Bimini Man and beyond."

"To Bimini Man and beyond," Luis repeated.

CHAPTER 18

▼

THE ESPLANADE

This was to be La Boheme's final performance and Amison's tuxedo, white kid gloves and silk scarf were ready by early evening. He stopped to have a drink with Marlene who excused herself after a while, explaining there were several functions she had to supervise. Not a word was exchanged about Mark.

It was a twenty minute walk along the river to the Esplanade which was lit up and alive with theater goers in formal wear arriving in a long line of limousines and taxis. He found Lou Santiago also in black tie waiting for him at a reserved table for five set with a spread of finger sandwiches, pastry and soft drinks at the promenade café.

"No martinis tonight?" Amison asked as he sat down.

Luis turned around. A wide grin broke out over his broad face, exposing his shiny gold tooth. "Good to see you. No martinis. This is serious."

Amison looked around. "Where are the others?"

"They'll be here." Luis looked at Amison. "You really go all the way, don't you?"

Three men in tuxes came over to the table at that point. The tallest of the three was Harold Levy who immediately stepped forward as Amison rose to his feet and gave him a strong hand shake followed by a friendly one handed bear hug, using his free one to discreetly drop a cold lumpy object into his jacket's inside pocket. "You'll need it," he whispered.

Jack O'Brien came up behind Harold. The CIA officer was of medium height and build with an expressionless moon shaped face surrounding a pair of cold blue eyes and a crown of short blond graying hair circling the bald dome of his head.

"Man, you look great in that monkey suit," Harold was saying.

"Any fishing?" asked Amison, trying to make light conversation.

"Not this time. But, maybe the next time, Jonesey. And tonight, it's business. That's why I'm here."

"Where's Marvin Childs and Vince Neals?"

"Oh, Marvin's minding the shop back north, counting the beans and making sure they keep coming in. And Vince is taking in some sun."

He winked and stepped aside. "You remember your old boss Jack, I'm sure. But you haven't yet met this other gentleman."

"Jack. It's great to see you again," said Amison. "You staying out of trouble?"

Jack O'Brien shook his hand limply and gave him a lame smile under his cold stare.

"I should be asking you that question, Jones."

His eyes looked as if they could shatter diamonds. "Aren't you getting close to retirement?"

Amison laughed. "I'm too poor to think of retirement. I'm going to have to work until I'm a hundred years old!"

"That's good to hear," the other replied almost without listening.

He nodded in the direction of the other person with him who was slightly taller, thin, and with a heavy thatch of frizzy gray hair. "This is Warren Kilpatrick, the president of the Everglades Bank and a trustee at Las Olas University. He also serves on the Alliance board. Warren and Frank Hoffman are old friends."

"Pleased, I'm sure," Amison murmured politely. "Frank has spoken often about you."

Warren asked Luis if he was attending the theater this evening.

"No," said Luis. "Don't get me wrong. I love this stuff, but I'm technically on vacation starting at midnight. I'm taking off after this meeting."

"Anyplace in particular?" asked Jack O'Brien.

"A place without rain."

"That's good. Have you informed our friend Jones of our difficulty?"

They all sat down at the table.

"He's familiar with some of the details, sir," said Luis.

Jack turned to Amison. "We have a small problem. You may be familiar with part of it. And by the way, I want to congratulate you on the Europol assignment that you are doing through Alliance. In helping them, you will be helping us."

Amison nodded but did not say anything. He could recognize Jack even if he never saw him. His low key voice had a perpetually threatening edge to it. "Essentially," Jack was saying. "The problem has to do with the Bencivenga family from Ciudad Bolivar in Venezuela. You have had some recent encounters with them, I heard. I also understand you are aware of what's going on in the hills around the Orinoco River?"

"Yes," replied Amison. "Poppy grows well in the hills there."

O'Brien nodded. "That's correct. The Bencivengas and several other families control the region through their business enterprises and through narcotics which has become one of the area's economic mainstays. The employment of one million Venezuelans is directly or indirectly linked to these family businesses. We made an arrangement with the Bencivengas and the other Orinoco families years ago. In return for their financial and political support to the Venezuelan government in Caracas, we would ignore their other activities so long as they were kept under control. This was back in the days when the price of oil had dropped and the Venezuelan government, a staunch U.S. ally I might add, was broke and on the verge of collapse."

"Did these activities include drug trafficking in Florida?" Amison asked.

Jack looked down and folded his hands. He slowly pulled his face up until he was looking evenly and steadily into Amison's eyes. Without answering directly, he said,

"The name of the game is oil, not drugs. The United States cannot afford a weak Venezuela and have its oil supply threatened. The Bencivengas helped us prop up their government, and we left them alone when they crossed the line. Let's just say that they were reimbursing themselves for their expenses.

"If the Venezuelan government fell, the country could break apart and signal the collapse of other countries in the Caribbean basin. We could lose the oil, and the drugs would still find their way here. We did enjoy a quid pro quo for a while. The Bencivengas guaranteed us a stable Venezuela and a steady flow of oil. We gave them limited U.S. market access for their merchandise. But, conditions have now changed."

Jack's voice turned more somber. "The price of oil has risen and politics inside Venezuela have stabilized. The Bencivengas and their circle of families are no longer needed."

"They used to call this 'Real Politick' in political science," Harold interjected. He received a cold stare from O'Brien.

"To conclude, we no longer support the Bencivengas. They have to go. Warren, you wanted to add something?"

"Yes," responded Warren Kilpatrick. "The situation in these parts is grim. The Bencivengas have made a deal with the president of Las Olas University, Frank Hoffman, to use its facilities as a hub for their drug distribution network. Had they used a trucking company or a chain of supermarkets, we might have let it go, at least for a while. We could talk to them. But using a large university that also is a major economic player in the Las Olas community creates a potentially explosive political and public affairs issue."

He paused to take a sip from his coffee and continued. "We were blind sided on this one," he said. "We didn't know that when the Bencivengas funded part of the Bimini Man project they were burying large quantities of heroin in the islands. We all felt he had a genuine interest in the project. And of course we needed money at the time.

"It turns out that the whole project is a fraud. We suspected that for some time, but we felt our hands were tied because of the race issue. The hype around the dig has created its own world. We would stand accused of being a racist university. We can't afford that."

"Is there a possibility that Frank was duped into this affair?" asked Amison.

"Duped or blackmailed," responded Jack O'Brien. "It doesn't matter. He has to go."

"What about Dr. Leslie Sandler, the project director?"

"Ah, yes, Sexy Sandler," commented O'Brien. "To paraphrase your friend Henry Alstrum, I would say she went down a few times too many, first for the old man, then for Frank, and then for tenure at Las Olas…Oh, she may have robbed a few bones along the way…I know the story. That only makes her a petty thief. But, she too has to go."

He stopped to take a breath and a smile broke over his face.

"They can redeem themselves," he explained. "Have them bring me the severed heads of the remaining members of the Bencivenga family on silver platters."

O'Brien winked to the others around the table. "And if they don't, you do. And shut Bimini Man down in the process."

The theater lights flickered and Jack O'Brien looked at his watch. "It's almost curtain time," he said.

Amison ignored his last observation. "What about the Bahamian government? Do you have a read on their position?"

"Yes. They're playing hardball. There are two realities here. The first is the dig which is good for tourism and for those true believers in Bimini Man. The second is that some identified Bahamian officials are on the Bencivenga payroll. When you find out, they too can be terminated with extreme prejudice."

"Is there a possibility that the dig team is on to something?"

Jack shook his head.

"Not a chance. He produced several photographs from his pocket. "These are pictures of the so-called fossil bones Luther Guenther shot before he died. He sent them to Leroux who gave them to Santiago. He had apparently penetrated the dig site. We also have aerial and satellite photos. They are being analyzed. They might be real, but they don't belong to Bimini Man."

Jack handed them over to Amison who put them in his pocket.

He turned to Kilpatrick and to Harold Levy, saying, "The curtain is rising and I have to leave."

"Anyone here going to the opera?" asked Amison.

They shook their heads.

"We just believe in giving to charity," laughed Harold Levy. "And since this is a fund raiser, I thought it would be a nice place to meet."

They all rose from the table, again shaking hands all around. "Good luck," said Harold over the heads of the others. I'll be in Philadelphia for a few weeks. Call me. You have the number. We'll go fishing when this thing is over."

Amison stood by silently as they left.

Sitting back down with Luis, he commented, "Whatever happens, Washington comes out red, white and blue and shining brightly."

"Right. I just wanted you to hear it from some higher-ups. However, keep in mind that once you're done, your life isn't worth shit, and neither is mine. So be careful."

"And Mark?"

"He'll be fine. I guarantee it."

Amison reflected silently on all that he had heard so far this evening and stared at the table.

"Well," he said, rising to his feet, and looking at the dressy crowd milling about the theater lobby and terrace restaurant. "I am going to La Boheme."

Luis rose to leave. "I've seen it. It's good. Culture is good. Enjoy the show."

Amison went to the ticket office where he picked up one of the two tickets that had been reserved for him. He took it and made his way to the side of the balcony where the seat was located and sat down, ignoring the empty one to his right. He settled down as the lights dimmed, and the overture began. He relaxed, his mind wandering with the music and the scenery.

Not more than ten minutes into the performance, he became aware that the seat next to him was occupied by someone with a raincoat folded over his arm. He was about to speak when he felt a blunt object being shoved into his right rib cage.

"It is so nice to meet you again, Mr. Jones," said a familiar voice.

Amison tried to turn but felt another jab.

"No, no," said the voice. "Please sit."

He turned his head slightly to match voice with face. The man was in a tuxedo and wore thick glasses. However, he wore no bow tie; his formal shirt was open at the neck and one of its button studs was missing.

"Dudley Haynes."

"Ah," said Dudley. "At your service. The last time we met we were enjoying breakfast in Bimini. Shall we go for a short walk?"

"I would prefer a long walk," said Amison. "It's better for the digestion."

"A short one will have to do. Kindly rise slowly and quietly."

The two rose together and made their way into the aisle. They walked side by side as the music and singing continued and walked out to the empty lobby and to the park outside. They reached a small secluded wooded area between the road and the river bank where they came to a stop several yards from a black limo that was parked with its dark windows drawn up.

"This is far enough," said Dudley. From the concealment of the raincoat draped over his arm he produced in his hand a silencer equipped pistol whose ugly black muzzle he pointed directly at Amison's chest.

"Slime floats," said Amison. "All the way from Bimini too. How did you get here so fast?"

"I flew over after Charlie Kane called. You must have found the sensor Ginny planted. Our timing was slightly off."

"So, who else is part of your little entourage?"

"I have friends, Mr. Jones. We little people must protect our interests."

"What interests, Dudley?"

"Why, our interests in Bimini Man, of course."

"You must have been the one who contacted Miguelito."

"Yes. How did you know?"

"You used the wrong limerick on me in Alice Town and your signals to Florida were intercepted. You were using five year old codes. All the codes were changed after our Miami fiasco. I bet you were the one who penetrated our communications five years ago."

Dudley smiled. "You are very smart. What a pity you must die."

Amison tried stalling for time. "Is Ginny your girlfriend?"

"No. She is Miguelito's girlfriend. She wanted my body, but I'm not interested in that sort of thing."

"Of course, you're not."

"We paid her over the years to keep track of your movements, just as I was paid to monitor your movements."

"Who is 'we', Dudley? Don Ignacio?"

Dudley laughed. "You will die without ever finding out. Now, turn around and I'll do it fast and easy."

"Now, would you shoot a man with no teeth?"

The question stopped Dudley cold. He stared dumbfounded as Amison raised his left gloved hand to his mouth and removed his front teeth and flashed them in his face. Flustered by the sight of the removable bridge, he flinched, causing his pistol hand to swerve.

He recovered too slowly. By the time he recouped his senses, Amison's right fist had flown out like a piston into his face. His nose broken, and blood gushing from his nose and mouth, he toppled over backwards and fell to the street, dropping the gun.

Amison caught the weapon and pistol whipped Dudley about the head who was now whimpering and crying in a fetal position.

Amison stretched Dudley out on his stomach with his face against the concrete and pressed his booted foot against the back of his neck.

Dudley was choking. "My god," he said in a gargled whisper. "You're not going to kill me, are you?"

"Of course, I'm going to kill you."

"Please."

Dudley was begging and crying by this time, his face still pressed against the ground. "I have a wife and children."

"No you don't. You're a fag. You know? Men in tuxedos look like penguins and I like penguins. But some guys look like cockroaches! I hate cockroaches! Now, I want to know. Who put you up to this?"

"You'll never get away with this. I'm not alone here."

"Listen, fuck face. You are alone. What the hell are you doing here, anyway? You're not even an amateur. You can't fight; you can't kill; you can't even take a hit. So, tell me Dudley. Who are you working for?"

He dug his boot deeper into Haynes' neck.

"For me, Jones!"

Amison strained to guess from where the voice came from but there was no need to do so. The voice came from someone lurking in the shadows. The body owning the voice stepped out from behind a tree, brandishing a pistol.

"Don't move and don't breathe, Jones. Just stand very still."

Amison barely looked up. He was furious at being out maneuvered, even if only temporarily.

"Fuck you, Vincent!"

He whipped out the gun that Harold had surreptitiously dropped into his pocket at the theater emptied it into Vincent Neals while firing the other weapon point blank into Dudley.

Vincent Neals clutched his chest and sank to his knees. He tried vainly to get off a shot but a second shot from off in the distance caught him behind the head and he collapsed dead on the street. But Dudley was still alive and wriggling like a worm.

Amison raised his foot stomped on his neck. There was a dull crack and Henry's medical assistant lay still.

Amison saw out of the corner of his eye a blue livery sedan pull up slowly along the drive near the embankment walk not far from the parked limo and dove for cover.

The limo's front windows went down and the driver side door opened slowly. A husky human form emerged, arms held high.

"Don't shoot," a familiar voice pleaded in a loud whisper. "This is your friendly clean-up man."

"Quinn!" Alison exclaimed, placing the two guns into his waist band. Mike Quinn went over to the car's trunk, opened it and pulled out two body bags.

Mike Quinn was his usual cheery self.

"Just don't stand there, man," he said. "Give me a hand."

The two men rolled the bodies into the open bags, zippered them with sobering finality and tossed them into the trunk.

"How did you know where I was going to be?" asked Amison.

"No problem. I've been shadowing you since you got here. A limo or a livery car is the best way to do a job in Fort Lauderdale on a Saturday night. Every other car is a limo. Who are the dudes?"

"Dudley Haynes and Vincent Neals. Old friends."

"Well. You certainly have a way with friends."

"I still want to know why you're here."

"Easy there, Jonesey. Harold Levy said to tail you because you tend to leave dead bodies in your wake and may need a cleanup man. That's what I do for a living. I clean up."

Amison's eyes turned to stone as he faced Quinn squarely. He was in no mood for jokes.

"I know what you're about," he said in a barely audible growl of a voice. "And we both know what happens when this mission ends. But until then you work for me, not for Levy and not for O'Brien. Understand?"

Only the darkness cast by the shadows of the night hid the redness that covered Mike Quinn's face.

"Understand?"

Quinn squirmed uncomfortably and for the first time, his smile degenerated into an embarrassed pout. He made a half hearted attempt to reply but gave up.

Finally, Amison softened.

"Oh well," he sighed. "I'm going back to see the end of the opera. What about the stuff for the dig?"

"Mostly done. I'll finish up tomorrow. When are you returning to Bimini?"

"Monday morning, early. How about you?"

"On my own. I'll be there to set up the charges," said Mike.

"Ok. Because I want this thing to be over by the end of the week. What are you going to do with the bodies?"

"No problem," Mike answered. "I'm going to dump them in the swamps a few miles west of here. It's alligator country out there. They'll be in time for Sunday brunch."

"Sounds good. Now, get out of here. I want to see the rest of La Boheme."

Finally, Mike Quinn blurted out. "Jack O'Brien didn't send me to be your tail. It was Levy. He said Neals was in town and out to get you. Dudley Haynes works for Neals."

Amison smiled for the first time. "Thanks Quinn. I didn't know that. But Vince is too stupid to make his own moves. If it wasn't Levy, someone else must have put him up to it. It could have been O'Brien."

"Shit, Jonesey. I work for the guy but I don't read his mind. Why the hell would he want you dead before this gig is up?

"Maybe for the same reason he wants me dead when the gig is done?"

"Then, he would have had me do the job by now, Jonesey."

Amison could not refute the man's logic.

"I guess I'm getting too paranoid over this."

Mike grinned. "No problem. Even paranoids have enemies. You know, I'm going to hate meeting up with you when this is over. It's nice working with you."

"Same here."

CHAPTER 19

▼

THE CENTURION CONNECTION

It was at least a friendly truce. Mike Quinn drove off while Amison straightened out his clothes and began walking to the theater, hoping to arrive in time for the last act. He was abreast of the parked limousine when its rear window slid down.

A vanity light came on and a voice called out. "That was cool work, Jonesey. Hop in. I'll drive you to the theater."

Amison peered into the limo's passenger compartment. It was Sol Weinberg, the Centurion Trust's generously proportioned CEO. Facing him in a rumple seat was Hank Lawrence. Behind the wheel was Tucker Anderson.

"Hello, Sol. Long time no see. And hello, Hank. Hello, Tuck."

There was a touch of coldness in his voice.

"I guess you guys didn't wait long to make your move, did you?"

Hank Lawrence was apologetic.

"I have to take care of myself, Jonesey. And old Tuck here is doing the same thing. This thing is turning into a blood bath and we have to survive. I'm trying to convince Sol here to consider buying up Alliance, Jonesey. I'm brokering a deal and save my ass from Harold. Tucker is pretty much in the same boat."

Amison stepped away and Sol Weinberg stuck his heavy pock marked face with the jowls, hound dog eyes and all out the window.

"We should have a chat, old buddy."

"How about coming out for a breath of air. We can both use it."

The Centurion chief instructed Hank to stay in the limo with Tucker and stepped out of the car.

"Do you want me to tag along?" Hank asked.

"No. You stay put. Jonesey and I want to talk in private."

Sol and Amison strolled over to the river bank where they sat down on a bench. Amison took some jelly beans out of his pocket and Sol produced an open bag of peanuts.

"Bet you can't eat just one," he said, offering him some.

"You're right." And he took three pieces. "How about some jelly beans?"

Sol took the beans. "Even exchange," he said. "I like your self control."

"What's on your mind, Sol?"

"How long have we known each other, Jonesey?"

"Too long?"

"We did a few good jobs together, didn't we?"

Amison pulled a cigarette from a pack in his pocket and offered it to the Centurion CEO. He then pulled out another and lit them both.

"We had good times, Sol. The last time we met was at your fish farm on the Amazon."

"That's right. You remember! That's when we fed a guy who swindled me to my favorite pirana. I also took Dominick, Vincent's brother, to my fish farm after old man Max bought the course. I thought he could bring us up to date on that Bimini Man business. Somehow, I thought you guys might be trying to sandbag me.

"He had a pair of brass balls, or so he thought. So, he learned to feed my pirana, one body part at a time, starting with his feet, then his legs, then his balls. He told me all I wanted to know. But he was so far gone, we had to lower the rest of him into the fish pond to end his misery. At least my fish were happy."

They both inhaled deeply. The evening air was cool, the sky was clear and the two men gazed at the moon's reflection on the river.

"One of the things Hank did in the months before leaving Alliance was to get me a seat on the Alliance board," Sol continued. "It's a voting seat and Hank wants me to back him for the president's spot at Alliance now that Harold has moved up."

"I thought Marvin Childs had first digs on it."

"He does, and so did Vince Neals. But you did me a favor with Neals. I owe you, and so does Harold. But the board has to vote. Kilpatrick prefers Childs. You may have to take care of Childs for me. What do you think?"

"I don't like Marvin," Amison replied.

"Neither do I. You know, Jonesey, why don't you throw your hat into the ring?"

Amison shook his head.

"That's not what my bag, Sol. I'm a street fighter. Or else, I'd be like you or like Harold. You guys have the big picture; I don't. Hank is an administrator. I can't stand offices and close spaces. But I'll support the Alliance chief whoever he is, like I always have."

Sol sighed. "I'm glad to hear that. So now, what are you doing with my land in Bimini?"

"Not protecting your interests, Sol; that's for sure."

Sol Weinberg said nothing for a while. Then he stuck the bag out again. "More peanuts?"

There was no response.

"I'll tell you what, Jonesey. I made a mistake allowing myself to be screwed by Harold. But that's fine. He needed quick cash and I was glad to accommodate. So I'm asking you for a favor for old times sake."

"What's that?"

"You're not stupid, Jonesey. But you don't have the big picture, as you say. I do. That deal Bencivenga, Levy and O'Brien made is going sour and they're playing for position with you and the heroin as the centerpieces. Bencivenga is going to be the odd man out because all he has is his idiot son for the heavy lifting. Harold has you and Mike Quinn, the dynamic duo, to pull off the heist, and maybe even Frank Hoffman when push comes to shove.

"Harold is also backing you to the hilt. That's loyalty. It also gives him a leg up. Jack O'Brien has Quinn also, and that's going to be a problem. He had Dudley Hanes and Vince Neals in his pocket but they're gone. Those other folks in that circle, Charlie Kane and Ginny Peters and a few others? They're worthless for the big job.

"So, O'Brien is short handed and if Quinn turns on him, he's done. That leaves you as the wild card. I have good ears working for me. You have the muscle and brains, and the team, with Quinn, Santiago and Tucker."

"Tucker Anderson?"

"You got it. I'm lending him to you. He's going to Bimini."

"What about Hank?"

"I'm keeping him in reserve. But I'm positive you'll also get Frank. If he doesn't smell the roses, he'll at least smell the poppy seeds."

"How the hell do you know so much?" Amison asked.

"You have a few friends and many enemies, Jonesey, but they all vouch for you and they talk to me, especially Leroux and Henry Alstrum. Word about the Bimini Man scam is filtering up to Washington about what's going on and some big shots at the CIA are unhappy and want O'Brien to retire. That's makes Europol nervous to the point that Leroux wants to break with Levy and O'Brien. Besides, he has his own plans for the heroin.

"That brings me to my point. I know you're going to make a run for the heroin. But the island and the stash belongs to me. That's why I bought the place to begin with. So, I'll tell you what. Do what you have to do and stay alive. I won't meddle unless I can help you one way or another. But if you get lucky and end up with the heroin, you owe me two billion dollars. Kapish?"

"I don't have that kind of money."

"You will. When you sell the dope, you'll have it and much more. That stuff isn't getting cheaper."

"You're not afraid of a double cross?"

Sol laughed.

"Here, finish the popcorn. You need it more than I do." He paused, and his sad, hound dog eyes caught Amison's.

"Look. You're not the double-crossing type, Jonesey. That's why you don't do the executive office bit. So stay alive and get me what I paid for. I don't give a shit what else you do. I need the money to buy Alliance."

"Is that your plan?"

"Not any time soon. Harold has too much staying power. When he goes, we'll see. But remember, if you dick me over, your friends die slowly, including that Bahamian chick you're banging. I have many hungry fish."

Sol Weinberg slapped his thighs and got up. "Come. I'll drive you back."

Amison waved him off. "No thanks. I'll walk. I need the air."

He decided not to return to the theater and went back to his boat. He was tired and thoroughly unhappy. He lay down for a quick nap and fell into a deep sleep.

The radio clock's alarm roused Amison early Sunday morning. Moments later a weather report announced that the Atlantic storm was growing more intense and was barreling across the northern Caribbean for the Biminis. He went out on deck and noticed for the first time that *Flyer* was gone. Thinking about his friend Mark, he assumed Luis had taken care of him. And Domino? His mind turned fleetingly to her. Wherever she was, at the very least, she was out of harm's way.

It was time to pay Bob Byrne a visit. He called to say he was coming over and fifteen minutes later a cab dropped him at the Bay Colony low rise condominium apartment complex. The development consisted of several middle income two story buildings filled with one, two and three bedroom apartments. Bob Byrne's place was easy to find. It was a breezy, ground floor, two bedroom apartment with a patio facing the front lawn. A wooden Eskimo sculpture stood on the lawn surrounded by an assortment of children's toys.

Amison was greeted at the door by a short Asian woman with long black hair. "You are Mr. Jones?"

He nodded as Bob Byrne came up behind her. "I see you've found us. Come on in. I have some interesting things to show you."

The entry foyer lead directly into a relatively spacious living room furnished in the usual light colors of south Florida homes. Aside from the TV, VCR, stereo and computer equipment strategically placed against the walls of the room beyond the reach of small, prying hands, the floor was filled with children's toys and games. Background screams and squeals explained the debris on the floor as two children, a little girl in pigtails and a slightly older boy in a cereal bowl haircut tumbled out of one of the bedrooms. They settled down on the floor and began playing with their toys until they were finally forced by their parents to acknowledge Amison.

After a few minutes, when Bob Byrne caught his breath, he finally got around to introducing Amison to his wife.

"Jonesey," he said, "You've never met my wife. This is Zara. Zara, this is my friend, Amison Jones."

"My husband has spoken a lot about you," said Zara, shaking his hand.

"I hope some of it was good."

"My wife, by coincidence, has taken a job with a private investigation company, Dalton Recovery."

"Yes," said Zara, smiling. "I am a receptionist and also do general clerical work. It is very interesting."

"You work with John Dalton?" asked Amison.

"Yes," she answered. "He is my boss."

"I haven't seen John in over five years. Give him my regards when you see him at the office."

Ojo, who was in the kitchen all this time, came out to greet his boss. He was wearing an apron, and was obviously pleased with his new surroundings.

"He has been cooking all our meals," said Bob. "He's a great chef and great with the kids. Too bad he can't stay. Perhaps the next time, you can rent him out."

"Maybe," said Amison. "Anyway, I'm glad things worked out."

Bob beckoned him to the other room. "Come into the dining room. We can talk there. Do you care for some soda, coffee, beer?"

"Coffee will be fine."

Bob spoke to his wife, but not in English, as she went to the kitchen followed by Ojo. "My wife is an Innuit Indian. We met in Alaska. The rest is history plus two wonderful kids; he pointed to the living room where the two children were busily dismantling a plastic toy.

"First," said Bob. "I want to thank you for this mission."

Amison's voice was grave. "I have to tell you this was not my idea. However, I'm glad you're aboard."

"Well, I have no complaints. Who arranged for my leave?"

"Apparently, it has all been taken care of. You're working for me."

"Who else is joining us?"

"Mike Quinn and Tucker Anderson. Luis Santiago is our mission chief. We may be able to count on Cecil Fergueson and Henry Alstrum, but I'm not sure."

"Wow! And what about Mark Stone. Is he in?"

Amison shook his head. "Too risky for him. His health is bad. I'd like to jettison you too because of your family."

"Shit, Jonesey, you can't do that. This is the chance I've been waiting for. This is the paid vacation I've been looking for. Besides, I understand some nice fees and expense money are being thrown in plus hazardous duty compensation and a hefty life insurance policy on top of my regular pay."

Amison leaned forward in his chair. "Listen to me, Robert. People have died since I signed on. And more are going to die. This is not Boy Scout camp!"

"That's a risk I want to take, sir," replied Bob quietly.

Amison leaned back again as Zara and Ojo returned from the kitchen with coffee and cake.

"I'm in," insisted Bob Byrne. "You're not going to talk me out of it. I've done too much background work on this mission since Friday to back out."

"Such as?"

"This guy, Dudley Haynes. I had a computer check done on him. He is actually Donald Henry Childs, one of two sons born to one Marvin Benjamin Childs and his wife Margaret. Her maiden name is Margareta Benito de la Cruz. The parents weren't born in the States. They arrived about ten years ago, but I didn't have time to find out where they were from. Son Donald went to school in England and into the English military where he trained as a communications specialist. He earned a general discharge. The record shows that he may have been gay. He moved to the Bahamas, surfacing seven years ago as a medical assistant. Is he important?"

"Not anymore. He's dead. What about the other son?"

"So much for old Dudley," said Bob. "The other son? We've drawn a blank, but a Childs working for Alliance? Are we looking at the same person?"

"Probably."

"I checked out the other names. "Cecil Fergueson and Henry Alstrum check out. Fred Peterson is interesting. He graduated from a Caribbean medical school and was appointed medical examiner by a Bahamian minister named Jonathan Sykes. He was put in charge of examining prisoners accused of peddling drugs. Most of them died mysteriously after those exams. He was married once, and divorced.

"I also checked out Marlene Stone and Leslie Sandler along with your buddies. Nothing there. I guess you guys have either been leading boring lives or you've been busy writing your memoirs."

"Memoirs, maybe," said Amison. "What about Mark's wife?"

"No real record. She and sister Leslie are foreign born and came over as orphans and were adopted by a couple who died at home of carbon monoxide poisoning fifteen years ago. Leslie was married briefly to a car salesman named Sandler who drowned shortly after the divorce. Marlene only marriage was Mark Stone and that was about ten years ago. There was no time to check INS records, so I don't know where they came from."

"How about social security numbers, passport numbers, that sort of thing?"

"We have all that. Everything dead ends. Maybe they had other names or maybe they got here without official papers. They could be from a foreign orphanage. If they came here young enough, they wouldn't even know and all the records could be buried somewhere.

"Now that George Gibson is something else. He's American born but we don't know to whom. Records show he was orphaned and lived in foster homes. He may have been raised with Marlene and Leslie's adopted parents but that's a guess. He has a petty criminal record. No violent crimes, mainly theft and bad checks. As he grew older, he did some embezzling at an assortment of jobs he held that involved money handling. So far, we have no proof he's related to Marlene. Maybe they're kissing cousins. You should speak to her; she might know something more."

Amison sat back. "I don't like him and I don't trust her. What about the clothing samples?"

Bob Byrne nodded. "I'm glad you asked. We have some eye-openers here. The clothing that came from Guenther and Douglas. The lab found semen remains and female hairs from two different women on the clothes they wore. There were also pubic and scalp hairs from the same women. This suggests that the guys, each at a different time, had sex with the same two women simultaneously shortly before they died. I sure wish I went to that party. More tests will have to be done to get a better picture of what happened. We requested DNA tests, but that will take time."

"We don't have time," said Amison.

"There was also a residue of jasmine-based perfume oil on the clothing. One or both women must have been wearing the same perfume."

"Cecil Ferguson's initial thought was that they died by drowning in the waters around Bimini," said Amison. Then he added, "But Henry Alstrum says the water he was able to remove from their lungs indicates they drowned in brackish water, the type we have here in the canals."

"That could be," agreed Bob. "The only logical scenario I could come up with is that a trap was set for them. They were on to something in Bimini. They traveled to Florida, maybe to make a report, met these women who talked them into having sex and invited them to an orgy where they were killed. Their bodies were put on a boat and dumped in the shallows of the Bahama Bank to avoid having a couple of murders discovered in Florida. The incoming tide carried their bodies to shore."

He noted the approval on Amison's face and went on. "I checked something else."

"What's that?"

"I was always curious about the Miami incident. So I asked a friend from the telephone company who has connections with the Bahamian telephone company to check their records of all calls between Bimini, Nassau and the States starting a few weeks before the Miami incident to the time of your wife's accident. There were a whole bunch of calls from Dudley Haynes in Bimini to Marvin Childs in New Jersey."

"How do you know the calls went to Marvin Childs?"

"They were routed to his private office line and to his home. And what's more, he made return calls."

"How about calls to Fort Lauderdale?"

"Those calls went to the Riverside, but we don't know to whom."

Amison shook his head and bit his lips. "Great friends I have."

"You should probably find new ones. What's our next move, chief?"

"We leave for Bimini tomorrow at dawn," said Amison. "I'll pick you and Ojo up at customs on the way out. Mike Quinn is going to meet us in Bimini."

"What are we doing in Bimini?"

"We're going to blow up the dig site first and then the *Casa D'Ora*. That's where I think all the heroin will have been stored by the time we arrive. Mike Quinn should have loaded up *Phoenix* with enough explosives to do the job by now. And oh, I almost forgot." Amison dug into one of his pockets and took out the pack of photographs he had received from Jack O'Brien at the theater the night before.

"We need a lab to analyze these pictures that were taken of the fossils at the dig. There's a possibility they may be fake."

"Do you mean we're blowing up a part of Bimini and risking our lives for some fake bones?"

Amison did not answer. The conversation changed to small talk as they turned their attention to the coffee and cake laid out before them. It went on for an hour as Zara, Ojo and the kids sporadically spilled into the dining room to play. He was uncomfortable and felt like an intruder. He did not belong here.

He finally looked at his watch and said, "It's late. I think it's time for me to go." He shook hands with Bob Byrne and bid goodbye to the kids and to Ojo. Zara escorted him to the door with her husband, holding what looked like two Indian charm bracelets in her hand. She gave one to Bob and the other to Amison.

"This is for you, Mr. Jones. If you pray, it will keep you safe so that you can look after my husband who will wear the other bracelet. It will protect him so that he can return safely to his family."

Amison thanked her and returned to his catamaran where he found Marlene Stone waiting at the bulkhead. *Flyer* was still gone.

CHAPTER 20

▼

INTERMEZZO

"Where have you been? I've been looking for you," she said.

"Out," he replied. "What's up?"

"Well, you could invite me on board."

He climbed on deck, and she followed him. She wore heels and a knee length flower print low cut dress over which she had on an oversized blazer from which a brass sleeve button was missing.

"Yours? Are you expecting to gain weight?"

"Marlene laughed lightly. "No silly. It's cousin George's. He dropped it on the grounds near *Flyer*. Have you seen him? The boat is gone too."

"Not since yesterday." "He held her hand up. "Missing a button?"

Marlene examined her sleeve. "George must have. I can't figure it out, Ruby. It looks as if it's been torn off. The material is ripped."

He held up her hand again, felt the sleeve and then put it down.

"Strange," he muttered. "Where's Mark?"

"Mark left for Bimini before dinner last night," she replied. "I guess you were unable to talk him out of the trip. George took him to the airport"

Amison did not reply. His better guess was that Luis had come over and spirited him away and that George had decided to take *Flyer* to Bimini, the klutz snagging his jacket on something while boarding the boat. He uttered a sigh of resignation.

"And by the way, Mike Quinn came over with some large bags and loaded them on. Are you guys going somewhere?"

Amison nodded. "Somewhere. I'm going below. Are you coming?"

They went below.

Amison had the distinct feeling she had not come just for a tour of his boat and that she had done this thing many times before with others. The perfume filling the air numbed his senses. He liked her habit of sometimes throwing her head back and to the side and then sweeping through her hair with one long motion of her hand. Her thick long hair diverted attention from a surface coarseness in her face.

"That's an interesting perfume," Amison said. "A special occasion gift?"

"Birthday. It's jasmine. Frank gave it to me. Do you like it?"

Marlene was well formed but not very beautiful. He recalled the old joke: "In a bar at closing time, everyone is beautiful."

She was sensually attractive. The form fitting dress she was wearing revealed a slender body with voluptuous breasts eager for use. Not too thin hipped. He could see that she wore stockings tied to a garter belt, but had no panties or bra.

She gave him a seductively wicked smile, saying, "Would you like to take care of me before you sail away?"

Amison beckoned her to follow him to his stateroom.

Marlene hitched up her dress and climbed into his bed, her legs and thighs slightly parted. Mutual instincts took over for the duration.

Was this a betrayal of his old friend Mark? Most likely. Something was not quite right. But sex was sex, and at his point in life he had to take all the opportunities offered.

"What do you think?" she asked, as she put her clothes back on. "Don't we make great lovers?"

"Yes. But I think you should settle down some day and have kids."

"With you, or with Mark?"

"Oh, you and I can mess around. I like that. It clears out my tubes. But I'm out of the baby making business. I've done it, been there and so on. We can have a few good years having fun and banging around. But, you're better off sticking to your old man."

"That's what I love about you, Ruby," Marlene said with sarcasm in her voice. "You're so much fun after sex."

"I tell you what, cookie. How about a night of heavy sex when I get back from Bimini? I'll spring for dinner."

"That's an offer I can't refuse. But I'll have to ask my old man first," she giggled.

Marlene put on her shoes made her way back to the main cabin where she gave Amison a long, lingering kiss.

"I'm going to make you mine yet."

He had no comment. He followed her silently up on deck where she blew him a kiss and jumped off the boat. Waiting until she was out of sight, he returned inside and called his daughter. A man answered who was not her husband.

"Gordon?"

"Dad?"

A big smile spread over Amison's face. "What the hell are you doing in New Jersey?"

"I graduated, Dad. I drove up this morning from Washington to do a little celebrating with Debbie, her husband and the kids. How are you doing? Debbie tells me you have a new assignment."

"Yes, I do," Amison confirmed. "But first, let me offer you my congratulations! That's terrific. I would give you a huge hug if I could."

"I know, dad."

"And so, the world now has another spook! What's your next move?"

Another voice came over from an extension phone with the sounds of children screaming in the background.

"He should settle down, become an accountant, get married and have kids." It was Debbie. "That's what you told me to do."

"I have a contractual commitment to meet," interjected Gordon. "When it's over, I might do something else. In the meantime, I'm on vacation for the next few days. Mitch here is taking a few days off, so we're going to play golf somewhere that has no snow."

Debbie interrupted. "Dad?"

"Yes?"

"Dad, about the jet's flight records at the time of Mom's accident. Gordon did some checking. I think we hit pay dirt."

"I called a friend at the FAA," said Amison's son. "That plane did a lot of flying but filed phony flight plans."

"How do you know that?"

"The pilot of record was a Michael J. Quinn. Does that mean anything?"

"Yes."

"It first goes from Paradise Island to Philadelphia International Airport the day before Mom's accident. No flight plan is filed. However, Philadelphia's control tower has a taped conversation with the Lear's pilot when landing instructions are requested. Paradise Island is indicated as the point of origin in the tapes. The jet discharges one passenger who goes through customs. Guess who it is."

"Who?"

"Harold Levy." There was dead silence. "Are you there, dad?"

"Yes. Go on."

"The plane flies out a few hours later, same pilot, but no passenger. This time a flight plan from Philadelphia to St. Louis, Missouri is filed. But the plane never goes there. Instead, it makes an emergency landing at Maguire Air Force Base right here in central Jersey, ostensibly for repairs. The question is: why didn't it return to Philadelphia if there was a problem? In any case, it stays overnight at the base where it's fixed."

"Any maintenance or repair records?"

"Nope. The problem was a switch that any amateur pilot could have figured out. I spoke to a mechanic who was on that shift when it flew in. He did the work. He thinks the pilot was a total jerk and should not have been flying.

"Anyway, the Lear is cleared for departure, but not before a chopper comes in and lets out three people: one short and portly and the other slightly taller and who some of the ground personnel salute. The third guy is big and rangy.

"The fat man and the big guy leave on the Lear. They sound like Vincent Neals and Harold. The one who was being saluted climbs back into the chopper and it takes off. Exactly to where, no one seems to know. That could be have been Jack O'Brien. He has a colonel's rank. Now, the chopper and plane connection takes place just hours after mom's accident."

"How did anyone know it was military?"

"Battle drab with serious weaponry? It wasn't civilian; that's for sure."

"Any input on the Lear's destination after it took off?"

"Well," continued Gordon. "It never went to St. Louis because there is no record of it ever having landed there. What do you think, dad?"

"I think you did just fine, son, and you too, Debbie. I'm just sorry I can't be with you guys."

"It doesn't look good, does it dad?" Debbie said from the extension phone.

Amison sighed. "Listen, I have to run. Love and kisses to the kids."

"Good luck, dad," said Debbie, "And take care of yourself. We miss you."

"Good luck, dad," said Gordon. "We all love you."

PART III

▼

THE DEATH OF
BIMINI MAN

CHAPTER 21

▼

JOURNEY'S END

Monday. Amison was up before dawn. The weather was cold and blustery and a strange feeling gripped his underbelly. Something was not right. He looked out to see if George Gibson was on his way but he was nowhere in sight. A call to Luis's private line produced a cryptic message informing him that the inspector was out on police business.

Waiting made no sense. He decided to cast off and a half hour later he picked up Bob Byrne and Ojo at the Port Everglades customs dock.

Under a colorless dawn sky, *Phoenix* raced out the inlet into the gray waters of the Florida straits. Drenching rain began falling and the men huddled in the cat's wheelhouse to stay dry.

Bob Byrne went out for air but it was bone chilling. He retreated to the relative comfort of the wheelhouse in time to field an incoming call on the vessel's marine phone. It was Luis Santiago.

The conversation was brief and Bob said spoke in mumbles. When it was over, he put down the receiver.

"There's been a snafu," he said.

"I figured. What happened?"

"Mark Stone disappeared. He hasn't been seen since early Saturday evening."

"Damn! Where the hell is he?"

"Luis doesn't know. Neither does Marlene. He never showed up for dinner. She thought he might have taken the last flight to Bimini because his bags were gone."

Amison concentrated on the helm and avoided looking into Bob's eyes.

"Maybe Mark did take that last flight."

"I'd like to think so," said Bob Byrne. "But it doesn't seem likely. Luis says his reservation was for Sunday. He thinks the most optimistic scenario would be that he committed suicide or fell into the river during a diabetic seizure. The river is being dragged now."

"Anything else?"

"Yes. The police went to question Mark's wife but they couldn't find her. Luis went looking for Mike Quinn but he wasn't around either. He probably left for the Biminis."

"What about the Bencivenga kid?"

"He was released Saturday evening. He's gone. What's going on, Jonesey?"

Amison could not muster a satisfactory reply. He gripped the cat's wheel tightly to keep his hands from trembling. At last, he freed a hand to fumble in a pocket for jelly beans but there were none to grab. He found his pack of cigarettes in another pocket but it was crumpled and empty.

"Damn!" He screamed out.

Ojo shook his head and retreated to the main cabin, leaving Amison subdued in the wheelhouse with Bob Byrne as the cat ploughed into dark swells against a low ceiling of fast moving black clouds.

Bob Byrne tried to make small talk.

"It looks like a weather change," he said. "The wind is usually on the nose this time of year. It's coming from the west. We're down wind racing. There's a new system brewing."

"You mean like a hurricane?"

"It's too soon for that," responded Bob. "But whatever it is, I don't like it."

"Neither do I. But what the hell. This means we'll be in Bimini for lunch."

By this time, Ojo had returned with a fresh pack of cigarettes and a sealed bag of jelly beans for his boss.

The cigarettes and jelly beans improved Amison's humor. The wind was, after all, good and it moved *Phoenix* at hull speed. The catamaran's diesels growled their defiance at the bad weather and the vessel was soon enveloped in a sightless gray void. The only noises to be heard were the muffled roar of the engines and the roar of sea water that raced between the hulls to create a foamy wake behind the transom. Somewhere in the distance a solitary sea buoy signaled ships with its lonely wail.

Bob had his ears glued to the radio's weather channel.

"The radio says the storm is northeast of Puerto Rico and may hit the Turks and Caicos by tomorrow," he said.

"We'll deal with it when it hits," Amison noted tartly. "We have a few days."

A stiff breeze kicked up. He brought the cat into the wind, pushed a button on the console and the mast rose into the air with the main and genoa sails unfurling simultaneously like giant wings. Ojo and Bob Byrne rushed to the after deck and worked the main sheet traveler and coffee grinder winches to achieve optimum sail trim while Amison turned off the engines.

Phoenix paused, heeled slightly, and then surged ahead on its easterly course.

"We're across the Stream," Amison announced a half hour later.

The weather threatened but held. The swells were mysteriously swallowed into the deep and *Phoenix* found itself in a flat, motionless slate colored sea without a seam on the horizon to separate it from the sky.

"Welcome to the Bahama Bank," said Amison.

The catamaran was by now skimming over the slate colored water at over twenty knots under a steady wind. Shortly before lunch, Bob sighted a low dark rise on the starboard horizon but could not tell if it was landfall or a storm cloud.

Amison looked through his binoculars.

"Bimini!"

The cloud cover made way for the sun and the air warmed. *Phoenix* catapulted ahead and slickers and sweaters were discarded for polo and shirt sleeve shirts.

Amison hit the controls that lowered the mast and turned on the engines while the others took up positions to furl the sails dropping to the pontoon decks. He looked at his watch.

"We'll catch the tide going in," he announced.

"Here," Amison instructed Ojo. "Take the helm. You know the way. I'm going to have a smoke."

The Bolivian took the wheel as the sun presided in a cloudless sky over a picture post card of baby blue waters lapping at palm shaded white sands as the Biminis slowly rose out of the sea. The cat was about to enter the cut leading to the harbor when they saw lying at anchor an old rusty freighter. It sat on the water like a huge water bug silhouetted against the sky. It was the *Casa D'Ora*.

Ojo negotiated the catamaran smoothly through the cut between the Biminis and brought it to rest at its usual bulkhead slip at Buccaneer Point.

Bob and Ojo tied down the vessel while Amison called customs to inform the duty officer of his arrival with the names of his passengers.

Looking skyward at the now cloudless sky and burning sun he said aloud, "This might end up being a nice day after all."

It was an empty gesture to a beautiful but questionable day. Amison's mind and heart was on Mark Stone and his whereabouts and he forced himself to believe his friend was safely ensconced at the Bimini Reef hotel.

A van routinely made the round trip between the hotel and the ferry landing but it was full. The ferry also was filled to capacity. People crowded the dock waiting for a ride, either on the van or on the ferry, and more could be seen across the cut at the Alice Town landing.

Amison pulled Bob Byrne aside.

"I want to find out if Mark is here. We're going to walk to the hotel. It's only a couple of miles down the road. Later, go to customs; find Frances Douglas and tell her you're with me. Have her check all manifests for passengers arriving Sunday. Then ask her to let you use the phone to call your wife for the results of the photo lab tests on those pictures I gave you yesterday. They may be in by now."

"Anything else?"

"Yes. I want to find out more about Frank Hoffman's boat, *Flyer*."

"I've seen the boat," said Bob Byrne. "It's a beauty."

"That it is. Ask your wife to use her connections at the detective agency where she works. I want to track the boat. I'd like someone to visit the Bahia Mar, Pier Sixty Six and Marina Marriott's fuel docks. *Flyer* is a guzzler and needs a lot of fuel. These are the only places where it can make a pit stop inside the inlet. I want a record of the times it fueled up. Even if cash was paid, there should be a record. A boat like that gulps diesel in hundred gallon shots. Someone should also stop at the bridge tender's office at the Seventeenth Street causeway bridge. The bridge tenders keep tabs on all traffic. I need to know about *Flyer's* movements from a few days before Luther Guenther was killed right down to the this past weekend."

"When is Mike Quinn getting here?"

"Soon, I hope. But when he surfaces, he'll know where to find us." He paused and added with a sneer, "That probably won't be good either."

They left Ojo on *Phoenix* and headed to the road to South Bimini's southern tip. Shade trees protected them from the sun as they began walking down the road on the long bluff overlooking the beach. The lunch hour brought a traffic lull and they were alone. They passed several wooden benches that served as rest stops for the occasional hikers who could stop and watch birds circling the western skies and screaming at passing ships in the distance. In the early evening lovers would sit on these same benches, holding hands and watching the sun slowly sink down under the sea.

Today, and closer to shore, the elusive billfish was being chased by party boats hounded by diving sea gulls looking for a meal. Further in the distance, a sailboat moved slipped silently over the horizon.

A noise at the beach caught their attention. Children released from their morning classes at the All Age School in Alice Town, and walking home from the ferry slip where they were let off, had gone down the bluff to the beach. They were clustered around something lying among the dead shells and debris at the high water line. Their muffled voices were not Amison's primary concern. It was the sight of sea gulls circling the children that peaked his curiosity. He ran down to the beach with bated breath followed by Bob Byrne to have a better look. A body was lying face down in the sand.

The children made way as he knelt down and gasped. It was Mark Stone.

A weariness overcame Amison and tears welled in his eyes. The sun did not blink and the sky maintained its cheery blueness while small breakers from the sea slapped mindlessly against the beach and tiny sand creatures crawled in and out of the body's soggy clothing.

"He was my friend," said Amison. "And now he's gone!"

He gazed inquiringly at the uncomprehending faces of the children and at Mark. "Goodbye old friend," he whispered. "We'll meet again some day. And when we do, whoever did this will be dead."

He happened to see something clutched in the Mark's hands. He worked the fingers of one hand open and removed a brass blazer button from which thread was hanging. An unraveled bow tie was held in a death grip in the other hand. He also noticed dirt and plant debris stuck in his pant cuffs.

Taking a few sample bits, he placed them into his pockets with trembling hands. He was shaking like a leaf, and Bob Byrne had to help him to his feet. Amison's shoulders sank and when he stood up he was for one fleeting moment stooped and shrunken like an old man.

The school children ran off and people began converging on the beach. By the time Cecil Fergueson and several officers arrived in a jeep and police van from Alice a large crowd had assembled. The police and two stretcher bearers had to elbow their way through the curious onlookers to reach the body. Some Triple A conference attendees were present and they quickly recognized Mark's body.

"He was a good person," Amison leaned on Bob Byrne.

"Good people shouldn't have to die, Robert," he cried. "They should be allowed to live forever."

Amison and Bob stepped aside to make way for Cecil and his men. Behind the crowd, he saw Frank Hoffman standing next to Leslie Sandler. A reporter was at the scene and wanted their picture.

"Dr. Sandler! If you would just look over here for a moment!"

Leslie turned and gave the reporter her best photogenic smile.

Someone else wanted an interview, but received a 'no comment' response.

Cecil shook his head in dismay.

"This is not good, Jonesey. This is not good at all."

Amison's hands were hanging limp with their palms open. "It's Mark. I don't understand, Cecil. He was fine. This wasn't supposed to happen."

Another officer came over and whispered something to Cecil who nodded. "Take the body to the barracks. We'll take a closer look at it there," he ordered. "Then get Henry Alstrum. He's at my home."

Turning to Amison he said, "I understand Bob Byrne came over with you."

And then he saw Bob next to Amison. "Welcome to Bimini," he said. "It's good to see you again."

To Amison he said, wringing his hands, "I'm so sorry. What a tragedy!"

He shook his head over and over again and wiped his brow.

"I'm truly sorry. Is there anything I can do for you right now?" he asked.

"Do you need a ride anyplace?"

"No, but Bob Byrne needs to go to town. Can you take him?"

"I'll have one of my men take him to your boat. He can ferry or dinghy over."

Cecil was about to relay commands to his men when suddenly George Gibson popped up out of nowhere.

He rushed up and down the area cordoned off by the police, proclaiming loudly to all who would listen that he was the deceased man's cousin and was claiming the body.

Amison tensed up.

"I'm going to kill the bastard!" he said.

"Is this man crazy or what!" Cecil exclaimed when he returned.

"Someone get him out of here."

Another officer grabbed George by the shoulder and lead him to the police van. He waved to Frank Hoffman as he was being lead away, but Frank ignored him. "This is terrible, terrible!" Frank moaned. "A great loss. Mark Stone will be truly missed. What a horrible shame he drowned. We're going to have to change the evening schedule to say something about..."

Cecil Fergueson looked up and broke in. "I beg your pardon, Frank. But I think it may be premature to call this a drowning or anything of that nature."

"Of course, of course," acknowledged Frank solemnly. "Is there anything we can do?"

Cecil shook his head. "Not right now. We may need you later for a positive I.D."

He looked back at Amison.

"Come over to the barracks tomorrow morning. And by the way, this is a bad time for celebrating, but Lang and Sykes are having a dinner reception Wednesday night. I think I can get you invited."

"I'll be at the barracks. Dinner, I don't know," Amison replied with disinterest.

Cecil nodded and turned to supervise the removal of the body and to encourage the crowd to move on, leaving Amison alone with Frank and Leslie Sandler. It was strange, he thought, but she wore the same jasmine perfume as Marlene.

"I want to speak to Jones alone," Frank told Leslie. "Do you mind?"

"Of course not, dear," she purred. "I'll see you at the hotel."

▼

CHAPTER 22

CLEARING THE AIR

Amison and Frank were alone by a bunch of boulders on the beach.

"You made a mistake getting involved here," said Frank. "You're going to get us all killed."

Amison took a deep breath and delivered a teeth jarring punch to Frank's jaw that knocked him off his feet and to the ground.

Frank sat dazed for a moment, his legs spread eagled, and rubbed his smarting face.

"I guess I had this coming, Jonesey. I hope it helps you work out your feelings. I'm not going to fight you over this."

He struggled to his feet and wiped off his trousers.

"You tear me apart, man," Amison said. "You're not the Frank Hoffman from the old days. Did you know that at one time you were a mentor and role model for me? What the hell happened to you?"

He threw him a look of utter disgust and began walking away.

Frank followed him, throwing up his arms.

"And who the hell are you? Saint Jones? Life's been very good for me. It's been very good for you too. And it's also been hell! But I can't cry any more than you can. I know what I've gotten myself into. Do you?"

I'm not in a mess. You are!"

"Ok. So, I created this mess and there's no way out. But I'm from under the same rock as you. I made a deal with my devils and you made a deal with your demons. If I could undo the past, I would."

Amison looked over his shoulder as he kept walking. "I'm glad you're not going to fight me, Frank, because I'm going to kill you the first chance I get."

"Is that a threat I'm hearing? Hey, man. Don't you turn your back on me!"

Amison whirled around, drew the service revolver he kept hidden under his shirt and leveled it at his former associate. His voice was dead calm.

"Don't push me, Frank. You want to talk about your hell? Man. Let's talk about my hell. You made that hell. And you know what else? I think you wanted me out of the way so you could get your hands on Leslie. You must think she loves you. Well, I screwed her the moment I hit Florida. And you want to know something? She's going to let me screw her even after you guys marry if it ever happens!"

Frank stopped in his tracks, lowered his hands and laughed hysterically.

"You crazy mother fucking bastard. What was that? A revenge fucking? What do I care what you do with Leslie. I'm not marrying her. The reason you're in a mess is because you never took care of your own wife when you had a chance."

Amison lowered his weapon slightly. "I don't follow."

Frank smirked and emitted an ugly laugh. "There's a lot you don't follow, old chum. Allow me enlighten you. I had a wife once, as you recall."

"Yes. She died ten years ago. I think she took an overdose of prescription pills for depression."

"She did. But she was murdered."

"How's that?"

"Jack O'Brien tried to have a thing with my wife. Actually, she started the fling. I was rarely around and he was. She even fantasized that she would divorce me and marry him. The problem was that he couldn't make it with her."

"Couldn't make it?"

"That's right, man. He's a fag, old chum! He likes clean young boys and an occasional woman for show. But he can't get it up. Even his tongue is limp. The relationship went south and O'Brien used his connections to have her prescription doctored. That's how she died. A drug overdose. She was a threat to his career and was murdered to keep his sexuality private. How do you think his career would go if people learned that a CIA hot shot was tuti-fruiti?"

"Why didn't you talk to the police?"

"You must be kidding. I know you were never the sharpest knife in the drawer, Jonesey. I would have been killed had I spoken to the police or anyone.

O'Brien knows I know. That means my life isn't worth a plugged nickel unless I play ball. So we have a standoff. I let Jack park CIA assets at Las Olas University, and he lets me live. I play ball with the Bencivengas, and they let me live. I play the game with Levy and he lets me live. I'm road kill once I lose my academic cover and stop playing ball. You're a total jerk, man. Instead of bugging me about my wife, why don't you focus on yours?"

There was a long pause. "Haven't you ever wondered about Bernice's so-called accident?"

"I wonder about it every day," said Amison. "That's one of the reasons I'm here. To bring her case to closure."

"Man. You are slow. I thought you would have figured this whole thing out long ago."

"Figured what out?

"Jack's relationship with Bernice."

Amison turned beet red. "Relationship?"

Frank looked amazed. "I always thought the reason you were putting the make on Leslie was because Jack was trying to have a fling with Bernice."

He was going to continue when he found himself facing Amison's gun barrel. "Fuck you, man! If you're going to kill me over the truth, you better do it right now!"

He could see a mix of rage and uncertainty in his old companion's face.

"I guess you really didn't know what was going on after all."

He went on to explain. "Shortly after he killed my wife, Jack started working on Bernice. You were gone a lot, and she had lots of free time. Not only did he try his luck, but he conned her into being a bag woman to move cash between the States and Nassau.

"Was she paid?"

"Of course. In cash, stupid! To make a long story short, he couldn't make it with Bernice either. To make matters worse, she got greedy and wanted more. That's when the decision to kill you both was made. Jack concluded that at some point you'd catch on. That's how the ambush outside Miami's harbor came about. And the follow up, her death, was to have been a suicide."

"You're lying!"

"Now, Jonesey. Don't go blind on me. Bernice was the bag woman for whom Mark took over so he could stay alive."

"How do you know all this?"

"I knew because I gave her money; Mark also knew about the affair. Your kids told me about the affair, and a few months before Bernice fell out of the Alliance building, she told Leslie about it."

"How on earth did Bernice learn about Leslie?"

"She's your wife, stupid. Wives know everything!"

"Damn! Why didn't my kids tell the police after the accident?"

"They feared for their lives, Jonesey. I didn't say anything because I didn't think at the time Jack would try to kill her. And actually, he didn't. His original plans were to simultaneously destroy you and your wife. You and your boat would be blown up outside Miami while Bernice would be lured to Philadelphia for a staged suicide. He used Vincent Neals as intermediary who hired the Bencivenga kids and Dudley Haynes and a few other stringers as mercenaries to take care of you.

"As you and Mark were turning the tables on the Bencivengas, Vince Neals and Marvin Childs were tossing Bernice out the window. Both plans went sour. Then O'Brien tried to have someone take you down in Miami for insurance. That didn't work either. The rest is history. He's still trying to kill you.

"I bet you're gunning for don Ignacio because you think he's the source of your malaise, old chum. But you're dead wrong. He's simply pissed at you for taking down his trawler fleet in Venezuela and may want you dead for that and for trying to foul up his heroin caper in the Biminis, but not for anything else. O'Brien is your man, Jonesey. He's our man. And the sooner he goes the better."

Amison lowered the gun.

"A Jamaican tried to put me away on the way to Philadelphia a few weeks ago. And then Dudley Haynes and Vince Neals tried to hit me Saturday night in Fort Lauderdale. I think I know why now."

"Well, good for you. Go to the head of the class. But in addition, I think Vince had his own agenda. His perception is that you planned the hits against his father and brother last year. Haynes has been on his personal payroll for years, along with Ginny Peters. Matter of fact, Ginny and Miguelito are a love item these days. My hunch is that everyone who's been trying to take you down works for either Vince Neals or Jack O'Brien or both."

"Vince and Dudley are dead, Frank."

"If that's so, then it leaves O'Brien and he knows by now. He's got to take you and everyone else down who was involved with or had knowledge of the Miami caper and your wife's attempted murder. That includes me."

"You know Frank. It's too bad we're not working the same side of the fence."

"You're not mad at me any more?" Frank asked timidly.

"No. I'm just disappointed. I'm disappointed because people I trusted kept me in the dark. What was that all about?"

Frank turned away from Amison's steady gaze.

"Fear? We were afraid of Jack and we didn't know what you would do besides return and kill everyone in your way. You know your temper."

Amison shook his head in dismay.

"I remember Harold telling me that the one thing we don't do in this business is touch family. When you get right down to it, it's all about family, isn't it?"

"You got that right, Jonesey. Just like when Harold had you send Ojo and his guys after Max and Dominick Neals last year. I happen to know you never touched Dom. Sol Weinberg did him. But let's face it, guy. It's about family. There's no sanctuary in this business."

"I guess not."

"So, what exactly are you going to do about this?"

A thin smile crossed Amison's lips. "I'm already doing things, Frank. Vince and Dudley are gone. I'm going to kill Jack and anyone else who was present when my wife was pushed out the window at Alliance."

His eyes narrowed. "And maybe you too if you were involved."

Frank stared at Amison who had again raised his gun. "Okay, jerk! You want to solve your problems? Kill me! Go ahead…go on. Squeeze the trigger, big man! Do it!"

He was screaming by now.

"Do it, damn it!"

Amison was speechless but he kept the revolver trained on Frank.

"I hear you've been screwing Mark's wife."

"Marlene? Of course I screwed her. Like I'm screwing Leslie. What the hell do you think women are on this planet for? To throw darts at? What do you do with your women, Jonesey? Play checkers?"

Amison could barely suppress a smile. He looked stupidly at his revolver, placed it back inside his shirt and walked over to a boulder on the bluff overlooking the beach and sat down, staring aimlessly at the sand and water.

Frank came over. "I'm in deep shit and can't get out, Jonesey. I'm devastated about Mark. He was a pain but he was my friend, even if I was tapping Marlene. And I'm beside myself for not saying anything about Bernice. But maybe Mark did drown accidentally."

Amison shook his head slowly. "No. He never left Florida alive. I think I can prove it. Mark died in Florida. He was taken out to sea on your boat and dumped near Bimini."

Frank scratched his head. "On *Flyer?*"

Amison got up, picked up a small rock and tossed it over the beach and into the water.

"As we speak, Frank, I bet it's in the harbor. Shit, Frank, this is going nowhere."

"That's right, Jonesey," Frank rejoined. "And killing me is only going to give you a leg up on thin air."

"This dig. It's a cover for a pending heroin shipment out of here, isn't it?"

"Of course it is. And cooperation keeps me alive. Do you know how much of that good stuff is buried here?"

Amison picked up another stone and threw it. This time, it hit the water and skimmed.

"Two billion dollars is the amount I keep hearing. How much do you say?"

"More than that by now. And that's at wholesale! And the price keeps moving up with demand and inflation."

"Is Bimini Man for real?"

Frank shrugged his shoulders. "What the hell do I know? I'm a con artist, not an archeologist. It's supposed to be for real, even if it is a cover. Leslie says it is."

"Well, let a hit man give a con artist a tip. You've been out-conned. The bones tucked away in North Bimini? They may not be real."

There was a long moment of silence. "Run that by me again?"

"Plaster and plastic. The whole dig is bogus. I thought you knew, or at least had an inkling."

Frank sat down on the boulder that Amison vacated and looked out to sea. "This is not good, Jonesey."

"No, it's not. Some people are going to look awfully stupid when the world finds out. Your bimbo took you!"

"You're not just pissed off at me for stealing your girl, are you?"

Amison laughed. "Yeah. I'm pissed. But that's not a heavy. We weren't married and she's only a broad. Look, I know you're in this for fame and fortune but it's a private party and you're not the guest of honor."

"Maybe I should deny everything and go back to Florida."

"No way, Frankie. Everyone knows. If you stay here you die and if you go home you go to prison. Leslie conned you. She and her Rastafarian buddies buried the dummy bones. There's nothing of value buried there except the heroin with you as the fall guy. The amazing thing is that you never figured it out. Mike Quinn and I are supposed to blow up the dig before the world wises up."

Frank made a face. "Who is Leslie working for?"

"Beats me. She can't be working for our dynamic trio because they are screwing each other as we speak."

"I figured that."

"I also want to know who did Mark and why," Amison insisted.

"Those who murdered the Europol agents killed Mark."

"You sure?"

"Positive."

He rose to his feet and tossed a rock. The tide had gone out too far and it could not reach the water.

"So, we're a couple of jerks. What now?"

Amison made a face. "We have few cards left, but together, we could manage to stay alive. I'm going to blow up the dig and the ship that the drugs are supposed to be loaded on."

"What ship?"

"It's an old converted freighter named the *Casa D'Ora*. It's anchored offshore."

"What about Bob Byrne, your new side kick?"

"He's good but he lacks experience in this game. Listen to me, Frank. We have no choice but to make a grab for the heroin for ourselves and kill everyone in our way. We're all earmarked for extinction anyway."

"Kill them with what? Dirty looks?"

"With guns, Frank. *Phoenix* is loaded for bear."

Frank paused. "I need time to think about this. I haven't killed anyone in years."

"Don't worry. You'll get the hang of it again."

"What about Quinn?"

"He's the explosives man. He has orders from O'Brien to kill me once we blow the dig. He'll have to go. Mike knows that I'm on to him. So it's a standoff. Now, what's with George Gibson?"

Frank sighed. "George is don Ignacio's watch dog and came with *Flyer*. There was no way I could afford the boat without Bencivenga's financing. George is dim witted and kills for fun. What's he doing here?"

"He told me he had to pick up some fishing gear in Bimini."

"We're going to have to take him down too. But how are you going to grab the heroin?"

"It's being moved to the *Casa D'Ora*. It doesn't have enough fuel to get back to Florida. I think it's going to be sunk on a ledge off the Bahama Bank with the heroin so that it can be retrieved later on. I'm going to help scuttle the ship."

"You are serious, aren't you?"

"You bet. I also told Lou Santiago. Are you in?"

Frank looked out to sea. "You do realize that Sol Weinberg owns the land. He has to be factored in."

"He already has. And I've settled with him. He wants two billion dollars for his aggravation. We keep the rest."

Frank squirmed. "I have to think about this."

"Don't think too long," warned Amison. "This is the chance of a lifetime."

"That's very true, Jonesey. We could even come out of this rich."

"I'll settle for alive. The longer this goes, the more I hate it."

"You're a phony, Jonesey. Now you're going to tell me should have stuck to teaching."

"Amison smiled faintly. "You think?"

CHAPTER 23

▼

DOMINO RETURNS

Amison returned to the catamaran where he found Ojo on board, scurrying about and doing performing all the small, unimportant tasks necessary to keep *Phoenix* afloat and ship shape. Ojo's presence was welcome but it could not begin to cure Amison's terrible loneliness.

Mark Stone was gone, Luis Santiago was not around and Frank Hoffman was a question mark. Cecil Fergueson was good company on occasion but without Mark and Frank, there was no one with whom to bend an elbow and share confidences and he had no real friends upon whom to rely.

He climbed aboard and sank exhausted into one of the banquet seats under the cockpit coaming behind the main cabin. Cigarettes and jelly beans were not the antidotes to his malaise and he chose instead to sit, arms folded, his mind blank, quietly staring at nothing in particular. His eyes followed a small spider climbing slowly up an almost invisible strand hanging from the lifelines until they found in their focus a pair of long, athletic legs the color of rich chocolate.

The legs were joined to shapely thighs covered by pair of blue shorts into which was tucked a white blouse. Fragrance from a familiar perfume teased his nose and made him stand up.

"Domino."

It was the only word that Amison could muster from his dry mouth. The two looked at each other and said nothing.

Finally, Domino asked, "Permission to come aboard, skipper?"

She threw Amison a friendly but provocative smile.

Amison stammered awkwardly. "I thought I'd never see you again."

He helped her on board and they fell into each other's arms and remained there in a long languorous embrace. When they finally disengaged, they sat down next to each other and watched the late afternoon bugs flying over the cabin top.

"Does this yacht serve rum, lime and ice?" Domino asked.

"Warm rum and lime", he replied. "No ice."

"You're always out of something," she commented softly. "I'll take warm rum and lime."

Ojo must have anticipated *Phoenix's* basic needs. He went shopping while his boss was gone and had bought ice at the police barracks. He stepped out of the cabin, smiled and waved several bags in his hands in front of them.

"Ice coming up." said Amison. He ran below for drinks, returning breathlessly a minute later with a tray of glasses, some limes, a small pitcher of ice and a bottle of rum, shooing Ojo back into the cabin where he discreetly stayed as long as they remained on board.

"To us," said Domino in a low sultry voice and raising her glass.

"To us," he repeated.

"I want to say," she began. "I'm sorry. I never realized how much you meant to me until I left for Florida."

Amison placed one finger on her lips, saying. "Never explain, never complain." After a while, he asked, "How did you know I was here?"

"This is not a big place, and *Phoenix* is hard to miss. Besides I kept contact with my sisters and with Cecil who said you were hanging around."

"Am I the only reason you're back?"

"No. My kids are with Frances and her two children. We want to get them out before the storm hits."

"I still have your money," Amison volunteered.

"That's good to know, Ruby. We might need it. I haven't been able to find a job in Miami."

She took a sip of her drink.

"I have plenty of money to tie you over."

"Thanks," and Domino smiled coyly. "I may not need much. I'm thinking of going into the fortune telling and beauty parlor business."

"You're what?"

Excitement filled her face.

"I've been saving money, Ruby. I'm going to start a business. I found a beauty parlor in Key Biscayne outside Miami whose owner wants to retire. It's for sale. It has ten stations for hair and nails. And you know what? I'm going to hire a fortune teller; there's room in the front. People go in for that sort of stuff."

"Shit, Domino, what do you know about fortune telling?"

"Nothing. I bought a book and the kit, the tarot cards, the tea leaves, the crystal ball with a round table and green drape to put over it, the whole nine yards. The stuff is at mom's house in Miami. The next time you see me, you're going to have to ask me for a date, just like you're a proper gentleman and I'm a proper lady."

"Well, since we're into lets's pretend, how about telling me my fortune?"

Domino giggled. "Don't tease, Ruby. This means a lot to me. Here, give me your hand."

Amison sighed and gave her his right hand.

"What do you see?"

"I see a man with sad eyes and a faraway look."

"That's because I'm far-sighted," he quipped.

"I see a glorious future for you, Ruby, and a long life." And then she added quickly, "If you don't fuck up," and she gave him a light, good natured jab in the ribs.

Amison threw her a shy smile.

"You think?" he asked hopefully. "Is there more?"

"Don't be greedy, honey." She pretended to look intently at his hand. "Ah, I see another woman in your life if you retire. And if you stay retired, you can help me in my business. I'm going to need a good partner."

Amison's hand suddenly went limp.

"Something is very wrong," Domino said. "I can feel it."

"I am having problems."

He proceeded to tell her everything that had happened to him since the last time they were together.

When he finished her only response was, "You are always in trouble. That's why I'm here. I told you before, you lead an over-active life. You should have stuck to teaching."

"I've been thinking about that."

"Or, we could have opened a beer, bait and tackle shop in the Keys, remember?"

Amison managed a smile. "Ice, extra," he said.

"Ice, extra," she repeated. "But there's another reason I'm here, Ruby."

"What's that?"

"I've been speaking with Cecil. He doesn't want you to pursue this mission."

"Damn it, Domino. The Bimini Man excavations are a fake. The whole thing is about heroin."

"So, let it be, Ruby. Who cares? Drugs puts food on the table for many people in the islands. Besides, I hear you're planning on stealing the heroin for you and your friends. Let's run off and forget about this. We can start a new life."

"Where, Domino? In Key West, a bullet away from Miami? In the Keys? How long do you figure we can hide? I'm dead here if I fail and I'm dead anyplace else if I cut and run. My passport to life is the heroin. If I can steal and hide it, then the greed of the world will keep me alive.

"But that's a long shot. You're not a party to this and you don't have to die. You have a family to raise. When were you planning to get your kids out of Bimini?"

"Tomorrow. Frances too."

"What about your younger sister, Eileen?"

"She's working at the Reef. She won't leave until the conference ends. But she's single and has no kids to worry about. You have to get out, Ruby."

"I can't," he said. "But you can."

"I know," Domino acknowledged softly. "You're on a death mission."

She took another drink and her mood changed. "We'll talk about that later. Right now, I want to call Frances, and then I'm yours until tomorrow."

The day was coming to an end and they decided to spend the night on the cat. A call by Domino to Frances ensured that the children were fine. The plan was to get on an early flight to Miami to meet the grandparents. The women agreed that their children would be on the flight and that they would join them a few days later.

Ojo always kept *Phoenix* stocked and when Amison and Domino were ready for dinner, they found the Bolivian in the galley putting on the finishing touches on a gourmet dinner complete with wine.

"Doesn't he ever talk?" Domino asked.

"Ojo? He's a deaf mute. He hears some sounds and can make noise but that's about it. He started working for me years ago."

"No family?"

"He has. Actually he comes from a pretty well fixed background, but this is what he seems to want to do. It works fine for me."

"How about girlfriends?"

"Oh, he's quite normal. Maybe too normal. He has a girlfriend in Bolivia. They may get married once things settle down."

"Have you ever thought of leading a normal life?"

Amison shook his head. "I don't know if that's in the cards for me anymore. But what about you, Domino? What do you want in life?"

"Every woman needs a family and home to care for, Ruby. That's all I want or ever wanted. I need to be owned by someone, so I can be a wife and mother with a nice home like everyone else. What do you want, Ruby?"

"I'm in too deep a mess to want anything more than to survive this thing."

"You can cut and run," said Domino.

"That's not going to work. Not anymore. I made commitments. Too many good people are going to be picked off one by one if I run."

"This is all connected to that damn Bimini Man thing, isn't it? It's going to kill us all."

Amison winced.

"Perhaps, we can put this away until tomorrow, Domino?"

"Can we at least drink to a happy future?"

"Yes. We can drink to a happy future, but with no guarantees."

Domino raised her glass. "To a happy future with no guarantees, then."

"To a happy future with no guarantees," echoed Amison.

They awoke early Tuesday morning to the sound of a steady rain and a persistent buzz on the VHF. Ojo was in his quarters and let Amison answer the phone. It was Cecil.

"Are you coming over?"

"Now? I'm having coffee." Amison replied.

"Henry finished his examination of Mark's body. I have to tell you, Henry went into shock when he saw Mark."

"I'll be right over." And he hung up. "Cecil wants me at the barracks. Henry is finished looking at Mark's body."

They dressed and rushed to the landing where they took the ferry to Alice Town and caught up with Frances Douglas at customs. Bob Byrne arrived a few minutes later with her children and those of Domino in the Zodiac that he had used the day before to get to town. It was now tied up at the Chalks landing.

The children were scheduled to take the morning flight to Miami. Despite the ashen skies and heavy rain, the seaplanes were running, but with delays. The tiny Chalks in-transit lounge that was filled with locals and tourists in sweaters and storm slickers waiting for flights to Miami, looking to evacuate the islands before the storm.

"I have incoming news," said Bob. A phone rang on the ticket counter rang and was picked up by a Chalks agent who called Frances.

"Long distance from Florida. My, you are popular today."

"I'll take it inside," Frances said. And she beckoned everyone to follow her to a back room sparsely furnished with a desk with a phone on it, a file cabinet and a few chairs. She picked up the phone on the desk while Domino kept the children entertained in a corner.

The call was from John Dalton in Fort Lauderdale and Frances signaled to Bob Byrne. He took the call and began scribbling notes furiously on a piece of paper lying on the desk. The phone conversation went on for several minutes and the women began readying their children. They could hear the old seaplane off in the distance as it bellowed through the cut, the throaty thundering rumble of its twin engines drowning out all other noises, as it laboriously taxied up the ramp.

There was a grin on Bob Byrne's face when he hung up the phone.

"I think we got something," he said. He showed his notes to Amison.

"Take a look at these dates. When did Guenther's and Douglas's bodies wash ashore?"

He was suddenly aware that Frances was in the room. "I'm sorry, Frances. I intended no insult."

"No insult taken," replied Frances. "My husband's body was recovered January ten, and Luther Guenther's was found December fifteen."

"That's it," he exclaimed. "*Flyer* fueled up once on December fourteen at the Bahia Mar. It fueled up again six hours later, this time at the Marina Marriott. The transactions were billed to Las Olas University in care of Frank Hoffman.

"*Flyer* filled up twice on the ninth of January, once early in the morning and then later that evening. Same deal. The bill goes to Las Olas University in care of Frank. *Flyer* tanked up again, this time early this past Saturday evening at Pier 66. The attendant said he recognized George Gibson on the Hatteras because that was one of its regular pit stops. But he said he was alone. Again, the billing was to the university.

"The attendants at the other fuel piers confirmed that George was on board with some guy with a Latino accent sporting a pony tail. Maybe that was Miguelito. I wonder if Mark was on the boat with George Saturday night."

"Could be, Amison replied. "And if he was, he must have been killed before the boat left Florida. George would have sailed to Bimini and dumped the body in the Bahama Banks where he knew the tidal current would drag it to shore."

"Should George be arrested, boss?" Bob Byrne asked.

"No. Let's monitor his activities. He's bound to make another move."

"What does it mean?" asked Domino.

"Mark died in Florida," Amison answered. "And his killer is here, with *Flyer*."

"The Hatteras is probably around somewhere right now." Bob noted.

"Do you think Luther and Dwayne were also killed in Florida?" Frances wanted to know.

Amison nodded, "That's how it seems."

They stood by pensively for a few moments. The children grew restless.

"We should do something," said Domino.

"We sit tight," replied Amison. "You girls get the kids off to Miami. Bob will help you. I'm going to see Cecil at the police barracks."

"What about Mike Quinn?" Bob Byrne reminded him.

"He'll be here. You can count on it. When he does, be nice and do nothing. He can kill you before you blink. Just watch him closely."

"What about penetrating the dig site?" Byrne asked. "We should be able to get in at night."

Frances shook her head. "We talked about it last night. It's too dangerous. Right now, we have to get the kids on the plane." She pointed to the wall clock. "And we have to take care of the passengers."

"I'll help you," said Domino. Then she asked Amison, "Are you going to see Cecil now?"

"Yes," replied Amison as they got up. "But I can wait until you're finished so you can drop me off."

"Cecil left his jeep here," said Frances. "I can drop you off at the barracks after we finish here. Domino and I are going to board up our homes. Bob can stay with me and we'll see what else we can find out about the dig."

"Try to do so without getting killed," warned Amison.

An hour later the four piled into Cecil's jeep and drove up King's Highway to the police barracks in the driving rain. Domino gave Amison a hug and kiss when they reached the barracks.

"What was that for?" he asked.

"It's just to say I love you," she answered.

"You and Frances were supposed to leave with the kids."

"I guess we didn't, did we." She looked at Amison inquiringly. "I'm free later today. Any plans?"

"No plans," replied Amison. "Meet me at the boat this afternoon. I'll think of something."

CHAPTER 24

▼

A MATTER OF EVIDENCE

Amison entered the barracks in time to hear George Gibson telling Cecil, who had just emerged from another room where Mark's body was being kept, that he had spoken earlier to Marlene on his cell phone.

"She's really broken up about Mark's death," he was saying. "She said she knew he would drown in a fishing accident some day because of his diabetic fits. Mark loved to fish, you know."

Amison and Cecil said nothing. Cecil whispered something to one of his men who left the room.

Cecil turned to Amison. "George tells us his cousin wants the body returned to Fort Lauderdale right away for cremation," he stated, nodding George's way. "Is that so, George?"

"Yes. The sooner the better."

Cecil rubbed his chin.

"I agree. However, there are forms to complete before the body can be removed from the Bahamas. We don't have any here, but I've already called Nassau, and they should be here by tomorrow morning. Is that all right?"

"I guess so," replied George. "But when can the body be flown out?"

"Not before tomorrow afternoon at the earliest. Naturally, you or Mark's family must make arrangements for a private charter. The Chalks' seaplane cannot handle the deceased."

"We also have to inform Sidney," Amison chimed in. "He's Mark's brother."

Cecil agreed.

"That's right," he echoed. "We'll get word to him."

These were not the responses George expected. But before he could open up his mouth, the same door from which Cecil had appeared opened again, releasing the smell of burning pipe tobacco followed by Henry Alstrum. He sat himself down at Cecil's desk. The pipe went out and he had to relight it, puffing away strenuously. "One of the few pleasures left to an old man," he said, blowing smoke into the air and throwing his legs on the desk.

"Make yourself comfortable," said Cecil. "Perhaps you would like my job too?"

Henry laughed. "I don't need more headaches at my age."

Suddenly, the smile left his face.

"Shall we talk about Mark Stone?"

Cecil interrupted, saying to George, "Can you wait in the next room, George?"

George was hesitant. "What about Mark's body?"

"It's not going anyplace," replied Cecil. "And don't you go, either. I want to talk to you after speaking with Mr. Jones."

George reluctantly left for the front office where Cecil made sure a constable was on hand to watch him.

Cecil mopped his brow and sat down on a spare chair.

"Incidentally, Jonesey. I called Luis Santiago who brought me up to date. He's quite broken up over this. He called Sid who I understand is enraged. He's looking for blood."

"I don't blame him," said Amison. He sat down near the desk and gazed out the window. "Tell me, Henry. Have you seen Dudley?"

"No. Have you? He's been gone since Saturday. Have you seen him?"

"He followed me to Fort Lauderdale. He and Vince Neals tried to take me down Saturday night. Incidentally, Cecil, I did get to see the beginning of La Boheme. It wasn't bad. Maybe with luck I'll get to see the ending someday. Anyway, Dudley and Vince are history. Mark is dead. Our body count is rising, gentlemen."

Henry's eyes widened. "You killed Dudley?"

Amison turned away from the window.

"You're going to need another medical assistant, Henry. But that's not the issue. I just keep wondering who exactly Dudley was working for. I thought you might be able to shed some light on that."

"I don't know, Jones. Do you know who you're working for?"

"I thought I did, but I'm not sure anymore. With what's going on, I'd be better off working for myself."

Cecil shook his head.

"I don't believe what I'm hearing. Can we talk about my problems in the next room before we start jumping to stupid conclusions?"

Henry pulled something out of his pocket. "It's strange. I found a tuxedo shirt stud on the body."

"And I found an undone black bow tie in his hand," Amison added, taking it out of his pocket and throwing it on the table.

"There was also a brass button from a blazer. When Dudley met up with me, he was wearing a tuxedo without a bow tie and his shirt was partly open. I also saw Marlene on Sunday. She had on George's blazer; it was missing a button. I'm placing Mark's time of death between the late afternoon and early evening on Saturday because Dudley was at the theater when the curtain went up."

There was a long moment of silence before Cecil asked. "Were only two people mixed up with Mark' death?"

"Possibly."

Cecil mulled the matter over in his mind and then asked, "Should we at least hold George for questioning?"

Amison turned away from the window. "No, leave him be for now. Henry, what did your examination find?"

Henry shook out his pipe ashes into an ash tray. "This is an odd case," he said.

"Odd?"

"Yes. First, Mark did not drown. When someone drowns, water is ingested into the lungs. Even without an autopsy, it's possible to push water out by pressing the belly. Very little came out of Mark's mouth. He suffered a forehead contusion, but it was from a fall and not from a blow to the head."

"Where did he fall?"

"In shallow water. A river bank perhaps. His head went into the water but not the rest of his body. He had to have died near an inland estuary subject to tidal currents because the water was brackish. It wasn't sea water. There are no such estuaries here. The closest ones are in Florida."

Henry looked pointedly at Amison.

"There are similarities between his death and those of Luther and Dwayne. But they were obviously murdered. Mark's case is different."

"Why do you say that, doctor?" Cecil asked.

"I couldn't find marks on his body suggesting a struggle."

"What about the bow tie, button and stud?"

Henry struck his pipe on the side of the table.

"It's a matter of evidence. Those things seem damning but they do not spell out a murder scenario. They could imply that one or two people were trying to hold him up, and in a delirium he put up a struggle. Mark was a diabetic who took daily injections. Both of his arms are scarred from old punctures. I found fresh puncture wounds on his left arm, indicating he gave himself a shot on Saturday. So I ran a toxicology test. The bottom line is that he overdosed, went into shock, suffered cardiac arrest and died.

"Now whether anyone, Dudley or George or both of them, had any intent to kill him is another question. They may have wanted to and their actions may have well accelerated his death, assuming they did nothing to try to keep him alive, but they did not kill him. He was gone when he hit the water. This could end up being a classical case of someone dying just in time to save himself the trouble of being murdered. Or, if Mark was clever enough and his timing was good, he might have staged his own murder just to pin the rap on someone else. We may never really know."

"Then how do you explain his body ending up here?"

"Ah. I can't help you there. You must speak to whoever brought him here."

"This brings me back to Guenther and Douglas. There's no further doubt in my mind that they were murdered, and in the same place in Florida. I can tell by the accumulation of dirt and other debris that stuck to his and to their clothes when they landed on the beach. That stuff isn't from here."

Amison's eyes lit up.

"Mark was around the hotel Saturday afternoon. If that's where he died, there's a good chance that Guenther and Douglas were also killed there."

"Could be. The killings were nothing fancy," said the doctor. "Just plain garden variety type murders by amateurs. They were killed in Florida, placed on a boat and dumped in the Bahama Bank west of here to float in with the tide. We have some bits of flora recovered from their trousers."

Dr. Alstrum pulled an envelope out of his pants pockets and emptied its contents on a sheet of white paper on the desk for all to see.

Cecil shook his head.

"I've never seen this before," he said.

"Right," agreed Henry. "That's because there isn't any in these islands."

Amison took one look and remarked. "This is potter weed. I removed some of the same from Mark's clothing when I found the body. It grows wild along the New River near the Riverside."

"Yes," the doctor confirmed. "Its full name is 'stachytarpheta jamaicus'. It's a wild weed with a pretty blue flower that originated in Jamaica and now grows in Florida. It does not grow in the Bahamas. Now, Jones, were you able to find out anything about those plant residues found on the clothing of Dwayne Douglas and the other fellow?"

Amison nodded. "It was the same potter weed. There's another thing. Semen and other body fluid deposits on their clothes indicate that each had sexual activity with the same two women shortly before they died."

"How do you figure that?" asked Cecil.

"Body and pubic hair and things like that. I had Bob Byrne arrange for a forensic lab to run the tests. Oil residues from a perfume were also found. DNA tests will confirm the evidence if they ever get done. Guenther was killed while having sex with the two women. When Douglas came into the picture a few weeks later, they did a repeat performance. As you noted, the bodies were found fully clothed, and their underwear was askew. Few men ever wear their shorts that way. Even if they get careless, they'll stop and get their shorts on right no matter how rushed they are. The poor bastards were killed having sex, and then their clothes were put back on in a hurry. Bob Byrne believes they were lured out of Bimini to Florida, maybe on the pretext of going to a Europol debriefing. The promise of an orgy made sure they'd make the trip."

"Who were he women at the sex party?" asked Cecil.

"I have my suspicions, but I'm not sure yet."

Cecil's eyes kept shifting from Amison to the physician and back to Amison. "Anything else?"

"Yes. We identified the vessel that carried the bodies to Bimini. It's *Flyer*, and it belongs to Frank Hoffman and George Gibson." It's a big Hatteras. We also know it left Fort Lauderdale Saturday night with George and Miguelito Bencivenga on board.

"How coincidental," said Cecil. "A yacht named *Flyer* put into the harbor early Sunday morning? It's still there. And of course, old man Bencivenga is in town on his yacht."

The doctor relit his pipe and puffed away. "I guess it's party time."

"This places me between a rock and a hard place," Cecil complained.

Amison inhaled deeply and blew circles into the air before crushing his cigarette in the ashtray.

"You're not in such a difficult position, Cecil. This is a old pirate story, nothing more. Instead of gold, we have heroin. In fairy tales we have good and bad guys. In a pirate's tale, we have only bad guys because everyone's after the gold. All we have to do is pick sides. Winner takes all."

Cecil Fergueson pushed his desk chair back so he could watch the rain from the window. Henry's pipe smoke filled the air again, and no one said anything for a long time.

"This seems to be the history of our islands, isn't it?" Cecil sighed.

"Cheer up," Amison said. "History books will make us look romantic."

Cecil rubbed his eyes and did not respond. He turned on the intercom and called the outer office.

"Will you please send Mr. Gibson back in?"

He rose from his chair as George entered.

"George, you're free to go. But stay in Bimini."

"I'm staying until Mark's body is sent back to Florida," George countered.

"You have a one-track mind, George," said Cecil. "I wonder why that is."

The man that Cecil sent out of the room earlier returned, asking to speak with him in private. They walked out and returned a few minutes later.

"I think we're done, George," Cecil declared. "Where are you staying?"

"The Reef Hotel. My partner, Dr. Hoffman arranged it."

George returned to the subject of Mark Stone. "What about the body? Will we be able to fly it back to Florida tomorrow?"

"I can't comment right now. But this gentleman will take you to the Reef."

Cecil pointed to the officer.

George rose to his feet with a disgusted look on his face and was escorted out.

"Strange bird," observed Henry, "And a dangerous one at that."

The others mumbled their agreement.

Cecil moved rapidly on to another subject. "Oh, Jonesey, I told you Jonathan Sykes and Reginald Lang are throwing a dinner reception. It's to honor Henry for his many years of service. Since I hear that you and Domino are an item again, it would be a nice function for you both. Would you care to attend? I can arrange for it."

"Why not," said Amison, winking at Henry. "Thank Lang and the commissioner for us. We would love to attend."

Henry added. "It would certainly be a treat to have you two there."

He looked at his watch. "If you don't mind, I have some patients to visit. I'll see you at the dinner tomorrow evening. And gentlemen. Let's keep an open mind on Mark Stone. I think it's important for George and Miguelito to be questioned. If they removed his body from Florida they know exactly what happened."

"Incidentally, Jonesey," said Cecil after Henry had left. "The bodies of Dudley Haynes and Vincent Neals were discovered yesterday afternoon in the outskirts of Fort Lauderdale."

Amison looked up open mouthed. "Where did you learn that?"

"Luis called me last night and we talked. That's what we do, Jonesey, we talk and compare notes. After all, we're cops. We're not very smart, but we're cops."

"Damn!"

Cecil returned to the chair vacated by the doctor. "What do we have, Jonesey?"

"We have three dead bodies on ice. We have an archeological hoax and a shit load of heroin. That's what we have, Cecil."

"To help you out," said Cecil, "I had one of my men call Marlene Stone in Fort Lauderdale. She'll be here tomorrow, weather permitting. She didn't know her husband was dead, or so she claims. We informed her. So did Luis.

"George never called her on his cell phone. Cell phones don't work from Bimini to Florida. He didn't use a regular phone because we have no direct dialing and there's no record of calls going through our telephone center to Fort Lauderdale since Friday. A call from a boat radio would have worked but he didn't say that. George is a bad liar."

"That's George," Amison said.

"By the way, how is Frank Hoffman mixed up in all this?"

"He's in over his head and out of his league."

"I figured."

"What about your old girlfriend, Leslie Sandler?"

"She's mixed up somehow with the Bencivengas. I think she's using the Triple A and Bimini Man to further her career and as an umbrella for the Bencivengas who helped finance the dig. I also believe that Sykes and Lang may be dealing with don Ignacio. I think Lang brought in Captain Jack and his Jamaicans in order to keep you and the local police out of the loop."

"Where do you fit in this?" Cecil asked.

"You and Leroux asked me to investigate two possible murders. I've done that. The fact that Guenther and Douglas were murdered has been confirmed. We have two motives. One is heroin, lots of it; the other is a coverup for an archeological excavation which is a fake and a cover for the movement of the heroin from here to Florida. My other orders are from the CIA and from Alliance. They are to close down the dig. I need your help for that, Cecil. What's your position?"

"I thought your government supported the Bencivengas. At least that's the way it was a few weeks ago when we met in Nassau."

"The agenda changed," Amison stated. "Venezuela and our government are no longer chums and Washington wants the Benivengas out of the picture. A quid pro quo with drug lords doesn't sell well these days. So, I'm here to clean house. Isn't that what you wanted, Cecil? That's what you told me when you were having that problem with Captain Jack."

"True. But street sweeping doesn't mean vacuuming away our living. Drugs are a big part of this economy. What happens after you clean up? How do the rest of us make a living?"

"Tourism?"

"Don't make me laugh!" exclaimed Cecil. "You're not stupid. We are a sleepy string of cays, tiny pearls upon the sea. Few know we're around. And fewer care. If the weather is nice, we get visitors. Big money comes in big yachts to fish, drink and get laid. They leave babies but no cash. And those who come on cruise ships don't spend money either. All they do is buy straw hats and T-shirts. The few long term visitors we get are either broke or fugitives. The world class money, we never see. It's buried in the Cayman Islands and spent on the Riviera."

Amison smirked. "And do you think drug dealing will put real money in most Bahamian pockets? I've been here five years, Cecil. Where are all the limousines and big houses in Bimini? Will you get richer if the heroin makes it to Florida and will it really benefit Bimini or only some offshore drug baron in a blazer wearing a piece on a yacht or at his club?"

"Are you any different?"

Amison shook his head. "No. Of course not," he replied quietly.

"Well, what do you propose?"

"You tell me, my police friend."

Cecil slapped his legs with his hands and got up.

"Let's leave it be for a while. I'm motoring out to *Flyer* this afternoon for a look see. How about joining me at about two?"

"Sounds good," said Amison, also rising. I'll meet you in there in my dinghy."

"And, don't forget the dinner reception tomorrow night. It's formal. I hope to see you and Domino there."

CHAPTER 25

▼

THE HARBOR

Gusting winds tossed horizontal torrents of water up and down the street outside the barracks and deep puddles turned into fast streams fed by the overflow from open storm sewers. The raised sidewalks and building overhangs provided little protection from the wind whipped rain that lashed the store fronts. Street flooding made returning to the ferry landing out of the question and Amison opted instead to make his way in the opposite direction to Domino's house, which was closer. The only people to be seen were negotiating zig zag courses around puddles that turned into small lakes. Some were making their way across the partially flooded Kings Highway to the marinas where the thunder of engines could be heard as boats were preparing to race the storm to Florida. Others were threading their way to the Chalks seaplane landing. Those staying behind were frantically boarding up their homes and businesses.

It occurred to Amison that Mike Quinn had not yet surfaced. What was he to do alone with the explosives on board *Phoenix*? He could place and detonate them himself, but without help a clean escape would be difficult. Ojo and Bob Byrne were reliable but he would still be short handed. And Frank's participation was still in doubt.

He reached the house ten minutes later. Domino was there with Frances, Eileen, and Bob Byrne, storm proofing their three small clapboard homes. Amison pitched in, speeding up the process, and the homes were sealed within two hours just as the rain, as if to mock their efforts, slowed to a drizzle.

"I'm surprised," laughed Domino after they were done. "You actually came to chase me down on foot."

"Well," said Amison rapidly, "You are my princess, whom I love and adore and cherish, and I need and want you! But, most of all right now, I need the boat you keep at the dock out there. *Flyer* is anchored in the harbor, and I'm meeting Cecil out there."

"I knew there was a catch," observed Frances.

"All men are sleazy," he grinned. "But tell you what. I aim to reciprocate by inviting all of you to a formal dinner at the Commissioner's residence tomorrow night. Cecil invited Domino and me. Do you guys want an invite?"

"Why thank you, Amison," and Frances smiled. "Cecil asked me yesterday to join him and his wife. We'll probably see you there. Perhaps Bob Byrne can join us also."

"Eileen, what about you? Or, are you going to play Cinderella?"

Eileen laughed. "No. I'm working overtime at the Reef Hotel. Most of the guests are leaving and there's talk we may have to board it up and send everyone away because of the storm."

"But what about the conference?" asked Domino.

Eileen shook her head. "It may have to be called off. We'll know by tomorrow."

Amison looked out the door. "It's not raining and there's no rain, and I need a boat. I'll bring it over to *Phoenix* when I'm done. I should be there by the time you come over. You can bring back the Zodiac."

"It's a Boston Whaler," said Domino. "I thought I'd pack some clothes including a dinner outfit that you could take with you on the boat."

"I'm going to go with Domino," said Bob Byrne. "I'm going to need my duffel for a change of clothes if I'm staying on dry land again tonight. Is that all right, chief? I may even go help Eileen out at the hotel."

Amison nodded. "I won't need you before Thursday."

Domino packed her things in an overnight suitcase that looked as if it had been in the household forever and walked out with Amison to where the runabout was docked.

"The ignition key is under the console, and the two tanks are full. It will take you to Miami if you want."

"One or two miles is all I need."

He jumped into the small boat with her valise, started the out-board motor slung over the Whaler's transom and sped away.

Amison reached *Flyer* before Cecil. It was hard to miss the Hatteras. It was one of the few boats left in the harbor. Its engines were still and it seemed deserted as could be determined by the empty davits on the bow from which the chase boat was missing.

He motored past the yacht on its starboard side and headed for Pigeon cay. The island blocked his view of the Bimini Man dig on a smaller patch of land and he wanted to motor around it. However, it was the muffled drone of outboard motors and the water's constant rocking motion that attracted his attention.

He inched the Whaler into a secluded mangrove cove at the edge of Pigeon Cay and from there he caught a glimpse of a long tender bound for the broad channel separating North and South Bimini to the south east.

Two more tenders appeared at timed intervals, following the same course. Their markings indicated they belonged to the *Casa D'Ora*. Amison guessed they would make their way through the channel bars, cut south and then west and then north around South Bimini to join the mother ship.

Smaller inflatable craft were ferrying what seemed to be sealed containers from the dig site to a waiting fleet of tenders. He was busy counting the boats when he heard the eggbeater sound of another outboard motor nearby. It was Cecil in his police runabout. Amison lifted a finger to his mouth to signal silence and helped Cecil climb on to the Whaler.

"Holy shit," Cecil whispered. "It's an armada out there. This must be the drug haul you are talking about. I never would have believed it without seeing it with my own eyes."

He started counting boats. "There must be ten tenders and thirty dinghies. That's about fifty men to crew the boats. Even if they do double duty, we're looking at sixty maybe seventy armed men. That's more than we can handle."

He pulled out a pair of binoculars to get a better view.

"Look there," he motioned.

Amison took the glasses. He saw anchored north of Porgy Bay, near the Sound, a large gray hulled cutter lying near another yacht. The cutter was Reginald Lang's command vessel and the yacht belonged to don Ignacio Bencivenga. Training the glasses on the cutter, he noted that it was armed and crewed. He slowly turned the glasses to the vessel's bridge where he spotted Lang on the bridge lazily leaning to one side and looking at the proceedings with a satisfied smile on his face.

Two more figures appeared on the bridge, one short, stocky and semi-bald, the other slightly taller and trimmer and with a full head of white hair. The shorter one was Jonathan Sykes. The trimmer taller one was Ignacio Bencivenga.

Amison smacked his lips grimly and returned the glasses to Cecil.

"All the rats are here, Cecil. Let's go see *Flyer*."

Cecil nodded. "You go ahead. I'll follow."

He returned to his boat and followed Amison. They moved away cautiously and quietly and circled back until they reached *Flyer's* transom, never noticing that all the while its chase boat was creeping up silently behind them.

A voice, speaking in a crisp South American accent, said, "Bienvenidos, senores Fergueson y Jones."

Amison turned to find himself staring at the front end of a shotgun barrel. At the other end stood Miguelito Bencivenga, shotgun in one hand and the chase boat's wheel in the other. A large diamond signet ring adorned the hand on the wheel.

"I would like to give you a special tour of *Flyer*, my friends. Por favor, tie a line to the end of my boat and climb aboard. If you make a bad move, I will blow away your brains, right away."

Amison motioned to Cecil. "Don't do anything stupid. This guy shoots, and he doesn't always miss."

"Thank you, senor Jones. It is always a pleasure to work with a professional like you."

They obligingly tied their boats up to *Flyer's* chase boat and climbed aboard under Miguelito's watchful eye.

"Tie the boat up to Flyer's stern," ordered Miguelito.

Again, Amison obeyed. He noticed up close that Miguelito was young, in his mid to late twenties and tall like Amison but more solidly built. Curly brown hair hung down his neck in a pony tail and a golden tan covered the exposed parts of his body. He wore a short sleeve shirt over a pair of worn slacks tucked into hiking boots. A long knife was strapped to the outside of his right boot.

Miguelito used the shotgun's muzzle to prod Amison and Cecil up the ladder and over *Flyer's* transom into the cockpit and then up another ladder from the cockpit to the enclosed bridge above the main salon.

Flyer was a spacious ocean going big game fishing machine with twin diesels that could push it at forty knots. Amison figured the vessel as configured must have had a two million dollar price tag when it was delivered new to Frank. This was much more than what a college executive could afford, and certainly more than what a university would be willing to spring for in the name of academic excellence.

He noticed also that *Flyer* had some interesting after-market weapons systems that could possibly be used to wipe out a herd of marauding whales but for which an average college president would have limited use except with which to face a hostile faculty. Moreover, for a vessel intended for fishing charters, its electronics had no fish finder, and *Flyer* had neither outriggers nor a tuna tower.

Thinking back, he thought that *Flyer* was close in appearance to the vessel he and Mark Stone had taken down five years ago. This could have been its sister ship. The Bencivengas must have ordered two vessels, selling this one to Frank. *Flyer* was more than a fast luxury yacht. Like *Phoenix*, it could double as a small warship.

Miguelito picked up another gun, a pistol this time, from a cabinet and herded them back down to the cockpit.

"Forgive me, gentlemen, if I offer you no drinks. I have no time because I must kill el senor Jones right away.

"You!" And he pointed the shotgun at Cecil, "I will let you live Gordo, if you behave. *No tengo*...ah, I have no grudge against you."

"Who's Gordo?" Cecil demanded to know.

"Shut up, Cecil. It means 'fat man'. He's going to let you live," said Amison. Turning to Miguelito, he asked. "Do you mind if we sit while you shoot? We are older and tire easily."

They sat down on one of the banquets lining the cockpit without waiting for a reply.

"Of course, you can sit. You can even say a prayer."

Miguelito sat down also on a opposite banquette opposite them.

"You seem calm very calm, senor Jones. Do you want to know why I am going to shoot you? Do you want to beg for life?"

"Yes," said Amison. "I'm curious, Miguel. Why do you want to kill me?"

"For money, of course. I want to marry."

"Ginny Peters?"

"Si. But my father does not approve. Pero, el senor Vicente Neals. He approves. He will give us ten million dollars for our wedding if we kill you?"

A broad smile broke across young Bencivenga's face.

"He gave us a one million dollar advance so we could get help from our friends."

He made a flourish with the ringed hand that held the pistol.

"Like Dudley Haynes?"

"Si. And Ferdinand Peterson."

Amison grinned. Little Ginny with the big boobs and the small brain. He had under estimated her. But Fred Peterson was a surprise.

It was Cecil who asked the next question.

"Who put the tail on Jones when he went to Philadelphia?"

"Oh that," laughed Miguelito. "It was el Senor Haynes with the assistance of la Senorita Peters. She is Dr. Peterson's ex-wife. And you must have met el senor Winslow, or Bug Man. He is la Senorita Peters's father."

Cecil winced. "Where is Ginny and her dad now?" he asked.

"They are at Bucanneer Point."

"Miguel", asked Amison. "Was it you or your father who put out the contract on my life?"

"No. It is your friends in Nassau, with the blessing of the CIA, who want you dead. They pay me. El senor Neals pays me. It saves my father money."

"How much were you paid to kill my friend, Mark Stone?"

Miguelito jumped up and waved his gun menacingly.

"I never killed your friend! We found him walking behind the hotel in a daze. He was loco and began fighting us when we tried to take him inside."

Tears gathered in Miguelito's eyes.

"I never had anything against el senor Stone. My father hated him and his wife hated him but he was a fine man. My friends George and Dudley liked him too. When he dropped dead at our feet, we had no choice but to put him on Flyer and try to fake a drowning. To leave him with our fingerprints all over his body could have gotten us arrested for a murder we never did. It was a terrible accident."

Amison wanted to believe the young man's story but he could not bring himself to do so. He changed the subject instead.

"Bring me up to date about these fascinating buttons on the console. I've only seen them on torpedo boats and sub chasers."

"Ah," replied Miguelito, smiling and smacking his lips. "That was my idea. *Flyer* carries four torpedoes in special chambers under the bow, and it can drop depth chargers from the back. We have four of them also. Like it?"

"I love it." Amison was humoring him with his usual sarcasm. "Now, I want to beg. Then I want to pray, and then I want a cigarette or a good cigar."

"Enough, enough!" cried Miguelito. "Here. Here. Here's a damn cigarette. He extracted a cigarette from an open pack that was in his shirt pocket, placed it between his lips, and lit it with a lighter that was in another pocket. He tossed it to Amison who took it and started inhaling deeply.

"You want know why I am really killing you?" continued the young man. "It is not my father who commanded me not to touch you. And it is not over drugs or anything like that. I would kill you anyway without being paid."

"I'm glad to hear that from a professional like you," said Amison.

"I'm killing you because you killed Paulito, my older brother, five years ago. Do you remember that?"

"Is that really why you were waiting for me the other day?"

"Si, yes. How come you didn't kill me when you had a chance?"

"Because I promised your father not to."

Miguelito seemed taken aback and fell silent. Finally, he leveled the shotgun at Amison, saying,

"And now, senor Jones, it is time for you to go. You know too much."

Amison finished the cigarette and crushed its remains on the floor of the deck. A slight roll passed under *Flyer* and someone appeared at the top of the transom.

It was Mike Quinn, soaking wet and covered with weeds and mire. He held a knife between his teeth. Miguelito swerved sideways and made a half turn, but too late. The knife was already in his chest. He dropped both guns and tried to extract the knife but he lost his balance. He fell off the deck but managed to hang on to a grab rail with his ring hand.

There was a sad, almost forlorn smile on his face as Amison rushed over and seized the hand to keep him from falling. It was too late. Miguelito slowly and silently slipped out of his grip and sank under the boat. Ripples marked the spot where he disappeared and Amison was left holding the diamond signet ring in his hand.

He unobtrusively placed the ring in his shirt pocket and turned to Mike Quinn. "Thanks. I was beginning to wonder when you'd show."

Mike Quinn walked over to Amison and the two men gave each other high fives. "No blood. Now, that's what I call a clean hit," he said.

Cecil found a pail and mop under the galley in the cabin and filled it with water. He passed it to Amison who proceeded to clean up the few drops of blood that had splattered near the rail.

"Are you living under water these days? Where the hell were you? How did you get here?"

"I flew over on the Lear and brought the cavalry with me."

"You what?"

"I took Anderson and Lawrence. They are going to help lay the explosives at the dig site."

"Damn!"

"Mark Stone is dead," said Cecil.

"That's too bad. He was a good man. Anyway, I hope you guys have some fresh clothes."

"Come over to the cat," Amison said. "We can do something."

"That's good, boss. Now. What's the next move?"

"Please forgive my stupidity," interrupted Cecil. "But what are you going to do about this boat?"

Amison slapped his back. "Loosen up, Cecil," he replied with a grin. "We'll put it to good use."

"You guys are crazy!" said Cecil. "I don't want to know what is going on."

"Then, don't ask. Do you want help getting off the boat?"

"No thanks. I'll help myself out. I'll see you at the commissioner's dinner."

Cecil climbed over the transom and down into the police runabout on the other side of *Flyer's* tender and headed back for Alice Town.

"Cecil is a great guy," commented Amison. "But he's straight and gets nervous in these situations."

Mike Quinn finished cleaning himself off.

"I don't blame him. I get nervous too. This fish factory is ready for a small war. It has torpedoes and depth charges. They may come in handy for us."

"I think it was originally designed to take down the freighter. That must have been Bencivenga's original idea. To sink the freighter with the heroin on board in the Bahama Bank and return for it later. But I'm going to beat him to the punch."

"How is that going to happen?"

"Are you working for me or for O'Brien?"

The cleanup man was non-committal. "It depends. I have nothing against you, Jonesey. This is nothing personal, but O'Brien pays my bills."

"Look at it this way, buddy. There's two billion dollars of heroin at wholesale and its value rises every day. Sol Weinberg wants the first two billion. He paid Alliance for the land, thinking the heroin was part of the deal. But he was crossed. What's more, Leroux wants in. But he's getting nothing beyond the answer to who killed his agents. I'm going to steal the heroin, sell it, pay off Sol Weinberg, and split the profit with all those who join me in this. You can be in or out."

"In alive? Or out dead?"

"That's for you to decide."

"Ok. I'm in. What's the plan?"

Amison grinned and extended his hand which Mike grabbed.

"Welcome aboard. Now, after we blow up the dig site, you'll use *Flyer* to get out of here. Move two charges over to *Phoenix* later and tie them to the stern. Ojo will help you. We'll follow the *Casa D'Ora* to a shallow ledge off the Bank and sink it with torpedoes."

"That simple, huh?"

"That simple."

"You're the boss. But what about the cutter? Is it just going to watch the show?"

"We'll take care of it."

"What's our time line?" Mike Quinn asked.

"Everything must be done by Thursday night. Stay put on *Flyer*. Miguelito's old man doesn't know his kid is dead and won't be looking for him for a while. Leave *Flyer* only to set the charges or to get over to *Phoenix* where Ojo will be on board. "I have a black tie affair tomorrow night, and all the important people in Bimini will be at the dinner. That means the security around the dig will be light. That's when you lay the charges. Bob Byrne is with us and he and Ojo will give you a hand while I'm at the party. I want everything to be in place by Thursday evening. That's when we kiss this place goodby."

"In the middle of the hurricane?"

"Why not? Do you get sea sick?"

"No. Just asking. What about Frank?"

"We'll have to ask him, won't we?"

Amison looked carefully at the shivering Quinn.

"Let's get you over to *Phoenix* for some dry clothes."

CHAPTER 26

▼

WAS CLEOPATRA BLACK

They left *Flyer* as rain began to fall again, motoring to the catamaran in separate boats, Amison in the Whaler and Mike Quinn in the chase boat. Ojo was there with Domino and Bob Byrne when they arrived. After a change of clothes and hot coffee, Amison extracted from his computer printer copies of the reconnaissance photos Jack O'Brien had talked about. Oddly enough, the photos had been sent by Harold Levy and they included several detailed nautical charts. He gave the copies to Mike Quinn.

"This will help you find your way in and around the dig site," he said. And he related to them what had happened from the time of his visit to the barracks to the encounter on *Flyer*.

"So that's where we are," he concluded.

Finally, Bob Byrne asked. "What are the stakes on this?"

Amison explained the deal he had made with Sol Weinberg.

"The price of heroin is going up," he said. "By the time we get to selling the stuff, who knows what our end will be. Certainly it'll be over a hundred million dollars for each of us. You'll have better odds here than with the lottery."

Amison looked at Domino.

"It's a fascinating prospect, isn't it, Robert? Are you in?"

Bob Byrne shrugged.

"We're damned if we do and damned if we don't. So we might as well go for the gold. I'm in."

Mike Quinn nodded. "We don't have much choice, do we?"

Amison made a face and avoided the subject.

"Right now, the thing to do is to batten down before the storm hits. Tomorrow, we'll move *Phoenix* to a hurricane hole east of here."

It was almost dark and still raining heavily. Bob Byrne and Ojo left with Mike Quinn to spend the night aboard the Hatteras and Amison and Domino lay back to relax for a few hours.

"Do you think we'll have a life together after this?" Domino asked afterwards.

"I'm sure," Amison conceded. "I even like your kids."

"I think they like you, too," she added. "Would we live here in Bimini, or do you want to go back to the States?"

"Where you are, I'll be," was his response.

She laughed, and poked his ribs.

"Liar," she said. "All pirates are liars."

"That tickles," he exclaimed, squirming under her fingers.

The sun never came out when they awoke late Wednesday morning. The rain continued to fall, whipped by gale force winds, and a weather advisory broadcast small craft warnings.

Domino called Eileen at the Bimini Reef hotel to find out if she was needed only to be told not to bother because the conference was canceled and the remaining guests evacuated during the night on emergency flights. However, when she called Frances at customs, Cecil who was there said the commissioner's reception was still on.

Cecil got on the phone after Frances. "I hope you guys are coming."

Domino looked at Amison who nodded affirmatively.

"We'll be there with flying colors."

"I've never been to a hurricane party!" Domino said.

Then Frances picked up the customs phone again to tell her sister that Marlene Stone had flown in last night on Chalks.

"That's interesting," reflected Amison after Domino hung up. "We have Frank, and Leslie, and Mark's grieving widow. That's a combination."

"I detect inside knowledge," said Domino. "Right now, shall we move the boat?"

"Yes, it's time." He looked out at the pouring rain. The wind had died down. He walked over to the sideband and sent a message over to *Flyer* for Ojo and Bob Byrne to return, and an hour later, *Phoenix* was moved with its mast down to a protected cove a short distance east of Buccaneer Point.

A path lead from the cove through the woods and brush to the road that ran from Buccaneer Point to the airstrip at the east end of South Bimini where the Lear was parked. There was plenty of time to get ready for the dinner.

A white dinner jacket, a pair of black slacks and a pair of higly polished black boots worked for Amison as did a black wrinkle proof chiffon gown and a pair of spikes for Domino, part of an all-purpose wardrobe she kept in a large drawstring bag. The only thing he added was a throwing knife tucked into his right boot.

They were lucky. The rain stopped when they arrived at the official colonial era government residence. Constables in kid gloves and dress whites greeted them at the door while light music played by an island band in the torch lit gardens behind the home created a tropical mood.

Cecil Fergueson was there with his wife, Charlotte, a pleasant faced woman in her forties. They were accompanied by Frances who, without her glasses, looked attractive in her evening wear.

Cecil reintroduced Amison and Domino to Reginald Lang who kept scowling and could not help but stare enviously at the couple. At Lang's was his adjutant, M. L. Wayne.

Captain Jack, in an open shirt, blazer, slacks and sandals, stood next to Wayne.

The conversation in the smoke filled air centered around the canceled Triple A conference. Lang managed to corner Domino over cocktails to explain that he was on an inspection tour of all government facilities in the Bahamas and had just acquired a new cutter currently in the harbor. He invited her to tour the ship with him after the reception.

Domino listened politely, and every now and then glanced anxiously over at Amison.

Jonathan Sykes appeared, a a short, bald owlish looking man. Next to him was Fred Peterson in dress whites with his jacket lapels covered by an assortment of medals and emblems.

Amison caught Henry Alstrum's eye as the physician mingled with the guests. Dressed in a freshly pressed blazer and looking slightly out of character and out of place, he was paired with Frances Douglas who had arrived with the Ferguesons.

There were late arrivals. One was Ignacio Bencivenga. The others were Frank Hoffman, in a white dinner jacket and black tie, and Leslie Sandler in a long pink gown.

He was about to greet Frank and Leslie when his attention was diverted by a murmur from the corridor. Marlene Stone, arm in arm with George Gibson, were being ushered into the reception area. Marlene wore a gown, but George wore the same blue blazer Marlene had worn Sunday. She had obviously brought it along for George to wear. Amison marveled about Mark Stone. If it was true that he was was not in fact killed, those around him were certainly going out of their way to be murder suspects.

Eileen Douglas, interestingly, showed up on Bob Byrne's arm. Amison thought they made an attractive couple and wondered what Bob would tell his wife when he returned home.

Frances saw Ignacio Bencivenga and almost spilled her cocktail. She made her way through the crowd to Amison and whispered into his ear.

"That white haired gentleman?"

She pointed sideways in Ignacio's direction. "Such a distinguished looking man. Who is that?"

"Ignacio Bencivenga," replied Amison.

"I thought so. He doesn't look like a killer."

Amison shrugged. "Maybe. Maybe not. We'll see."

Instead of returning to where Cecil and his wife stood, Frances remained next to Frank, engaging him in small talk.

Amison wondered if Bencivenga was growing curious about his son.

"You are a fascinating woman, Frances," Frank told her. "And I'd like to spend the rest of the evening with you, but I'm in a bit of trouble here and must speak to Jonesey."

"Of course," smiled Frances. "I understand," and she started to move away.

"Oh, no," protested Hoffman. "This is nothing personal. Please stay. I just must speak with my old buddy."

Frank pigeon holed Amison.

"I need your help here."

"Why? You're good. Can't you handle two women at a time?"

Amison chuckled and looked at Frances.

"Not here!" Frank responded in a whisper.

"This is something like a school home coming," commented Amison as he drew Frank and Frances to a corner of the reception hall. "Everyone you don't want to see is here. Now Frank, tell me about your next cool move."

"Look, I'm in deep shit here."

"I told you that before."

"No. I'm talking about Marlene and Leslie. I can't have them talking together for long. You guys need to engage Leslie while I get Marlene and George to stick with one another."

"You're going to owe me for this, Frank."

"Ok, ok! What?" asked Frank impatiently.

"Mike Quinn is in town and he did Miguelito, but the old man doesn't know it yet."

"Quinn? He's going to kill you."

"Well, I think I gave him a better deal than O'Brien. Hank and Tucker are also in town. So, what do you think, Frank?"

Frank paused. "I do believe I'm due for a career change. What do you want me to do?"

"Mike Quinn is working from *Flyer*. You're going to work with him and help us sink the freighter. This way, you can keep an eye on him."

A uniformed officer, who served as protocol officer for the evening, announced dinner.

Amison pressed on. "Well, how about it?"

"All right. All right. I'm in. Now, go do your thing."

Frank fell back in the crowd with Frances in hand as Amison intercepted Leslie, Marlene and George after making sure that Domino was still chatting with Lang.

"Good evening, George."

Turning to the women, he said, "If it isn't two of my favorite women."

He saw Ignacio Bencivenga tagging along behind them as they walked to the dining hall.

"It's good to see you again, don Ignacio. I hope you find archeology interesting."

"You look well, senor Jones," commented the old man pleasantly. "What a pity you never accepted my offer."

Amison managed to sandwich the two women between himself and don Ignacio while Domino elbowed the old man out of the way and slid over to his side with Reginald Lang tagging along.

When they sat down at the long table, George took a seat to Ignacio's immediate right while Frank sat himself down next to George with Frances on his other side. Lang ended up flanking Domino to his left. The rest of the entourage ended up on the other side of table, leaving the two end chairs for the commissioner and Henry Alstrum.

Jonathan Sykes gave the blessing and Amison muttered under his breath, "Let the games begin."

The dinner was a white glove french service affair with a uniformed waiter for every two guests. The preliminaries, the usual toasts, salutations and dull speeches were mercifully short, and Amison was glad when waiters started serving the main course, a local fish dish with a cheap white wine.

Finally, the commissioner rose to his feet, raised his glass.

"I want to propose three toasts. The first is to our own Dr. Henry Alstrum. The Bahamas is healthier because of him. My second is to Bimini Man and our many foreign friends who come here with money by land and by sea. And my third is to Amison Jones, a visitor from the United States and the scourge of drug traffickers. He has made Bimini a better place."

Soft laughter made its way around the table.

When he was corrected by Cecil who explained that Amison was a resident of the Biminis, the commissioner added, "Well, he is still important, isn't he?"

A murmur of agreement went around the dinner table.

"Tell me, Mr. Jones, what do you think of Bimini's African past?"

Amison just smiled and replied, "Today, anything is possible."

Reginald Lang took over for Sykes.

"I understand, Mr. Jones, that a few people are disputing the findings at the dig. A certain Professor Mark Stone, for example, I am lead to believe. Is that correct?" Cecil cleared his throat.

"Sir, with due respect, we do not know what his beliefs are. The poor gentleman is recently deceased."

"Oh, what a shame," rejoined the commissioner. "Accidental, I'm sure."

"We are not sure at this point, Excellency," answered Cecil.

Frank interrupted. "Again, I think it's inappropriate for us to discuss the late Dr. Stone here. His widow is with us this evening."

"Thank you, Frank," said Marlene in a low voice from the other side of the table.

"You're quite right," said the commissioner.

There was another murmur around the table as waiters began serving.

Cecil whispered in Sykes' ear.

"Dr. Alstrum made an initial inquiry and believes that Professor Stone may have died in Florida."

The commissioner breathed a sigh of relief.

"I'm truly sorry to hear that Professor Stone died, but if he died elsewhere, what is he doing here?"

Sykes spoke in low voice but loud enough for everyone to hear.

"That's what we are trying to determine," said Cecil.

"That's good", continued the commissioner. "But perhaps the body should be returned to its original jurisdiction."

Cecil objected. "With due respect, Commissioner, we would like to request that autopsy be done in Nassau."

Jonathan Sykes was adamant.

"Out of the question!" he insisted. "Let Florida handle it if that is where he died. We don't need an investigation here. It's bad for business."

He smiled at Marlene.

"My deep condolences on your recent loss."

Addressing all the guests at the table, he continued. "We have all worked hard to get the Triple A to hold its meeting here. A shame it had to be canceled. Perhaps it can be re-scheduled at a later time. We have labored five long years with the Las Olas University dig team to bring this project to a successful conclusion. We also owe a special debts of gratitude to our good friend, don Ignacio Bencivenga, who has helped finance this archeological expedition, to Dr. Frank Hoffman and to Las Olas University who organized the project, and to Dr. Leslie Sandler, the project's lead archeologist."

Ignacio Bencivenga and Frank Hoffman bowed their heads in recognition while Leslie smiled broadly.

"But I am interested in Mr. Jones's views. Don't you agree that Bimini Man is good for Bahamian tourism?"

"Definitely uplifting for the Bahamian spirit," added Amison.

"What does that mean?" Lang asked. "Do you question the dig team's findings?"

Amison took a sip of wine and leaned back in his chair.

"I don't question anyone's opinion. Facts have infinite interpretations."

Leslie smiled. "Would you care to elaborate?"

Amison cleared his throat. "Oh, you're the expert, and I defer to you and to Dr. Alstrum. Your minds are much better than mine."

Henry Alstrum cleared his throat. "There is a school of thought that says that all civilization has African roots. For example. Some people think that even Cleopatra was black."

"Was she?" Amison asked.

The commissioner looked past Amison to Domino.

"What do you think, dear lady?"

Domino looked Sykes in the eye. "Would you, a white Caesar, have loved Cleopatra if she was black? Or, would you, a black Caesar, have loved her if she was white?"

"Or, would you, as a white man, have married Cleopatra knowing that she was black?" added Frances Douglas.

"Or would you only have had sex with her?" Eileen asked conclusively.

"Touche!" said Cecil.

Reginald Lang shot him a dirty look.

"What I mean to say is," Domino went on, "that if love is not colored by race or by one's origin, then Caesar's skin tone and Cleopatra's complexion would not matter. Isn't it the same with Bimini Man? Is it so important to prove that he was of one race or another? What difference does it make?"

Lang shook his head.

"Dr. Hoffman's and Dr. Sandler's work in Bimini proves once and for all that the Bahamas is the lost civilization of Atlantis, and that it's inhabitants were African."

Amison nodded.

"Interesting theory, isn't it? What do you think, Dr. Hoffman?"

Frank choked on his drink and Frances slapped his back.

"Whatever works for you works for me," he said.

Henry reached for his pipe. He could no longer resist having a smoke.

"I think," he said, "that Bimini Man stands as a symbol to the fact that there is still much we do not know about our origins. More research and more discoveries will be needed before any firm conclusions can be made."

"I agree completely," Leslie added in support. "This archeological expedition is the first step of a long road to acquiring more knowledge of what went on here a long time ago."

Everyone nodded in agreement. The conversations went back and forth this way until don Ignacio hit a water glass with a spoon to attract attention.

"I wish to propose a toast," he said, standing up and raising a glass of wine.

"To el senor Jones. You are to be congratulated on having made Bimini your residence. You have picked the best pearl in the middle of this great ocean."

He smiled and sat down.

All eyes turned to Amison who responded to Ignacio's toast without standing up.

"Thank you, Don Ignacio," he said. "It's good to see you are well. I offer a salute to Bimini. 'To Bimini Man and beyond,' I say."

Everyone raised their glasses and chanted, "To Bimini Man and beyond."

Bencivenga stared unblinkingly and said nothing but Sykes asked, "Might I ask what special interests you have in the Biminis?"

"Certainly," replied Amison. "Europol has asked me to investigate the deaths of two of their agents. Beyond that, Centurion Trust owns the Bimini Man dig land. It wants guarantees that nothing besides Bimini Man will be removed from the dig site."

The room fell strangely silent. "But I'm sure you have it under control."

The conciliatory and matter-of-fact tone of his words returned the conversation to a semblance of cordiality and the evening wore on.

At last, Amison turned to Domino and said, "It's late. I think we should go." And to Sykes and Lang, he said, "Thanks for the invite. It was great."

"Of course, of course," said the commissioner. And please rest assured that the government of the Bahamas will do everything possible to guarantee the safety of Centurion's investment in the Biminis."

Amison and Domino said their goodbyes and left. Outside the air was cool and damp and overhead street lamps cast a reflected glow on the wet pavement.

Domino whispered into his ear, "I think some people are uneasy about you."

"Not as uneasy as I am."

Cecil joined them minutes later. Charlotte and Frances were still in the powder room when they were met by Lang and his adjutant.

"The commissioner wants all the bodies gone by tomorrow," said Lang. "Can it be arranged?"

"What about Dwayne Douglas? He's a Bahamian," said Cecil.

Frank came out behind Lang with Leslie at his side and sensed trouble.

"Hitch a ride with Marlene and George," he said. "I'll see you at the hotel."

"Don Ignacio is with us."

"Great. Take him along."

He stayed with her until she was joined by Marlene, George and Bencivenga and then positioned himself next to Amison.

"Stay cool," he advised. "Dwayne's widow is here."

Lang burst out laughing.

"That's the answer," His widow is here. Give her body to her so it can be buried. And get rid of Guenther's body. Sykes will sign the papers. And if Stone's widow wants to leave with her dead husband, that's fine too. Understand, Fergueson?"

"Yes, sir," replied Cecil.

Lang walked away and called for his jeep, leaving M. L. Wayne.

"I don't like you, Jones," he declared. "I never did. I think Lang is too generous. I want you out of here by morning. You have a choice. You either sail out of here or you get to share your friend's body bag. I'll take care of you myself."

"Tell me," said Amison."Did you receive top honors when you graduated from the college of idiots?"

"Easy, Jonesey," cautioned Frank.

Bob Byrne, who came out into the street at this moment with Eileen, took up a position directly behind Wayne.

Wayne cursed and pulled a gun.

"Don't do anything stupid, guy," Amison warned.

The adjutant hesitated for a moment, and Cecil stepped between him and Amison.

"Back off, Wayne. Let's not rush into things."

Captain Jack had come outside to lend Wayne support.

"Do you want me to take care of this guy?"

He was about to move when he felt a gun barrel pressed against his temple.

It was Frank with two pistols were in his hands. One was against Sanford Jack's head; the other was trained on the adjutant.

"Let's relax, shall we?"

Sanford Jack backed away.

"Stay cool, folks. Let's keep it cool."

M.L. Wayne took stock of the odds against him. He grabbed the sea captain and lead him away and Frank returned his pistols to their holsters.

Reginald Lang returned at the tail end of the exchange. Sensing there had been a confrontation, he spoke to Cecil directly.

"Fergueson. You can obey orders or resign. Have a good evening, gentlemen!" Lang, Wayne and Captain Jack climbed into a jeep that had arrived for them and drove off.

Cecil scratched his head. He was annoyed and fuming.

"Shit, Jonesey. How did this fight start?"

"Over buried treasure. That's what this is all about."

"Man, you really blew it. You're an arrogant bastard! "Can't you be sensitive? Can't you have more understanding?"

"Sensitive? Understanding? I am blocked at every corner with folks out to kill me, and you want me sensitive and understanding? Give me a break, man? I have a job to do."

"Damn it, Jonesey! Lang, Wayne, Alstrum, me; we stand for the Bahamas. Who do you stand for? Some huge mother fucking country that thinks it can tell every little nation what to do? What gives you guys the right to barge into our lives and rearrange our furniture?

"You come here like you own the place. You take our land, kill our fish, pollute our water, fuck our women and treat our men like shit. Your people can't kick their own drug habit, so you come down here to kick ass! And you want our help? Our cooperation? Well, fuck you, Jones!"

"That's fine with me," said Amison, "Forget the drugs. And forget Bimini Man, because plaster-of-Paris bones are all you'll find. And forget the Bahamas because it's going to be the world's laughing stock. You won't cooperate? Then wait until the media does a job on you with the picture of a baboon holding fake bones in its claws claiming to be descendants of a lost civilization. So, you make up your mind real fast as to what you want for the Bahamas."

Charlotte and Frances emerged at that moment but did not hear the conversation. Frances slid over to Frank's side and took his arm.

"It's ok," Frank said. "Everything's under control, isn't it Jonesey?"

The women knew instinctively from the deteriorating tenor of the dinner talk that words had finally flown between Cecil and Amison. Henry showed up at the same time, puffing nervously on his pipe. He had managed to catch a few words about Dudley Hanes from Lang and Wayne before they drove away.

"I suppose everyone now knows where they stand," he solemnly declared.

He looked sheepishly at Amison. "I'm sorry, Jones. But you know where I stand. I have to support the Bahamian government. It's a pity, but that's the way it has to be. Good luck, anyway."

"I'm truly sorry too, doctor," Amison replied quietly.

There was nothing else to say. A good night, even a grunt, would have been useless at this point.

Everyone left, leaving Amison and Domino to walk in the silence of the night to the dock where their boat was tied to a piling. They climbed aboard and returned to *Phoenix*. Even the moon and stars had ducked for cover.

CHAPTER 27

▼

A MARRIAGE PROPOSAL

"What a bad ending to a nice party," Domino said in the boat on the way back to the catamaran.

"It wasn't good," said Amison. "I noticed that Fred Peterson never opened his mouth. That worries me."

Domino said nothing. After a while she inquired, "Are we spending the night together?"

Amison looked at her. "I was counting on it."

The rain began falling but it was invisible in the darkness. Her back was to him and he could not see the concern that lined her face. They reached the cove where *Phoenix* was concealed when she blurted out, "We're reaching the end of the line, aren't we?"

"End of the line?"

"I mean, what's going to happen to us after this is all over?"

"Love? Travel? Adventure? We could buy a house? Whatever you want?"

"Life with you is an adventure. But I have a family and I need a home. There has to be something beyond love, travel and adventure. And there is this little thing about your wife."

"Well, let's first finish this thing. Alive, there's a future. Dead, there isn't. You can bet I'm not going to leave you. I'm quitting the business. We'll find a place to live and raise the kids. We'll live wherever it makes you happy."

"What about *Phoenix*?"

Amison hesitated for a moment. "We'll sell it," he said.

"And the heroin? If you and your buddies get your hands on it, what makes you different from the others?"

"Maybe I'm not different."

"At least you're honest."

Domino was close enough to see the anguished look on his face. She kissed his head.

"We'll talk about it later," she said softly.

They reached the catamaran and Domino was about to open her mouth to say something else when he placed a finger on her lips.

"There's someone on the boat," he whispered. "The boarding ladder is down."

"It might be Ojo or one of your other buddies," Domino suggested.

"No. They would pull up the ladder behind them."

They climbed on deck where he motioned Domino to stay behind him while he placed himself between her and the companionway. A slight rustling sound came from inside the cabin and a tall, athletic figure in a jet black spandex body suit filled the companionway holding a silencer equipped semi-automatic pistol.

Amison lunged forward, throwing the intruder off balance. He followed up with a quick kick to the stomach and the stranger doubled over, dropping the pistol. The intruder tried to retrieve the gun but a kick to the head threw him backwards on deck. Amison picked up the pistol and passed it to Domino who had stepped out of the shadows.

Looking closer at the intruder in black camouflage, Amison exclaimed, "Well, Dr. Peterson. Is this pistol and silencer part of your medical kit?"

Shaken by Amison's blows, the medical examiner slowly and painfully stumbled to his feet.

"Have a seat, Fred. I want us to have a heart to heart conversation."

Domino held the pistol with both hands and kept it aimed at Peterson's head while he sat down on one of the banquets along the sides of the cockpit with Amison taking a seat opposite him.

"Now, tell me what you're doing here."

Peterson sat up, rubbing the back of his head, unable to look directly at either Amison or Domino. Amison sighed.

"Whose boat did you use to get here, Fred?"

"I used Cecil's skimmer. I told him I had left my medical bag at the reception. He loaned me the one he keeps in the canal by his office."

"How did you find *Phoenix*?" asked Amison.

"I waited around yesterday and watched you guys move it. I didn't know exactly where you were going, but with the mast down I concluded you would be looking for a hurricane hole. This is the only one around here that can fit a boat this size." Amison rose to his feet.

"Fred. What did you propose to do with that pop gun?"

The medical examiner looked fearfully at Domino and nervously ran his tongue over his dry lips.

"Lang sent me to kill you. But Sykes gave the order."

"They're too dumb to be working on their own."

"They have a deal with Marvin Childs of Alliance."

"That's a new one on me," said Amison. "Tell me how that works."

"It just sort of happened. Five years ago Dudley Haynes and George Gibson had the idea of outsmarting everyone and stealing the heroin for themselves. They got together with me, Ginny, my ex-wife, her dad and Miguelito Bencivenga. I had connections in Nassau through Lang and Sykes and Dudley had connections with Marvin Childs. Ginny and her father were in the picture because you kept your boat at their marina and they could keep an eye on you. And Miguelito knew what was going on because he was the one who was moving the heroin from Venezuela to the Bahamas. We also knew he wanted to kill you. That also worked well with Lang whose wife you screwed and whose woman you stole."

Fred looked painfully at Domino who remained poker faced.

"Were you supposed to kill anyone else?" he asked.

Fred looked nervously at Domino. "Yes. I was going to take her down, and Captain Jack was going to take care of her sisters, Ojo and Bob Byrne."

"Does old man Bencivenga, O'Brien or Levy fit in your picture?"

"Only O'Brien. He thinks we're working for him since we promised to kill you.

For some reason he wants you dead in the worse way."

"How about Frank Hoffman, Leslie Sandler and Marlene Stone?" asked Domino.

"Yes, they go too but Sykes does not want them to die in the Bahamas."

The doctor looked pleadingly at Domino and then at Amison.

"Are you going to kill me?"

"Maybe and maybe not. Tell me. Is Cecil clean?"

"Yes."

"And Henry Alstrum?"

"He's a Europol man. He's clean but he's loyal to Leroux."

"I hear what you're telling me." Amison said. "And it's too weird to be a lie. How did you guys know I was going to Philadelphia?"

"Marvin Childs told us."

"Fascinating. What's the connection between Marvin Childs and Bencivenga?"

"I thought you knew. Marvin and don Ignacio are brothers. Dudley is Marvin's son. Marvin is a spoiler. He figures that if we get lucky, he'll get a piece of the action and then use us to go after Harold and take over Alliance. He hates Harold for destroying the Neals family. He also knows that Harold is very fond of you and wants to keep you around. With you gone, Harold loses his best man."

"Now tell me something I don't know. What's supposed to happen with Bimini Man?"

"The entire dig site has been wired. It's going to blow tomorrow at midnight!" Amison was shocked.

"That's what I was supposed to do."

"Your assignment is a sham. Its only purpose was to get you out in the open to be killed. Either I or Mike Quinn were to do the job before the dig goes up. If he failed or reneged, I was to take over. Quinn works for us."

"Mike Quinn seems to work for everyone," Amison noted.

His concentration was broken by the medical examiner last comment. Peterson pulled a knife from an ankle holster at the same time that a red dot appeared on his forehead followed by a single shot from the water.

Amison and Domino hit the deck as Fred's knife slid out of his hand and he fell to the deck.

Amison stuck out his hand to feel Fred's head and mumbled, "Dead,"

They waited a few minutes, listening to a boat motor start up not too far away. Its noise grew fainter as the craft sped away in the darkness.

"Shall I go down below for another gun?" asked Domino.

"No."

Amison jumped to his feet and helped her up.

"This was for Peterson, not for us. The shooter won't be back."

"Do you think it was someone who was at the party?"

"Not hardly. Except for Fred, they don't know where we are."

Domino was crying. "Was it necessary for him to die like that?"

Amison shrugged. This wasn't a social call. But I had no plan to do him in."

She shuddered. "You lead a violent life, Ruby. I don't know if I'm ready for it. I can't take this killing casually as you do."

"I don't take it casually, Domino. I take it seriously. This is the business I'm in."

"But this makes you no better than the killers you hunt down."

"That's right." agreed Amison. "I'm not. I'm part of society's garbage disposal service. We are the insects under civilization's manicured lawns that keep them neat and green. Many of us don't live long enough to see our kids grow up and most of us will never know our grandchildren. That's the business I hope to leave when we marry."

"Is that a proposal, Ruby?"

"Yes," he replied with determination in his voice. "Yes."

"Well, that's the sweetest thing I've heard in a long time."

They stood silently under the Bimini, damp and shivering while the rain continued to fall.

"Let's go down below where it's warm," Domino said.

"Good idea." he noted. "But first, let's place poor Dr. Peterson back in Cecil's boat, start the engine, and send it on its way back into the harbor. Someone will find it before long."

Thursday morning arrived with non-stop rain and wind from the storm that had spun to the north of Bimini and was supposedly breaking up. Stumbling on deck from the warmth of the cabin, Amison discovered the spent shell casing that had gone through the medical examiner's head. He put it in his pocket and returned to the cabin where Domino was preparing coffee and listening to the radio's weather channel.

The storm was weakening but a news bulletin announced that the islands should brace themselves for a possible storm induced sea surge.

"Most of Bimini is at sea level," Domino said. "The last thing we need is a tidal wave."

"We'll deal with that when and if it happens," he grunted.

"That's the problem with you. You don't plan. You insist on working things out as they happen. We need to talk when this is over," she said curtly.

"That's works for me," Amison countered. "You pick the time and place."

Domino finished her coffee and left abruptly in her Whaler to check her house in Alice Town. He listened to the fading noise of the Whaler's motor in the distance and wondered how Mike Quinn, Ojo and Bob Byrne were making out.

He shuddered. If Peterson's story was true, Ojo and Bob Byrne were at risk. So were Hank and Tucker. Quinn might have killed them all by now.

It was panic time. Amison concluded that search parties would soon be looking for Miguelito once Fred's body showed up in Cecil's dinghy, and he worried that others might be aware of *Phoenix's* whereabouts. He had not slept well and was exhausted. He lay down to rest inside the cabin with a revolver by his side and fell into a fitful sleep.

It was lunchtime when he awoke to the clatter of more rain beating down on the boat and the chop-chop sound of a helicopter overhead which he dismissed as a figment of his imagination. He was now worried about Domino who had not yet returned.

Amison called her home on the VHF, but there was no answer. He tried the Reef Hotel to see if by chance she might have gone there despite the fact that the hotel was shut down. A security guard informed him that the facilities were closed until further notice. Guests who decided to stay in Bimini had been booked in Weech's. Neither was Frances Douglas at customs. A recording advised that the office was closed. Neither could he reach Frances and Eileen at their homes.

A signal came in on *Phoenix's* sideband radio as he was putting down the VHF. It was Mike Quinn.

Everything was on schedule, according to the coded signal. The explosives were set to go at off at Eleven that night. The signal went on to inform him that Ojo and Bob Byrne had left a few hours ago to return to the catamaran.

"They never made it back," Amison replied, also in code.

"Do we start looking for them?" inquired the signal.

"No," answered Amison. "Stay put. I'll go out. Is the cutter still around?"

"Yes. It let out more anchor line, and so did I. The water is rising. How is it at your end?"

"Same here. Stay in touch." Amison instructed. "I'll reach you later."

He hung up and went back to the VHF to call Weech's. The front desk confirmed that rooms were reserved for Ignacio Bencivenga, George Gibson, Leslie Sandler and Marlene Stone but that none of them were there.

Amison asked for Frank but he had no reservations there. Something must have happened to him.

"Any new guests arriving?" Amison asked.

"As a matter of fact, yes," the front desk responded. "Ginny Peters and her father checked in. They said it was too dangerous to stay at Buccaneer Point. They took adjoining rooms."

This was news. He checked his revolver to make sure it was loaded and went out on deck. He made his way to *Phoenix's* bow where a spare inflatable with a small outboard motor mounted on its stern was sitting on the starboard hull. He lowered it to the water and sped off to a landing near Weech's where he lashed the dinghy to a piling and walked over to the rooming house on the other side of the road.

CHAPTER 28

▼

CLOSING THE ODDS

The rain started up again, and the street was empty. He went around the building to enter from the rear at the same time that someone was ducking out.

Amison drew his gun and called out, "Hey, Bug Man!"

Bug Man turned and pulled an ugly snub nosed revolver from under his shirt. It was too late. An ear splitting clap of thunder rocked the island the instant Amison fired. Bug Man twisted around and fell dead face down in the mud.

The odds were improving, Amison thought grimly to himself. But did he have enough bullets and luck to win? At any rate, he entered Weech's without looking back. He crept up a flight of stairs and slowly made his way down a dark corridor with its bank of partially opened doors. The hotel guests had apparently left for the day, leaving their doors ajar, as was the custom in Bimini, for the housekeeping staff to enter and fix the rooms.

One door was closed. He listened and heard a female voice humming. It was Ginny. He made sure his gun was ready and knocked on the door.

"Is that you? Come in, Miguelito, the door is open."

He opened it to find her seated at a vanity on the far side of the room applying makeup to her face.

"What happened? I thought you would be here earlier," she said.

Her voice trailed off when she saw Amison in the mirror. Caught unawares, she was surprisingly quick to regain her composure. Ginny stood up and came forward to give him a kiss.

"Ruby," she said dreamily. "I've missed you. I just got back from the States. Are you staying a while?"

"A while," said Amison, "And I did say I was coming back for a little action." He stood still as she slithered up against him and like a perfumed serpent and started hugging and kissing him in a tight hip grinding, open mouthed embrace that almost loosened his false teeth.

"What about Miguelito?" asked Amison.

"Fuck him," she retorted with a sneer on her face. "I gave him his hast week! I even had to bail the dumb shit out of jail over some gun fight he got into. He owes me money for that. I want you now."

Amison gave her an even more resounding kiss and placed his free hand behind her and slowly pulled up the back of her shift. She had no under garments.

"Well, well," he exclaimed, "What have we here?"

She pulled away and sat down on the edge of the bed with her legs slightly spread so that he could see enough but not too much.

"Are you going to do me with your clothes on or are you going to take them off? We don't have much time."

She sat there, humid and ready. She leaned back slightly with her elbows on the bed and one leg slightly raised to reveal a body ready for action. Whatever other qualities Ginny possessed, she was a direct woman and did not require a veneer of imaginary romance to hide her cravings.

But Amison had other things on his mind. He moved nearer to the bed.

"Tell me about how you've been working with Miguelito and with Bug Man and your ex in Bimini to set me up."

Ginny Peters sprang to her feet like a coiled serpent, but Amison punched her in the face, and she fell back on the bed. She assumed a fetal position and started pounding the bedspread and crying.

"You bastard! You son-of-a-bitch! You no good bastard!"

Amison continued. "Now that you know me better, we can talk freely."

Ginny was sobbing hysterically by now. She took her right hand and reached for what Amison thought was a tissue or handkerchief and spun around.

Instead of tissue, she was holding a small pistol in her hand.

"You ass hole!" she cursed. "Why did you have to spoil a good thing? Miguelito was right. You're only good dead. He'll kill you if I don't."

"No he won't, cookie. He's dead."

Ginny started trembling. "You're lying!"

"So is your ex-husband and your ex-husband's friends. And so is Bug Man. I just saw him They are all gone. You're alone, woman."

"You come here to tell me this? You're a bigger ass hole than I thought."

She raised the pistol but a shot rang out from behind Amison.

A small reddish hole appeared in the middle of Ginny's forehead from which blood slowly oozed out as she collapsed on the bed.

Amison turned to see Luis Santiago in ill fitting slickers standing in the doorway with a toothy grin.

"You know, Jonesey. You're a nice guy. How come so many people want to kill you? Is it bad breath?"

"What the hell are you doing here, Luis?"

His brother-in-law gave him his usual toothy smile.

"I'm still your handler even though I'm a thief like you. Cecil called to say that Captain Jack had a small army. He said you needed help so I came over to back up Hank and Tucker. They've fanned out with Quinn and are hitting the Jamaicans one by one when they run into them. That will improve our odds a bit."

"I thought Hank doesn't do guns."

"He uses a knife. He also has a gun. He said he'll shoot them in the back."

Amison smiled. Good old Hank. Always dependable in a pinch.

"How did you wise up to Ginny Peters?"

"I'm a cop, I keep telling you, amigo. Her marina has been under surveillance for the longest while. It ends up that Bug Man isn't her dad. He's a contract killer for the CIA and Ginny works for him. Ginny flew here yesterday from Florida. I followed her in a borrowed chopper this morning as soon as the weather broke."

"Whose chopper is it?"

"Sol Weinberg's. He's the one paying the bills on this trip. He wants to protect his investment."

Luis went over to Ginny and felt her pulse.

"Dead," he said. He went over to the window where he saw Bug Man's body sprawled on the ground below.

"You work fast, Jonesey."

"He drew on me."

"Excuses, excuses!"

He called Cecil Fergueson's office from the phone near Ginny's bed to have him come over for the bodies.

"I have Florida warrants for them," he said. "They were killed resisting arrest."

He looked up at Amison. "You know? I've had some thoughts about Mark."

"What about?"

"The poor guy was in his last days, and he knew it. My gut feeling is that he was going to fake his own murder so that Marlene wouldn't be able to collect on his will and get the hotel."

Amison shook his head. "That's what Henry believes. Miguelito was there when it happened. He confirmed the scenario. However, forget the past. We have some problems here. The Bimini Man site was pre-wired to blow by our mutual friends tonight. Apparently, Quinn was paid to do that job.

"If he set new explosives, the dig area is overloaded. O'Brien's and Alliance's mission to have me blow up Bimini Man was a ruse to hire me to have me killed. They had already made their own arrangements. If our blast sets off their charges, all of North Bimini could be destroyed unless the incoming surge floods the cay."

"Shit, Jonesey. I thought the mission was real. What about Leroux's mandate?"

"That part is legitimate. I think he was really concerned about what happened to his agents," Amison replied.

"He'd like to get his hands on the heroin but he's not mixed up with anyone in this. I'm supposed to be his man to get him a piece of the action. It's the explosion's overkill that concerns me."

Luis whistled. "You're right, Jonesey. We have a problem. Have you heard from Quinn?"

"Yes. He says the place is ready to blow. And incidentally, I offered him a piece of the action if he threw his lot in with us. He said he's in but I think he's playing all ends against the middle for security."

The police inspector winced. "What do I tell Cecil?"

"Nothing until we hear more from Quinn. The saving grace is that he took out Miguelito. Cecil will tell you about it. And Peterson, Ginny's ex-husband, is dead. A sniper in the harbor shot him in my boat when he came to take me out. I set him adrift in Cecil's skimmer."

"Cecil will be thrilled," said Luis. "And so will don Ignacio be thrilled when he hears about Miguelito. I hear he's on the island."

"Right. Now here's one for a chaser. Old man Bencivenga and Marvin Childs are brothers. Marvin's kids have to be Dudley and George. That would be in line with Mark's Atlantis story."

Luis grinned and remarked. "Old Mark wasn't that crazy after all."

Amison sighed.

"No he wasn't. That's history. There's something else, Luis. Domino and her sisters are gone. So are Ojo and Bob Byrne. And Frank, who finally agreed to work with me, is also nowhere to be found."

Luis looked concerned. "That's not good at all. Shall we wait outside for Cecil and the meat wagon? He'll search the area."

"You wait. I'm going back to the boat. Quinn is on *Flyer* waiting to hear from me."

"Are you sure he's thrown his lot with us?"

Amison threw Luis a cynical smile.

"I'm not that concerned any more since the odds changed. Dudley Haynes and Vince Neals are gone, and so are Miguelito, Fred Peterson, Ginny Peters and Bug Man. We'll manage."

"Never underestimate your enemies, Jonesey."

"I never do, Luis. The worst ones are the dumb ones; they're too stupid to plan."

"Assuming Quinn works with us, can he be trusted?"

"It's kind of like the story about the guy and the snake," Amison said.

"What guy and what snake?"

"This guy goes into the woods and sees a snake with a rock on its head. So the snake says, 'Can you please take this stone off my head', which the guy does, and then the snake bites him. And the guy says, ' What did you do that for?' And the snake answers: 'Because I'm a snake!' Like it?"

CHAPTER 29

▼

RESCUE

Amison left Luis and made his way back to the catamaran. No one had returned and there were no messages from Mike Quinn. An hour passed and the rain picked up. He was in the cabin cleaning loading two of his long barreled magnums when a noise outside alerted him.

He got up and peered through the companionway. Several shapes stood at the edge of the clearing near the boat and at the same time he heard an outboard engine drawing closer in the cove.

So much for concealment, he muttered to himself. He ran back into the cabin and ran out again, this time with the two magnums.

"Don't shoot!"

Hands on land and a pair of hands in the cove, all holding automatic weapons, reached for the sky. The men attached to those hands were in camouflage slickers.

"It's the cavalry to the rescue," announced a familiar voice.

Amison looked closer. The whole gang was there. Cecil, Frank, Hank, Luis and Tucker. Mike Quinn was in *Flyer's* chase boat. Cecil called over to him.

"Give us a hand, Jonesey. There's quicksand here!"

Amison put down his guns, jumped off *Phoenix* and carefully lead them through the quagmire to the boat.

Mike Quinn was his usual enigmatic self.

"I figured something was up and that you'd be needing help," he said.

"We've been beating the bushes and improving your odds," Tucker exclaimed, nodding in Hank's direction.

Hank was beaming. "I've been learning about guns."

"The dig site was already wired, Mike. Did you know that?" Amison asked.

Mike Quinn grinned.

"I knew. I set the first round of charges a long time ago. I didn't want to spoil your party but I've been here before. However, don't worry. The new charges are far enough apart so that they won't set off the others. There'll be two separate 'bangs' and you'll love the fireworks. The first set goes at Eleven and the second set will go at Midnight."

Amison felt better. He turned to Cecil and asked, "How did you guys find me?" "Come on, man, give me some credit. I was born here."

"Well, now that you're here, what's up?"

"We don't have time for chit chat. Frank came to see me when he couldn't find Frances and Luis told me everything that's been going on. We arrested one of Captain Jack's guards a few hours ago," Cecil explained.

"He told us they caught two guys snooping around the dig site last night. They must have been Ojo and Bob Byrne. He also said they nabbed Domino, Frances and Eileen early this morning."

"Who is 'they'?"

"Wayne and some of the Jamaicans from the freighter. Lang was at the barracks with the commissioner and old man Bencivenga when someone found Peterson's' body in my boat circling the harbor. I have to tell you, they went crazy."

"I did that job," said Quinn. "I saw a boat leave the docks in your direction, so I followed."

"It's good you did," said Amison. "He pulled a knife. Now, where are they being held?"

Cecil pointed eastward with his rifle.

"At the old customs shack at the edge of the airstrip where Mike's Lear is parked, not far from here," he replied. "I have a truck. Shall we go?"

They left the boat, cut through the brush to the road, climbed into Cecil's truck and drove off. They were almost within sight of the customs hut when they came to a stop. Two bodies with West Indian features lay lead by the side of the road, each with a bullet hole behind the head.

"Someone was here before us," noted Luis, looking around.

"Not us," Tucker whispered. "Hank and I did some reconnaissance here earlier. We didn't see anyone."

They hid the truck in a wooded area at a crook in the road and advanced quietly off its shoulders in the tall grass. Reaching the edge of a clearing about a hundred yards from the customs shack with the Lear standing alone on the runway in the distance, they saw four guards with automatic weapons taking turns walking in a wide circle.

They were suddenly caught by surprise when a fifth guard who was hidden in the brush jumped out from behind them with an automatic rifle poised to fire. There was a dull pop from the side and the guard stopped short in his tracks and fell on his back. Amison turned in time to see Hank waving.

"Shit, Jonesey," Quinn commented. "That guy can shoot when he has to."

Amison was all business.

"Luis, you bring up the rear and watch our backs."

Cecil came over to Amison and asked, "What now?"

Amison whispered, "We get to kill the guards. Where are they from?"

"Jamaicans from the ship. Lang and Sykes wouldn't use Bahamians for this type of job."

They spread out silently in an assault line and crept forward. Amison and Mike Quinn reached two of the guards and in a synchronized sequence from a grotesque ballet, drew knives, they jumped them from behind and slit their throats a single fluid movement. Frank in turn dispatched his target by throwing a knife into his back.

Cecil was not as lucky and had trouble with a guard who started grappling with him. Luis ran to his rescue, yanked the guard's head back and sliced his throat. He took one look at the blood splattered Cecil and laughed.

"You'll live, Cecil. But that's going to be some cleaning bill. I hope Nassau pays it."

Cecil grimaced with pain and hugged his wounded left arm. Leaving him to bring up the rear, the rest advanced in the high grass only to be discovered by two more guards. The guards had the draw on them but never had a chance.

Two shots rang out from the woods and they were both killed instantly.

"Shit," exclaimed Frank, trying to catch his breath. "Who did that?"

"Don't look a gift horse in the mouth" said Amison. "Just keep moving. The guy's either a lousy shot or he's with us."

They reached the shack and Amison peeked into one of the windows. The three sisters were inside, gagged with their wrists bound to ropes slung over a ceiling rafter and tied to an iron collar bolted to the floor. The ropes were taut so that their arms were drawn over their heads and their feet could barely touch the ground. Their dresses were ripped down the front from top to bottom and hung in tatters around their shoulders and hips. Their bras and panties had already been torn off.

Three Jamaicans were inside the hut along with Captain Jack. They alternatively sat and walked around, sometimes pawing the women and taking breaks to guzzle rum from several open bottles on the ground. A gasoline powered chain saw lay next to a red fuel jug on a wooden bench nearby.

Two more ropes hung over the rafter. One had a knotted end that held a pair of hands, wrists and arms complete to the armpits, still oozing blood. The rest of the body, two halves of a torso, a severed head with its eyes and mouth open for what might have been one last mindless scream, was on the cabin floor. The feet, legs, thighs and arms had been sawed off. This had once been Ojo.

The second rope held Bob Byrne, who was gagged and bleeding from several superficial saw wounds.

"Fuckin' Indian," Captain Jack was saying. "He wouldn't talk. That will teach him."

"Are you going to let us do the girls before we kill them?" one of the leering guards asked.

"We're all going to take turns while this guy watches. Then, we're going to carve him up piece by piece," said Captain Jack.

Obscene laughter filled the room. "Why don't we see if these broads can dance. Can we work them over a little?"

"Well…"

"Oh, come on, just for a little fun!"

Captain Jack said nothing. "Use the saw," he said finally. "That will wake the girls up."

A guard grabbed the chain saw off the bench and started it up. Its roar drowned out the knock at the door.

The man holding the saw approached Domino and touched her lightly in the buttocks. She jolted and started to shake her body to avoid the blade. The other men, aroused by her involuntary bump and grind, gathered around.

"Let's give her a little fucking right now. We can do the others later. They'll be nice and hot from watching. They'll be begging for it."

"Loosen the top rope," said another Jamaican, dropping his pants.

"I want to wrap her legs around my ass and do a dance. She's going to love it."

There was another knock, louder this time, which again the men inside the cabin ignored. Finally, there was a third protracted and insistent series of loud knocks at the door.

Sanford Jack looked at the door impatiently.

"Who the hell is that?"

"It must be one of the brothers who wants to get in on the action," said a guard.

There was one final knock and it swung open. Amison stood in the doorway, his magnums drawn. He fired slowly and deliberately as he waded into the hut.

The two side windows were shattered by Frank and Mike outside who emptied their weapons into the guards.

The three Jamaicans fell where they stood, leaving Captain Jack alone in the middle of the hut to nurse a gaping arm wound.

Amison fired another shot and hit Captain Jack's other arm. He could now only watch helplessly as Frank and Luis entered and untied Bob Byrne and the women while Cecil and Mike Quinn kept watch at the door.

"Cut them down," commanded Amison. "I'll take care of the captain."

Without another word, Amison pulled a knife from his boot and with one single stroke he slit the skipper open from crotch to chest. With another he gutted him, dropping his intestines to the floor.

Captain Jack fell on his back, his arms alternatively flailing at the air and gripping his disemboweled belly in a desperate effort to keep more entrails from spilling out.

Amison, in a fit of uncontrollable rage, placed a leg over the skipper's open belly and ground his booted foot into the man's body until he could feel the bones of his spine. Sanford Jack screamed hoarsely as blood erupted from his mouth and body and splattered over Amison's trousers. A few more wrenching screams and it was over.

Amison collapsed panting and shaking on a bench as the women were covered up and carried outside where they broke down and cried hysterically. Bob Byrne was in shock, having lost blood, but his wounds seemed superficial.

Amison regained his control quickly and beckoned Cecil to go and bring the truck over for the women and Bob Byrne.

"Go back and get the truck while we drag the other bodies inside the cabin."

"You won't have to," a soft voice said. "I drove it over."

They turned around to see Henry Alstrum standing at the door.

"Damn," said Cecil. "It was you out there."

The doctor looked at everyone sheepishly.

"Like you, my friend. It was time for me to take a position for the Bahamas."

"Welcome aboard," Amison declared. "You're just in time. We have casualties who need mending."

"What do we do with the bodies?" asked Frank.

"Leave them in the hut," said Amison. We're going to burn it down."

The still sobbing women and Bob Byrne were helped into the truck by Hank and Tucker while Frank grabbed the red fuel jug and doused the floor with gasoline. He lit a match, tossed it and the hut filled instantaneously with flames.

They were in the truck hanging on from all sides, and headed away when they looked back and saw the hut engulfed by fire and smoke.

"The fire will burn itself out long before anyone gets here to try to figure out what happened," Amison noted. "It was a drunken party gone bad. That's what people will think when they get here."

"What now?" asked Cecil.

"Have Henry take you and everyone to Alice Town but drop me, Frank and Mike off at the boat. We're going to move *Phoenix* to the End-Of-The-World Bar. It's time for me to be seen."

"You'll be killed," said Cecil.

"I hope someone tries. That's why I need the visibility"

"What about me?" asked Bob Byrne who was slowly recovering his senses.

"You're going back to Florida alive. Your wife and kids need you alive. Can you fly jets, like a Lear?"

Bob nodded.

"Great. Then, you take the Lear with Hank and fly the women to Florida as soon as they get patched up."

"But the dig…"

"Fuck the dig! You're still part of the team. I want you to take the women out of here. That's an order!"

"Go with it," Luis counseled. "You have to save the women. We're staying here to finish the job."

Bob Byrne pouted but finally agreed.

Cecil had a deep flesh wound that needed attention, but the women were not as hysterical as before.

"Poor Ojo," Domino cried. "They didn't know he couldn't talk."

They drove a few minutes until they reached the narrow path leading to *Phoenix* where Henry let off Amison with Frank, Mike Quinn and Tucker Anderson.

"You're a doctor," said Amison. "You go do your thing now."

The truck drove off to Buccaneer Point where Cecil commandeered the ferry to make a run across the cut. By now the rain seemed to have stopped for good and weather was clearing.

Amison dispatched Mike Quinn with Tucker on the chase boat to *Flyer*, asking them to stand by while he and Frank prepared to move the catamaran.

"Hey, Quinn?" He called out as Mike Quinn departed.

"Yeah?"

"Thanks."

Mike looked back and grinned. "I'm the cleanup guy, remember?"

CHAPTER 30

▼

SHOWDOWN

The cat was underway in minutes, deck lights shining in the waning night. Less than a half hour later, it was secured at an outside slip at Brown's Docks near the End-Of-The-World Bar. Night fell and the wind was light but the water level was steadily rising and *Phoenix's* deck was almost flush with the dock.

Frank looked around.

"I take it we're walking into a trap."

Amison nodded and sat down on a cockpit banquet while Frank relaxed on the lazarette by the stern. Overhead, they heard the Lear as it roared away to Florida with Hank, Bob Byrne and the girls.

A half hour passed and someone did appear on the dock. They sat motionlessly. The stranger on the dock looked to see if anyone was around before jumping aboard only to find himself slammed on the back of the head by Frank's revolver butt.

The intruder fell with a groan and crawled about aimlessly until Amison placed a foot on his back.

"I think this is your partner, George Gibson," he told Frank.

George was armed. Feeling around his body, Amison removed a pistol and while he lay in a daze, he removed the bullets. When George came to, he found himself staring at his own gun in Amison's hand.

"Well, well. What a pleasure. What brings you here, George?"

Amison sat him on a banquet along the side of the cockpit, pulled up a pail, turned it upside down and sat on it facing him. Frank climbed down from his perch on the lazarette and took a seat opposite George.

"Hello, George," said Frank.

George seemed totally confused at seeing Frank and Amison together.

"How would you like to play Russian roulette, George?" asked Amison.

George was terrified and looked imploringly at Frank who asked him, "Would you like a drink, George?"

George opened his mouth to answer and Amison pushed the pistol's silencer end into his mouth.

"What I want now are some answers, George. Why are you here?"

Amison squeezed the trigger. There was a click, but the weapon did not fire.

George tried to speak but his voice was muffled by the gun barrel in his mouth. "I need the portfolio Mark gave you in Fort Lauderdale," he said after Amison removed the pistol from his mouth. "Marlene wants it."

"Why?"

"It's Mark's revised will." George gulped. "Mark wrote Marlene out of the will. It leaves the hotel to Sidney and his life insurance policy to you."

Frank laughed.

"That's why Marlene let you screw her, Jonesey," he said.

Amison glared at Frank and then back at George.

"Ok. Now tell me. Am I looking at Dudley's brother, Marvin Childs' son, and Leslie and Marlene's cousin?"

"Yes," replied George. "My father's brother is don Ignacio. Leslie and Marlene are his daughters through his first wife."

Frank and Amison exchanged glances.

"How did Mark die, George?" Frank asked.

George voice broke. "It was an accident. But you won't believe me so I'm not going to tell you. Mark hated me but I meant him no harm. Marlene loathed him but she would never have killed him. Neither would Leslie even though he tried to stop her tenure at the university."

He started crying.

"Mark had a diabetic fit and died. I never killed him, Jonesey. I swear, I never did."

He moaned and started rocking back and forth.

"I think we have more company," said Frank as another but very familiar shape appeared on the dock.

"My lord!" exclaimed Amison. "Domino! You're supposed to be on the Lear."

"You're here, so I'm here," she replied simply. "Permission to come aboard, skipper?"

"You'll have to let yourself on, cookie. We have George Gibson here."

Domino gingerly jumped aboard, giving him a look. "Oh?"

She gave Amison a kiss. "I'm going to Florida like my sisters, but on *Phoenix*. I'm going below to freshen up. I want to look beautiful for my future husband."

He almost choked, apparently having forgotten his marriage proposal. Domino went below, returning minutes later in a long, wrap around sarong type dress.

There was movement on the dock.

"Are you expecting guests?" Amison asked George.

His voice trailed off as four people materialized on the dock from the shadows, the barrels of their poised weapons glistening in the reflection of *Phoenix's* deck lights.

Amison recognized the accent.

"Buenas noches, senor Jones. May we come aboard?"

It was Ignacio Bencivenga, in blue blazer and white slacks and protected by a large golf umbrella held high over his head by M.L. Wayne.

Wayne held an automatic pistol in his free hand.

Leslie and Marlene flanked Don Ignacio and they too were armed with pistols. They kept them pointed at Amison and Frank while they helped their father aboard.

"I want you to meet my family," said don Ignacio, "and your executioners…my daughters, Marlena and Isabella. You have already met my nephew, George."

"I see you've also brought Frankenstein."

Amison pointed to Wayne who did not respond.

Leslie, who was about Domino's height, slid behind her, put a strangle hold with one hand around her throat and pressed the muzzle of her pistol firmly against her temple.

"I want you to think carefully, senor Jones," don Ignacio said. "If you do not do exactly as we say, your lady will also die."

The old man looked around and sat down.

"I think you should raise your hands, senor Jones and senor Hoffman. Very high in the air. Tell them to raise their hands high, Marlena."

Marlene waved her gun at Amison and Frank who were facing one another. They followed her motioned instructions while George Gibson grabbed his gun back from Amison and scurried to her side.

"Frank tells me you're a little pissed with him. Is that so, don Ignacio?" Amison asked.

"This mess is all his fault," Bencivenga declared. "He could not keep you under control, senor Jones."

"But it didn't have to be that way," said Leslie. "I told Papa that Frank had what it takes to be university president and that Papa should arrange it through his ties with the board of trustees. Once Frank became president, he would help expand Papa's businesses in Florida. Papa was very generous. You ruined everything for us, Ruby. I was going to marry Frank."

Amison grinned. "But I thought Frank was screwing Marlene."

The two women glared at each other.

"Isn't that true, cookie?"

"Ruby, I told you before not to call me that."

Ignacio Bencivenga waved a trembling finger at Amison.

"You are an evil man, senor. Marlena is my younger daughter, my baby. When she married your friend, senor Stone, I helped finance the restoration of his hotel. He seemed nice, a former military man, well educated, and now a professor, even though he once worked against us. I wanted my daughters to marry well. But I was wrong about both men. They were fools.

"What is worse, Marlena's husband did not give me a grandson after all these years, even after I promised not to have him killed after I found out about my Pauli. I originally wanted you, senor Jones, for a husband for either my Isabella or Marlena but that I knew it would never be. You are not nice, but at least you like women and would not betray a trust."

"I feel honored, don Ignacio. Now that I know about your daughters, how do your nephews fit into this family tree?"

"Marvin Childs is my brother who came to your country and changed his name to what it is today. I arranged a job for him at Alliance through the Neals family. It gave me a window into what the CIA and Europol were up to. His sons were, shall we say, comme ci-comme ca from birth and not too bright. As they grew older, I arranged an identity change for one with my good friend, Jonathan Sykes. I had the other raised in Florida. Marlena looks after him."

Amison smiled. "Let me ask you this, don Ignacio. Who killed Luther Guenther and Dwayne Douglas?"

"Marlene and I did them together with the help of Ginny Peters," volunteered Leslie.

"They had to be killed, don't you see? They were with Europol. Dudley tricked each of them into going to Florida for a meeting and George took them to the Riverside on *Flyer*. Luther Guenther was first. George introduced him to Ginny who invited him to a room at the hotel where he could watch us making it together in another room through a see-through mirror. Then, we would come into the same room and give Luther a real party. I sat on his face and let him do his thing while Marlena worked his other end. At the moment he had his orgasm, I squeezed his head between my thighs until he suffocated to death. We then took his body and put it back on *Flyer* where George took it to here to make it look like a drowning. We did the same thing with Dwayne Douglas."

"And Mark Stone?"

"I never killed Mark," Marlene insisted.

"I know you never touched Mark. It was an accident. George told me about it."

"You idiot," Marlene screamed at George.

"I told you to leave him alone. He wasn't going to live long."

"I wanted to be a helper," George cried. "I was only trying to make you happy."

"Imbecile!" Marlene screamed again. "You've made everything more difficult."

"My poor child," said don Ignacio soothingly but sadly. "I wanted the best for my daughters."

"I thought I was really on to something," said Leslie with tears in her eyes. "All my research pointed that pre-historic humans lived somewhere in the Bahamas. When Papa arranged to finance the dig project, that was the greatest thrill of my life. Success would have meant a place in history."

"And tenure," added Amison. "But it really doesn't matter now, does it?"

"Yes," Bencivenga murmured. "It matters little now. The heroin is safe aboard the *Casa D'Ora,* and before the night is over Bimini Man will be a memory and my daughter will have her fame. And we will be rich. And you, gentlemen, will be dead."

"We may be dead, don Ignacio," said Amison. "But, your plan won't work."

"Yes," Frank echoed. "Your plan won't work." He whispered to Amison. "Why won't it work, Jonesey?"

"Yes? And why not?" Don Ignacio asked.

"Because you're the ultimate hypocrite. You set Leslie up, your daughter, for fame and fortune with a fake story about Bimini Man as a cover for all that heroin that you were hiding. You made deals but everyone double crossed you. You hired family and friends for your crazy project but they went off on their own.

And now you're here alone, don Ignacio, with your daughters and your idiot nephew."

Bencivenga smiled. "You forgot my son, Miguelito."

"Ah, Miguelito. He's dead, don Ignacio. Do you want what's left of your family to die?"

The old man's face turned red upon hearing the words. He began to shake.

"He's lying!" said George.

"Ask him to prove it!" cried Marlene.

"I have proof," said Amison. He stood up slowly. "Reach into the left side pocket of my shirt," he said. "The proof is there."

George Gibson went over cautiously and found Miguelito's signet ring in Amison's pocket and held it up. The old man recognized it and screamed.

"Kill him. Kill the woman! Kill them all!"

"George, shoot him," said Leslie.

George was at a loss. "They may still be armed," said Marlene.

"Marlena, check them," her father commanded.

"You'd like that, wouldn't you?" said Frank.

Marlene curled her lips in a cutting smile.

"I know how these guys operate," she said, leveling her gun at both Amison and Frank.

"You have guns in your belts behind your back. I want you to remove them and toss them on deck."

"I thought you and I had a thing, Marlene," said Amison, reaching cautiously for his revolver.

"You're wrong," said Frank, carefully removing his gun. "Marlene is mine."

"No. She's mine now. Leslie can be yours."

"Shut up!" Marlene yelled. "Throw down your guns."

"I would have preferred Leslie, but I'll settle on Wayne here," said Amison. "I've never tried men before."

"I'm going to try don Ignacio if he'll have me," Frank added.

"Frank!" exclaimed Leslie. "Marlene!"

"Shit," said Amison to Leslie. "What about us? Remember that wonderful night in Fort Lauderdale?"

Frank looked at Amison. "Jonesey, you didn't."

"My lips are sealed, Frank. I'll never tell."

"Ruby! Frank!" cried Leslie.

"What the hell is going on?" said Wayne, anticipating trouble.

"I'm going to have to kill you for this, Jonesey," said Frank.

Marlene screamed. "What the hell are you guys doing?"

"Fuck you, Frank!" said Amison.

The two men tossed their weapons gun butt first at an angle toward the ground. Before anyone could react, each had caught the other's revolver by the handle and started firing.

M.L. Wayne fell with a bullet between the eyes from Amison. Don Ignacio fell in a hail of bullets from Frank's gun while Amison shot the gun out of Marlene's hand and then took aim at George.

"Okay, George," said Amison quietly, "You're the man of the hour, now. What's it going to be?"

He grabbed Marlene around the neck and used her as a shield between himself, George and Leslie, who still held Domino by the throat. Ignacio Bencivenga was still alive and struggling feebly to aim and fire his gun.

George took careful aim at Amison to avoid hitting Marlene and squeezed the trigger. There was a click, and George stared stupidly at his weapon.

"Sorry, George," said Amison. "I removed the bullets"

Leslie, distracted by her father crawling about, relaxed her hold on Domino.

That was all Domino needed. She drove an elbow into Leslie's rib cage and spun free. Reaching down between her thighs, she drew a knife and with a toothy grin frozen to her face, she plunged it into Leslie's side.

Don Ignacio's hands shook. He fired and hit Marlene by mistake and she fell.

His second round accidentally hit George, dropping him on the spot. The old man tried to shoot himself but fainted before he could fire again.

Leslie staggered but remained on her feet until a shot from the dock dropped her down the companionway steps.

Amison, Domino and Frank turned to the dock and Mike Quinn who stood there with a double barreled shotgun in one hand and a revolver in the other.

"This is your clean-up man reporting for duty, folks" he said. "I want to thank you all for doing a great job for me. Now good buddies, it's time for the grand finale."

CHAPTER 31

▼

EXODUS

Amison pointed at Mike Quinn's poised weapons. "I guess you decided not to join us after all, huh, Mike?"

"You catch on fast, Jonesey."

"Where's Tucker?"

"Waiting on *Flyer*."

Mike Quinn smiled sadly. "It was a great offer, Jonesey. But I can't go for it. It pains me, Jonesey; it really does."

"Why, Quinn?"

"Promise, commitment, loyalty, old times, Jonesey; I don't know. Jack and I go back a long way and he looked after me when I was sick a few years back and unable to work. He's no bargain, but then neither are you. I've taken the king's shilling and I think I have to do the king's bidding."

He paused and a look of mischief crossed his face.

"But when you get right down to it, I've done enough for him and everyone else. I'm going to keep all that heroin for myself. I guess the bottom line is that I'm as greedy as you. This means I'm going to have to kill you all, including Tucker."

"This entire project was Jack O'Brien's making, wasn't it, Mike?" Frank asked.

"Not really. Many people had the same idea, but they just couldn't get together as a team. They used Bimini Man for their own agendas. The only thing they had in common was their quest for the heroin. It was the pot of gold at the end of the rainbow. I like you guys, but I'm as close to that pot of gold as you are and I want it for myself."

Amison shook his head sadly. "You flew the Lear five years ago, didn't you?"

Quinn lowered his eyes. "Yep. I knew you'd find out sooner or later. That's why I gave you that tip on our flight to Paradise Island. I was Jack's pilot, but I had no idea what was going on until it was all over. And I was never very proud of that day. I'm sorry, Jonesey. I truly am."

"And you were the guy who took a pot shot at me that night in Miami five years ago."

"Yep. But I missed." A strange smile spread over Mike's face.

Amison sat down. Domino was about to go over to him but Mike Quinn waved her away with the shot gun. He went on.

"Vince Neals and Marvin Childs pushed your wife out the window. Harold and Jack were in the next office. Harold was afraid of being blackmailed by Jack, so he did and said nothing."

"What was he afraid of?"

"He had a brief fling with Bernice right after you met her. She got pregnant and had to go for an abortion. Harold was afraid you'd kill him if you found out. Jack knew about it because he was the one who arranged for the abortion."

Amison turned his head up and studied the few stars that began peeking through the thinning cloud cover. His voice was flat and dry.

"Do you plan to kill everyone?"

"Yes. No hard feelings, though. I'm on my own on this gig, like an entrepreneur, Jonesey. Isn't that the American way?"

Amison sighed. "I guess so, Mike. I guess so."

"Look," said Mike Quinn. "I'm a sporting man and I don't like killing you and Frank in cold blood. I personally like you guys and you deserve a sporting chance. So, I'm going to count to 'three' before firing. That should even the odds."

A thin smile curled across Amison's lips. "You think?"

Mike Quinn raised and aimed the shotgun and started counting when a shot rang out behind him. He whirled around to fire but there was only a click. There was a second shot and Mike's knees buckled and he fell on top of the shotgun.

Frank stared open mouthed.

"Well, I'll be damned. Luis Santiago!"

Amison felt a sense of relief but still could not move. Frank patted him on the back, picked up the shotgun and opened it.

"Shit!" he cried. "It was never loaded!"

Luis jumped on deck and yelled.

"How the hell did I know it wasn't loaded?"

There was a mortified expression on his face.

"Don't worry, Luis," said Frank. You did what you had to do. Was it your shot that took down Leslie?"

"You bet. I watched the whole play. It was better than the theater. However, I had backup in case you had trouble."

A creaking noise from the dock diverted their attention. They looked up and saw two men in slickers standing near the boat with several jeeps and vans pulling up behind them.

"Well, it was quite a party," said a familiar voice. "And we certainly learned a lot, didn't we, doctor?"

It was Cecil Fergueson with Henry Alstrum.

It took a while for all the stretchers and body bags to be loaded and removed to the vans. One by one, the vehicles left for the barracks and things slowly returned to as normal as they could get on the catamaran.

"I'm going," the physician declared. "We might just be able to save a few lives. To the rest of you, good luck. And you too, Jones. We'll meet again."

He waved and left quickly with a stretcher in one of the vans while Cecil gave instructions to his other men to help clean up the boat before leaving.

"Where were you guys when we needed you?" Amison asked.

Cecil yawned. "We thought you had everything pretty much under control."

"It was very educational," Luis agreed. Looking around, he added. "Actually, you guys looked pretty good with all those folks trying to kill you. Maybe you should do this for a living, Jonesey. What about you, Domino?"

"I'm ready to retire," said Domino.

Amison sat down with Domino and Frank started helping Fergueson's men mop the deck.

Several more officers arrived in a jeep.

"Is there anything else you want us to do here, chief?" one asked.

"We found bodies at the old airstrip. So we still have a lot of cleaning up to do there. But that has to wait until the storm is over for good."

"Fine," said Cecil. "That will be fine."

"Are there any charges being lodged against anyone?" asked another.

"No. This is the end of a long family feud. Adjutant Wayne, he just got caught in the crossfire, and Domino and these other folks are spectators to a family tragedy."

The officers left and Cecil got up to leave.

"I'm going home. Domino, can I drive you?"

Domino shook her head. "I'm going to Florida to see my kids," she said. "I'm booking passage on the good ship *Phoenix*."

Cecil turned to Luis Santiago.

"Are you hitching a ride with Jonesey to Florida?"

Luis shook his head. "I'm flying Sol Weinberg's chopper back." He turned to Frank and said, "Tucker is on *Flyer*, waiting for you. I don't think he knows what Mike Quinn was up to."

Cecil began walking away and Amison called after him.

"The dig site is going to blow at eleven," he said. "Quinn placed the detonator switches on automatic. There'll be a secondary blast at midnight."

Cecil never looked back. "Let it blow. That end of the island was evacuated days ago. There's nothing left there except some old bones. I'll be fast asleep by then."

Amison turned to Domino and asked. "Are you sure you want to do this?"

"Yes. I don't how this is going to end, Ruby. But I'm in until it does."

Frank checked his watch. "I think we have to go."

"I'll have the chopper over the freighter to mark its location until your vessels close in," said Luis as he left.

"That would work," Amison commented. "*Flyer* will torpedo the vessel and I'll lock on to its position the moment it goes down."

Frank asked. "Anything else?"

"No," said Amison. "*Flyer* leaves westbound through the cut while we go east through the shoals. We'll leave first as soon as we hear the blast at the dig site and make a lot of noise so that the cutter takes off after us. We'll drop the two depth charges that Mike tied to the stern of my hulls. Hopefully, they'll disable or slow down the cutter.

"But whatever happens, when we take off and the cutter starts following, *Flyer* takes off. The *Casa D'Ora's* crew is probably ready to go and standing by for instructions. They'll get an order to leave once we take off. That means we have to work fast. Fire your torpedoes at the ship's mid section. That should break it in two and keep the holds intact."

He noticed Frank's puzzled stare and asked. "Anything else?"

"Where do you think the *Casa D'Ora* will be headed?"

"It has to bear north between the shoals before cutting west to deeper water. Bob Byrne thought it didn't have enough fuel to make it all the way to Florida because it was never intended to return. So go up the North Bimini shoreline and when you catch up with it, don't wait. Sink the damn thing and move on. I'll catch up later."

Frank left and and Amison took a deep breath and looked at his watch. It was almost Eleven. The night sky was clear and it began to look as if the storm had indeed passed to the north. He watched Domino moving about in the cabin and sat down near one of Phoenix's coffee grinder winches and lit a cigarette. Somewhere up in the sky the chop of a departing helicopter could be heard.

Domino came out after a while to sit next to him.

"I heard the story about your wife, Ruby," she said. "I'm terribly sorry."

She slipped her hand over his.

He hesitated for a moment. "It will be ok," he replied. "Everything will be fine."

"It was a terrible thing that happened to you both."

Amison looked at her. She seemed exceptionally beautiful. He placed his arm around her and walked her to the front of the boat.

"I had it coming, and I should have seen it coming. I was rarely around. I'm just kind of surprised my kids never told me."

He took a deep breath.

"I'd like to marry you, Domino. Will you marry me?"

Domino replied but saw he was not listening. They sat there for what seemed an eternity and she knew his mind had left Bimini for somewhere else. But in fact his mind and ears were focused on a sound coming from the north end of the island.

"I know that sound," he said.

It was a dull, subdued thunder, like an advancing heavy artillery barrage.

Amison rose to his feet. Two words left his mouth. "Tidal wave."

The gathering thunder was from a tidal surge on North Bimini's outer shoreline at the top of the island beyond Porgy Bay and the Sound. The surge was cresting and pushing against the mainland. The sound of rapidly moving water grew louder and closer.

"Let's go!" exclaimed Amison. "The water is rising."

The catamaran was tugging madly at its lines and the dock to which it was tied was already under a foot of water. There was no storm, no rain and little wind, and the stars were out, but the water lapped higher and higher at the sides of buildings facing the harbor and started flooding into Alice Town's adjoining streets.

"Oh, my God. My life. My home!" cried Domino.

Amison bounded for the wheelhouse.

"We're leaving! Signal Frank to get going!"

His voice had an urgent ring to it.

"I'm starting the diesels," he said, settling in behind the wheel.

"Drop the lines and stay near the transom. You're going to cut the straps holding the depth charges. You won't hear me so drop them as we pass over the shallows east of here if you see the cutter in pursuit. And hang on tight."

The engines turned over with a throaty rumble. Domino cut the dock lines and *Phoenix* literally leaped into the harbor.

Amison was familiar with tidal surges. They formed around ocean storms and shoved mountains of water n the same direction of the tidal current. This was a low intensity tidal surge. It was sweeping over the island's north end and spilling into the lagoon harbor to create dangerous swell conditions.

He maneuvered *Phoenix* to the middle of the darkened harbor where swells were making the boat sway from side to side as it crossed *Flyer's* bow. He could make out the cutter's dark outline further off behind the Hatteras. Both were swinging and tugging at their anchor lines. A flashing signal from *Flyer* told Amison that their departure had been noted and that they too were getting under way.

Phoenix continued to glide across the harbor which was suddenly filled with noise from loose objects falling in the water and from flimsy structures crumbling under the surge. Now and then splashes could be heard as anything loose on the few boats left swaying at their anchors fell overboard. Bimini's power generation system failed, and lanterns and flashlights flickered in the night and mixed with yells and screams as people groped for higher ground.

An explosion shook the island. It was followed by an orange ball of flame high above to the north that left a lingering glow in the moonless night. There were lesser, secondary explosions but they were muffled by the low wall of water that surged over the top of North Bimini and over the cays in Porgy Bay, engulfing the remains of the archeological excavation.

There was a smile on Amison's face.

"Perhaps we'll see a monument to Bimini Man some day," he said to no one in particular .

Amison took the VHF sender in his hand and moved *Phoenix* with increasing speed eastward across the harbor. "Hey, Lang, Sykes, do you read me, over?"

A static laced voice responded. "Identify!"

"Is this you, Lang?"

"Yes. identify yourself."

"Hello, fuck face! This is the vessel *Phoenix*. Come and get me, mother fucker!"

With those words, Amison turned on *Phoenix's* running lights and revved up its powerful diesels, pushing the throttle levers fast forward for more acceleration. *Phoenix* shook and shot forward like a rocket.

The cutter, ts engines on and idling, had already lifted anchor, and was in hot pursuit in moments, barely missing *Flyer* along the way.

This was what Amison was counting on. He turned around and saw the cutter gaining. He also caught a glimpse of *Flyer* which was proceeding slowly down the harbor past Buccaneer Point and westward to the cut.

The cutter opted to chase down the cat, leaving the Hatteras free to go after the *Casa D'Ora*.

Phoenix was doing thirty knots with little wind resistance. But the sea surge had raised the lagoon's water level so that the cutter could move faster without fear of grounding.

Amison cursed. Foam and spray covered the catamaran which was now passing the area that had been shallow water. Domino feverishly cut the stern lines holding the depth charges and the drums fell in the vessel's wake. The land cleared away on both sides and the cat made a bee line for open water with the cutter on its tail.

Suddenly, there were several explosions and two ghostly gray white geysers could be seen momentarily against the night sky. The cutter's lights dimmed and Amison could see it was no longer following. A happy grin filled his face as he poked his head out of the wheelhouse and shouted.

"We grounded the thing. I bet it buried its propellers."

He could hear the rat-tat-tat of the cutter's machine guns trying to pierce the darkness, the sound growing fainter as the distance between the catamaran and the stranded cutter grew.

Domino made her way next to Amison in the wheelhouse.

"Hang on!" he yelled.

Phoenix made a sharp turn to the south. It rounded South Bimini and bore north to close in on the *Casa D'Ora* which was already on the move, partially lit by the chopper's strobe light above. Visible also were running lights from another fast boat on the freighter's the far side.

Amison guessed it was *Flyer*.

Machine gun fire from the freighter sprayed the area and struck *Phoenix* like a hail storm. Several rounds hit the wheelhouse, tearing at its aluminum sides and shattering its port windows.

The staccato thunder of the freighter's guns grew louder and more insistent as *Phoenix* took a position on its port side.

Flyer was no longer in sight and Amison could not tell if it had taken a hit or if it was lining itself up to deliver its torpedoes on the other. Overhead, Luis had to shut his lights and leave to avoid the gunfire which was now aimed directly at the chopper.

The steamer was now heading for deeper water. Not waiting any longer, Amison gunned his engines and aimed the cat into the larger, lumbering vessel. There was an explosion on the freighter's starboard side.

Flyer scored a hit, but it was not enough to stop the ship as it ploughed on. He his teeth, slammed down the engine throttles and the cat sprang forward. It was about two hundred yards away from the freighter when he pressed a button on the console. Hatch covers strategically positioned near the bow of each hull opened, raising and exposing rocket launchers. He pushed another button and two missiles burst out.

By then *Phoenix* was ploughing through the water so fast that it was too late to come about. Amison turned and grabbed Domino who leaned limply against him. "Let's go!" he yelled. "Jump!"

She did not respond.

He threw her over his shoulders, rushed out of the wheelhouse and jumped overboard seconds before *Phoenix* followed the missiles into the freighter's side. The old ship shuddered, creaked, groaned and broke in two. A deafening roar followed and the *Casa D'Ora* disappeared in a blanket of smoke that was blacker than the night.

There was another explosion from a point further north that Amison suddenly remembered was the detonation set for midnight.

When the air finally cleared, the *Casa D'Ora* was gone and he was alone in the water with Domino. Treading water, he floated around until he could make out a vague shape in the darkness.

It was *Flyer*. A piece of flotsam drifted by which he grabbed with one hand and tried kicking his way to the vessel, supporting Domino in his other arm.

Moments later *Flyer* was within earshot. A roving strobe light from its bridge panned the water until it passed over them. The Hatteras drew closer and Amison could hear the sound of life slings being dropped into the water.

Domino was brought up first followed by Amison. Frank happened to look at a spot in the distance and pointed into the night.

"Well, I'll be damned. Look, old chum. Your boat...*Phoenix*, it's still there!"

Amison turned. It looked like a phantom but he could make out the giant bird's shape. It was the catamaran. It dove through the freighter's severed halves. If not totally whole, it was at least afloat.

But *Phoenix* was of little interest at the moment. He went over and knelt where Domino was lying.

"We made it, sweetheart," he said. "We made it together. Next stop, Florida, and after that, there's just us."

Frank placed a hand on his shoulder as Tucker came over and took her pulse. He looked at Frank and shook his head. They searched for words to tell Amison who, with his eyes closed and tears streaming down his face, began to rock her back and forth in his arms.

Tucker placed his hand on Amison's shoulder.

"She's gone," he said softly. "She's gone, Jonesey."

Amison recoiled so violently that he and Frank drew back.

"Don't mess with me," he screamed. "Or I'll kill you!" He pulled a knife and brandished it at them.

Tucker winked at Frank. "He's right. Domino is fine."

To Amison, he said, "We're going home. So you look after her, you hear?"

"I'm telling you she's going to be all right," Amison kept repeating while he continued to cradle Domino.

"She just needs some rest. She's going to be fine."

Frank and Tucker exchanged glances again. Frank's eyes grew misty and he sniffled.

"Sure, Jonesey, sure," he said.

And Tucker added, "You stay with her while we bring *Phoenix* along side and tow it back to Florida."

They secured the catamaran to *Flyer,* carefully avoiding Amison who rocked slowly back and forth with Domino in his arms.

"Do you think those folks back in Bimini made it?" Tucker asked.

"Yes," Frank replied. "They're island people. They'll cope."

A calm returned and the sea, flat like glass, reflected the stars above. It was time to go home.

▼

RETRIBUTION

Amison's grief was irreconcilable. He wanted revenge and he wanted it fast. It was small comfort that Hank had delivered Bob Byrne and Domino's sisters safely in the Lear. There was an empty space at his side and no one to fill it. Moreover, he had scores to settle.

He was spilling his guts to Tucker Anderson at the Floridian a few weeks later when Luis Santiago caught up with them.

"You know Jonesey," Tucker noted. "You still have a wife to look after."

Amison scowled.

"She's part of the problem, Tuck."

Luis sat down and asked, "What's up, guys?"

"I'm waiting for the repairs on *Phoenix* to be completed," Amison replied.

Luis took a sip of coffee. "Forget the boat, Jonesey. There's still work to do."

"I have to agree," said Tucker. "There's an old saying, if you don't mind my saying. We don't get mad in this business; we get even. Forget everything and set your sights on Jack O'Brien. He has to be taken down."

"Oh, I'll get to it, Tuck. Matter of fact, I'm working on it."

"Look at the bright side, Jonesey," Luis suggested. "We're still alive and kicking, Jonesey. So, it wasn't all bad."

Tucker looked at his watch.

"Yes, and there's all that good heroin waiting for us at the bottom of the sea. So, life can't be all that bad. Well, I have to go. You guys take care, you hear?"

He got up, dropped some money on the table and left Amison and Luis alone. Amison sighed.

"The man's right, you know. We have to keep our eyes on the bouncing ball."

"I suppose. Have you spoken to Sid?

"Yes. He called the other day to tell me about Bernice. He doesn't want to have a funeral for Mark until everything else is settled."

Amison put down his coffee and banged on the table.

"Damn! Luis. I wake up mornings and I feel Domino next to me. I hope things work out. I'd probably kill myself if they didn't."

"Don't you go suicidal like you did when Dolores died. It took you years to get over it. You made a bad call when you remarried. You've hated the world since then. So snap out of it, man!"

Amison's eyes hardened.

"Just like I'd never forget Domino, I'll never forget my first wife. And I'm not suicidal, Luis, not by a long shot."

His face softened and he threw Luis a sly grin and a wink.

"I hate the world and I basically hate people, but I love living."

"Have you spoken to Deborah and Gordon?"

"No. And I don't plan to any time soon. However, I've spoken to Estrella, Ojo's cousin. She's working at the Riverside now but she said she'd drop over and see Debbie the next time she visits her relatives in New Jersey."

"It's a sad day when a father becomes estranged from his own children," Luis observed.

"I realize that," said Amison. "But there are a few problems that still have to be sorted out before we start talking again."

"Talking about problems. What are you going to do about Jack O'Brien and the guys at Alliance?"

"I have a plan. Sid Stone said he'd help. I'm going to need your help also."

He leaned forward and detailed his ideas to Luis.

When he was done, his brother-in-law's jaw's dropped, exposing his gold tooth. "You're as crazy as they come, Jonesey. You're going to be all right. Now, what about the *Casa D'Ora* and all that heroin?"

Amison punched him jovially on the shoulder.

"I'll tell you exactly what I told Sol Weinberg. I know where the boat sank so you better be nice to me."

They parted company and Amison returned to the Riverside where he was acting as a surrogate for Sid who was busy up north in New Jersey. He hated office work, but felt he owed Sid a favor.

He was uncomfortable at the keyhole desk in the executive office. He found it difficult to press his long legs into the space provided between the side drawers. It might have been the right size for Marlene but it was wrong for him. The chair was too small for his lanky frame, forcing him to hunch forward on the edge of the seat and place his elbows on the desk blotter to hold the soggy slice of pizza that was lunch.

His elbows ached and he stopped to study the old tatoo on his bare arm. Damn! He thought to himself. Doesn't that thing ever wear off?

He shook his head in a vague motion of disgust and scratched his head. So this was how life winds down. The private intercom phone rang. It was Charlie Kane.

"I have Sid Stone from the nursing home in New Jersey on the line, Mr. Jones. Do you want to speak to him?"

Again, he cursed silently. He never liked nor trusted Charlie Kane, the slope shouldered, pot bellied, former Washington civil servant with the face of a gopher. But the man had been recommended by Jack O'Brien and placed in the job. That situation too had to be resolved.

But it was as Luis once told him, "What the hell. Jack sees us, and we see him. Charlie is stupid. We'll use him."

"Put him through," Amison said.

The conversation was about Bernice. It was brief. He fancied he heard a double click on the line and smiled.

He finished the pizza before exiting through a side door to the administrative offices with a wall of one-way glass to offer a view of what was going on out at the registration counter and in the lobby. He found Charlie Kane there who was about ready to leave.

"Where are you headed, Charlie?"

"Lunch," the manager replied.

"Oh yeah? Take a long one. You deserve it. You're a hard worker."

"You mean that?"

Amison slapped the man on the back. "You're Ok, Charlie. Now, before you leave, call Continental and get me on the first flight Monday morning to Newark. I'm going to see Bernice."

"I'm glad she's better, boss."

Amison smiled and looked quizzically at his manager.

"Yes. Are you doing anything special Monday?"

Charlie shook his head. "Vacation. John Talbot will be covering."

"I know that." Amison added. "I need you to take me to the airport. Do you mind?"

"No, boss. Not at all. That will be fine."

He waited until Charlie had left before returning to his office and going out-side through a back door where he called Sid on his cell phone from the street to say he would be arriving late Monday morning.

He returned to the hotel and holed up in the large second floor suite reserved for him by Sid, emerging only for meals at the Indigo. It was not a bad apart-ment, he had to grudgingly admit. It seemed like years ago that he and Mark Stone had sat at a table at the hotel's Indigo café having their last meal together under that same balcony.

He awoke before dawn Monday, cleaned himself up, packed a small duffel, donned an old blue suit over a short sleeve shirt and red tie and stuffed a pair of surgical gloves into his jacket pocket before descending downstairs to the lobby. He looked to the left where John Talbot was standing behind the registration desk facing the empty lobby. He quietly ducked out through the livery entrance where he found Charlie Kane waiting near an old, beat up brown sedan with its engine running.

"Let's go."

Amison jumped into the front seat on the passenger side and Charlie jumped in behind the wheel, his jacket opening up just enough to reveal the butt of a pis-tol sticking maliciously out of a shoulder holster.

It was early, and the brown sedan was the only thing moving on the streets. Overhead, the skies were shrugging off the night in advance of a pulsating ball of flame rising over the sea to the east. The bright sun's glow broke against the city's gleaming towers that threw cool, protective shadows over the expensive mansions and yachts below lining the New River and its tributary canals.

"It's early," Amison declared, checking his watch. "Let's stop at Chinnock's on the river. I want to see what they're doing with *Phoenix*."

"Are you planning a trip on the cat?"

"Not right away. But I want to have a look see anyway."

They headed west along the road that paralleled the New River until they passed a clearing and a deserted boat ramp that lay between a municipal marina and the boat yard. An inflatable Zodiac equipped with an outboard motor was tied to a piling off to the ramp's side.

Charlie Kane pointed to the unoccupied dinghy, failing to notice that Amison had put on his surgical gloves.

"Who would have left an expensive thing like that unattended?" he asked.

"Let's have a look," Amison suggested innocently.

Charlie drove the car to the edge of the ramp and put it in neutral. He was about to open the door when Amison reached into the manager's jacket and removed his gun. Caught by surprise, the Riverside's hotel manager sank back into the driver's seat. "What are you doing, boss?"

Amison held the weapon against his sweating temple. "I don't know, Charlie. What's with the gun?"

"I...I have a permit. I thought I might need it in self defense."

"Poor Charlie Kane." Amison shook his head sadly. "You're a good man, but I don't think I need you any more. And if I don't fire you now, I'd just have to fire you later."

Charlie started sweating.

"I don't know what you mean. What did I do?"

"It's not nice to eavesdrop," Amison reminded him.

Charlie started crying.

"I didn't do anything," he blubbered repeatedly.

"How else could you have known that Bernice was all better unless you were listened to my conversation with Sid?"

Charlie opened his mouth to answer only to find the pistol's business end rammed into it.

Amison shook the gun barrel around in Charlie's mouth. "Are you right handed or left handed, Charlie?"

Charlie Kane made a feeble effort to raise his right arm when the gun went off with a dull pop that scared off a flock of birds grousing nearby. The bullet went through the roof of his mouth and out the top of his head and lodged itself in the car's upholstered ceiling.

Amison removed the pistol from the hotel manager's mouth and let him slump forward against the steering wheel. He placed the gun in the dead man's right hand, got out of the idling car with his duffel, opened the windows, and pushed it down the ramp and into the river where it sank.

It was over. Amison gathered his duffel, went over to the Zodiac, threw it into the dinghy, climbed in and started the outboard motor. Minutes later, he arrived at Chinnock's where he was greeted by Luis who helped him secure the inflatable to a vacant dock and walked with him over to the street. Luis was already dressed for work, immaculate as always in a highly styled dark silk suit, tailored to his burly athletic frame, a french cuffed shirt with contrasting tie, and a pair of expensive lizard loafers.

"Dressed for a special occasion, Luis?"

Luis smiled. "This is a special occasion," he said.

"You know, Luis," Amison reflected as they walked through the boat yard which had not yet opened for the day. "Style is important. Now Charlie Kane. He had no style."

Luis scratched his bald head and threw Amison a Cheshire cat grin under his dark pencil thin moustache.

"Jack is going to need a classier pigeon the next time, more in keeping with the Riverside's image."

Amison looked at Luis inquiringly. "You think?"

"I know. That's why I'm Broward County's homicide police inspector. Now let's get you to your flight."

Luis dropped Amison off at the airport in time for the Newark flight. Amison grabbed his duffel and made his way to the Continental boarding gate where a few minutes later he found himself staring into Jack O'Brien's cold blue eyes. So, the late Charlie Kane had indeed blown the whistle. Good.

"What an unexpected pleasure," said Amison. "I thought you were dead?"

"No. Just recently retired," said Jack. "And my being here is a coincidence. I settled on this flight after I couldn't get one to Philadelphia. I have a rental car at Newark Airport to drive the rest of the way. I have a Tuesday meeting with Harold Levy at Alliance. What are you doing here?"

"Oh, I'm going to pick my wife up. She's being discharged today."

"She's all better, I take it."

"She's fine, and she has her memory back."

"That's great," Jack said. "Thank god. I'm glad to hear that."

They boarded together and took adjoining seats in the half-full cabin and continued their small talk during take-off. The flight was smooth, but Jack, who sat in the window seat was irksome. He kept trying to press for details about the Bimini affair and then started discussing his own post retirement plans.

"You know, this retirement thing?" Jack was saying. "At first, I was resentful when my resignation was accepted. I never thought they would. After all, I was the guy who put the whole Bimini mission together. You'd think they'd show some gratitude. Anyway, I'm treating this as a new lease on life. In many ways I'm glad I never married. Too busy. I never would have had time for a wife and kids."

"That's too bad, Jack." Amison was barely listening. He was trying to read the Sun Sentinel's early morning edition over Jack's shoulder.

A news item about a proposal to build a monument to Bimini Man's memory on the dig site caught his eye.

Jack put down the paper and sighed nostalgically.

"I liked the old days better. When the CIA goofed then, we simply killed a few people, staged a coverup and started over again. No one gave a damn."

"But I have to say," Jack went on. "Retirement is the best thing happening to me. Harold asked me to join Alliance. If the job comes through, it will keep me in the thick of things. By the way, you never told me about the location of that load of sealed heroin that went down with the *Casa D'Ora* off Bimini. That heroin is government property, you know."

"But you're not with the government any more, are you?"

"That's correct; but I'm going to be around for a long time."

Amison sounded cheerful. "Not a problem."

He pulled a blank card from his suit jacket's inside pocket and scribbled down some numbers and passed the card to Jack.

"These are the coordinates, right at the edge of the Bahama Bank. However, I know the precise location."

"That means the haul is either in one hundred feet of water or down over a mile under the Gulf Stream."

"That's the luck of the draw, Jack. You may want to keep me alive for a while."

"Perhaps you and I can make a deal once I'm with Alliance."

"Perhaps."

Jack's lips were parched and he ordered a double bourbon. He finished the drink and was soon fast asleep and snoring.

It was the mid-morning when they landed in gray, snowy weather. Jack collected his bags at the luggage carousel and the two left the terminal on a shuttle bus to the Hertz rental depot where Jack had his car waiting.

"Tell you what, Jonesey," he said. "I'll drive you to see Bernice and then drop you guys off at your daughter's house before heading for Philadelphia. What do you say, huh?"

"Sounds good to me."

"But you drive. I'm tired."

Amison accepted, wondering all the while where Jack might have hidden a gun. This was still the same old Jack, skilled, dangerous, casual and courteous.

The shuttle dropped them off at the car, and Amison, out of habit as the slightly junior traveling partner, did the honors stuffing their bags into the trunk while O'Brien waited in the car studying a road map. They were off less than a half hour later.

Jack mumbled something about wanting to take a short detour to a government office at the Gateway in downtown Newark to pick up a file for his Philadelphia meeting.

Amison smiled and said nothing. He pulled the car off the highway and threaded his way through the city's shopping district to the Gateway building adjoining the Hilton hotel and Newark's Pennsylvania train station.

They parked in front of the building and Amison waited in the car until Jack returned. He went directly to the car trunk, opened it, put something inside and then shut it after a few seconds. Jack finally appeared on the passenger side and climbed in.

"I bought a box of sweets for Bernice," he said. "I hope she'll like them."

They were back on the highway in minutes and heading west on the interstate in light snow when Jack complained about having to go to the bathroom.

"That damn drink," he said.

Amison drove on a while and then left the highway for a fast food restaurant where he stopped to allow Jack to find a rest room.

With him out of sight, Amison went to the rear of the car, opened the trunk and rummaged inside. He closed the trunk a few moments later and returned to his seat before Jack returned. They drove off again and Jack fell asleep again, waking up when the car pulled up in front of Sid's nursing home and rehabilitation center an hour later.

Sid Stone owned a chain of pharmacies, beauty salons and a general distribution business. He owned the nursing home and improved its bottom line by installing a full service rehabilitation facility equipped to handle transients as well as chronic cases like Bernice's.

"I'm going to drive around back," said Amison. "This way she won't have much of a walk."

He followed the road around the side of the building and to its rear and parked at a loading platform where an EMS vehicle was stationed with its back against it. Sid was standing there to greet them. He was over six feet tall with a full head of straight, dyed black hair and dark probing eyes set in a large bony head.

He peered into the car and looked first at Amison and then at Jack.

"What a surprise," he said. "Frick and Frack together."

"I met Jack at the airport. He's heading for Philadelphia to meet with Harold Levy. He kindly offered to drive me here to pick up Bernice."

"How cozy. I'm sure she'll be thrilled by all this company. Why don't you guys leave the car where it is. You won't be here long."

He pulled his long frame away from the car and opened the door.

Amison turned off the ignition and they got out of the car.

Jack O'Brien pointed to the trunk. I bought something for Bernice, a box of sweets. Give me a moment to get the box."

"No problem," said Amison as Jack went to the back of the car, opened the trunk and retrieved the box and cradled it in his left arm.

They followed Sid Stone into the building where they walked down an empty hallway to a service elevator that took them down two floors to another network of halls on either side of which were private hospital rooms that appeared empty. The only noise to be heard was their footsteps echoing in the deserted corridors.

"No full house?" asked Jack.

"Not these days. That's good for the world, but not so good for us," said Sid. "I have your wife down here Jonesey. This is where we have the best and the largest suites where she's able to walk right out to our gardens in the back."

They walked down another hallway, passing a short, muscular man with dark porcupine hair and swarthy Indian features who was mopping the floors.

Sid complimented him.

"Nice work, Gonzo." Turning to Jack, he said, "Gonzo is a Bolivian Indian."

Gonzo smiled and winked at Amison who nodded as they were lead to a room whose door was slightly ajar. Sid's voice dropped to a whisper.

"This is it," he motioned to the door. "I'm going to leave you guys here. Come upstairs whenever you're ready to leave. And take your time; she's still weak."

He walked away and left them alone.

Amison took a deep breath. "I'm going in," he said in a low voice. "Wait here until we're ready. I don't want my wife to see two people at the same time."

"I understand," responded Jack O'Brien.

Amison knocked softly upon the half open door.

"Come in," A female voice replied weakly.

Amison entered the dimly lit room, closed the door softly behind him and put on the surgical gloves that he had in his pocket.

Minutes went by and Jack kept standing outside. Finally, he opened the door and slipped in.

"Hello, Jack," said a faltering female voice from the direction of the bed. "I can't believe it's been five years since Vincent and Marvin threw me out that office window while you and Harold sat and watched."

Jack moved on instinct. He quick-drew a pistol from the gift box, aimed at the bed and squeezed the trigger. There was a click. He never noticed that the bed was empty.

Amison stepped out of the shadows. "I'm sorry, Jack, real sorry. My wife died a few days ago. It's too bad. I had wanted to hear you talking about all those times you had with her while I was away. I also wanted to hear how much money she moved for you as your bag woman."

O'Brien noticed that Amison was wearing his gloves. He spun around, aimed the pistol at Amison and squeezed the trigger again.

There was a second click!

"So you were going to kill Bernice because she knew too much and also knew you were a queer. Well, fuck you, you goddam faggot!"

Jack was not listening. He stared at the gun in his hand and slapped it before quickly squeezing the trigger again.

A third click!

He threw the weapon at Amison who swerved and then floored him with a single punch. He kicked him in the groin for good measure as he hit the ground.

Jack doubled up in pain but was flattened on his stomach by a swift kick to his legs. Amison kept him down by placing a foot in the middle of his back.

"The gun was empty, Jack. I took care of it when you went to the bathroom."

He knelt down over him.

"Now, Jack, I think it's time you retired for good." He knelt down and grabbed both sides of O'Brien's head and raised it a few inches off the floor. "But first, I want you to meet the voice you heard."

Estrella Gomez stepped out of a closet.

"This is Estrella, Jack. She's Ojo"s cousin. And Gonzo outside? He's another one of Ojo's cousins."

Estrella was close to tears.

"This is the man who came to Philadelphia five years ago," she cried.

Jack's voice was hoarse as blood started dripping from his mouth.

"Okay, Jones, you got me. But listen, I can deal. Let's forget the past. We can forget about this and Bimini. I can cut you a deal on the heroin."

Amison glared down at him.

"Everybody wants to cut me a deal, and everyone wants my heroin. Why is that, Jack? Huh? Tell me. Well, I don't deal, old chum."

Jack tried to move his head, but it was useless. The vise-like grip only tightened. "What do you want?" He asked hoarsely.

"I want you dead!"

"Harold Levy will kill you if I don't show tomorrow. Charlie Kane gave him my itinerary," Jack confided in a last ditch effort to save his life.

"Charlie's dead. Tell me something I don't know."

"Damn it, Jones. I'm telling you everything."

"Neat. Now, say 'good bye,' Jack."

"I'll tell you all I know!" screamed Jack. "There are others who want you dead."

"I'll read a telephone book."

Amison pounded Jack's head against the floor and blood hemorrhaged from his nose and mouth.

"I don't like you, Jack. I never did. Happy retirement, Jack!"

He placed his hands around Jack's head and wrenched it around, wringing his neck like a chicken's. One good twist and a hard yank was enough. There was a sharp crack and Jack O'Brien was dead.

Groping inside the dead man's pockets, he found and retrieved the piece of paper with the *Casa D'Ora's* coordinates, removed his gloves and stuffed them back into his pocket.

"Give me a hand up, Estrella," Amison growled. "I'm getting too old for this stuff."

Estrella helped him to his feet.

"How did I do, senor Jones?" she asked timidly.

"Fine. Fine. You did well."

Sid Stone entered with Gonzo at that moment and surveyed the room. "Well, well, what do we have here?"

"Jack fell down and broke his crown," said Amison.

"Cremate him with Bernice. They would have wanted it that way."

"Will do," said Sidney. "Now, I think you should leave. Take the Hertz. Drive it to Philly and get rid of it there."

CHAPTER 33

▼

REVENGE

Amison arrived in Philadelphia where he dropped off the rental car in O'Brien's name. A cab deposited him in front of the Alliance building a little past midnight in time for a late winter snow storm. He had called Harold a few days before that he might drop by and so he was not totally unexpected. Harold indicated that and Marvin would be working around the clock to finalize a report for a scheduled board meeting and that they would both be there. He also told Amison that Jack O'Brien was looking for a cushy deal at Alliance and that it would be a good idea if he never showed up.

Amison snuck into the building through the company's garage and made his way up to Harold's new offices on the forty fourth floor.

Harold was there alone and buried in newspapers with accounts of the events in Bimini. The Alliance chief was excited by the turn of events. He was especially impressed with the story about white supremacist terrorists who went to Bimini to discredit the Bimini Man dig. When that failed, they blew up the excavation site only to be drowned in a tidal wave that covered parts of North Bimini as a storm blew by.

Another story reported that a scientific research ship, the *Casa D'Ora*, sank in the storm with all hands on board. Rumor was that the fossil remains of Bimini Man were either swept away by the tidal wave or were entombed within the ship at the bottom of the sea.

Influential people like Hiram Goodwind from the Triple A were proposing that a monument, an obelisk, be erected in North Bimini to commemorate Bimini Man and were out searching for funds. Praise was heaped upon the brave citizens of the Biminis and their heroic leaders, Lieutenant Wayne, Commander Lang and Commissioner Jonathan Sykes for their valiant efforts in confronting the terrorists in the face of many casualties.

M.L. Wayne, whose injuries were fatal, received a military hero's funeral in Nassau. A West Indian weekly announced that Reginald Lang, severely injured when the cutter under his command engaged a terrorist gun ship, was promoted before being retired on a pension. Jonathan Sykes was invited to London to be knighted by the Queen while Cecil Fergueson moved on to become a police chief in Nassau.

His wife Charlotte must have been overjoyed, thought Amison.

Another piece, this time from the Nassau papers, reported that Henry Alstrum retired. The vacant position of naval commander was posted, and it was reported that one Robert Byrne, an American, had applied for the job.

"Hey, look at this!"

Harold pushed some papers in front of Amison. The Miami Herald reported that the U.S. government was increasing its contributions to the Bahamas for its role in the drug wars and was giving Venezuela a bridge loan to tide it over hard times. Jack O'Brien was to have been assigned as project manager but had decided to retire instead.

"I thought he wanted a job here at Alliance," Harold said. "He's supposed to be here later."

"He won't be here," Amison said. "He's permanently retired."

"I like that."

There were other noteworthy articles that Harold summarized for him from the Chronicle of Education. Frank Hoffman received a hero's welcome, returned to his duties as president of Las Olas University which in turn posthumously promoted Leslie Sandler to full professor for her outstanding achievements.

A major publisher asked Frank to write her biography, giving him a one million dollar advance, and the university's board of trustees unanimously voted to name the school of archeology for her and to co-share the costs of building the Bimini Man memorial monument in Bimini.

Frank Hoffman concurred with all recommendations after which he announced his resignation to take a one-year sabbatical leave with full pay, with an invitation to return to the classroom as a tenured senior professor of cultural anthropology at the same executive salary he enjoyed as president.

"You know, Jonesey?"

"What?"

"I'm sorry about your nigger girlfriend. What's her name? Domino? Well. Black meat is always easy to find. I was thinking about the broads you hang out with. if I were you, I'd find some with lower mileage. Maybe a white one for a change."

"I'll keep that under advisement, Harold."

"Well, that closes the book on this mission," said Harold. He took a sidelong look at his appointments book before slam-ming it shut.

"But it doesn't end it for you and me," he said abruptly. "I want to know where that damn ship went down."

Amison leaned back in his armchair. "I'll tell you, Harold. But I still have some unfinished business. It concerns someone in your company and my wife. There is that quid pro quo deal we made that has to be brought to closure. I help you and you help me."

Harold drew his large frame forward. "Ok. How do I help you?"

"There's a mole at Alliance."

"A pause, Then. "Do you have a name?"

"Yes. The mole is Marvin Childs."

Harold burst out laughing. "I already know that."

Amison looked up.

"Listen," Harold said. "Moles are important in this business. They provide an essential service. They report on us, true; but if we know who they are, we can tell them what we want them to know, and can find out valuable information about their foreign handlers. Marvin Childs works for several foreign interests. The Bencivengas may be out of the way but they have other clients. Moles provide a back channel means of communication when we cannot, for political, public relations, military, or diplomatic reasons, deal directly with the people we want. Look, you are a well paid pebble, a pawn. We're on this side; someone else is always on the other side. You're in the middle. You pick a side but still stay friendly with the other side to minimize risk and maximize opportunities, and…."

Amison leaned over the desk, interrupting him.

"Don't start believing in your bullshit, Harold. It's not good for your health. I hear that Marvin is Bencivenga's brother."

"I know that," said Harold impatiently. "That's why we hired him. Jack O'Brien wanted it, so we complied."

"Then why the charade in Bimini?"

"Washington mandated it, and you were the only one with balls enough to pull it off without compromising our foreign policy interests."

"One of our rules was broken," said Amison. "Someone tried to kill my wife."

"What the hell do you care, Jonesey?" Harold sneered. "You never loved the woman, and besides, you can have any chick you want."

"Then I should have been the one to call the hit, Harold."

"Shit, man. Jack O'Brien was putting the make on the broad and she knew too much about everything. She had to go. Jack O'Brien gave the orders. Marvin and Vincent threw her out the window. The whole thing was never my idea. I loved your wife like a sister. She was my wife's best friend. Hell, Jonesey, we raised our kids together. But I had to go with Jack's call, or else it would have been bad for Alliance. Besides, Bernice isn't dead. She's only in a coma. And I made sure you were well taken care of, didn't I? You had five good years in the Bahamas. Man, You're rich!"

"I understand your position, Harold," Amison noted. "And I'm not holding you responsible. I owe you my career. It's all O'Brien's doing. He was also trying to place a frame on you. But he's dead. So. He won't be here. And Bernice is dead too. So neither of them can talk. You're safe, Harold."

Harold looked up with interest. "Both dead?"

"Yes. Now Jack said you were the one who pushed Bernice out the window. And I spoke with Marvin earlier who said the same thing. But you know what? They lied. You're clean in my book."

Harold stared at Amison with unblinking eyes.

"Well, I guess I'm going to be out more partners when it comes to splitting the heroin."

"Not if Marvin lives, Harold. He's been after your job for years and made a deal with Sykes to take over Alliance. That's why you had so many problems, Harold. You were being buddy fucked by your CEO. And now that Sykes is knighted, you won't be able to touch him, but you can hit Marvin."

"Of course, of course."

Amison went on. "The problem is Estrella, the cleaning girl was in the office shortly after Bernice flew out the window. Estrella found your Cuban cigar ashes in the room, and she's still alive."

Harold looked at him indulgently. "Then, you'll take care of her, won't you Jonesey, as usual? I pay big bucks."

"I will," Amison reassured him.

Harold heaved a sigh of relief. "I think we have to go downstairs and have a chat with Marvin, don't you?"

"That's why I'm here, Harold. I'm out to protect you. I'm your hit man."

"You think the Neals family is wise to what happened last Thanksgiving?"

"They're not only wise, they're smart. Now, I've taken care of Vince Neals for you."

"You have?"

"Yes, Harold. He tried to take me down that night at the Esplanade. He's dead."

"I'm beginning to understand," said Harold. He extracted two long cigars from a humidor and gave one to Amison.

"Cuban. Care for one?"

Amison thanked him, took the cigar and placed it in the inside pocket of his suit jacket. "I have a slight cold, Harold. I'll smoke it later."

Harold grunted, snapped off his cigar tip with a gold cutter and lit it. "Nothing like a good cigar," he said.

"I'm beginning to understand too, Harold."

"What's that?"

"I mean, your personal interest in the Bimini Man dig. I finally figured out your private agenda. And I have to hand it to you, you're one hell of a clever guy."

Harold beamed and kept puffing away. "That's why I run this place."

"And you want to keep running Alliance. As for me, I'll be happy with only five hundred million dollars after we grab the heroin. You can keep the rest. Shall we pay Marvin a visit?"

Harold nodded. "Yes. We have some housecleaning to do."

Amison got up and ambled over to the desk where Harold kept a set of quill style ball point pens held vertically in a gold and silver holder. He picked up an apple from a fruit bowl on a corner credenza and stuck it into one of the pens.

Harold sighed. "You know Jonesey, you're probably right." He rose to his feet and slapped his thigh. "Damn! I know you are right. Let's do it.!"

"Great. Make the call."

"How about the *Casa D'Ora?*" asked Harold.

"No problem. But this first."

Harold got on the inter-office line. Marvin was having dinner in alone. Harold told him he had some good news and wanted to come down. The two left the office and took the executive elevator down to Marvin's office on the forty third floor where Amison greeted the accountant like an old friend. They sat down and Amison settled in the same armchair he occupied in early February.

"Why don't you tell Marvin what you told me?" said Harold after the usual pleasantries were exchanged.

Amison waved a hand.

"I'll make it short," he said. "I'm the guy who killed off your entire family from Venezuela."

"You what?"

"That's right, Marvin, in case you were trying to figure exactly what happened to them. I learned that you and Ignacio Bencivenga were brothers. So first, I want to extend my condolences. I was forced to terminate your brother in Bimini."

Marvin looked at Harold. "Ignacio, dead? You never told me that."

"It was part of the job, nothing personal," said Harold. "Orders, you know."

"But, you were there also. You never told me."

Amison could see the man was agitated.

Harold Levy shrugged. "That's life," he said.

Amison went on.

"That means your nephew, Miguelito, your two nieces, Isabella and Marlena, are gone. And lastly, I want you to know that your two sons, George and Dudley, are also gone!"

"Enough, enough!" cried Marvin.

"You should know I learned that you tried to murder my wife."

Marvin Childs sprang to his feet. He grabbed the derringer channel changer on his desk and aimed it at Amison. He squeezed the trigger, but nothing happened. He tried again, and again nothing happened. He kept struggling with it for a few moments while Amison got up.

"I emptied that damn thing earlier, Marvin," said Harold. "You don't know how to use it anyway."

Marvin threw the derringer at Amison who sidestepped and then grabbed the smaller man by the scruff of his neck. Marvin looked at Harold who threw up his hands in a helpless gesture.

"What can I do, Marvin? Jonesey says he wants to help me with housecleaning. And you know, the more I think about it, it's probably not a bad idea. It's not like I don't have a replacement for your job. I'll call a head hunter in the morning."

"Harold. Open the window for Marvin," Amison requested, tightening his grip around Marvin's neck.

Harold obligingly went to one of the tall double hung windows and raised it. He He watched Marvin squirm with glee.

"Look Marvin," he said, pointing to the window. "It's open. Fresh air is good."

Marvin screamed, broke loose and bolted for the door, but Amison caught him and threw him into Harold's outstretched arms.

"Give me a hand, Harold," said Amison. "Place one hand under his armpit, and grab him under the legs with the other. I'll do the same on my side."

"Harold, you...!"

Marvin started to blurt out something, but Harold struck him in the face with his fist, smashing his nose and teeth. Marvin started to choke in his own blood. He began crying and begging as he was carried like an invalid to the window.

He became hysterical. His head was out the window and he could see the snow covered street forty-three floors below, his view only partially obstructed by the two stone gargoyles guarding the ledge two floors below.

"Say, good night, Marvin," said Amison. "A One, A Two, and away we go..."

They swung him back and forth two times and tossed him screaming out the window on the third swing.

Amison and Harold looked at each other. "Now, that's the way, Harold. You've got to toss a body way out so it doesn't hit anything on the way down. Shall we do dinner?"

"I could use a dinner and a good stiff drink."

"Great. Close the window, Harold."

Without thinking, Harold went to the window and leaned way out to see where Marvin had landed.

Amison snuck up behind him, lifted his legs in the air, and Harold toppled out of the window with a curse.

Amison yelled after him.

"Bon voyage, Harold."

The Alliance chairman's large frame crashed into the ice covered ledge between the gargoyles where he wrapped his arms around the stone monsters to break his fall.

Amison poked his head out the window and looked sadly at Harold whose eyes eyes met his for one fleeting moment.

"I going to miss you, old friend. We had good times together."

Amison was on the verge of tears.

"Why did you have to be here when those mother fuckers threw Bernice out the window."

His grief turned to rage.

"Damn you, Harold." he yelled at the top of his lungs. "Rot in hell!" Harold was too heavy. The gargoyles snapped off the ledge and carried him head first like a rocket down to the to the snow covered street where he landed next to Marvin. The statues shattered into jagged fragments that formed a shadowy halo around the bodies .

Amison closed the lights, went to the window and looked out. It was snowing heavily and already the bodies were partially covered. Sanitation trucks would be coming through in a few hours to plow the streets and bury the bodies under fresh mountains of snow. They could lie there undisturbed and undiscovered for hours, maybe days.

He inhaled. The air was clean. It was cold, but it reminded him in some ways of a distant tropical island after a rain, where the air smelled fresh and where he met a girl whose face he could not remember, a long, long time ago.

CHAPTER 34

▼

REDEMPTION

The Spring semester was history and the summer sessions were about to start at Las Olas University. Frank Hoffman's tenure as its president was over.

Amison had not seen him in a month and so he e decided early one morning to visit Frank's office. It was one of those bright days when nothing could go wrong. But he found the office darkened with its windows closed and shades drawn. Frank was alone and standing by his desk surrounded knee deep by boxes and stacks of books waiting to be packed and moved. He was stuffing personal papers and belongings into a carton when Amison appeared.

"No more parties?"

Frank looked up. He seemed pensive and preoccupied.

"I know I'm a hero but I feel as if I've been defrocked."

Amison tried to commiserate with him.

"Life sucks, that's for sure."

Frank sat down behind his desk. The walls around him were bare. The diplomas and citations that once decorated them were gone.

"Jonesey, old chum," he said quietly. "It's good to see you. Where have you been?"

"Oh, nowhere. Just finishing up old business."

"Have you spoken with your kids?"

"No, not really. I will, but not right now."

Frank was not paying attention.

"How's *Phoenix*?" He asked mechanically.

"Just about ready for a new adventure. What about *Flyer?*"

"Same here. We'll be ready for another small war if someone ever calls us."

"At least, you'll have a place to live if you leave the Sagamore House."

"Oh, I don't care where I live right now. I can settle for a trailer."

"It's not all that bad, Frank. You still have a job. You're a teacher again, and you keep your executive pay."

"That's terrific, old chum. But that doesn't feed my ego. I need more. What are your plans?"

"Sid invited me to move *Phoenix* to the Riverside permanently in return for helping him run the place."

"That sounds like a good idea," said Frank. "The neighborhood's good."

Amison noticed a revolver lying on top of Frank's desk.

"Are you going hunting, Frank?"

"I'm pissed off, and I have no one to be pissed about. I feel like crying, Jonesey, and then killing myself, and then crying again."

"But if you kill yourself, you won't be able to cry. Why don't you just have a good cry. Better. Get drunk, and then have a good cry, but don't shoot yourself."

"I fucked up," said Frank. "I have no family, no career, no real job. I'm a lousy professor teaching courses I don't want to teach to students who don't want to learn."

"Well,"consoled Amison. "You have those great memories."

He walked over to the windows, drew back the shades and opened the windows. Light entered and a cool breeze drifted into the office and the merry voices of the students filled the air.

"What you need is a new woman to keep you company," suggested Amison. "I could use one too. Now what I really want is a gal in her thirties or early forties, single, big boobs, no kids and no cats."

"Shit," said Frank. "I'm too old to start looking for women again, and so are you. But if you're interested, I know someone who can sell you a six foot female doll, anatomically correct. In the meantime, I'm thinking of leaving Florida for good."

"That's not a bad idea. How about a deep sea charter business in the Keys?"

"I''d rather start a medical school somewhere in the Caribbean. I know where to find some fast money…Hey, where are you going?"

Amison was walking to the door. He looked back at Frank.

"I'm going to the Floridian. They stop serving grits at Eleven. Are you coming?"

"Yeah, wait for me."

"Take your gun, Frank. Never forget what you really are."

They left the office and went out into the sunlight. They walked to the Floridian and encountered Luis Santiago along the way. Dapper as usual, he was stood against a lamp post near his unmarked sheriff's sedan. The inspector winked at them.

"Breakfast, amigos?" he called out.

"Breakfast."

A window table was waiting for them at the Floridian. They sat down and a waitress came over with coffee and doughnuts and a large order of grits for Amison.

"By the way," asked Luis later. "I have a vague idea where the *Casa D'Ora* went down. Did any of you get a good fix on it?"

"I didn't," replied Frank. "Our systems caught one of the *Casa D'Ora's* shells and were shut"

"I did," said Amison. "The GPS computer wasn't hit. It recorded our position at the moment of impact with the freighter."

All eyes turned to Amison as he raised his coffee cup.

"To Bimini Man and beyond," he announced.

"To Bimini Man and beyond," said Frank and Luis, and they raised their coffee cups....

..."And so that is the story of Bimini Man," said Cecil, mopping his brow.

"It started with a bang and ended in a whimper."

The sun was sinking over Alice Town and he reminded the students, "We should be going; it's late."

The students stirred slowly, but eventually they stood up and went down to the dock and filed aboard the waiting launch.

Bill and Lorraine Small were the last to board. Alice Town's flickering lights were barely visible through the haze hanging over Porgy Bay's glassy waters and everyone shivered in the early evening chill.

"What happened to Domino's sisters?"

"Oh, they settled in Miami and never returned to Bimini."

"It's so sad what happened to Domino. She really didn't have to die," said a student.

Cecil grinned. "Actually. She didn't die. She was wounded and went into shock. She recovered and broke off all contact. I think she realized there could be no real future with Jonesey. I heard she moved to California.

"What about the others?"

"Hank Lawrence took over Alliance after Harold Levy died. Tucker Anderson became the public safety director at Las Olas University, and Jonesey took over the management of the Riverside. Mike Quinn was one lucky Irishman. He lived, thanks to Henry Alstrum, and moved to the Keys. Bob Byrne left Florida and took a commission in the Bahamian navy.

"And interestingly, Miguelito Bencivenga did not die in Porgy Bay. He swam to shore and recovered enough to eventually make it back to Venezuela.

"And here's the real scoop. George Gibson died but don Ignacio Bencivenga and his two daughters, although badly wounded, did not die. They were flown to a hospital in Nassau and shipped back to Venezuela when they were well enough to travel."

"Does this mean that they might make a try for the heroin?" Bill Small asked.

"That remains to be seen," Cecil replied.

"Do you think Ruby will ever fall in love again?" Lorraine asked.

"Hard to tell." Cecil winked in the descending night. "That's another story."

END

0-595-27360-2